# X-MEN 2

D1040337

*Also available from Del Rey Books:*

X-MEN by Kristine Kathryn Rusch and Dean Wesley Smith

SPIDER-MAN by Peter David

HULK by Peter David

# X-MEN 2

**A novelization by
Chris Claremont**

**Based on the story by
Zak Penn and David Hayter
and Bryan Singer,
screenplay by
Dan Harris and Mike Dougherty**

A Del Rey® Book
BALLANTINE BOOKS • NEW YORK

to Beth

A Del Rey® Book
Published by The Ballantine Publishing Group
TM & copyright © 2003 by Twentieth Century Fox Film Corporation. All rights reserved.

www.delreydigital.com

ISBN 0-345-46196-7

Manufactured in the United States of America

First Edition: March 2003

OPM 10 9 8 7 6 5 4 3 2 1

# Chapter One

*Mutants. Since the discovery of their existence, they have been regarded with fear, suspicion, and often hatred. Across the planet, debate rages: Are mutants the next link in the evolutionary chain . . .*

*. . . or simply a new species of humanity fighting for their share of the world? Either way, one fact has been historically proven: Sharing the world has never been humanity's defining attribute . . .*

—Charles Xavier

" 'We are not enemies, but friends,' " the tour guide said as she led the group through the East Wing entrance of the White House. " 'We must not be enemies,' " she continued, pausing to let them gather inside the foyer beneath one of the presidential portraits that lined the wall. " 'Though passion may have strained, it must not break the bonds of our affection.' Abraham Lincoln."

Alicia Vargas had made this speech hundreds of times, yet she had a knack of making it sound as though she'd just thought it up. She was a short young woman who looked barely out of college, with big, wide-spaced eyes,

1

an open face, a ready smile. That way, you'd miss the fact that those lustrous eyes never stopped moving from person to person among the group she was shepherding along, or that the drape of her blazer masked the Sig-Sauer pistol resting in its snap-draw holster at the small of her back.

Alicia Vargas was Secret Service, just like the tall, broad-shouldered, stone-faced men in business suits who stood at intervals along the walls. At the reception desk and at the doorways leading to the interior of the White House were their equally imposing uniformed counterparts in the Executive Protection Service. When the decision was made to continue public tours, in spite of the ever-present threat of global terrorism, the Secret Service had insisted that its people take over the job of guides. They understood the political and public relations realities of the office, but their job was to protect the man who held that office, and from that perspective, they argued, you could never be too careful.

Offering up another smile, Alicia indicated the portrait that hung behind her, the sixteenth in the line of chief executives that began with George Washington and culminated today in George McKenna.

"President Lincoln said that in his first inaugural address. It's one of my favorites. I like to think, especially with all that's happening in the world, that those words are more important than ever."

With an apologetic gesture, intended to put the tourists at ease, she led them toward the security desk.

"I just want to repeat what you were told at the Main Gate. Obviously, with the President in residence today, we want to be especially careful. One at a time, please approach the desk, present a photo ID, place your bags and purses on the conveyor belt, and pass through the metal detector. Your possessions and all cameras will be returned to you when you leave. I know that sounds harsh, but I hope you understand."

One man in the back caught her eye. He was wearing a Red Sox baseball hat, pulled low. He wasn't doing anything wrong; far from it. His body language was totally relaxed and easy. Maybe that was it. Most people visiting the White House came through the door excited, upbeat, impatient, and impressed. Then, seeing the airport-style X-ray console and the metal detector, even the best of them got nervous, wondering if they'd inadvertently brought something that would sound an alarm and get them into trouble.

Red Sox didn't seem to have a care in the world.

Quickly, as she ushered the first woman in line through the cage, Alicia recalled the scene at the Pennsylvania Avenue gate, where the tour had been admitted to the grounds. She'd watched them come through on the surveillance screens and now that she replayed the scene in her mind's eye, there had been no Red Sox hat in the group.

Turning back to look for him, she registered a faint sound, the *bamf* of imploding air, like when a balloon pops.

Red Sox was gone.

From the East Wing entrance, a broad hallway—called the Cross Hall—runs lengthwise through the heart of the building. Originally, this had been the area where the everyday work of the household was done—the rooms housed butler's pantries, closets, and the like—but successive renovations and the growing need for space had transformed them into formal receiving rooms: the Roosevelt Room, the Vermeil Room, the China Room. At the moment, none of them was in use, which is what caught Special Agent Donald Karp's attention when his peripheral vision registered some kind of movement in one of the doorways.

When he turned to peer down the corridor, all he saw was shadow inside the deep alcove—that was one of the problems caused by the comparatively low, vaulted ceiling, it made the hallway hell to light properly. He knew it was probably nothing, but he was bored and in the mood for even a minor break in routine. Once before he'd opened an office door and found a couple of mid-level staffers behaving far too friskily for their own good. They'd been lucky they weren't fired on the spot, but they really should have known better.

To his surprise, as he stepped closer to take a proper look, someone *was* there—though for some reason he wasn't sure until the figure stepped clear of the shadow, a lean-bodied man whose stoop-shouldered stance belied the fact that he was roughly Karp's height, wearing non-descript clothes and a Red Sox baseball cap. Boyoboy, would he have fun roasting Alicia's ass for being so careless as to let a tourist stray from the group.

He reached for the man's shoulder.

"Excuse me, sir, are you lost? I'm afraid you can't leave the group—"

The man rounded on him—and Karp gasped, goggle-eyed, to find himself face-to-face with a demon. Skin so dark a blue-black it was as if the man were cloaked in his own personal shadow, the only points of color his gleaming yellow eyes. The ears were pointed, the teeth had fangs, and the hand that grabbed Karp's wrist possessed two fingers instead of the normal four.

Training took over. Without a conscious thought, Karp went for his gun—and a forked tail wrapped tight around his throat, cutting off his cry of alarm. The tail spun him like a top into the alcove, and he felt a blinding pain as the side of his head cracked hard into the arched stone. After that he never felt the blow to the side, chop to the neck that finished the job of knocking him unconscious.

It was all over in a matter of seconds, but those seconds made the difference.

From the East Entrance came Alicia Vargas' shout—she was already through the hallway doors, coming at a dead run with sidearm in hand, ahead of the other agents and uniformed officers.

Karp's partner was closer. He lunged for the intruder, who tripped him up with a sideways sweep of the legs—ditching his shoes in the process to reveal elongated, weirdly articulated feet with a two-toed configuration that matched his hands. The intruder leaped across the hall for the opposite wall, somehow grabbing hold of the falling agent's gun and pitching it clear. His leap landed him up by the ceiling. To Alicia's astonishment he stuck there, three-quarters upside down, as though fingers and toes were tipped with Velcro.

Above the chandeliers, he was suddenly hard to see, and Alicia realized with a shock that he was blending with the ceiling shadows. Against a dark background, the intruder's indigo skin made him functionally invisible.

With a snarl, he was gone, scampering faster than her eye could swallow, around the corner toward the executive offices of the West Wing.

Alicia had a mini-mike clipped to her sleeve; she used it now.

"Code Red," she cried. "*Code Red.* Perimeter breach at visitors' checkpoint! Agent Vargas in the Cross Hall, ten meters in from the East Entrance. Intruder is hostile, two agents are down. Threat to Braveheart!"

At the rear of the mansion, in the opposite wing, President George McKenna was working the phones, applying a measure of charm—with just the faintest edge of threat—to a senator hoping to make some political ink by throwing a monkey wrench into the latest administration initiative. The President was a rancher by temperament and wished, as he found he often did since assuming the Oval Office, that he could solve the problem by simply hog-tying the man and planting his brand indelibly on that arrogant posterior. He liked cows better than legislators. At least they knew their place.

He looked up with irritation as the door to the outer office burst open and Sid Walters, the head of his protection detail, strode inside. He was about to lose his temper—which was legendary—when he realized that Walters had his gun in hand and, from the look on his face, he wasn't going to be interested in any comment the President had to make.

"Say again," Walters snapped into the mini-microphone clipped to the cuff of his shirtsleeve, "how many are there?"

"What the hell—" the President began, but all questions and any thoughts of protest evaporated as a half-dozen more agents rushed into the room to form a living shield around his desk. The two biggest stood on either side of him. Four of the team were in suits, with pistols in hand, but these last two were in full combat gear, helmets and flak jackets, with MP5 submachine guns in their hands. McKenna had been to war, he'd been shot; he knew at a glance that this was no drill. These men believed he was in deadly danger, and they were prepared to give their lives to save him.

McKenna heard a tinny voice demanding attention, belatedly realized he was still holding the phone.

With a calmness that astounded him, that he never dreamed he possessed, the President raised the receiver to his ear.

"Trent, I'm sorry, I can't talk right now, something's come up. I'll call you back, soon as I can, all right?"

Without waiting for an acknowledgment, McKenna hung up. He sounded so normal, not scared at all. The analytical part of him knew that fear would come later and that it would be very rough indeed. *If* there was a later.

He looked at the pictures on his desk, thankful now the first lady was in San Francisco and the kids were at school. Nobody home but him.

"Sid?" he said.

"You'll be fine, sir. You have our word."

The West Wing was a madhouse, agents trying to evacuate the presidential staff at the same time they were hunting down the intruder. There was no pretense of order; that had vanished with the first gunshot. The guards weren't polite and they weren't gentle. Their goal was to get everyone clear as fast as possible. Thing was, they were just as scared as the civilians.

Internal surveillance cameras were proving worse than useless; their quarry moved too fast, with an agility that put monkeys to shame. By the time the guys watching the monitors could yell a warning, it was already too late.

Toby Vanscoy found that out the hard way. He was clearing a suite of offices, herding people toward the Press Room because it had a clear route to the outside, when a scream right next to his ear alerted him to the danger.

He reacted as he'd been trained: He took a split second to confirm the target, then opened fire. His weapon was a Sig-Sauer P226, one of the finest handguns in the world, and like every agent in the President's detail, he was rated expert. As fast as he could pull the trigger, he emptied his fifteen-round magazine, and impossible as it was for him to admit—in the heartbeats he had to do so—not one of his rounds came close.

The intruder bounced off the walls, he leaped from floor to ceiling, he ran as easily upside down as he did on the floor, he almost seemed to dance around Vanscoy's shots until, so smoothly that it seemed choreographed, he hurled himself through the air in a somersault that ended with both feet hammering Vanscoy full in the chest.

It was like being hit by a battering ram. Vanscoy flew backward through the air, holding on to his gun but losing the replacement magazine he'd been trying to load, to crash through the set of double doors that led to the main suite of offices.

The intruder followed, straddling Vanscoy's body only to find a half-dozen agents blocking his way. He glanced over his shoulder to see a half dozen more taking position behind him. Scarlet dots flared all over his torso as he was illuminated by their laser sights. The agents all had good cover; he was wide open. They could fire at will with minimal risk to their colleagues. They pinned him with pistols, with automatic weapons, with a sniper rifle centered right on his head. It was a drop-ceiling overhead; if he tried to stick to it, the removable panels would simply collapse. They figured they had him.

The intruder looked down, almost in surprise, at the grating sound of Toby Vanscoy's voice. Battered and broken as he was, the agent had his own weapon in a two-handed grip, aimed right up at him.

"Hands behind your head," Vanscoy ordered. "Get down on your knees! Right now!"

*"Right now!"* repeated the lead agent from the group ahead of them. "No tricks, or we'll fire."

The intruder snarled, baring fangs. Vanscoy pulled the trigger, hammer falling uselessly on an empty chamber . . .

. . . and the intruder vanished.

"Mr. President," snapped Sid Walters, one hand pressing against his earbug in a vain attempt to make sense of all the chatter jamming his radio, "we've gotta go!"

Hank Cartwright, his deputy, grabbed Walters' arm. "We don't know the sitch, Sid. We don't know how many there are. We've got a solid defensive position, we've got the firepower. We're better off staying put!"

Walters turned on the other man in a fury. He was boss, he called the plays, there wasn't time for debate— but before he could say a word, both entrances to the Oval Office crashed open to admit the agents who'd been stationed outside. They were coughing and choking, shrouded in gouts of thick, oily smoke.

That same instant, the intruder appeared in midair, right in front of Cartwright. Without missing a beat, the assassin lashed out with a powerful kick to the chest.

Even with Cartwright's flak jacket and equipment blunting the force of the jackhammer blow, it was enough to throw him off his feet and into the agents behind him.

Walters managed to snap off a shot, but his target disappeared. Before he could react, he felt the intruder's tail around his neck, and then he was flying himself, tumbling over one of the couches and in among the agents who'd fallen in the doorway. As he struggled up, searching desperately for a weapon, one part of his mind kept repeating over and over, like a mantra: *He's got a tail! He's got a* tail! Even with the creature right in front of him, real as life, he still couldn't believe it. *He's got a* tail!

Again and again and again, the intruder disappeared, to materialize somewhere else in the office, turning the confined space of the room to his advantage as he made mincemeat of the President's bodyguard. It all happened so fast Walters would have to register the events in retrospect. At the moment, sick at heart, he simply realized he was too slow. There was nothing he could do to save his President.

Alone now, with no one to protect him, George McKenna sat in his seat of power and stared into the inhuman eyes of his assassin. The eyes were strangely drained of color, and it struck him that they were dead. What little hue they possessed was an afterthought, lacking anything resembling humanity.

The intruder had a knife, big and gleaming. Wrapped around its hilt was a brilliant red ribbon marked with flashes of gold. Poised on the edge of the desk, he rose above McKenna. The President had never been more scared, and yet never more calm. A line from somewhere or other popped from memory: "When the end is all there is, it *matters*." If this was his end, he'd do the office proud.

The gunshot made him jump in his chair.

The intruder cried out, dropping the knife as he clutched at a shoulder suddenly turned scarlet from the impact of a 9mm shell. Instantly, his expression changed. He looked suddenly shaken, confused, and as McKenna watched, the creature's eyes changed, gaining color and vibrancy and . . . awareness.

Absurdly the thought came to McKenna: *He doesn't know where he is. He doesn't know what's* happening!

The intruder looked around and saw Alicia Vargas standing in the doorway, pistol leveled.

Before she could take a second shot, he was gone—with the same characteristic *bamf* that came from air imploding inward to fill the empty space left by his body when it disappeared. And also, the President realized, the faintest scent, reminiscent of sulfur and brimstone.

"Sir?" Alicia asked as she hurried over to him, avoiding the bodies of her fellow agents, her eyes never at rest as they swept the scene for the assassin or any like him, her gun cocked and ready. "Are you all right, Mr. President? Are you hurt?"

"I'm fine, Alicia, I'm fine." It was a lie and both of them knew it, but he was the President and this was the time for lies like that.

"What the hell *was* that?" he wondered aloud.

"Damned if I know, sir. But I sure hope he doesn't come back."

"Amen." The knife, superbly balanced, had landed point first, its weight stabbing deep into the wooden desktop. As he touched the ribbon, McKenna realized that the black flecks were writing.

"What the hell is *this*?" he asked aloud.

On the ribbon, printed in black, was a demand—or perhaps, he thought, suddenly heartsick, a declaration of war: MUTANT FREEDOM *NOW*!

# Interlude

He came in to Alkali Lake the back way, over the mountains from the north. He cut through a saddleback notch and made his way down to the glacier by a trail so poor even a bighorn sheep would think twice about trying it.

Before reaching the base of the escarpment he went to ground, taking cover in a jumbled pile of scree and rocks that gave him a superb view of the glacier and minimal chance of being seen himself. The last stretch was open country; he'd have to wait for the right moment to make his approach. He didn't mind. When he had to, he could be inhumanly patient.

There was a road up to the complex from the south, as miserable in its own way as the path he'd followed. Blacktop asphalt, barely two lines wide, beat to shit by the pounding of too many heavily laden trucks over too many years with hardly a thought given to maintenance. It wound its way better than seventy miles through the snowy mountains, with a decent-sized town at the far end that catered mainly to the hunting and camping crowd who wanted something wilder than Lake Louise or even Jasper. There was a hamlet some fifty miles farther that consisted of a saloon, some gas pumps, and a batch of cabins that rented by the hour.

Trouble was, if he took the road, they'd know he was coming.

He was a short man, with a stocky, powerful physique, as though the frame of an athletic six-footer had been squashed down to five and change. To look at his face, you'd think him a young man, his features weathered by a life spent mainly outdoors. His dress—jeans as worn as his boots—marked him as an itinerant wrangler or cycle bum, blue collar for sure. This was a man who worked with his hands, not his mind.

His hair was dark, sweeping back from his forehead in a wave that looked natural on him but somehow . . . wrong for a human being. He wore his sideburns long, right down to the line of his jaw, in a fashion more in keeping with the nineteenth century than the twenty-first.

His eyes were the giveaway. Like his hair, they were right for his face, yet at the same time they had no right belonging to one so apparently youthful. These eyes missed nothing and had seen too much. They were the eyes of a hunter. A predator.

His name was Logan, but the only reason he knew it was that it was printed on his dog tags. A name, a serial number, a blood type. No indication of nationality or branch of service. The only clue, if you could call it that, was that the information was printed in Roman letters. Not Arabic, not Cyrillic, not Chinese or Japanese kanji. He had no past worth the name, only a present filled to bursting with questions. Here was where he hoped to find some answers.

But first he needed a storm.

He got a beaut.

It came in during the night, boiling off the Continental Divide with winds and snow to spare, a howling monster that seemed bent on scouring the landscape down to bare rock. The rocks afforded a fair measure of protection from the wind, but there was nothing he could do about the cold. The temperature was close to freezing before the storm. Once the blizzard started, it quickly dropped past zero. His jacket was fleece lined, but against this kind of elemental fury, that was no help at all. Hypothermia set in almost immediately. It was a pain, but he'd endured far worse. As often as he froze during the night, his healing factor kicked into gear and brought him back to life.

The weather system proved to be as fast-moving as it was intense. Toward morning, a shift in wind velocity told him it was time to get moving. Timing was perfect. The fury of the storm had probably nailed any of the installation's remote sensors positioned to watch the "back door." And any living sentries were just as likely to be hunkered down in their bunkers, dreaming dreams of "Baywatch."

He was in place by dawn, a spectacular sunrise that went hand in hand with the equally impressive—although far more bleak—vista that spread out below him. Dominating the scene was the dam, a thousand feet high, three times that across, holding back a lake that stretched for miles. A huge generating station at its base told the reason for its existence, to provide an inexhaustible source of hydroelectric power. Thing is, there were no towering pylons marching away downriver to carry all this energy to a hungry populace. What was generated here stayed here, to be used by the Alkali Lake Industrial Complex.

There was a fence blocking access to the crest of the dam, but it was no obstacle. The poles and links were so rusted and twisted by the fierce mountain weather that he simply stepped over. He found an older sign than the first, barely held to the fence by a scrap of wire, informing intruders that this was a government installation, a military base, and top secret besides, and warning of the most dire consequences if anyone was of a mind to trespass.

Below the dam, the forest had been cleared for the better part of a mile to allow for the construction of the base. The layout of the complex was circular, like a defensive laager, and the scale was as impressive as the dam itself. This place had been built to last.

So why had it been abandoned?

The whole base was covered with snow, drifts piled over doors and windows. What roads he saw were cracked and blistered, with weeds and flowers and the occasional small tree sprouting to reclaim the land that was rightfully theirs. Windows were mostly broken. No vehicles. No tracks in the snow save his own.

Once he made his way inside, it wasn't any different. Long hallways and empty offices. They'd packed up the incidentals but left a fair amount of furniture, all of which had suffered from the assault of the elements, summer and winter. But the basic structure of the buildings—thick metal walls—was surprisingly sound. It was composed of a succession of strong points, compartments that could become individual fortresses all their own, almost as if the builders were as worried about an assault from within as from without.

He wandered without obvious direction, trusting his feet and his instincts to lead him. Most of the time he trusted them far more than his intellect. To him, thinking was a liability—took too long, led down too many wrong paths. His body was a much more dependable instrument.

He caught a strange scent but wasn't worried. It was only a wolf, which seemed as curious about him as he was about the buildings. They stood watching each other from opposite ends of the room for a few moments before the wolf calmly turned tail and padded down a nearby flight of stairs.

Intrigued, Logan followed, into a darkness so complete even his extraordinarily sharp eyes weren't of much use. He pulled a mini-Maglite out of his jacket pocket, which revealed a large, circular room, as bare and nondescript as everywhere else in the base.

Suddenly the wolf howled, the noise amplified and echoed by the cavernous space. It was a primal sound that went straight to Logan's back brain, as it was intended to, as it had since men and wolves first shared this wilderness, and he reacted accordingly. He spun into a crouch, ready for a fight, and bared his teeth in a flash of familiar pain as three gleaming metal claws, each as long as his forearm, punched out of the body of his clenched right hand. They made a distinctive *snikt* sound as they emerged, like a rifle bolt being engaged. They were forged of a metal called adamantium, and they could cut steel as easily as air. The claws had bionic housings built into each forearm; his healing factor handled the wounds they made each time they were used. That same metal was laced through his skeleton, creating an amalgam with his bones that made them virtually unbreakable.

He hadn't been born this way. Someone had done this

to him. His whole life since, the parts he remembered, anyway, had been devoted to finding out who, and why.

The wolf was sitting in another doorway, but as Logan swung his light around he lost all interest in the animal. He crossed to the wall and raised his right hand to chest height. There were three marks in the metal, deep, parallel gashes, as though someone had slashed at the steel.

He placed his fist by the doorjamb. His claws were a perfect fit.

He had an answer. Once upon a time—a very long time ago—he had been here.

He looked down, but the wolf was gone, with a fast-paced click of claws on concrete to mark its hurried exit to the surface.

With an equally distinctive snakt sound, his claws went away. Reflexively he wiped the little bit of bloody residue from between his knuckles and took one last look around the empty room.

He wasn't done searching, but he was done here. Time to go home.

# Chapter Two

Against a backdrop of barren, snow-swept rock, a mother wolf faced off against a hunter. She had young to protect and the blood on her muzzle spoke eloquently of her determination and ferocity. The hunter was short by modern standards but powerfully built, wrapped snugly in layers of fur that afforded protection both from the elements and the wolf's fangs. His low forehead and prominent brow marked him as Neanderthal man. He had a spear in one hand, a club in the other. The sharply pointed stone tip of the spear was likewise flecked with blood. Each combatant had taken the measure of his foe; neither would back down until the other was dead.

It was a typical weekday afternoon at New York's famed American Museum of Natural History; the bulk of the visitors were schoolchildren on a variety of class trips. A clutch of them were gathered before the diorama, only half-listening to their teacher as they made whispered comments and comparisons between themselves, choosing sides as to who would win this reconstructed fight.

The teacher herself was, in her own way, as striking as the display. It wasn't just her height, six feet even, or, surprisingly, the dramatic shock of hair that fell straight as a waterfall to the middle of her back, colored so pure an arctic white that it gleamed like silver, providing a stark contrast to her coffee-colored skin. What marked her most was her carriage, a bearing and manner so naturally graceful you couldn't help but think of her as royalty. She had a beauty that was breathtaking, but remarkably, she didn't seem to notice. There was no posing to her presentation, no posturing, no flaunting of the gifts nature had so amply bestowed; she was a woman totally at one with herself. She had a ready smile, and although her voice seemed soft, you had the immediate sense that when she spoke every child in her charge would hear her and, more importantly, would listen. And lastly, there were her eyes, which were a rich, cobalt blue, the same as the sky just before it goes purple at sunset. She was a mass of contradictions whose individual elements should all have been at odds with one another; yet, when combined, the end result was the closest thing to perfection that could be imagined.

"Contrary to popular belief," she said to the children, "Neanderthals are not the direct ancestor of modern-day humans, but rather distant cousins who died out some thirty thousand years ago. . . ."

With a sweep of her hand, which seemed to leave a distinctive puff of breeze in its wake, she ushered her class along to the next diorama, presenting a scene of Cro-Magnon hunters ganging up on a towering woolly mammoth. They'd backed the mammoth into a corner, where it couldn't easily maneuver. Already a couple of stone-tipped spears were stuck in its flanks; all the men looked poised to hurl more. The mammoth had put up a powerful fight—a couple of hunters lay broken on the snow—but barring a miracle, the giant creature was doomed.

"They were replaced," the teacher continued, "by a more advanced race called Cro-Magnon man, also known as *Homo sapiens*, also known as human beings. In other words, children, they were replaced by all of us.

"It was once theorized that Neanderthals were wiped out by years of conflict with these successors, but new evidence found in our own DNA suggests that these two species may have interbred, eventually evolving into modern humanity. In effect, they *became* us."

One of her kids, a twelve-year-old named Artie, flashed a smile at a little girl standing nearby. She was with her parents and she didn't look at all happy. Her dress was stained with ice cream and Kool-Aid, and she was far more interested in getting some more snacks than in looking at boring old statues and such. When Artie smiled, she responded by sticking out her tongue.

He did the same, only his tongue was black and forked like a snake.

The girl stared goggle-eyed for what seemed like forever before jumping back against her mother and, to that woman's surprise, burying her head against her leg and whining in fright.

"Artie," the teacher said quietly, looming over him. He tried his best smile; she wasn't interested. "Not here."

"I didn't mean any harm."

"You scared her."

"She started it!"

"She's a little girl, you're almost a teenager. I expect you to know better."

"That is so bogus, Miss Munroe."

"I beg your pardon?"

"Hiding what we are."

"Yes, in a way. But also necessary. That girl doesn't

know you, Artie, or any of the other students in the class. She didn't react to who you are, but to what she saw. And it was different and it was scary. It's very easy, almost natural, for people to react to the surface presentation of things; it's a survival instinct that some believe is hardwired into our genes. It's why people have problems with different cultures and different faiths and different skin colors and different ways of behavior. What's 'same' is comfortable. What's different could be a threat."

"Are we a threat, because we're mutants?"

"Am I a threat because I'm black? Or that little girl because she's Hispanic?"

Artie shrugged. "Of course not."

"Exactly. As Martin Luther King said, we want to be judged, not by the color of our skins—or, in our case, the makeup of our genes—but by the content of our characters. Artie, mutants are only people with some extra, unique genes. We're still human."

While she was talking with Artie, the bulk of the class had moved on to the next diorama, and as Ororo Munroe, known to the other teachers as Storm, strode after them she sighed inside that she'd allowed herself to be distracted. This was a presentation she'd wanted to avoid.

Although the museum had been assiduously upgrading its collections over the years, to stay current with advances in the evolutionary and archaeological sciences, this was one of the exhibits that had been left over from the old days. Against a panoramic background of what was meant to be the Great Rift Valley of eastern Africa were a succession of mannequins and visual presentations, tracking the development of mankind from the apelike *Homo habilius* all the way up the evolutionary line to the present day. Along the way, however, there was a diversion to a second grouping of figures, labeled *HOMO MUTANTIS*? Some were based on informed speculation, while others were clearly purest fantasy. But they were all awful to look at.

A few of the younger students, grouped around Jubilation Lee, exchanged some gently rude banter about ancestry and the obvious resemblance between the display figures before them and some of their classmates. Their way of coping was to hurl wisecracks, but a couple of others just stood and stared, making the obvious connection between past and present, the one perhaps being prologue to the other. Mutant powers tended to catalyze at puberty, and while all of them had been cataloged as carriers of the active gene, not all of them had manifested their powers. They were clearly wondering now if they'd end up looking anything like these nightmares.

"The tribe where I used to live called this part of Africa 'the forge of Heaven,'" Storm told them all, standing right before the diorama but staring past the figures, ignoring them in favor of the vista that lay beyond. In her mind's eye there was no painted backdrop but a stark, sere landscape that stretched far beyond the visible horizon. It was mostly grassland, when there was rain, not much in the way of anything larger like trees. Those were found in the higher elevations, toward Mount Kilimanjaro. "It's a harsh and unforgiving country where anthropologists believe that life on Earth was born," she continued. "Only the strongest, the most intelligent, the most *worthy* of creatures can survive here. That's nature's way. She tries all sorts of possibilities—dinosaurs great and small, mammals much the same—until she finds a species that works. At the same time, we have to accept that some things . . . don't."

"Old news," Artie said flatly, end of story.

"Precisely," Storm responded cheerily. "What you see here is our snapshot of the world tens of thousands of years ago. What they were has no more relevance to what you are than that Neanderthal does. What matters is who you *choose* to be. The kind of person, the kind of life you want to live.

"Come on, class," she finished, shuffling them along, "let's go rejoin the others."

Around the corner, down on the main floor, some older students from Professor Charles Xavier's School for Gifted Youngsters were checking out a reconstructed skeleton labeled SABER-TOOTHED TIGER. Their comments were mostly about a notorious mutant who'd adopted the same name and was currently the object of a hugely unsuccessful worldwide manhunt.

The teacher responsible for watching them was only partly paying attention. His eyes and the bulk of his focus were on a slim, striking redhead who stood across the hall. She was a head shorter than he was, which made her about five-foot-seven to his six-plus, with legs that went on forever, a figure to die for, and a face to match. Her eyes were the green of a spring forest and had a sparkle that would put the finest emerald to shame.

His own eyes, she had never seen. He kept them hidden behind specially designed glasses whose lenses were made of a ruby quartz so dense the crystal seemed almost opaque. Sometimes he wasn't even sure there were proper eyes at all within their sockets anymore, although he had perfect twenty-twenty vision. Instead, there were beams of pure force that Xavier had labeled "optic blasts," powerful enough to knock a tank end over end or punch holes through mountains. Unlike the others with their powers, Scott Summers had no control over his. He couldn't shut off his beams; they blasted away 24/7, as they'd done since he was a teenager. Even closing his eyes didn't help. For some perverse reason, his eyelids—or his hands—were able to block the beams; he couldn't do damage to himself. But the beams themselves were so powerful they'd take advantage of the slightest gap. A twitch of the eye, the slightest relaxation, meant instant disaster. So, to keep from devastating his surroundings, he had to wear these glasses—or a visor that even allowed him to manipulate the strength of the blasts—constantly.

The eyes, so the saying goes, are the window to the soul. He didn't like to think how that might apply to him.

Aside from that, Scott Summers was a fair package. Good lines to his face, the kind of clean-shaven, handsome features that may have started out slightly pretty but which improved markedly with age. His hair was brown, with a hint of auburn, and when he spoke there was a faint echo of Nebraska in his voice. He was a natural leader, the sort of young man who would seem at home taming a frontier, although he himself would scoff at the description.

He was hopelessly in love with the redhead, Jean Grey, and had been since the moment they'd first met.

She saw him watching and flashed him a smile that made his heart sing and ache all at the same time, and wish they were alone. Then her eyes slipped past him and the students they were minding to a clutch of tourists just down the gallery, and her lips tightened, her smile quickly becoming a work of fiction and artifice. Scott immediately intuited what was happening. Once more her mental barriers had turned porous and Jean was finding herself caught in a rapidly rising tide of thoughts and emotions. That was how she described it to him, late at night, usually with wine, on the increasingly rare occasions when he could get her to relax. The hardest part about being a telepath, she explained, wasn't "reading" other peoples' thoughts, it was keeping them out of your own head. If your control slipped, if the shields failed, it was so easy to be overwhelmed, like standing in a puddle one second and being lost in the middle of a raging ocean the next.

But Jean had another problem. She wasn't simply a telepath, but a telekine. She could manipulate physical objects with the power of her thoughts and will. And when she was stressed, like now, that second aspect of her abilities as a mutant gave the conflict within her a tangible, material dimension.

Just like now.

The glass wall of the display behind her was trembling, displaying visible ripples like the surface of a pond being stirred by an autumn breeze. As Scott stepped forward, he could see the window warp in its frame, the metal creaking quietly in futile protest. In another moment it was sure to shatter—and Jean hadn't noticed. The interactive display TV monitors flashed with static.

"Hey," he said gently, slipping his arm in hers.

"Hey," she said, visibly relaxing as she reacted to his presence, before her eyes widened, her mouth pursing in tired frustration, as she realized the reason. The glass behind her was still once more, and solid. The voices had silenced in her head. For a while.

Scott didn't need telepathy of his own to sense what

she was thinking, although her face masked that fury superbly. She had an impressive temper and, from God knows where, a wealth of profanity that beat anything he'd ever heard. She was a doctor, and she was proud. She didn't like being weak or vulnerable.

"You okay?" he asked.

Her eyes were half-closed, which undercut what she told him in answer: "Yeah," she said, giving him a reassuring squeeze. "I'm fine. It's just a headache."

Scott felt a tug on his other sleeve and turned to see one of the students holding up a sketch she'd made of an iguanadon.

"Scott," she reminded him, "you were talking about the extinction of the dinosaurs. . . ."

He nodded and indicated the tiger display. "I need to talk to Dr. Grey real quick. Can you draw me a picture of that big cat?"

She sniffed, hugely uninterested. "It's a saber-toothed tiger."

"Right."

She took his cue and scampered off to join the other kids. Scott looked back to Jean, who chose to look anywhere but at him.

"It's not just a headache, is it?" he challenged.

She didn't want to talk about it, but this time he found he didn't want to hold back.

"I wasn't sure how to say this," he began, and then he paused, concern vying for dominance with his prairie rectitude. He understood her desire for privacy. In the orphanage, growing up, you played every emotion, every thought, tighter to your chest than a winning poker hand. But she was in pain and it wasn't getting any better and that was more than he could bear.

"Look, Jean," he began again, "ever since Liberty Island you've been—"

"Scott," she tried to interrupt. He didn't let her.

"—*different.*"

"My telepathy's been off lately," she confessed. "I can't seem to focus. I can hear . . . everything."

He shook his head, ruthlessly exploiting the opening she'd given him, hoping she'd understand, praying it would pay off. "A month ago you had to concentrate just to levitate a book across the room. Now when you have nightmares the entire bedroom shakes. It's not just your telepathy."

She left her arm in his, her grip tightening around his fingers, while she splayed her other hand against the glass in front of her, as if to reassure herself that she hadn't done it any lasting damage. At the same time, as she watched the room behind them both in the window's reflection, he was reminded of how science teachers used to warn about looking at a solar eclipse. The only safe way to gaze at the sun was through a reflection; do it directly, you'll go blind. Jean had that same apprehension about people. And it was growing.

"The dreams are getting worse," she told him. "I keep feeling that something terrible is about to happen."

She leaned her forehead against the glass and spoke so softly Scott couldn't tell if the words came from her lips or from her thoughts.

"I don't want to lose you," she said.

He wrapped his free hand around her and pulled her close against him.

"I'm not going anywhere," he told her.

She relaxed against him, but only a little bit, leaning her head into the junction of his neck and shoulder but keeping her eyes open and on the glass, with a stare that seemed to go on forever, as though she was searching for something.

He wondered, and hoped she had grace enough not to pry, if what she was searching for had a face. Handsome and hairy and Canadian, Logan had rolled into their lives like an avalanche and wreaked just about as much havoc. It drove Scott a little crazy to think that, only a few months ago, there'd been no Logan to complicate their lives—and yet, without Logan, he and Jean and Storm wouldn't have stood a chance when Xavier's former colleague and friend, who now called himself Magneto, had tried to reshape the face of the world. All as part of a misguided attempt to guarantee the future safety and prosperity of mutantkind.

He believed as an article of absolute faith that Jean loved him. It was the keystone of his world, as he hoped his own love served for hers. But he could also see what happened when Jean and Logan came near each other. That kind of primal attraction was impossible to hide, and trust Logan not to even try.

They hadn't heard from him since he left the school, to follow some leads Professor Xavier had provided about his mysterious past. And Scott knew there hadn't been a day since when Jean hadn't thought of him. The questions he had were, *how* did she think of him? And what was she going to do about it?

And when that moment came, what would Scott do?

"Are we interrupting again?" Storm said softly as she came around the corner and into view.

Because the two women were best friends, Jean didn't react to her arrival as any sort of intrusion. She took a moment to gather wits and self-possession, gradually disengaging from Scott—her hand staying closed around his right to the last—using her telepathy to partially cloud the perceptions of the kids so they wouldn't easily recall how vulnerable she looked.

"So," Storm continued cheerily, "how was the giant squid?"

"The children liked it," Jean replied. "Scott was bored."

"It was boring," he agreed wholeheartedly. And then, taking refuge in responsibility, "Guys, if we don't want to get stuck in rush-hour traffic—"

"We should get moving," Jean finished.

Storm absently acknowledged their decision. She wasn't quite paying attention, though, as she finished a quick headcount of their charges. She didn't look happy.

"Wait," she said in a tone that made clear she wasn't really surprised, just disappointed. "We're short."

Jean concentrated, and Scott know she was casting a mental net across the whole of the museum.

"We should find the professor," she said.

In the museum's basement was the food court, with seats galore and offering a surprisingly eclectic collection of items, ranging from burgers to sushi. Off in a corner all their own, polishing off the remains of a modest feast, were Xavier's three missing students. Two boys and a girl, all in their midteens.

One of the boys was slightly taller than the other, both their bodies built pretty much the same, both of them slightly taller than the girls. The taller boy had pleasant, regular features, with curly blondish hair that looked like he generally used his fingers in place of a comb, in a vain attempt to establish some kind of order. His companion's face was sharper, a little more technically handsome, thick brown hair swept straight back from his face. He had a Zippo lighter in hand, and the way he kept snapping it open, igniting a flame, snapping it closed, to the beat of a doo-wop song only he could hear, went with the hair and manner to present him as a reincarnated fifties rebel.

The girl was southern; that was obvious the minute she said a word. She was pretty, on her way to beautiful, with eyes green enough to put Jean Grey's to shame. Her shoulder-length dark hair had a dramatic streak as purely white as Storm's that rose from the peak of her forehead, in absolute contrast to the rich auburn that covered the rest of her skull. Unlike the others, she wore gloves at the table, and long sleeves and a high collar, and the coat that was slung back on her shoulders had a hood so that when it was pulled up the only part of her body that showed any skin was her face. She also sat a little apart from the others, as if she was wary of touching or being touched.

"So I'm asking," said the dark-haired boy with the lighter, John Allardyce, "what would be worse, to be burned to death or frozen?"

The girl made an appropriately dismissive face, this was so *not* why they had snuck away from the crowd, but John could be worse than a mastiff with some topics. Try as you might, there was no way to get him to back off.

In any event, Bobby Drake wasn't in the mood. He looked intensely perplexed, facing a problem that taxed his obviously meager mental resources, while Marie fidgeted under John's stare, and Kitty wondered how big a fight she'd start if she just snatched that damn lighter away. The boy loved that Zippo more than she did her stuffed snugglies! Too totally creepy for words.

"Gosh," Bobby began, which made John chuckle because only a lamoid straight would use a word like "gosh," "I dunno, John. Seems like being burned would be awfully painful. . . ."

John flicked the lighter again, his eyes momentarily caressing the flame before returning to Marie, who tried to look bored to tears as she met that gaze but knew she wasn't quite pulling it off.

"It is," John said.

Marie turned her eyes away and knew the moment she did that she'd made a mistake. There was another crowd of teens sitting at the next table, a little bit older, taking advantage of this out-of-the-way alcove to sneak some smokes. One of them looked up at exactly the same moment, and for that moment their gazes locked. He smiled, Marie let the edges of her mouth quirk in response, then she turned back to her friends in time to hear Bobby start to turn the verbal tables on John.

"But you know," Bobby said, "there's something pretty agonizing about freezing to death. You don't just drift off to sleep like most people think."

"Damn," Marie muttered, "I was *so* hoping for a nap!"

"Enlighten us, snowman," John instructed.

"It all starts with shivering. Just a little at first as the body struggles to keep warm. Your skin turns a pale blue."

"Guys, not again," Marie pleaded. "Change of topic, okay?"

Being guys, they ignored her.

"Then," Bobby continued, "the moisture in your lungs starts to freeze, so that even breathing is painful."

"This conversation," she tried again, "is painful!"

Marie snuck another sidelong glance at the other table, to find two pairs of eyes staring back. They looked nice, they looked interesting, they were a pleasant change to this pissing match she had heard too many times before. So when they smiled, she didn't try to hide her response.

Neither of the boys at her table even noticed.

"Those shivers," Bobby said, "turn into violent convulsions as your blood begins to crystallize."

The other boys got up from their table.

"Wouldn't you be, like, *so* dead by then, Bobby?" asked Marie in a tone that broadcast boredom.

"Worse," he replied. "Your brain starts to scream for oxygen and you can't stop yourself slowly, inexorably sinking into complete and utter . . . *insanity*!"

John looked wholly unimpressed. Marie actually yawned.

"Insanity, huh? I s'pose that might be considered an improvement over this little colloquy."

"Hey," said one of the boys from the next table.

All three of Xavier's students looked up. Marie turned around in her chair to find the boys standing over her. This was *so* not what she wanted. It had never occurred to her that they'd take a little bit of flirting as an outright invitation.

"He said, 'Hey,' " said one of the others, after an uncomfortable silence.

"Hey," Bobby replied with a grin, hoping to defuse the situation.

But it didn't work. The others had responded to what they thought were a set of definite cues. When Marie didn't greet them enthusiastically, they weren't happy to discover they'd perhaps made a mistake, and adolescent pride wouldn't let them back down.

The second boy spoke again, jabbing a thumb toward his friend, who took a drag on his cigarette—ostensibly to show how cool he was, but more likely to hide a sudden attack of nerves. "He was talking to *her*," the boy said, meaning his friend and meaning Marie.

"What's your name?" the first boy asked.

She had more than one, but the situation was making her a little bit nervous as well, and the boys were crowding her awfully close. So she answered with the name she'd chosen for herself, rather than the one with which she'd been born.

"Rogue," she said.

That prompted a snort from the third newcomer.

"Cool," he said, meaning exactly the opposite, as in "look at these prep school jag-offs throwing off street names, figuring we'll be impressed." "This is Slash," boy number one, "And I'm Bobcat! Nice ta meetcha!"

He finished by reaching for Marie's arm.

Bobby intercepted him, placing his hand on the older teen's wrist and speaking as easily as could be. "You really don't want to touch her."

"Excuse me," said Bobcat.

"Or what?" echoed Slash, "you gonna hurt him?"

Bobby shook his head. "Nope. But *she* might."

The two teens looked at him, looked at Marie, looked at each other—and burst out laughing. To them, it was such an outrageous idea, there was no other response, which was precisely what Bobby had in mind. It made the Xavier's students look a little silly and gave these guys a way out without losing face. Crisis averted, no harm done.

But John Allardyce wouldn't let it go.

"You know," he said, his voice dripping unmistakably acid contempt, "there's no smoking in here."

That was a challenge. No way would the others back down now.

"No shit?" Slash sounded incredulous, returning an equal measure of insult. "Really? You got a problem with that?"

John flicked his lighter—open, closed, open, closed— while never taking his eyes off Slash.

Slash gestured toward John's lighter with his cigarette. "Got a light?" Challenge, served and returned. Another opportunity for all concerned to back off.

John wasn't interested. He was enjoying himself.

"It's a simple question," Slash said, finishing with the silent but unmistakable comment "asshole."

John shrugged, so bored. "And I'll give you a simple answer." Suggesting, just as plainly, that these mooks were too damn dumb for anything better.

Slash let his temper show, spacing his words for emphasis: "Do . . . you . . . have . . . a . . . light?"

John kept flicking the cap of his lighter. "Sorry, pal," he said, "can't help ya."

Marie sighed.

"Knock it off, John," Marie hissed at him.

"Please," Bobby echoed in frustration, figuring that before this was through he was going to have to grab his friend and hustle him bodily out of here.

"Yeah, John," Shadow chimed in, "listen to your girlfriends."

John, not about to yield center stage, winked at Marie.

"I'm sorry, guys," he told them all. "Besides the fact that this is clearly marked as a nonsmoking environment"—he pointed to a sign—"I couldn't bear knowing that I contributed to your collective slow, tumor-ridden deaths."

For final emphasis, he flicked his lighter shut. But he'd miscalculated as Slash snatched it away.

"What's this?" he demanded, spinning it between his own fingers. "A fashion accessory?"

His pals laughed and smirked, enjoying how the tables had suddenly turned in their favor. John, all humor gone from his face, lunged for the lighter, only to be shoved hard by Bobcat back into his chair.

Slash struck a flame and lit his cigarette, making an exaggerated show of blowing a lungful of smoke into John's face.

Later, much later, they all told themselves they should have seen this moment coming, they should have been prepared, they should have stopped him. Truth was, though, they never imagined it *could* happen. John, of all people, knew the nature of his mutant power and how important—how *essential*—it was to use it properly. They didn't think he was serious, and once it started, there was simply no time.

John was a pyrotic. His mutant ability was to control flame. Before any of them could stop him, before they realized the danger, he amplified the tip of the burning cigarette to white-hot incandescence and sent it flashing all the way to the boy's fingers and beyond. Instantly what was left of the cigarette was reduced to ash. Slash opened his hand, even as the tips of his fingers blistered from the sudden, scorching heat, but it was far too late as raw flame raced up his sleeve to ignite his jacket and hair and set him aflame from head to toe.

Slash screamed—mostly in terror, there hadn't been time yet for any pain to register—and reeled away from the corner, slapping at himself in a doomed attempt to extinguish the flames. A succession of other screams were heard as patrons of the food court reacted to what was happening, scrambling to get clear of the young man or pull their own children to safety, calling for fire extinguishers, starting a stampede for the sole exit.

John stayed where he was, watching with a smile.

With a curse, Bobby leaped to his feet, reaching out to Slash with his right hand, which suddenly turned transparent, as if the skin had turned to crystal-clear ice. The temperature in the corner dropped so low, so fast, that every breath around their table left clouds in the air, but more importantly a stream of frost embraced Slash like a blanket to smother his flames.

Marie stood, but before she could get clear of the corner the second boy—Bobcat—made a grab for her. In her hurry, her coat had slipped off her shoulder, baring a stretch of bicep. Bare hand closed on bare arm, flesh made direct contact with flesh, and all of a sudden Bobcat looked like he'd just been hit in the belly by a battering ram.

His mouth opened wide, but he couldn't find the air—or even the will—to shriek his heart out as veins distended on his head and throat and Marie bared her own teeth in a grimace of sympathetic pain, giving voice herself to the raw terror the young man felt. In midscream, she wrenched free of him, breaking contact with such force that Bobcat collapsed forward onto the table, and Marie stumble-spun into John's arms, which made his day.

Bobcat pulled himself up and cocked a fist to deliver a blind-side punch to John's head.

The punch was never thrown.

The three Xavier students looked around in amazement to discover that every person in the food court was frozen in place. They looked accusingly at Bobby, but he only shrugged in helpless demurral: This wasn't his doing.

Then the penny dropped, and four sets of eyes turned as one to the doorway, where Charles Xavier sat grim-faced in his chair. Clustered close behind him were Jean, Scott, and Storm, and, farther back, the rest of the tour group. One look at the faces of their teachers told the students how badly they'd just screwed up. "The next time you feel like showing off, don't!" the professor said curtly.

Standing, Charles Xavier would have matched Scott Summer's height, but he was in a wheelchair and had been for as long as the young man had known him. He was twice Scott's age and more, but he carried those years easily, and the wiry strength of his body made no concession to his disability. He spoke with a rich English accent he'd acquired as a student at Cambridge and although he possessed a smile as generous as his nature, he generally presented himself in a manner as formal as his attire. When he looked you in the eye, he gave the impression that your whole being had suddenly gone transparent. Scott was one of the few who knew that wasn't hyperbole. Xavier was a telepath, perhaps the foremost on Earth. He could read minds as easily as anyone else might read a book. Jean was his prize pupil.

He had founded his school to provide a venue where

young mutants could learn not simply to use their powers properly and safely, but also responsibly. The core curriculum was as much about the ethics of being a mutant as the practicalities. At the moment it was plain that he was wondering why he even bothered.

As the students gathered their gear and trudged across the court, a look suddenly swept across Jean's face, as if she'd heard something from outside the building. Xavier's concentration was occupied keeping the patrons of the food court "off-line"; he hadn't noticed what she had.

There was a television set suspended from the ceiling, turned off. A faint flicker of energy appeared around Jean's eyes, and the set came on. The channel quickly changed to Fox News as a title banner at the bottom of the screen announced the news that the midday anchor was breathlessly repeating aloud: MUTANT ASSASSINATION ATTEMPT. Behind the anchor there was a secondary window showing a live shot of the White House, surrounded by Secret Service and a detachment of Marines in full combat gear.

". . . we repeat," the anchor was saying, relief as palpable on her face and in her voice as terror, "the President is unharmed. We are awaiting confirmation from the White House, but informed sources have told Fox News that an attempt was made on the President's life less than an hour ago by an assailant who has been tentatively identified as a *mutant*!"

No one said a word for what seemed like the longest time. Scott finally broke the silence.

"Professor, " he said quietly, "people, I think it's time to go."

Xavier drew a deep breath and nodded his head.

"I think you're right," he agreed.

A moment later, the food court came back to life—with a startled yelp from over by the soft ice cream machine as the attendant found his hand covered with chocolate/vanilla twist. Slash couldn't recall why he was on his hands and knees—or why he smelled like he'd just walked through a smoke factory—as he sucked on a set of scorched fingertips, but right then and there he made a silent vow that he and cigarettes were done. As for the rest, they had no idea that a minute was missing from their lives, or that the table in the corner had been occupied by a pair of boys and a girl. Or that those three teens had ever even existed.

Outside, Scott pushed Xavier's chair while Jean and Storm kept the children in line as they hurried past a succession of momentarily "frozen" patrons on their way to the parking lot.

Marie had her coat wrapped close around her, her hood pulled up to hide her face, and while she kept pace with the group, she kept a definite distance between herself and everybody else. Bobby tried to walk beside her, but she made it clear she wasn't interested, and he had sense enough to back off.

# Chapter
# Three

A straight line from Xavier's School on Graymalkin Lane in the town of Salem Center to the Empire State Building runs forty-five miles. An hour by Metro North from Grand Central Station, generally two by car at rush hour.

Scott made better time than that. There wasn't much traffic on the roads, everyone seemed to be glued to the nearest TV, waiting for word from Washington on the President's condition and what might happen next. Lacking definitive hard news—beyond the initial announcement of the attack and the fact that the President was alive and unharmed—talking heads filled the airwaves with blather and speculation, almost all of it fixated on the as-yet unconfirmed report that the assailant was some kind of mutant, and almost all of it hostile. Was this a follow-up, people wondered, to the recent mutant terrorist attack on the World Unity Conference on Ellis Island? Had any other nations been attacked? Was the President the only target? Was this a conspiracy? Was it a declaration of war?

The questions fed on one another like a brushfire. Even the President's hurried appearance and brief statement from the White House Press Room didn't make much difference. It was as if there was this incredible reservoir of anxiety where it came to mutants, held back by a dam of faith and hope that the government had a handle on the situation, that maybe mutants weren't so bad. With this one terrible blow, the dam had cracked and people across the country, across the world, were venting their fears about what would come next.

As more details about the attack were revealed, this proved a far more damaging blow to the national psyche than the Ellis Island incident. That had involved some incredible machine whose fantastic energies had lit up the New York skyline more vividly than any fireworks display. No one had really understood what was going on, save that official spokesmen said it was really dangerous.

This, though, was a man with a knife, who'd penetrated one of the most secure locations in existence. If mutants could get that close to the President, where only a miracle had saved him, nobody was safe.

The irony was, the mutants—young and old, students and teachers—driving through the wrought-iron gates that marked the entrance to Xavier's School for Gifted Youngsters felt just the same. Fearful that a suddenly uncertain present was giving way to an ominous and threatening future.

Xavier's ancestors had settled this part of Westchester County when Salem Center itself was little more than a tavern and trading post. They'd laid claim to a five-mile stretch of land along the north shore of Breakstone Lake and held on to it ever since. Some generations prospered, others struggled, as what began as the wilderness frontier gradually evolved into one of the wealthiest counties on the globe, home now to billionaires and ex-presidents.

But the enduring constant for the family was that they never let go of their land.

The original mansion had been Georgian in style, two stories high with pillared porticos offering a magnificent view down the sweeping lawn to the lake. A century or so later, it was replaced by the current structure, a late Victorian stronghold of dark, gray stone, meant to look as solid and eternal as the lake itself. They built big in those days, so what was entirely excessive for a family residence became ideal for a school. There were wings and battlements and turrets galore and a layout so eccentric every new arrival was told suitably spooky stories about kids who'd gotten lost, never to be seen again. The newbies scoffed, of course—until one of them actually did get lost. Then they paid more attention to the maps and the rules.

Classes had already been canceled for the day because of the field trip, which left the students free to find their own ways of coping with the news.

Theresa Roarke angrily stormed out of the common room, snarling to everyone within earshot how fed up she was with the doom and gloom that filled every channel and radio frequency. She'd grown up in Northern Ireland; terrorism was a fact of life for her. She learned early to cope with the moment but not to obsess. Feel angry, fine. Feel scared, fine. Wallow in it, not on a bet. Especially on so beautiful an afternoon. Especially if that afternoon could be shared with a certain boy.

Tracy was everything her name and antecedents implied: sandy red hair and aquamarine eyes, pert features, a dusting of freckles across a classic peaches-and-cream complexion, a face and figure that nicely mixed cute and pretty. She was a girl of big gestures and big emotions.

She had a voice like an angel, if that angel liked to hang out in honky-tonks and sing Motown, and she could dance everyone else in the school, teachers included, into the ground.

On the surface, Jamie Madrox was her polar opposite, matching her fierce passion with an almost infuriating calm, still water where she was a roiling cataract. He was Canadian, from Saskatchewan, where the land is flat and covered with wheat. He was a farm boy and proud of it, he liked growing things, and soon after arriving at Xavier's he took over the care and feeding of the estate's formal garden. He was the only kid in school who could keep up with Tracy; that came from running mile after mile across the prairie, and from winters pounding up and down the community rink playing ice hockey. But what she really adored about him was his mouth. She tended to slash and burn anyone who crossed. She had a temper and a tendency to scorch those who ignited it. Jamie, though, had that trademark Canadian knack for irony. He'd smile at the person making fun, as though he was too dumb to realize what was being said, and then respond with such outward politesse that it took the other person a minute to realize how deftly the insult had been turned back. By then, of course, everyone else was in stitches laughing. There was always the possibility of a fight, but then again, Jamie was a farm boy and he had a farm boy's physique.

He and Bobby Drake were roommates. Jamie didn't mind that Bobby had adopted his style.

Tracy was waiting for him by the fountain that some Xavier ancestor had decided would be the perfect design element for the patio. The fact that it was a monstrosity, totally at odds with all the architectural elements around it, evidently hadn't been a consideration. At one time or other, just about every student in the school had fantasized about using his or her mutant powers to make the fountain go away, but until somebody acted on those impulses, it was the ideal place to meet.

She'd been picking flowers, and as Jamie approached she held them out for him to take a sniff. Too much pollen, or dust or something; he knew right away he was in trouble. He started to back away, but the sneeze caught him in midstep. The way he reacted, it might as well have been a rocket engine firing. Off balance, he went straight down on his butt, landing hard at the very moment the force of the sneeze doubled him over . . .

. . . and, just like that, thirty identical copies of him filled the patio.

He took a great breath, desperate to calm himself before another such outburst triggered a second attack of doubling. That was his power, to take the kinetic energy of any physical blow and use it to manifest duplicates of himself.

Tracy's power was the embodiment of her code name: Siryn.

She was startled enough when Jamie fell. Seeing him megadouble for the first time spooked her completely.

She screamed.

Jamie covered his ears, but that didn't do much good as the sonic waves lanced right through the bones of his skull. The air around him shimmered with the raw force of her outburst, flowers and shrubs bent as if they'd been hit by a sudden gust of wind, and every lightbulb within eyesight instantly shattered.

Tracy stopped, covering her mouth with both hands in shock and shame as the echo of her shriek hung between them a few moments longer. She looked around at the shattered bulbs, the cracked and crazed windows, and she bolted.

Jamie knew better than to follow. He wiped his upper lip and took a big sniff to stop his nose from bleeding. Tracy hated losing control, and whenever she did she demanded to be left alone until she worked through it enough to come back and apologize.

He looked up, saw Scott Summers looking down from an upper-floor turret window, where Jamie knew the staff had their lounge, and shrugged. The course of true love—yada yada yada.

Scott offered a small smile he knew the boy down below couldn't see and traced his fingers lightly over the hairline cracks that Siryn's scream had caused in the windowpane. If Jamie's doubles lasted long enough, he'd put them to work replacing the glass. Afterward, when he had the time, Scott would have to see if he could make the panes more resistant to sonic attack.

*Everything all right?*

His smile broadened inside at the sound of Jean's thoughts mixing with his. It was the strangest and most wonderful sensation, to know that they were standing on opposite sides of the room yet to feel her inside himself, as real and tangible as could be. When she spoke to him telepathically, he processed it the same as verbal speech, but it came with so much more besides. He had a sense of her emotions, as well, layer upon layer of subtle textures that made the most innocent exchanges incredibly intimate. For someone as private, as guarded, as he, the miracle wasn't that she could share herself so with him, but that he didn't mind.

greatest potential of going active with puberty. He sought them out and recruited them to his school. Here, they received a first-rate academic education; they also learned how to use their powers and the ethics of doing so responsibly.

At the same time, Xavier knew there were mutants—some, like Lehnsherr, already well established—who had no regard for the constraints of society. To oppose such mutants, Xavier had established a strike force, which he code-named X-Men. The founding members were Scott, Jean Grey, and Storm. One other mutant had been involved in the confrontation with Magneto on Liberty Island, but Scott wasn't sure if he qualified as a recruit. He didn't seem interested in joining the team; it was more a marriage of necessity. His name was Logan; code name, Wolverine.

He'd left right afterward, and Scott hadn't shed any tears, metaphorical or otherwise, to see him go, because it was becoming more and more apparent that the man had taken a bit of Jean's heart with him.

Scott blinked, belatedly realizing that Xavier had spoken to him. He blinked again while he shifted mental gears to let the part of his consciousness that was paying attention move to the forefront. He had his own talents when it came to multitasking.

"My opinion," Scott said, taking another moment to shrug his shoulders even though he'd actually made up his mind the moment he first heard the news reports. "Magneto's behind this."

Surprisingly, instead of the professor himself, it was Jean who disagreed.

"No, Scott," she said. "I don't think so." Mentally

she provided an update on Jamie: *He's fine and back together.*

Xavier spoke now, thoughtfully: "While Eric is certainly capable of organizing something like this from prison—for him, such an act, such a gesture, is too . . . irrational. It does nothing to further his goal of mutant prosperity."

"You mean superiority."

"You're right." Xavier nodded. "If Eric had his way."

"Think of the repercussions, Professor," Scott said. "It pushes us into a corner, it forces everyone to choose sides. Mutants, good or evil, no more middle ground, no more equivocating."

"You know how the government will respond," Storm said. "They'll reintroduce the Mutant Registration Act."

"Or worse," Xavier agreed.

"He's a survivor of Auschwitz, Professor," Scott said, returning the topic to Magneto. "Maybe this is his own little version of the Reichstag Fire. Maybe he figures, by provoking an extreme response against mutants, we'll have no choice but to embrace his cause. Mutant superiority, mutant hegemony, guarantees mutant survival."

"Do you really believe that, Scott?"

"He does, Professor. That's what matters. I know he's your friend. I know this school is as much his creation as yours, but he's seen—he's survived—the worst we can do to one another. I think that's made him willing to do anything, *anything,* to prevent it from happening again. If that means destroying the village in order to save it, he's there, locked and loaded."

"The White House assassin's the key," Jean said.

Scott nodded agreement. "If the Feds had him, they'd have announced it. That means he's on the run."

"Could he have been working alone?"

"The only way to determine that," Xavier decided, "is to find him before the authorities do. Using Cerebro, I've identified his signature and have been able to track it to the vicinity of Boston. Jean, Storm, I'd like you to take the *Blackbird* and make contact. Hopefully, through him, we can defuse this nightmare before it gets any further out of hand."

Normally, the President's "body man"—his personal aide—ushered visitors into the Oval Office. Today, it was a Secret Service agent, hard-bodied and hard-faced, chosen for his intimidating size and strength to match.

"Mr. President," he said, stepping aside to allow the guest to enter as the President crossed the carpet with hands outstretched.

"William," he said. "A helluva day!"

"I came as soon as I heard, sir," the older man replied.

William Stryker stood a little shorter than the chief executive, but broader in the shoulders and the body. Looking at the pair of them, eyes instinctively went to Stryker as the more commanding presence. He had a full head of close-cropped hair that was still more pepper than salt, marking a distinct widow's peak on a broad forehead above deep-set eyes that missed nothing and gave away even less. This was not a man to face at poker, nor at chess. His cheeks were clean-shaven, but he favored a neatly trimmed mustache and beard around his mouth. He was a rugged man and utterly direct, so much so that people's first impressions cataloged him as having no subtlety or grace whatsoever, akin to plastering the shell of a Rolls-Royce over the body and soul of a Mack truck. It was a facade Stryker cultivated deliberately, and well. He made his career on the backs of adversaries who'd underestimated him. It was a mistake they rarely made twice, because he just as rarely allowed them to survive.

Without preamble, he leaned over the President's desk and idly rubbed a finger across the gash made by the mutant's knife.

"It was close, wasn't it?" he said, in a voice as accustomed to being heard on a battlefield as in the halls of Congress. "Far closer than anyone's admitted."

George McKenna didn't reply at once. He waited for the door to close, for the two men to be alone—that is, if he didn't count the two Secret Service agents flanking the fireplace and a young woman standing over in the corner. Obviously a secretary, so unassuming and inconspicuous it was easy to forget she was even there. Which made Stryker smile to himself as he turned toward the President. From where she sat, she had a better view of the room than the two men, which meant in any combat situation she'd be the key player. The report he'd read mentioned that a female agent had shot the mutant and probably saved the President's life. No doubt this was her.

McKenna finished pouring brandy and handed one of the cut crystal snifters to Stryker, indicating a seat on the couch. McKenna, being President, took the chair beside it.

"What do you need, William?" the President asked, meaning "What do you want?"

Stryker flicked his glance to the watching agents, which provoked a humorless chuckle from the President.

"They're here for the duration, I'm afraid," McKenna said, making a fair attempt to keep the comment light and casual. He was handling this better than Stryker had expected. "In fact, I had the devil's own time keeping them from posting agents in my own damn bedroom."

"I can imagine the first lady's reaction, sir."

"So could they. I think that's why they caved." The President took a small sip of brandy, letting the prompting expression on his face repeat the question he'd asked.

"Your authority, sir," Stryker replied, "for a special operation."

McKenna took another swallow of brandy and leaned back in his chair.

"And somehow I thought you'd come to talk about school reform."

Stryker uttered a short, barklike laugh. "That was top of your schedule for today, as I recall. Funny you should mention it, though."

He looked up, irritated, at the sound of a discreet knock. This time it was the President's aide who stuck his head in. McKenna himself, Stryker noted, wasn't surprised. The meeting wasn't to be as private as he'd first assumed.

The new arrival was a face as well known on the nation's airwaves as the President's himself, as befit someone who'd made his own run for the White House in years past. Robert Kelly, senator from Massachusetts, was ambitious enough to try again, young enough to wait, smart enough to bide his time. In the meanwhile, he continued to build a strong activist record in Congress, reaching out to conservative and liberal constituencies alike with a success that hadn't been seen since the campaign of RFK.

Stryker, who was good with details, noticed that the senator was in much better shape than he recalled. The man had a tendency to indulge himself in just about everything and used to have a knack for making a custom-tailored wardrobe look rumpled and off the rack. Not anymore. There was a crispness to his appearance and manner that echoed Stryker's own.

"I'm not sure if the two of you have ever officially met," the President said. "Senator Robert Kelly of Massachusetts, William Stryker—"

"Of No-Name, Nevada," Stryker finished.

"Mr. Stryker," Kelly said, smiling at the small joke as the two men shook hands.

"Call me William . . . Bobby," Stryker replied, intentionally using the diminutive. Kelly didn't appear to notice. His grip had improved, too. Used to be he'd close his hand around the other person's fingers in what Stryker thought of as a sissy shake. This one was palm to palm, man to man, strong and secure.

"Mr. President," Kelly said as he sat on the couch opposite, in a way that allowed him to relate to both McKenna and Stryker without moving. The President, in his chair, was able to do the same. Stryker, though, oriented as he was toward the President, was forced to turn right around to face Kelly, partially turning his back to McKenna. It was a superb tactical move, immediately putting Stryker in an awkward position. Stryker, who was far more used to doing this to others, wasn't happy, but he'd be damned if he'd allow either man to see.

"I appreciate your allowing me to sit in on this meeting," Kelly said.

"I value your input, Robert, as I do William's. He's with the . . . intelligence community . . ."

"Which element?" Kelly asked.

"It's not important," the President said.

"It's just that I'm ranking member of the Joint Intelligence Committee—"

"Robert," the President said, allowing the faintest edge to his voice, "it's not important."

"Yes, sir. Sorry, sir."

"As I was saying, his task force has been studying the mutant phenomenon for us since . . . well, before my time in office."

"So I've heard, albeit only as rumors. For a man as influential as you, William, you leave damn small footprints."

"I must be slipping," Stryker said with a smile. "The idea is to leave no footprints at all."

"You definitely have some interesting ideas . . . and methods."

"I get the job done, that's true. I've followed your career with interest for years, Bobby. As I recall, you were a staunch supporter of the registration act. I must confess though, your ideas on the mutant problem appear to have . . . changed recently."

"For the best, I trust."

"Myself, I trust in God."

"Since Senator Kelly has been at the forefront of *both* sides of this issue," the President interjected, "I thought his perspective would be worthwhile."

"You're the commander in chief, sir," Stryker said.

"So, what are you proposing, Mr. Stryker?" Kelly asked directly.

Stryker didn't answer at first. His pause, and the look he gave the President, made plain that he considered this a need-to-know matter and that Robert Kelly wasn't on his personal list. The President frankly didn't care.

"You spoke about a special operation, William," prompted McKenna.

With a curt nod, acknowledging and accepting the President's authority even when he bitterly disagreed with it, Stryker opened his case and spread a set of glossy surveillance photos on the table, right at the end where the President could see them but Kelly could not.

"Working with the National Reconnaissance Office, my people have gathered these surveillance photos of a mutant training facility near the town of Salem Center, in Westchester County, right by the Connecticut border."

"How did you develop the information?"

"Discover the installation's existence, you mean? Primarily through interrogation of one of the terrorist prisoners captured after the Liberty Island incident."

"Eric?" Kelly asked sharply. "Eric Lehnsherr?"

"Code-named Magneto, yes," Stryker replied.

"You have access to him?"

Intrigued by Kelly's surge of interest, Stryker nodded. "My group developed the technology that built his plastic prison when, I might add, Mr. President, your defense department couldn't find room for the allocation in their own budget."

"At the time," the President said slowly, "the need didn't seem pressing."

"Priorities, sir, I do understand. Threats are easily identifiable in hindsight. The challenge for a prudent and responsible leader is identifying clear and present dangers to the nation and dealing with them *before* there's a disaster."

He indicated another set of photographs.

"It appears," he said, "I'm not the only one with access to the prisoner. This man"—he pointed to a bald-headed figure in a wheelchair—"we've identified as Charles Xavier.

The leader of this training facility and a longtime associate of Mr. Lehnsherr. Apparently Xavier has . . . friends in the Justice Department. Since Lehnsherr's incarceration, he's paid several visits."

Kelly leaned forward for a closer look at the pictures. His tone and manner were discreetly skeptical.

"What is this place?" he asked.

"Ostensibly, a school," responded Stryker with a humorless chuckle. "For 'gifted' youngsters."

He tossed a fresh set of photos on the table, for both men to see.

"We retasked a keyhole spy satellite to get these," he said. "I believe you'll agree the results are worth the expense."

For pictures taken from two hundred fifty miles above Manhattan, with camera lenses powerful enough to read the lettering on a pack of cigarettes and enhancement technology that allowed them to work as effectively at night as during the day, the results were extraordinary, and devastating.

"What's that?" asked McKenna.

"A jet."

McKenna gave him a sour look. "What kind of jet?"

"We don't know—but as you can see, it comes up out of the basketball court."

In a sequence of images, as the President passed the eight by ten sheets across to Kelly, they saw a court behind the main house slide apart to allow an elevator platform to rise to the surface from what had to be an underground hangar. The plane that was revealed was unlike anything the President had ever seen, twin engined and twin tailed with forward-swept wings. It rose into the air on vertical thrusters, shifted to horizontal flight, and was quickly gone from sight, as its flight path and the satellite's orbital track took the vehicles in opposite directions.

"I've talked to the Air Force," Stryker said. "I've talked to DARPA"—the Defense Advanced Research and Planning Agency. "They don't even have aircraft with capabilities like this on their drawing boards. And it clearly represents the ultimate in stealth technology as well. We examined every radar record we could find, civil and military, for the time and course indicated. Not a trace."

Stryker waved his arm to encompass the Oval Office, with a pointed look at one wall where the bullet holes from the attack hadn't yet been patched.

"You gentlemen ask yourselves: How could this have happened?" he snorted in disgust. "How could it *not* have?"

Kelly held up another photo. "These are *children.*"

"Being trained, being indoctrinated, for what purpose, Senator?" retorted Stryker. "How many miles of news footage are there from the Middle East, showing children dressed up as terrorists?"

"These are American citizens, none of whom—that I'm aware of—have committed any crime."

Stryker turned to the President: "Sir, if we had been allowed to do our jobs before this attack—"

"What would you need?" McKenna asked.

"Just your authorization."

"To do *what* precisely?" Kelly demanded, because he knew the President would not.

Again Stryker ignored him, concentrating solely on McKenna. "Don't misunderstand my goals, Mr. President. I just want to go in there—to see precisely what they're up to. If they have nothing to hide, they have nothing to fear."

"It's illegal," snapped Kelly.

"Not if they're terrorists," replied Stryker calmly. "For over a year now, we've been tracking this mutant in particular. His origins are European, but we believe there is a possible affiliation with this institution."

He pulled a last photo from his case and held it out to the President.

"This was taken three months ago," Stryker finished, but there was no more need for him to make his case. The moment McKenna saw the picture, his decision was made.

The figure in the picture was humanoid—that is, two arms, two legs, central trunk, bilateral symmetry. Two big digits on hands and feet, skin of indigo blue, hair a slight shade darker. Gleaming yellow eyes, fangs, pointed ears, and a long, pointed tail all combined to give him the look of a modish gargoyle come to life. He was snarling.

He was the assassin who'd almost killed this President.

"Listen to me, William," said McKenna, in the same still tone of absolute command he used with the joint chiefs. "You enter. You detain. You question." His voice took on a faint but unmistakable edge. "But the last thing I want to hear is that we've spilled the blood of an innocent child, mutant or otherwise. You understand?"

"Absolutely, Mr. President," Stryker replied.

The meeting over, Stryker had already reached the hallway outside the President's suite of offices by the time Kelly caught up with him. Repairs were much more evident here, as were armed guards.

"You made a powerful argument, William," he said.

"The evidence made the case, Bobby." Stryker indicated a lovely Asian woman who'd obviously been waiting for him. She wore a discreet but attractive business suit and carried herself in a way that made Kelly think, *Bodyguard*. She wore light sunglasses that allowed a view of her eyes but not of their color. "Please allow me to introduce Yuriko Oyama. She's my director of . . . special projects."

They shook hands. But when Kelly relaxed his grip, she tightened hers, just for a moment, enough to mean business.

Kelly obliged her with a wince, and once his hand was free he shook it a few times, wriggling his fingers to make sure they still worked.

"That's quite a handshake," he told her.

As Stryker and his assistant started for the exit, Kelly matched their pace. After a couple of steps, Stryker—eager and determined to be rid of him—stopped and confronted the younger man.

"What can I do for you, Senator?" he asked.

"Eric Lehnsherr's prison" was Kelly's quick reply. "If possible, I'd like to arrange a visit."

Stryker snorted. "It isn't a petting zoo, Senator. In this conflict, he's the enemy. You're just a spectator. Do us both a favor, and sit this one out, all right?"

"Are you trying to turn this into some kind of war?"

Outside the Oval Office, Stryker didn't bother to hide his deep contempt. "Senator"—and the way he said it turned that title into a profound insult—"I was piloting black-ops missions into the jungles of North Vietnam while you were suckling your momma's titties at Woodstock."

"Am I supposed to be impressed? We lost that one—
*Billy.*"

Contempt turned instantly and completely to fury, but
Stryker kept it confined to his eyes and his voice. He
moved in close to Kelly, speaking in a clipped, parade-
ground cadence that no one else would hear, jabbing his
thumb right to the base of the other man's breastbone
hard enough to hurt. If looks could kill, the man facing
him would have been burned to ash. Kelly, though, paid
no attention to either.

"Don't you *dare* presume to lecture me about war,
Senator. You don't want this to turn into a war? Sonny
boy, we're already there. The trouble is bleeding hearts
like you who are too damn dumb to realize it!"

"I appreciate your concerns. I'm simply suggesting
that perhaps your operation deserves a second thought."

"And I'm saying that you have no idea at all what's
going on around you. I really do hate to break this off,
but I'm afraid you're making me late for a rather pressing appointment. Good day, Senator."

He and Yuriko strode quickly away. As Kelly watched
them go, his expression darkening with every step, a
cloud seemed to pass across his eyes. Iris and pupil disappeared as the whole substance of his eyes suddenly, and
momentarily, turned chrome yellow, the same shade as
the assassin's.

Then, with a blink, they were back to normal. No one
around him had noticed.

His own steps were hurried and purposeful as the senator took his leave. He had some pretty urgent appoint-
ments himself.

# Chapter Four

In the 1950s, with the world perpetually poised on the brink of Armageddon, strategic planners had to devise a means for the government of the nation to survive a global thermonuclear war. The presumption was that Washington and its environs, which included the Pentagon and a whole host of major military installations, would be prime targets. What was required, therefore, was a location sufficiently far away to escape the brutal impact of multimegaton hydrogen bombs, yet convenient enough for the President and senior members of the civilian and military hierarchy to get there before the region was destroyed.

The choice was the Appalachian Mountains, due west of the capital, along a stretch of peaks that formed one wall of the Shenandoah Valley and also demarcated the border between Virginia and its neighbor West Virginia. The installation was built using the same principals employed in the construction of the headquarters of the North American Air Defense Command, inside the heart of Cheyenne Mountain, Colorado. A couple of mountains were hollowed out at the base, so that the ancient stone itself would provide the bulk of the protection for the people sheltering within. The compartments that filled this newly emptied space rested on gigantic shock absorbers. It was guaranteed by the designers and builders that only a direct hit would do any substantial damage. It was outfitted with state-of-the-art technology and hardware, together with resources to sustain the survivors for years if necessary.

Thankfully, it was never used.

With the ongoing collapse of the Soviet Union, and the consequent lessening of the traditional nuclear threat, this secret haven became gradually less important in the strategic scheme of things. It was considered an icon of a bygone age, like the battleship. Most in government simply forgot about it.

Not William Stryker.

As it became increasingly clear in recent years that the mutant situation, which he'd been addressing with increasing passion and vehemence, was something that had to be taken seriously, the question then arose: What to do with the mutants if things went bad? Where could the government possibly incarcerate a mutant criminal?

Mount Haven was Stryker's answer.

And Eric Lehnsherr became its first inmate.

As befit a man who styled himself the "master of magnetism," his cell was plastic, suspended by pliable plastic cables and beams in one of the chambers of the mountain that had been hollowed out but never fully converted. What had been left was a monumental box of a space, easily a thousand feet square, buried more than a thousand beneath the surface. The stone of the mountain itself was nonferrous, and the chamber's walls had been lined with molded plastic that was as strong as steel. The cell was transparent, as was all the furniture. The only opaque items were the inmate's clothes and the sheets and blankets on his bed, as well as the few items of reading material allowed him.

He was under constant surveillance, scanned by a vast array of cameras and electronic sensors and a full complement of guards. Their orders were strict and absolute. No metal of any kind was to be permitted into the stone chamber, much less the cell itself. No significant amount of metal—whether furniture or vehicles or even weapons—was to be permitted within a half mile of his cell. One positive surprise effect of his incarceration was a quantum leap in the practical design and technology applications of plastics.

The prisoner's clothes were a form of wearable paper, fastened with Velcro. As a condition of employment, guards had to have their metal fillings replaced by porcelain. You violated the rules, you got fired. No exceptions.

No one knew the true extent of Lehnsherr's power. No one wanted to find out the hard way. Better to conceive of the worst-case scenario and take all precautions from there.

Thing was, the man himself didn't look so fearsome. In person, the face possessed a dignity and a humanity that the holographic image Scott beheld at Xavier's lacked. His intelligence and his commitment were immediately clear. He was a man whose soul had been tempered by the most inhuman furnace, the great kilns of Auschwitz that had claimed his parents, his family, the life he knew and the one he'd dreamed of. He had survived there. He would survive here. Of that, plainly he had no doubt.

Access to his cell came through an umbilical walkway, a plastic tube that extended like an airport's jetway from the nearer wall. He didn't set down the book he was reading, T. H. White's masterwork about the life of King Arthur, *The Once and Future King*, until he heard the bolts cycle and the docking port at his end slide open.

Close up, the bruises on Lehnsherr's face were evident. The look on the face of the man entering the cell made it plain that he was the one who had inflicted them and was looking forward to delivering more. Mitchell Laurio had been chosen specifically to look after the prisoner at a time when it appeared certain his next visit to a prison would be as an inmate rather than a guard. Two felony indictments had been quashed to bring him here—for brutality, of course—and the day he started he was told the recorders would be turned off whenever he was in Lehnsherr's cell. He wasn't allowed to break any bones, he couldn't kill the old man.

Outside of that, he was told, anything goes.

This was nothing new to the prisoner. He wasn't yet even a teenager when he received his first beating from an SS guard. He also remembered what he'd done to that guard, years later, to repay him.

He met Laurio with a level gaze, eyes as deep and unreadable as an ocean abyss.

"Mr. Laurio," he said almost pleasantly, in his rounded, cultured voice that had its own distinct touch of England. "How long can we keep this up?"

Laurio cracked his knuckles. "How long you in for?"

"Forever."

"Not necessarily forever," Stryker said pleasantly from the walkway as he followed Laurio into the cell. "Just until I have what I need."

"Mr. Stryker," Lehnsherr said, his tone giving no sense of how he felt, his body language almost relaxed. "How kind of you to visit. Have you come back to make sure the taxpayer's dollars are keeping me . . . comfortable?"

"Simply a case of the punishment fitting the crime. Heads of state don't take kindly to being attacked. Quite a few of them wanted you killed. Without, I might add, benefit of a trial."

"How fortunate for you that, merely by labeling me a terrorist combatant, the government removed all need for such legal niceties."

"The ACLU is still filing briefs on your behalf. You never know, they may find the right judge, he may accept their writ of habeas corpus."

Both men knew that day would never come. Lehnsherr was here until he died, or found another way. The same rules as Auschwitz.

"In the meantime . . ."

Lehnsherr's eyes narrowed fractionally as Stryker withdrew a plastic case from an inside pocket of his suit jacket, and from that a small pipette of glowing yellow liquid. The prisoner started up from his chair, a reflexive gesture of resistance, which was just what Laurio was waiting for.

A swift, sharp application of his billy club to the back of the legs collapsed Lehnsherr's knees out from under him; an equally cruel jab to the side made the prisoner gasp. Laurio grabbed Lehnsherr's right arm in a brutal hammerlock, forcing the trapped hand almost all the way up to the other man's neck, clearly disappointed not to hear even a whimper of pain as he did. With his free hand he forced Lehnsherr's face flat against the table and held it there as if gripped in a vise, turned so that the base of his skull was exposed to reveal a scar right at the brain stem, in the shape of a perfect circle.

Lehnsherr bared his teeth, ever so slightly, his sole gesture of defiance as Stryker leaned forward and delicately, carefully, placed two drops directly on the scar. They bubbled, like hydrogen peroxide foaming away bacteria on a wound, and were absorbed.

Lehnsherr's face relaxed, his eyes wide, pupils dilating to their limit. Stryker nodded approvingly: After the initial exposure, results were virtually instantaneous.

Laurio yanked Lehnsherr up by the collar and deposited him back in his chair. There was no readable expression whatsoever on the prisoner's face; but for the metronomic rise and fall of his chest he might have been a mannequin.

Stryker put away the pipette and its case and perched himself on the corner of the table, reaching down to catch Lehnsherr by the chin and tilt the other man's face up to his. Lehnsherr didn't react to him at all. Perfect.

"Now, Eric—may I call you Eric? Course I can, 'cause thanks to my little serum here, we're the best of friends. And friends have no secrets from one another, am I right? So while we have this special time together, I'd like to have one final talk about the school that you and Charles Xavier built. And especially that wonderful machine you both call Cerebro."

Back at the school, Bobby Drake was flirting. He'd started with a shared Dr Pepper, to go with popcorn and a mix of Skittles and M&M's in Marie's favorite colors, while they gathered with a clutch of other kids in a corner of the common room to watch some DVDs. They tried broadcast, but most of the networks were still showcasing their in-house talking heads with more pointless blather about the attempted assassination.

She wasn't in the mood for talking, she never was after one of those encounters she called "imprinting," so he handled most of the conversation himself. He was a Boston boy and proud of it and didn't mind sharing. He talked of baseball at Fenway and how like every true believer he dreamed of the day the Red Sox would reclaim the World Series for their own, or at least stomp the hated Yankees on the way to a pennant. He talked about rowing on the Charles and sailing out of Marblehead and giant dunes that filled the shores of Cape Cod. Every now and then he'd pause, offering her an opening to talk about her home in return, but she wasn't interested.

She didn't seem bored, either, which he took as a good sign.

Somewhere along the way, their fingers brushed. Marie flinched, even though she was wearing gloves and there was no danger, but Bobby was ready for that. He covered the gesture by challenging her to a bout of thumb wrestling. She didn't believe her ears at first, who the hell thumb wrestles anymore? When Bobby assured her it was the done thing in Beantown, she muttered, "That 'splains a lot." But when he waggled his hand at her, cocking his thumb in challenge, she responded with a grin, shifted herself on the couch to face him, and held out her own hand.

She trapped him in a heartbeat. She was faster than she acted and way stronger, easily able to wiggle free whenever he tried to pin her and then turn the tables. He kept coming back for more, though, and she continued to let him, stifling the occasional giggle.

Neither of them realized they were being watched or, worse, recorded. Catching a nuance of expression, Peter Rasputin applied his eraser to paper and then tweaked a couple of pencil lines to make art more like life. He was sketching, which is what he did every chance he got, which was a strange sight to see in a young man the size and build of a small mountain. He stood six-foot-eight, with a physique and the natural athletic talent that would make any NFL head coach weep for joy. He played passable sports—not because he wasn't any good, but because he wasn't interested. His great and abiding love was the images that flowed down his arm from eye to pencil and from there to paper. He'd started drawing almost as soon as he could hold a pencil. It was what defined his life.

Right now he was having some fun with the lovebirds.

"Is that them?" asked a much smaller figure craning over his shoulder. Flea was on the short side to begin with, so when the two of them were together it was like parking a toy airplane beside a working 747.

Peter grunted. He was usually nonverbal when he was working, which was pretty much all the time. The other kids were used to it.

The picture was recognizably Bobby and Marie, even though Peter was intentionally erring on the side of caricature. They were in the early stages of a kiss. From the expression on Marie's face, she looked embarked on a course of major league passion. Bobby may have had that idea at the start. Right now, he was being electrocuted. Arms and legs akimbo, hair extended to full length, eyes bugging from their sockets in a classic Tex Avery pose, his body surrounded by a corona of shock waves and speed lines and appropriate other pyrotechnics.

"This," Flea chortled, "I would pay to see."

Peter blinked, shifting mental gears to reengage himself with his surroundings, and shook his head.

"No," he said, origins immediately revealed by his Russian-accented English, "because it would be wrong."

"Then you better say something, big guy," Flea said with irrepressible glee, " 'cause they're goin' for the gold!"

No more thumb wrestling. The couple were just holding hands now. Neither was initiating the move; they were moving together of their own accord as fascination overcame common sense.

Peter opened his mouth, aware they'd likely hate him for it, but never got the chance to do any more as the roar of an unmuffled Harley rumbled over the house. The sound rose in a steady crescendo as the bike raced up the long drive toward the house and just as suddenly went silent, right outside.

By then, Marie was on her feet, the bowl of popcorn and treats flying off her lap, Bobby completely forgotten as she charged the front door with a cry of "Logan!"

"Miss me, kid?" the Canadian growled as he sauntered inside.

She answered by hurling herself into his arms, and for that first minute, they just held each other, before she pushed against him just enough to clear some room between them, assumed what she hoped was a languid and uninvolved expression, and drawled, "Not really."

Logan laughed, and her expression immediately changed as she intuited that he hadn't done that in quite a while. Before she could ask about him, though, and perhaps as a way of deflecting those questions, Logan jutted his chin toward the boy standing just inside the foyer.

"Who's this?" Logan asked.

"This is Bobby," she told him, with just enough of a

hitch to her voice to make his eyes crinkle with amusement. Along with his healing factor, Logan possessed exceptionally acute physical senses, and they told him volumes about Rogue's feelings for the boy, probably more than she admitted to herself. A faint flush to the skin, a change in pulse and respiration, the faintest of goose bumps at the hollow of her throat said there was something serious at work here.

The cues radiating off the boy were even less subtle.

"Her boyfriend," Bobby said flatly, looking the older man in the eye.

Logan held out a hand, Bobby took it, and immediately there was the faint crackle of ice and a burst of frozen vapor into the air between them. Rogue muttered under her breath, but Logan sensed she was also pleased. The two men in her life were fighting over her. *Cool!*

"They call me Iceman," Bobby said, unnecessarily.

Logan looked totally unimpressed. He flexed his hand to shake free the last bits of ice clinging to his skin hair and looked toward Rogue.

"Boyfriend?" he inquired innocently. "So, ah, how do you two—"

Rogue blushed crimson and turned away, and Bobby colored a little bit himself.

"We're working on that."

"Ohhh-kay," Logan said. "Lemme know how it turns out. Meantime, I need the prof—"

"Well, well, well," called a throaty contralto from the stairs. "Look who's come back."

Logan returned Storm's smile, hers unrestrained, his much more guarded.

"Isn't that what the prodigal son does?"

"We certainly won't fault your timing."

"Eh?" Logan wondered.

"We need a baby-sitter."

"I'm outta here, darlin'."

"No, you aren't, my friend." She gave him a proper hug and a kiss on the cheek. "It's good to see you, Logan."

"Likewise," he replied, but he no longer had eyes for her. She didn't need to be told who'd followed her down the stairs.

"Hey," he said to Jean.

"Hi," she told him. "Welcome home."

Storm picked up the cue that neither of the others were aware they were broadcasting and flicked her fingers in the general direction of Bobby and Rogue. A puff of breeze whirled across the foyer to give them a gentle push back toward the common room. They took the hint, with all manner of semisecret giggles at how the tables had suddenly been reversed.

"I'll go preflight the *Blackbird*," Storm said, but she might as well have been speaking to herself.

"Bye, Logan," Rogue called out as Bobby pulled her through the double doorway.

"Later," Logan replied absently.

"Nice to meet you, sir," said Bobby.

"You, too, kid." Then, at last, once they were alone, to Jean: "You look good."

"You, too," she said, descending the last few steps to the foyer. They kept a distance between them because the signals their bodies were giving were pushing hard to bring them together. She took refuge in business. "You heard about what's happened in Washington?"

"Haven't stopped except for gas since morning," he answered with a nod. He'd pushed the bike to its limits, on back roads and interstates, covering better than a thousand miles over the course of the day.

"Storm and I are heading for Boston," she continued. "Cerebro has tagged the mutant who attacked the President. Professor Xavier wants us to try and make contact. We won't be gone long."

"I just got here."

"And you'll be here when we get back—unless you plan on running off again."

"If this hitter's the real deal, you could use some muscle taking him down."

That made her laugh. "We can handle ourselves, thank you very much."

He shrugged, posing nonchalance. "Then I guess I can probably think of a few reasons to stick around."

"That's my guy."

"Find what you were looking for, Logan?" called Scott, entering the foyer and catching sight of them both.

Logan didn't spare him a glance. "More or less," he said.

Jean broke their eye contact and strode across the floor to Scott, hating the moment and hating her reactions even more. She didn't like being out of control, of herself, of situations. She was a doctor, with a doctor's abhorrence of surprises and chaos. Logan was the personification of chaos. Sometimes she couldn't stand the little runt, he couldn't hold a candle to Scott in any respect—or so she told herself. Yet she couldn't get him out of her thoughts. And the thoughts she had of him made her nervous.

"I'll see you later," she said to Scott.

"Be safe, okay?"

"Always," she said, and gave him a powerful, passionate kiss that was undercut a moment later as she couldn't help looking back at Logan. "You, too," she said, telling herself she was talking to them both, while both men knew that wasn't quite true.

Logan tossed Scott the keys to the bike.

"Good wheels," he said. "Needs gas."

Without missing a beat, Scott grabbed the keys out of the air and tossed them right back.

"Fill her up, then."

"If you say so, bub," Logan muttered under his breath. He watched the taller man walk away and permitted himself a grin while jumping the keys up and down in his palm. He liked surprises, and Scott was proving more full of them than he'd ever imagined.

*I'm downstairs, Logan,* came a familiar voice in his head.

He didn't move at first. He stood in the foyer, breathing in a slow, deep cadence, filtering out the myriad scents filling the air around him until just one remained. She favored Folavril, Annick Goutal. He'd know her anywhere and, more importantly for him, find her anywhere.

He knew he was keeping Xavier waiting. Didn't bother him a bit.

He found the professor in what was literally the heart of the underground complex, buried deep beneath the mansion proper and extending for hundreds of yards under the estate. He'd wondered from the start how something this big could have been built in complete secrecy, but when he considered the capabilities of the man responsible, it no longer seemed like such a mystery.

At the end of a main hallway stood a circular door that would have done justice to a Federal Reserve bank vault.

Its diameter was twice Logan's height, and it was easily a couple of feet thick. Through that portal, a gallery walkway led out to a circular platform in what he assumed was the center of the room, but there was no way of knowing if that was really true. The curvature of the interior walls near the doorway suggested that the room was a great globe, but a wicked trick of design and lighting made it impossible for anyone, even Logan with his enhanced senses, to perceive its true dimensions. He couldn't see the far wall, or the summit, or the base, and the anechoic properties of the tiling deadened sound to such an extent that there wasn't even a ghost of an echo. He thought of pitching a penny but suspected he wouldn't hear it make contact.

Psychically, this was a "clean room." The only thoughts that entered were the ones Charles Xavier permitted or sought out himself.

Xavier was seated in his wheelchair on the central dais, adjusting the controls of the main console. There was a skeletal helmet on the panel, connected to it by a pair of umbilical cables that ran from either ear flap. That, Logan knew, was the receiver. The room itself was a focusing chamber for Cerebro, a titanic array of sensors, daisy-chained multiprocessors, and resonance amplifiers all intended to magnify Xavier's already considerable telepathic abilities to a quantum level.

Without looking up from his work, Xavier said aloud: "Logan, my repeated requests about smoking in the mansion notwithstanding, continue smoking *that* in *here* . . ."

Idly Logan took the cigar from his mouth and looked at it. He hadn't indulged during the entire last leg on the cycle; he'd lit it up on the walk downstairs without a second thought to the propriety—or the consequences. A man with a built-in healing factor doesn't have to worry about lung cancer.

Xavier finished silently, mind to mind: . . . *and you will spend the rest of your days under the belief that you are a six-year-old girl.*

With the thought came an image: Logan in a frilly party dress, something out of the Barbie collection, with layer upon layer of silk and crinoline petticoats, bows galore, ankle socks, and patent-leather shoes.

Both men registered the *snikt* of his claws extending, from the hand that held the cigar, but Logan made no move.

"I'll have Jean braid your hair," Xavier said aloud, and mentally tweaked the image to match, in a way that was so ridiculous and over the top that Logan couldn't help snorting in rough, rude humor.

They'd each had their moment and taken the measure of each other. Xavier probably could impose his psychic will on Logan, but he also now knew that, either right at the start or some inevitable time down the line, the berserker in Logan's soul would square accounts—and he would likely die for it.

Logan thought then of the kids upstairs as he put his claws away and crushed the burning embers against the palm of his left hand. The students didn't have a healing factor.

"Please, Logan," Xavier said, "come in."

"What's the phrase? 'Enter freely and of your own will'?"

"Dracula to Jonathan Harker, welcoming him to his castle. Is that how you see me?"

"You're the telepath, you tell me."

"I don't go into other people's minds on a casual basis."

"You don't like to pry?" Logan didn't believe him.

"It's not as easy as you think, or as pleasant. The danger is, it could be: easy *and* pleasant. To play the voyeur, to play the puppet master."

"Power corrupts."

"Power should breed responsibility. That's why I built this school."

Xavier rolled his chair into place at the console and set the helmet on his head. At once the chamber itself began to hum.

"You sure I should be here, Prof?" Logan asked. From the way the others talked, Xavier didn't allow visitors when he used his toy, but the door had closed behind him.

"Just don't move, all right?"

He did, though, the couple of steps remaining to take him to the platform just behind and beside Xavier, following the push of an instinct that had never played him false. He gasped as the fabric of the platform seemed to dissolve beneath him. There was a sensation of falling, like going over the top of the first riser at the ultimate roller coaster to start the plunge straight down to oblivion—or something even wilder.

Then, just as suddenly, he was at rest again, in the same position with Xavier as before, in the center of a giant three-dimensional representation of the world. Dotted across the land masses, lightly dusted here and there over the oceans, were uncountable numbers of white and scarlet lights that reminded Logan of fireflies or stars blazing in the heavens. There were a fair number of red, but they were no comparison to their counterparts.

"These lights," Xavier said with the same hushed reverence reserved for speaking inside a cathedral, "represent the whole of humanity. Every living soul on Earth."

"Lemme guess," Logan said. "The red ones are us."

Obligingly the white lights faded away. Only scarlet remained.

"These are the mutants," Xavier acknowledged, impressed by Logan's quick insight. "Many of them don't even realize yet who they are, what they will become. We're not quite as alone as some of us might think."

"I found the base at Alkali Lake." He thought of the slash marks on the wall, and decided to keep the thought to himself, partly to see if Xavier was peeking. "There was nothing there."

Surprisingly, as far as he could tell, the other man didn't even try.

Around them, the globe appeared to rush toward them, giving them a vastly expanded bird's-eye view of the northeastern seaboard of the United States, the fabled BosNYWash megalopolis. Then Xavier blanked all the extraneous signals as well, leaving just a small scattering, which Logan deduced, from their placement and intensity, were himself, the professor, and the others who qualified as X-Men. There was also a jagged scarlet line running from Washington all the way to Boston.

"That trail," Xavier pointed out, "represents the path of the mutant who attacked the President."

"Jean said you were sending her and Storm after him."

Xavier nodded. The scene above them resolved even more tightly on the Boston metropolitan area. Here, though, the trail, the contact waypoints, became more scattered and indistinct.

"I'm finding it hard to lock in on him," he confessed.

"Can't you just . . . I dunno, concentrate harder?"

"If I wanted to kill him, certainly."

"You can do that?"

Xavier spared him a long and measured glance. "Easily."

"Guys I know would pay a fortune for a skill like that."

The scene changed again, zooming in again to a neighborhood in the South End.

The single scarlet light was blinking. After a moment, latitude and longitude points were displayed and, a moment after that, the appropriate cross streets.

"There," Xavier said. "It appears our quarry has finally stopped running and gone to ground."

He closed his eyes, and—presto!—the illusion vanished, and Logan found himself once more on the central platform with Xavier. An eddy of fresh air told him without looking that the door had cycled open. He wasn't interested.

"I need you to read my mind again."

Xavier took his time before replying, and Logan ignored the fatigue that caused it.

"And I told you it isn't that easy," he said at last. "I'm afraid the results will be no different than before."

"We had a deal."

"Logan." Xavier spoke more sharply than he'd intended, and he took a pause to dial his irritation back a notch. "The mind is not a box to be simply unlocked and opened, its contents parceled out willy-nilly for the world to see. On one level, it's a beehive, with a million separate compartments. Yet on another, all those compartments are bound together, interconnected in a multidimensional holographic maze that would put the Gordian knot to shame. One moment of your life, one image of your memory, doesn't lead in sequential, linear fashion to the next. It splinters off into a thousand different directions, each valid, each needing to be investigated. That takes time, that takes care.

"And that's just a normal mind.

"The problem with yours is, someone's already taken the Alexander the Great approach to untangling the mysteries—or perhaps to tangle them beyond all recovery."

"I'm messed up. So what else is new?"

"Logan, sometimes there are things the mind needs to discover for itself." As Xavier placed the helmet back on its pedestal, Logan felt a faint tap on the inside of his consciousness, akin to someone rapping a knuckle on his forehead. *You have a healing factor,* he "heard" Xavier say without speaking aloud, *a most remarkable ability. Trust it to do the same with your psyche as it does so well with your physical body.*

"Don't be in such a hurry," Xavier finished aloud. "You might make things worse."

There was a fresh scent in the doorway: Ivory Soap and Old Spice, with a faint Armani chaser that had to come from Jean. Scott was standing there expectantly, dressed for the road. He wasn't pleased to see Logan in here, any more than he had been to see him with Jean. As if Logan gave a tinker's damn.

"I promise you, Logan," Xavier said as he wheeled himself from the chamber, "we'll talk more when I return. In the meanwhile . . ."

"You need a baby-sitter, Storm mentioned."

"If you would be so kind as to chaperone the children tonight, Scott and I are going to pay a visit to an old friend."

"Yo, Charley," Logan called as Scott pushed the chair down the hall. He knew Xavier hated such familiarity, but he figured, since he'd backed down over the smoking, he was entitled. "When you see Magneto, give him my regards. Tell him to rot in hell. For what he did to Rogue, he got off easy."

# Chapter
# Five

As she strode a bit too briskly into the hangar, almost fleeing the exchange that had just taken place in the foyer, Jean Grey couldn't help but take a moment to admire the magnificent aircraft waiting for her.

It was black as deep space, a paint scheme perfected by the Massachusetts Institute of Technology to make a plane visually undetectable once the sun went down. The lines of the great jet were so sleek she seemed to be cutting through the air even while standing still, the slightly canted nose flowing aft past where the fuselage flared naturally into the main body of the hull above air intakes for the tremendously powerful ramjets. These engines were so powerful that Jean could stand upright in the intakes with room to spare. The wings themselves were swept sharply forward, in defiance of traditional design philosophy, creating an airframe that compensated for its inherent instability with the ability to perform combat aerobatics over a breadth of speeds and altitudes that its nearest rivals couldn't hope to match. If it had any rivals worth the name.

They called her the *Blackbird*, as a tribute to the greatest achievement of one of the premier designers in aviation history, the justly famed Kelly Johnson, head of the equally renowned Skunk Works aeronautics team of Lockheed Aircraft. In the early 1960s the Skunk Works built an aircraft that was a generational leap ahead of anything else in the air. Only in retrospect, as years turned into decades, did the flying community realize just how spectacular an achievement that was. For the whole of its operational life, which extended right to the dawn of the twenty-first century, the SR-71 regularly flew higher, faster, and farther than pilots had ever gone before.

This vehicle was what came next, the product of a bunch of geniuses with a crazy idea and a man with the wherewithal to bankroll it to fruition. The geniuses were aeronautical engineers, downsized with their industry as the Cold War gradually came to an end. The money, of course, came from Xavier, who required something quick and stealthy, with a host of revolutionary capabilities, to transport his prospective team of heroes.

As before, the gearheads built far better than they realized. This *Blackbird* could take off like a helicopter and punch her way into a suborbital trajectory at velocities that would take her from one side of the globe to the other in barely an hour. Even better, the same structural integrity that allowed her to traverse the atmosphere to near-Earth space and back again also permitted a moderate immersion in shallow water. She couldn't move well beneath the surface, but you could definitely hide her there.

Jean was a competent pilot, but Scott and Storm were the ones who loved to fly. It was a toss-up which of them could handle the plane best. Scott had the knack for teasing the best out of the machine, but Storm's elemental powers gave her an awareness of the atmosphere the others could only imagine, allowing her to instinctively find the ideal path through the air.

She was in the left-hand pilot's seat as Jean climbed aboard, pulling the hatch closed behind her.

"Where we at?" Jean asked, taking the copilot's seat and locking her four-point harness closed. They'd both changed for the flight, into their X-Men uniforms, snug-fitting suits of what looked and felt like designer leather but which also served as highly effective body armor. For some reason, Storm had chosen to accessorize hers with a cloak that Jean had to concede looked pretty damn good on her and didn't seem to hinder her movements in the slightest. Jean had left her own outfit as is. It made her smile to recall that Logan had hated his on sight, though he didn't look half bad in it, either.

She caught Storm staring and blushed, realizing she hadn't heard a word the other woman had just said to her, or sensed a thought.

"Checklist," Storm repeated, shaking her head in amusement. In all the years they'd known each other, Jean had never let herself become so flustered.

They were a well-practiced team, and their work was quickly done. After making sure there were no planes in their vicinity, they damped the interior lights and cracked the surface hatch. Overhead, the basketball court in the athletic yard split in two and slid apart, allowing the great aircraft to rise almost silently into the night sky. Both women gave a wave to the kids they knew would be watching from their upstairs bedrooms, and then, as they cleared the surrounding trees and the roof of the mansion, Storm turned the nose toward Breakstone Lake and shifted to horizontal flight mode.

In less than a minute they were a mile high and miles

removed from the school, slipping into the stratosphere at a speed that would carry them to Boston in a quarter hour, tops. The shape of the *Blackbird* made her as impossible for a radar to detect as the paint scheme foiled visual sighting. This meant plane and crew had to be extra vigilant for any other aircraft sharing the increasingly crowded Northeast sky. Occasionally that meant taking a more circuitous route, to avoid even the risk of contact.

Immediately after takeoff, both women felt the familiar presence of Xavier's thoughts among their own.

*I'm sending you the coordinates of your target's current location,* he told them telepathically. *Scott and I are en route to Mount Haven Prison. We'll be incommunicado until we leave the facility. Once you land, you have to rely on your own skills to track him.*

"We'll be fine, sir," Storm assured him aloud.

"Let's hope he cooperates," Jean muttered, thankful for the refuge of potential action as she struggled to keep her conflicted thoughts to herself.

Storm engaged the autopilot, but Jean paid no attention as she stared out the canopy window. For all she actually noticed, a blank wall would have served just as well.

Storm's eyes narrowed as the tempo of the great ramjets increased, the surge of power making itself felt as vibration through the body of the aircraft as well as through sound. She checked the throttles and the flight dynamics liquid crystal display for a status update on the engines.

The airframe shuddered slightly as they passed the sound barrier, and miles below, amid the hills that crowded the Connecticut and Massachusetts border, she knew people would be looking around in surprise at the distant thunder of their sonic boom.

Storm disengaged the autopilot, shifting to manual flight mode, and retarded the throttles, but that did no good; their speed continued to increase, and at the rate they were gaining altitude, the *Blackbird* would be sub-orbital in mere minutes. Great for a hop over the pond to London and the professor's Scots associate Moira Mac-Taggart; utterly useless for a short-haul trip of a couple of hundred miles to Beantown.

The problem, she realized, wasn't with the controls. Someone was bypassing them to manipulate the air-frame and mechanical systems directly.

"Jean," she said, and when her friend didn't reply, she repeated herself, a little more loudly, accompanying her call with a touch of Jean's arm that carried with it just the gentlest shock of lightning.

Jean jolted awake like a student who'd been caught napping in class, denial vying visibly on her face with embarrassment for prominence.

"Sorry," she said quickly, "I'm sorry," shaking the cobwebs from her brain and releasing every hold her teke powers had placed on the aircraft.

This time, when Storm slowed down the engines, they complied, and she turned the *Blackbird* into a sweeping descent out over the Atlantic that would quickly bring them to their destination.

"You okay?" Storm asked Jean, who at first didn't seem quite sure how to answer.

"All of a sudden," Jean replied, trying to make what had just happened a joke, "damned if I know."

"Something wrong?"

"It's nothing." Jean shook her head, wriggled in her

sheepskin-covered seat to make herself more comfortable, even though both of them knew it was anything but. "I was thinking, y'know, if only we could make the flight go faster. I guess my wish fulfillment kinda got . . . carried away."

"Ah" was Storm's only comment. It spoke volumes.

"What?" Jean demanded.

"Nothing. I asked, you answered, end of story."

"*What*, Ororo, for God's sake!"

The other woman shrugged. "Maybe it's just that Logan's back in town."

Jean slumped in her chair, as much as her harness would allow. "Oh, God, it shows."

"Jean," Storm said flatly, "the *sun* 'shows' every morning when it rises. It has nothing on you."

"Why me?" Jean muttered, covering her eyes with her hands. "Why him? It isn't fair."

"You annoyed or tempted?"

"Truth, both."

"Ouch!"

"Tell me something I don't know."

"He has the look," Storm agreed with a throaty chuckle.

"Then take him off my hands, please, before there's a disaster." To illustrate her point, she waved her hands to encompass the flight deck and remind Storm what had nearly happened mere minutes before.

"Grown woman like you, grown man like him, you saying you can't set a proper example for the children?"

"You're gonna bust my butt forever about this, aren't you?"

Storm turned serious. "I like him, Jean. But what I feel, it's minor league. You two, you're the show."

"It's pure chemistry," Jean told herself as much as Storm. "I've never experienced anything like it. I see him, and the brain disengages completely. It's"—she searched for the right word—"primal. And I can't hide it from him, I can't bluff that nothing's happening—or that nothing's going to happen. And then there's Scott . . ."

Her voice trailed off. Storm reached across the center console and gave her friend's hand a squeeze, but she knew that was scant comfort.

"Have faith, Jean. You'll find a way to work things out."

"I hope so, Ororo. Really I do. For all our sakes."

The radio crackled with Xavier's voice. Storm answered.

Washington is a company town, that "company" being the federal government. And despite the promises and strenuous efforts of both political parties and numerous national administrations over the past few decades, the sheer size of that government has grown well beyond the physical capacity of the District of Columbia. Nowadays, working Washington is considered anything inside the Capital Beltway, with associated office parks springing up even farther out from the city itself, in such bedroom communities as Rockville and Gaithersburg and Reston.

In Rockville, Maryland, there was a new clutch of moderate high-rise buildings, ostensibly associated with the National Institute of Standards and Technologies, a couple of miles and one town over. Impersonally modern, they looked just like a score of similar structures scattered across the nation. Midlist government glass boxes.

This time of night, the only staff on duty were the security officers and the cleaning crew. Even in an age of terrorist threats and heightened awareness, these weren't considered viable targets. The bulk of the surveillance was handled remotely, at a central office keeping watch through a phalanx of cameras slaved to a computer monitor system. There was a manned reception desk in every ground-floor lobby, another couple of uniformed security guards to patrol the floors, but that was it. Big Brother was responsible for the bulk of the work.

The officer at the desk didn't think twice when Yuriko Oyama strode through the doors. Her group were the odd ducks among the building's federal tenants, working all hours of the day, all days of the week; something to do with auditing, they explained. The guard didn't figure he was paid enough to be more curious, especially since all their credentials were in order. He did figure this was his lucky day, a treat for the eyes just before his shift changed.

Yuriko flashed her ID and strode to the waiting elevator, totally aware of how intently the desk guard was staring at her backside. She was a fine-looking lady, and the guards had eagerly added the many sequences of her coming and going to their pirate surveillance disk of local hotties. The guard paid her the compliment of never taking his eyes off her, waiting till the elevator doors were closed to pack up his station and prepare to hand it off to his replacement.

On the top floor, Yuriko passed the cleaning crew without a second glance. At the end of the hallway there was a single door as nondescript as the building itself. No lock, only a hand scanner. She pressed her right hand against the plate and the door obligingly unlocked.

Inside was a suite of offices that could have belonged to any midlevel bureaucrat working for any midlevel agency. The only personality to the rooms was that there was no personality whatsoever.

As she proceeded to her destination, she passed behind an opaque glass wall divider, and a remarkable transformation occurred. With each step, Yuriko's features began to ripple and flow like wax exposed to direct heat. Black hair took on the color of flame, amber skin darkened to a blue that was almost midnight. Features that were pleasantly Asian became haughty and aristocratic and altogether Caucasian, a face as predatory as a hunting eagle yet possessing beauty enough to launch the thousand ships of fabled Ilium. The clothes seemed to flow into the body until what was left seemed mostly naked, save for an arrangement of ridges and scales that afforded a measure of protection and the illusion of propriety.

Her eyes were chrome yellow. Her name was Mystique.

In William Stryker's office, she sat in Stryker's chair and activated Stryker's computer monitor. On its screen appeared the legend >VOICEPRINT IDENTIFICATION PLEASE.

In Stryker's gravelly voice, Mystique replied, "Stryker, William."

Obligingly and instantly, the monitor flashed >ACCESS GRANTED.

Working fast, because that was her nature and because she was on a clock, Mystique called up the directories, selecting RECENT ITEMS from the main menu and then a folder labeled simply 143. That in turn led to a series of files: FLOOR PLANS, LEHNSHERR, INTERROGATION SUMMARIES, AUGMENTATION . . .

She read quickly, printing everything on screen. As she proceeded through the documents, the set of her mouth tightened and her eyes narrowed. This was worse than she'd ever suspected.

Downstairs, a second Yuriko strolled into the lobby, barely acknowledging the man at the desk. Since he'd just come on duty, he had no idea there were two of her loose in the building.

In the office, a few minutes later, Mystique looked up suddenly at the faint *klik* of the door locks disengaging. Her time was up, right on schedule.

The real Yuriko walked to her desk and began to hunt through the main drawer for something, seemingly unaware of the other presence in the room. Then, without warning and with a speed that defied description, she whirled around to level a Glock 19 at the intruder.

"Who are you?" she demanded. "What are you doing here?"

A uniformed janitor stirred into view, hands waving before his body, fear plain on his face. He wanted no trouble.

*"Lo siento, a puerta fui abierto!"* he said.

Yuriko reached out for the man's ID, hanging from a lanyard around his neck, comparing face to photo. Then she used her own terminal to access the night's crew roster to make sure both were legitimate.

With a wave of the hand, she dismissed the janitor and returned to her desk without giving the man another thought. It never occurred to her to wonder what a janitor was doing in her office without his cart of supplies.

Mystique considered that as she strode quickly down the outer hallway, right past the man whose face she was using. The real janitor stared at her in disbelief—it was like watching your mirror image pass you by—and reflexively crossed himself. Mystique was thinking about Yuriko. This caper had gone down far more easily than she'd anticipated. That gave her hope, an emotion she hadn't allowed herself since Magneto's capture. Before long, if all went well, maybe it would be Stryker who was on the run. And the society he championed that lay in ruins.

The *Blackbird* approached Boston low and late, literally skimming the surface of the harbor at an hour when they had sea and sky all to themselves. Their objective was a stretch of waterfront near the Marine Industrial Park that was in the nascent stages of urban renewal and gentrification, a city planner's attempt to upgrade this part of the South End into a reasonable facsimile of the more respectable neighborhoods across I-93.

They found a derelict slip with more than sufficient underwater clearance for their needs and gentled the *Blackbird* to a landing. They disembarked first, then signaled the autopilot to submerge the jet to its resting place on the bottom. There was a good ten-foot clearance to the top of the vertical stabilizers, the aircraft's tallest point. Even at low tide, there was little chance of contact with the kind of small surface craft that cruised these waters, and even less of being seen.

Hopefully, the women wouldn't be around here long enough for either to become a problem. They both put on trench coats to cover their uniforms.

As they made their way through the deserted and randomly derelict streets, Storm played with the atmospheric balance around them to roll a dusting of mist over this part of the city. She didn't want a real fog, that would be too blatant, cause too much disruption to the local community; her goal was just enough to make it easy for them to slip out of sight if they had to.

The coordinates Xavier had provided led them to a church.

In better times, this had been a house of worship worthy of its parish. Constructed to last by stonemasons and old-world artisans who were building more for their children's children than for themselves, it still presented a proud and dignified front to the desolation that surrounded it. The spire towered over the scattered clumps of row houses that remained and the long-abandoned factories that gave their owners and tenants work. Much of the stained glass, produced by contemporaries of Louis Comfort Tiffany, still remained, although it was probably only a matter of time before it was looted or destroyed.

The wall of one of the buildings opposite had been tagged with some fresh graffiti: CLEAN THE GENE POOL! KILL MUTANT SCUM!

Storm didn't appreciate the sentiments.

"They'll never let us lead our lives," she said, and this time she let her anger show. She clenched her fist, and from off in the distance, out to sea beyond the entrance to Boston Harbor, came the kettledrum beat of thunder.

They circled the church without approaching it, and Jean used her teke to try every doorway they passed. To their surprise, all of them appeared to be stoutly locked.

"Somebody taking care of this old place?" Storm wondered aloud.

"I caught a couple of thought flashes from that bar up the street."

"From the guys we saw through the window?" Storm made a face. "You're a braver woman than I am."

"Tell me about it," Jean agreed, matching her tone to her friend's disgust. "Thing is, this church has a rep. It's supposed to be haunted. By its very own demon."

"Get out."

"No lie. They believe it. Even the local tough guys steer clear of St. Anselm's."

"I've never met a demon."

"After you, then."

An artful combination of telekinesis and a push of wind popped the bolts on the main doors, which swung wide to their stops, creating an echoing *boom* throughout the body of the church. From the rafters, coveys of pigeons exploded into view, startled from their nighttime slumber.

The women said nothing as they made their way down the nave. Most of the pews had either been taken or were trashed in various corners, leaving a large open space leading to the transept and the altar. Up in the shadows below the vaulted ceiling, a pair of chrome yellow eyes watched their progress. And then, in a faint *bamf* of imploding air, they disappeared.

Just as suddenly, Storm stopped, looking steeply upward and to her right.

"What?" Jean prompted.

"A shift in the air," she replied quietly, matter-of-factly.

"Movement?"

"More than that. A sudden vacuum there." She pointed to where the lurking figure had been. "And an outrush of air from something popping into being." She turned her arm to the altar. "There."

*"Gehen sie raus,"* came a whisper from the deepest darkness ahead of them, in a voice calculated to chill the soul. They saw a lit candle set beside an open Bible. As they watched, the flame flickered from a sudden breeze and the topmost pages stirred.

"He's gone again," Storm said, and Jean nodded as they both heard from a balcony high overhead: *"Ich bin ein Bote des Teufels!"*

"We're not here to hurt you," Storm called out. "We just want to talk!"

Even as she spoke, she turned in response to another faint and distant shift in the air patterns, so that she started facing one way and finished having turned right around toward the entrance.

*"Ich bin die ausgeburt des Bösen,"* the lurker cried in something close to a primal howl.

Storm had a sudden, awkward thought. "You know," she told Jean, "we're assuming he speaks English."

"Not a problem," Jean assured her. "He's a teleporter."

"I noticed."

"That must be why the professor had so much trouble locking on to him with Cerebro."

"Will it be any easier for us to catch him?"

"Not a problem."

Another howl, much closer, although try as they might neither Storm nor Jean could see him in the gloom of the church.

*"Ich bin ein dämon,"* he called.

Jean rolled her eyes and shifted her stance into a picture-perfect ValGal Barbie.

"Are you bored yet?" she asked Storm.

"Totally," was the reply.

"You want to bring him down, or shall I?"

Storm narrowed her eyes in momentary concentration and snapped her fingers. Obediently, a bolt of lightning erupted from her hand, sizzling up one of the support columns and into the rafters of the church's single spire, where it struck with an explosion of light and sound, a clap of thunder that pounded the air and stone around them like a hammer.

They had a momentary glimpse of a vaguely human shape before it vanished. But when it reappeared almost instantaneously, at the far end of the nave, right above the altar, Jean was ready. As soon as she had a sense of his mental signature, she reached out with telepathy and telekinesis together, freezing his thoughts at the same time she locked him in place a dozen feet above the rubble-strewn floor. Trapped, he still fought her, defiant to the core.

"Got him?"

"He's not going anywhere." Jean brought him closer. Then, to the prisoner's surprise, she smiled—genuine, winning, friendly—and held out her hand. "Are you?"

"Please don't kill me," he pleaded in English, with a soft German accent that marked him as an educated man. It had a mellow timbre, the kind more suited to cabaret songs than playing the matinee-movie monster. "I never intended to harm anyone!"

"I wonder how people ever got that impression," Storm remarked wryly. "What's your name?"

"Kurt. Kurt Wagner."

"I'm Ororo. Call me Storm," she told him. She flashed a sideways look to Jean to complement her thought. *This is our assassin?*

*Appearances are deceiving,* Jean projected back at her. *But—which way?*

*Your call.*

With that thought from Storm, Jean cut loose the prisoner. He dropped lightly to the floor, landing on the balls and toes of his outsized feet. He looked poised to bolt, but Jean took it as a positive sign that he hadn't immediately teleported. She kept her hand held out to him.

"I'm Jean Grey. We're here to help."

Kurt Wagner followed Quasimodo's lead and lived up in the spire, on the level below the belfry. The walls were solid there, and he'd replaced the panes of broken stained glass with the precision and craftsmanship used for the originals. By day, when the sun was shining, both women recognized, the room would be ablaze with color. He used candles for illumination instead of electricity; their light was less likely to be spotted from the street. The height of the steeple gave him a panoramic view of the neighborhood. He had privacy and a decent chance of spotting any intruders. For a teleporting acrobat like him, whose natural coloration made him invisible in shadows, this was an ideal hideout.

The furnishings were spartan, a function more of choice and aesthetics than of poverty. True, the pieces were mainly scavenged from the derelict and abandoned homes nearby, but they'd been restored with the same painstaking care and attention to detail as the windows. A bed, a table, some chairs, a pantry, a bookshelf. Dried food mostly in the pantry, chosen for ease in storage and in preparation. The books were an unexpected mix. Religious works mainly, a well-thumbed Bible sharing space with a copy of Rafael Sabatini's *Captain Blood* and George MacDonald Fraser's classic pastiche, *The Pyrates.*

Above the headboard, a Catholic crucifix. On the table, a set of rosary beads, polished from handling. Icons and images galore, of Christ himself, of the Blessed Virgin. The beads were lying on a pile of newspapers, all headlining the attack on the President and showing an artist's sketch of the assassin that was a devastatingly faithful likeness.

On the wall, though, something completely different—a series of circus posters, from venues all over Europe: Paris, Florence, Barcelona, Munich, Prague, Krakow. They all were pictures of Kurt, showing him on the trapeze, celebrating the performances of the INCREDIBLE NIGHTCRAWLER! As well, a couple of movie one-sheets: Burt Lancaster in *The Crimson Pirate*, Douglas Fairbanks, Jr., in *Sinbad the Sailor*, and almost in a place of honor, Errol Flynn's film adaptation of *Captain Blood*, the role that made his swashbuckling career.

Jean shook her head. A man of obviously deep religious faith who loved classic pirate stories. Didn't fit any profile she'd ever read of your basic assassin. He picked up the rosary as she asked if she could examine his wound, but even though she knew she was hurting him—she couldn't help it—the only sound she heard from him was a cadencelike muttering that she soon realized was a prayer: "Our Father, Who art in Heaven, blessed be Thy Name . . ."

The 9mm shell had missed the bone as it passed through his shoulder, but it had still done its share of damage. Kurt had administered some decent first aid; he'd stopped the bleeding and applied sufficient antiseptic to prevent any major infection. Without proper treatment, however, his athletic ability would be crippled, and she told him so in a way that also told him she was willing and able to provide it.

"You'll be fine," Jean told him as she finished suturing the wound and began wrapping it in the necessary bandages. "The worst you'll have is a small scar."

"You are not the authorities," he said with a hint of a question.

Storm snorted, "Not hardly."

"You wear uniforms."

"We like to look cool," Jean told him. "I'm sorry if I'm hurting you."

"I know it cannot be helped." He shook his head, a little bit of misery, a lot of confusion. "I just don't understand—any of this. I could . . ." He paused, glancing at the papers on his table, trying to come to terms with images and memories that made no sense to him, yet could not be denied. "I couldn't stop myself," he said desperately. "It was all happening to someone else, like a bad dream. That would be nice. But then—I move my arm and realize that is a lie. It *was* real. It was *me*!"

He twisted and rolled the rosary beads in his two-fingered hands until he held the crucifix that anchored the strands together. On his face was a terrible and haunting desolation.

"I fear He has left me," he said with a grief, a sense of loss, that was palpable. "I even found a mark, perhaps like the mark of Cain. See? Look here!"

He tilted his head, sweeping aside the thick indigo curls to reveal a mark at the base of his skull. It was a scar, Jean recognized, that reminded her of kinds of insect bites or the welt left by some topical irritant akin to what was found on poison ivy or oak. It was placed right above the brain stem, and it formed the shape of a perfect circle.

"What do you think?" Storm asked Jean.

"Let's get him back to the professor," she replied, her concern and worry as plain for Storm to see as the intricate markings that covered Kurt Wagner's body.

Normally he sleeps without dreams. A quiet time, restful, a relief from the cacophony of input assaulting his physical senses every waking moment. So much to process just to determine the appropriate levels of threat. Every person he meets, a potential enemy, to be sorted into its appropriate box in that split second of initial contact.

Lately, no peace, anything but, no chance to recharge his batteries, psychic or physical, forcing him to stay awake to the point of absolute exhaustion, when he doesn't have any choice about it anymore. Yet that carries its own price, because it leaves him with fewer defenses against the nightmares that invariably come.

He hears himself scream with rage, giving himself completely to the berserker in his soul.

He's fighting fighting fighting, against what he never knows. People? Things? Demons? Monsters? Fate itself? All of that? None?

He has no clothes, the better to see the marks drawn on skin that's been stripped of hair, the better to see the livid scars that follow the marks as he's opened from crown to crotch, shoulders to fingertips, hips to toes.

He sees himself in the reflector overhead, lying on a

table, dissected like a frog, skin peeled back, organs laid bare, watching his heart beat, his lungs pulse. He hears voices, dissecting him as clinically as their scalpels, hears a voice, his voice, asking over and over what was happening, why were they doing this? Hears laughter, they aren't interested, they don't care, they think this is funny. Hears threats of bloody vengeance give way, impossibly, to words he never imagined saying, begging, pleading for mercy.

He can't wake up. He has to watch.

Knowing that he was conscious through whatever was being done to him. They didn't use anesthetic, they wanted him to experience every bloody moment.

They took lots of notes.

Someone holds up a set of claws.

He pops the claws from his hand—snikt!

He slashes the claws into the wall, making an indelible mark on the armored plating too thick for him to cut all the way through.

He's in a tank, lights are flashing red and green, the lights resolving into what's supposed to be a pair of eyes in a face too terrible to be remembered except as repeating images of pain and horror. The tank is filled with liquid, covering him, drowning him, turning bright yellow as the face spits venom at him like a cobra, burning him inside and out.

Rage now, beyond comprehension, beyond control.

He's fighting fighting fighting

No more yellow anymore, but lots of red

He's alone

No more floors beneath his feet, only earth, then rock, then nothing but air as he tumbles from a precipice

Then water as a cataract sweeps him away

*Then earth and rock again as he grabs for salvation and pulls himself ashore*

*Then, miraculously, mercifully, snow, falling fast and hard, burying the world, burying him, allowing him to sleep, to heal, to*

*forget*

Snikt!

Snakt!

# Chapter
# Six

Logan woke up on the floor, amid the ruins of yet another bed.

Reflexively, he started to raise his hands to rub his face, smooth his hair. Then he paused in midgesture and opened his eyes to see if his claws were still extended. No fun to accidentally slice open your own scalp, even if the wounds healed in next to no time.

His hands looked normal, with only the damage that surrounded him and the dull and familiar, and fading, ache between his knuckles.

He spit some feathers from his mouth, plucked scraps of pillow off his chest.

The bed was basically splinters, the mattress and linens shredded. The floor was badly scored as well. His flailing hands had cut through the parquet to expose the joists beneath. He moved carefully as he shifted his weight to sit up and determined which sections of the floor were still capable of supporting him. He wondered a moment why no one had come to investigate, then remembered that he was the only adult left in the mansion. Considering the looks he'd gotten from the students, and the stories Rogue had no doubt been telling, any kids close enough to hear what had happened in here more than likely had sense enough to make themselves scarce.

That made him grin, although there was little humor in it.

He'd left his clothes on the far side of the room. They were untouched by his unconscious berserker outburst, but as he approached to get dressed he had to admit they didn't look much better than the room. He made it a point to travel light. Anything that couldn't be carried was expendable, and he wore his clothes to their limit before replacing them. The boots and the leather jacket had some mileage left; the jeans were near the end. That didn't used to matter to him, because he never used to care what others thought when they saw him.

He took his time under the shower, muttering darkly that the spray wasn't as powerful as he liked. Truth was, what he liked was a fire hose at full pressure, enough to scour his flesh the way it could be used to flay paint off a wall. He started as hot as he could bear, which wasn't quite hot enough to burn, then went for cold. That wasn't satisfactory, either, for a man used to mountain rivers and lakes where the water was usually a degree or two shy of turning to ice. The immersion left him tingling all over, totally raw and feeling better.

He'd known the moment he awoke what time it was. Another instinct, an uncannily accurate awareness of time and space and of his self. It was almost impossible for him to get lost, and he always knew immediately if something had changed around him while he was unconscious.

Past 3:00 A.M.

Silently despite the boots, he prowled the empty halls of the mansion, registering the photographs and paintings and antiques displayed along the walls even if his mind took no active notice of them. Quizzed, he could have described his environs perfectly, but the objects themselves meant virtually nothing to him. Tools he understood, but he had no use for ornamental artifacts.

The sound of a television led him to an upstairs common room. He'd assumed at first that somebody had left it on, but as he approached he registered an active presence, early adolescent and male, and wide awake.

Before going to bed, Logan had used Jean's terminal to review the files of every student in the school. He told himself he was simply being responsible, but he acknowledged that it was also another way of getting close to her, which made him shake his head in dismay. This wasn't like him, yet the impulses and the emotions were too primal, too powerful to be ignored. Or denied. Guaranteed trouble, no doubt about that. No hope of a happy ending. He didn't care.

Anyway, if Jean was going to entrust him with the kids here, he'd do his best to be worthy of it. That meant putting names to faces, and powers to names.

This one was Jones. He had a first name but nobody used it, Jones included.

He was sprawled on the couch, picking at a full bowl of popcorn. He'd watch the big plasma screen until he got bored, then he'd blink his eyes. The channel would obligingly change. Watch a while, repeat the process. It happened often. Jones had a low threshold of boredom.

He noticed Logan's reflection in the screen but didn't look around. He didn't much like what he was watching, but he wasn't about to miss a moment of it.

"Can't sleep?" he asked.

"How can you tell?" Logan retorted.

" 'Cause you're awake."

No arguing with that ironclad logic, that's for sure. Kid had a mind like a steel trap.

"What's your excuse?" Logan asked.

"I don't sleep."

"Your loss. You guys got any beer?"

"Try the kitchen."

He did, and found one of the professional Sub-Zero fridges filled with all manner of healthy food: yogurt and greens, fruits and eggs and meats. Primarily organic, the produce of local farms and green markets. Minimal snack food. He grimaced, recognizing the influence of both Jean and Storm, and wondered how often the students made a break for the local Mickey Dee's.

The other one held fruit juice, mostly fresh squeezed, bottled water, and dozens of cartons of chocolate milk.

Grumpy now, Logan shut the door,

He wasn't alone in the kitchen anymore. Bobby Drake sat at the table, methodically excavating a quart container of ice cream.

"Hey," the youngster said, making an effort to keep his voice steady. Logan had sensed him coming, but clearly Bobby hadn't realized it was Logan in the room until the man had closed the refrigerator door, and by then pride wouldn't allow for even the thought of flight.

"Hey," Logan replied offhandedly, poking through cabinets and the walk-in pantry. "Got any beer?"

Drake's laconic response brought an amused twist to Logan's lips. "This is a school," Bobby said.

"So that's a no?"

Bobby smiled broadly and pointed to the fridge. "We have chocolate milk."

Logan growled and emerged from the pantry carrying

a six-pack of Dr Pepper bottles. He pulled two from the cardboard holder and took a chair opposite Bobby. He made a small gesture with one bottle.

"Want one?" he asked. When Bobby nodded, he added, "They're warm."

Without a word, Bobby reached across to take the proffered bottle in hand. Air crackled and frost formed on his fingers and the fluted glass. He gently blew on the neck.

"Not anymore," Bobby said as he handed back the ice-cold Dr Pepper.

Logan popped the cap and took a long swallow. Just the way he liked it.

"Handy," he conceded.

Bobby gave a nod of acknowledgment as he repeated the process with his own bottle.

"So," Logan asked bluntly, with a sidelong look to the boy from beneath lowered brows, as he held up his right hand and, for show, popped the middle claw out, *snikt*, and in, *snakt*. Bobby's response was a choked spit-take that sent soda bursting from his mouth and nose, followed by a desperate grab for paper towels as he struggled to regain his self-possession. Through it all, Logan hardly moved, apparently engrossed in an examination of his knuckles for any sign of the blade's extension.

When Bobby had settled back into his own chair, Logan gave him his most dangerous smile and administered the coup de grâce: "What's with you and Rogue, eh?"

Xavier didn't like Mount Haven. It gave him a headache.

He knew the reason: ultralow frequency harmonics whose pitch was specifically calibrated to inhibit any form of extrasensory perception, including his own telepathy. He could overcome it, of course; that was no problem. It just took a little more effort and exacted a more than equivalent cost. Far easier, while he was here, to keep his thoughts and his powers to himself.

What disturbed him was the notion that the designers knew what they were doing. It suggested a far greater familiarity with mutants than most people realized. Over the past months since Magneto's incarceration Xavier had made discreet inquiries to learn as much as possible about the government department responsible for the establishment of the prison, but painfully few of those questions had been answered. Perhaps the time had come to dig deeper.

Following the security protocols, his wheelchair had been exchanged for a plastic counterpart back at the main entrance. Under escort, he and Scott had proceeded to the cell block for the final series of identity and security checks, this time under the supervision of Magneto's warder, Mitchell Laurio.

With the peremptory manner of a man used to instant obedience, Laurio waved Scott back from Xavier's chair.

"I'll take it from here," he said.

Scott didn't like the tone, didn't like the man, and for a moment the two men bristled with challenges.

"Scott," Xavier said quietly, forcefully, to defuse the tension, "it's all right. I won't be long."

"Nice coat," Laurio said to Scott over his shoulder as he wheeled the chair toward the hatchway leading to the umbilical tunnel.

"Thanks." There was a little more of a flat, prairie Nebraska twang to Scott's voice, the kind you expect to hear from a gunfighter marshall whose job was to bring order to a lawless frontier.

"Nice shades." Meaning "I'd like to take them away from you, pretty boy."

"Thanks." Meaning "You're welcome to try."

The hatch opened onto a small platform where both men had to wait while the tunnel unfolded toward the cell itself, suspended in the middle of the room. Even through the translucent walls of the tube, it was possible to get a sense of the chamber's immensity, and especially the tunnel's height above the floor. It was designed to make visitors uncomfortable as they realized their lives depended on the strength and integrity of the network of rings and cables that held the tunnel aloft. Most quickened their pace. Laurio slowed his down, his own way of emphasizing that *he* was in charge here. He was the *man*! He left Xavier alone with the prisoner.

Lehnsherr had his back to Xavier and didn't turn around when he spoke.

"Have you come to rescue me, Charles?"

"Not today, Eric. I'm sorry." There was a quality of genuine regret to Xavier's voice, as though someday that circumstance might change and there would be a rescue.

"To what do I owe the pleasure?" Lehnsherr asked, and he sounded genuinely amused.

"The assassination attempt on the President. What do you know about it?"

"Just what I read in the newspapers." He turned to face his friend. "You shouldn't even have to ask."

Xavier couldn't hide his revulsion, he didn't try, as he beheld the bruises on Lehnsherr's face. The way the other man held his body revealed more eloquently than words that the damage wasn't simply confined to his face.

"What happened to you?" Xavier asked, aghast.

"I . . . fell," Lehnsherr said without irony. "In the shower."

"This isn't funny!"

"No." For emphasis, a shake of that leonine head.

"This is unconscionable."

"I'm a terrorist, Charles. An enemy of humanity. Given that status, and the circumstances of my capture, it's been made repeatedly clear to me that I should be . . . grateful for my treatment."

"Told by whom?" Xavier demanded, already formulating his protests to the authorities. "Who is responsible for this outrage?"

"You remember William Stryker?"

"I haven't heard that name in years."

"I've had frequent visits from him lately. His son, Jason, was once a student of yours, wasn't he?"

"More a patient than a student. Unfortunately, I wasn't able to help him. At least not the way his father wanted me to."

At the mansion, Jones donned a set of Bose headphones and cranked the volume, his flickering eyes changing channels faster than ever.

The assault force closed on the mansion from three directions, two by silenced helicopters flying a map-of-the-earth profile that had the wheels of their Sikorsky *Blackhawks* literally brushing the treetops while the third unit used SCUBA sleds to approach from the lake. The teams had been handpicked by Stryker himself,

culled from the finest special operations cadres on Earth—
American SEALs and Army Rangers, Great Britain's Special
Air Service, Russian *Spetznatz*, German GSG-9, Israeli
Pathfinders, and some Vietnamese. They'd trained for
this op for months, not only familiarizing themselves
with the layout of the mansion but also exhaustively
learning how to protect themselves from the myriad of
powers and abilities they might encounter. Now, with all
the adult staff of Xavier's School absent from the estate,
the time had come to put that preparation to the test.

In quick and practiced succession, as the first units
rappelled to the ground from their hovering aircraft, all
the mansion's power and communications lines were in-
terdicted and the security network neutralized. On command, the school would be completely isolated. Even
cellular and radio communication would be off-line.
From high overhead, an orbiting C-130 Hercules kept
the entire estate under constant electronic surveillance,
using thermal imagery to mark the position of the students. Only a couple of signatures indicated contacts
who were awake. For the rest, it was already too late.

In the observation booth at Mount Haven, Scott
leaned closer to the phalanx of monitor screens. He'd
seen the bruises, too, and Xavier's reaction to them, but
there was no sound.

The guard at the console shrugged apologetically.

"It happens," he said, by way of explanation, not for
Magneto's condition but for the lack of audio.

"Here?" Scott asked pointedly. "With *this* prisoner?"

"We got backups on backups," Laurio growled. "You
got nothin' to worry about. Joey, put in a call for a

techie. Let's get this fixed before Movie Star here makes a federal case."

Both guards laughed, and Scott felt the hair prickle on the back of his neck. This was wrong, and he called out to Xavier with his thoughts as loudly as he could. He yelled inside his head, but the figure he could see plainly on the screen gave not the slightest indication that he heard any of it.

Lehnsherr picked up a pawn from the plastic chessboard on his cupboard, then exchanged it for a knight.

"And now you think that taking in the Wolverine will make up for your failure with Stryker's son?"

He placed the pieces back on the board and turned slowly to look at his friend.

"You haven't told him about his past, have you?"

Reluctantly Xavier shook his head. "I've put him on the right path, but Logan's mind is still fragile."

"Is it?" Lehnsherr obviously thought differently. "Or are you afraid you'll lose one of your precious X-Men?"

Xavier didn't reply at once. He looked distracted, brow furrowing, head cocked slightly to the side in concentration as though trying to make sense of some noise or other right at the edge of his awareness. He blinked, marshaling his telepathic resources against the low-frequency harmonics and the realization that the headache that was merely infernal now would be brutal by the time he was done. But this increased psychic sensitivity didn't give him the answer he sought. Instead it gave him insight into something far more serious.

"Eric," he cried, shocked at the scraps of memory he was perceiving and all their terrible implications, "what have you done?"

"I'm sorry, Charles," Lehnsherr replied, swinging his hand across the chessboard to knock down both kings at once. He was a proud man who had sworn long ago never again to become a victim. That he had failed, utterly, was a hard admission to make. "I . . . couldn't help myself."

"What have you told Stryker?" *About my school,* Xavier thought desperately, *about my X-Men?* He recognized the source of that burr in his awareness that had been bothering him, and called out a warning to Scott in turn, with all his own considerable strength.

"Everything," Lehnsherr said with the simple finality of a death sentence.

Both men reacted to a faint hiss from all around them. From apertures on every wall a cloud of mist could be seen flooding into the cell.

Xavier had time for one last, desperate outcry—"*Scott!*"—before oblivion claimed him.

On the monitors, Scott saw Xavier lunge forward in his chair, heard a faint echo of that call in his thoughts, watched his mentor collapse. It was over in seconds.

"What the hell?" he cried.

He looked up, heard an almost inaudible *pop,* and reacted to the impact of something small striking the middle of his chest. He didn't know what it was, but that didn't matter as his body reacted of its own accord to this sudden and unexpected ambush.

He quickly registered a new presence in the room. A young woman, Asian, beautiful, wearing a guard uniform and carrying a dart pistol. That told him they wanted him alive. In that same instant, he also assumed that the dart hadn't done its job, working on the presumption they'd want to neutralize him as quickly and efficiently as they did Xavier. It probably hadn't been strong enough to penetrate his leather coat and his uniform beneath. He knew they wouldn't make that mistake twice. He had to act first.

All these thought processes occurred in the split instant it took him to complete his turn. He identified the woman as the primary threat, and he wasn't overly gentle with his response. He tapped a control on the wing of his visor, the ruby quartz depolarized, and a beam of scarlet force exploded through the lens.

For the woman, it was like being hit by a battering ram. He caught her full in the belly, doubling her over and hurling her into the wall behind her. The whiplash of the impact cracked her skull against a projection and she dropped to the floor, bloody and unconscious from a nasty scalp wound. The same beam shattered the pistol and knocked off her lightly tinted sunglasses.

The guard at the console made a grab from behind, but Scott elbowed him in the face, used the same fist to deliver a sharp jab that dropped this adversary from the fight. That left Laurio and his partner.

A snap shot of optic blasts took care of the partner, but Laurio proved a lot faster than Scott expected from a man of his bulk. He tackled Scott before the young man could bring his eyes to bear. Laurio had seen how Scott manipulated the beams, and he was doing everything he could to keep the mutant's hands away from his visor. Without the power, Laurio likely figured this to be an easy fight.

Now, though, it was his turn to be surprised. Scott's slim and rangy figure was as deceptive in its own way as Laurio's. There was a wiry strength to him that matched the guard's, and a willing ability to take punishment. Laurio delivered a couple of hard shots to the body that were usually good enough to take the fight out of anyone, but all Scott did was wince with the shock and hit back just as hard.

Unnoticed in the struggle, the woman—Yuriko Oyama—stirred. Her wound had stopped bleeding and, covered now with fresh skin, was healing with a speed reminiscent of Wolverine.

Scott used a knee to lever Laurio aside, quickly rolling the other way to yank a nightstick from the belt of the guard. Both men came to their feet together, but Scott had the advantage as he hammered the handle of the stick into the pit of Laurio's gut. The bigger man staggered, gasping for breath, and Scott followed up with a roundhouse swing to the jaw that drew blood from mouth and nose as it threw the guard against the wall.

Instinct warned of another attack, a fresh threat; training prompted an instantaneous response. But quick as Scott was, Yuriko was quicker as she slapped the nightstick from his grasp. Scott gasped in pain as if he'd just been hit by a bar of steel. In blinding succession, she struck him in the hands and forearms and body, leaving him unable to defend himself actively with his own martial skills or his optic blasts. He wasn't sure how this had happened; he knew how hard he'd hit her, was certain when she fell that she was out for the duration. Yet here she was, attacking him, seemingly in better shape than ever.

Without pause, she set herself and launched a sweeping, flying kick for his head. He saw it coming, tried to avoid it, watched her compensate impossibly in midair, felt a murderous shock to the side of his skull as her boot connected. On the way down, she gave him another kick for good measure.

She reached down to check his throat pulse, satisfying herself that it remained strong, then turned to the monitors to check on Xavier. With a smile of triumph, she threaded her fingers together and cracked her knuckles. Mission accomplished.

Inside the cell, Eric Lehnsherr watched his old friend fall. The gas had been specially mixed for Xavier's genetic structure. It was effective against Lehnsherr, too, but it just took a little longer.

He coughed, thinking as he did about every time he had seen the white cloud pour from the vents of the "showers" that claimed so many at Auschwitz, remembering the feel of lifeless flesh still warm beneath his fingers as he and the other *Sonderkommando* dragged the dead from gas chamber to crematoria. The hair was cut from their heads, the gold was pried from their teeth. Everything that was perceived to be of value was taken from them, before their wholesale murder and afterward. Especially their dignity.

Never again, he had sworn then.

He knew his captors thought that the most hollow of boasts.

He also knew he would live to make them regret it.

"I'm sorry, Charles," he said with his last conscious breaths. "You should have killed me when you had the chance." Then he looked toward the distant observation booth, but the face that marched into his mind's eye was Stryker's. "So should you," he finished, and then he let his own consciousness go.

\* \* \*

At the mansion, the cavalcade of images cascading before Jones' eyes suddenly and unexpectedly paused. Something else had caught his attention, an image on the screen but having nothing whatsoever to do with it. Jones peered closely at the screen, then clambered up the back of the couch to see who'd entered the room behind him.

It was a man dressed just like the commandos Jones watched on TV. Black from head to toe, face decorated with camouflage paint and a knit wool balaclava. Battle fatigues, combat boots, weapons and equipment harness, night-vision goggles. His name, though Jones didn't know it, was Lyman. He was in command of the assault force.

Finding himself facing a boy who was barely a teenager, Lyman wavered.

Wondering if this was some prank, or test, or maybe a new teacher, Jones swung his legs over the couch and padded, barefoot and in pajamas, toward the stranger.

"Hi," he said. He wasn't afraid. In this mansion, he truly believed he had nothing to be afraid of.

His eyes widened slightly in disbelief as, without a word in response, Lyman pulled a pistol from its holster and fired.

Jones felt a sting in his neck, grabbing at it reflexively in time to pull free the tranquilizer dart but not before the drugs took effect. He collapsed to the floor, his eyes fluttering, the TV changing channels so fast behind him that the flickering images registered more like static.

Lyman used hand signals to motion the rest of his team forward. Silently, weapons leveled, they spread throughout the mansion.

\* \* \*

In the kitchen, Logan sat slumped deep in his chair. Until tonight, he hadn't slept since leaving Alkali Lake, and the nightmare that had sent him wandering through the mansion had been worse than a knockdown, drag-out bar fight. As a consequence, his healing factor was so busy fixing the damage that, even though he looked awake and was carrying on a decent conversation, he was mostly in a kind of hibernation. Whatever enhanced awareness he possessed right now was limited to this room and the boy across the table. Even that was pretty piss poor.

They quickly polished off one six-pack of soda, Logan chugging four while Bobby was still nursing his second, at the same time picking at the mostly melted remnants of his container of ice cream.

"My parents think this is a prep school."

"Hey," Logan said pleasantly, amused that he was co-herent since he was speaking through a mental haze that put a pea-soup fog to shame, "lots of prep schools have their own campus, dorms, kitchens."

"Harrier jets? The *Blackbird*?"

"It's a free country."

Logan leaned back in his chair, establishing a balance so precarious that Bobby was sure he would fall. He thought of saying something, thought better of it. Logan struck him as the kind of guy who always knew precisely what he was doing.

"So," Logan growled, "you and Rogue, eh?"

"Marie," Bobby corrected.

"Whatever."

"It's not what you think." Logan quirked an eyebrow, making Bobby wonder with a suddenly racing heart just what the man thought. "I mean," he stammered, closing his eyes in misery, "I'd like it to be. . . ."

Which, from the look he got now, could not have been more totally the wrong thing to say if he'd tried.

"It's just," he explained hurriedly, sure that he was making things worse with every word, but having no idea how to stop or make things right, "that it's not easy—when you *want* to be closer to someone, but . . . you *can't* be. Y' know?" He paused, utterly miserable as Logan's expression changed and sharpened before his eyes. He'd screwed up, big time, no doubt of that at all. "You probably don't understand."

Logan wasn't listening to the boy anymore, and he wasn't in hibernation, either. He knew exactly what was happening and he was furious at himself for allowing it.

There was a green dot right in the center of Bobby's forehead. The boy hadn't noticed.

Bobby yelped in terror and sprang back from the table as one set of Logan's claws extended and slashed through the air right in front of where he sat. They both heard a small *clink*, and a dart, sliced perfectly in two, dropped into the ice cream.

The targeting laser shifted at once from Bobby to Logan as Logan erupted from his chair. Too late the intruder realized his fatal mistake. He'd been thrown off by Logan's size, especially slouched so deeply in the kitchen chair. He assumed he was dealing with a pair of students.

He had a submachine gun, a Heckler & Koch MP5, and managed to squeeze off a round before Logan reached him. Good shot, too; the bullet grazed Logan's shoulder. He barely noticed as he grabbed the weapon's barrel, forcing it upward as the intruder squeezed the trigger on full auto. Bullets peppered the ceiling and walls. Bobby sensibly dived for cover beneath the table, and the temperature of the room turned Arctic.

Without realizing what he'd done, Bobby generated a cold so intense that it overwhelmed all the heat signatures in the room. Aboard the circling Hercules, the remote observers suddenly couldn't tell what was happening there.

Logan wrenched the gun from the other man's hands and flung it aside. They traded punches, to no effect, but the man was able to grab a combat knife from its scabbard on his vest. He was bigger than Logan and possibly stronger. Their struggle had given him the advantage of height and leverage, and he used both to push the gleaming blade straight for Logan's eye. The man's gaze flickered slightly, to acknowledge the sight of the gash across Logan's shoulder—which was healing rapidly. But mainly he concentrated on the task at hand: Kill the enemy.

Then he realized he could see that same flat, utterly merciless expression in Logan's eyes, and he knew in that awful moment that it was over, that he'd never had a chance, that up till now, Logan had been trying to take him alive.

He heard a *snikt* from the hand he couldn't see and felt an awful, stabbing pain in his chest that reached all the way to his heart . . .

. . . and felt no more.

# Chapter
# Seven

In Kitty Pryde's dreams, the Cubs were sweeping the Yankees for the World Series in straight shutouts, Sammy Sosa was making people forget that Babe Ruth had ever existed, and she and her mom and her dad had front-row field-level seats for every game, right behind the Cubs dugout. Her folks were together again, they were a family, and her life was back the way she wanted it. She watched Derek Jeter whiff a fastball straight up into the air. She knew from that moment of contact it was coming for her, and she leaped to her feet, eyes on the ball, glove poised to grab it.

But she started to lose it in the sun. She squinted her eyes as she'd been taught, but she couldn't filter out that wicked glare. She also couldn't understand why the sun was turning green. Then, to make matters worse, somebody grabbed her across the face, a gloved hand covering mouth and nose, choking off her cries of excitement as they turned to protests, choking off her air.

She lashed out at him, still determined to catch the ball, but the emerald radiance was brighter, unbearably so, and next to it in the sky, bigger than anything she'd ever seen up there, she saw a gun.

Her dream popped like a soap bubble and she came

instantly, totally awake, one part of her mind automatically cataloging everything around her while her active consciousness came up to speed.

She was in her dorm room at Xavier's, which she shared with Tracy Cassidy. It was night. The lights were out, except for right around the two girls, and they were no longer alone. Two men, one looming over her, the other over Tracy. Both wearing combat gear, full commando rig with night-vision goggles and laser sights on their weapons. The laser was what she'd reacted to.

Both men were bringing their pistols up to shoot.

Tracy screamed.

In terms of raw decibels, a military jet on full afterburners would have been quieter. The cry covered the full range of the ultra-high-frequency spectrum, and it went through the surrounding ears like a shower of white hot needles. Glass shattered throughout the room— not only lightbulbs and mirrors but the focusing lenses of the soldiers' lasers and their goggles as well. Siryn was living up to her name and then some, generating a sound so powerful it overwhelmed the anechoic baffles built into the walls of her room to protect the rest of the school and students from just such an incident.

Down the hall, where the boys lived, Peter Rasputin and Jamie Madrox found themselves jolted awake. Alone in the room he shared with Bobby Drake, John Allardyce flailed so wildly against unseen enemies that he pitched himself out of bed. The same went for Marie and every other student in the school.

Nobody yet understood the reason for Tracy's outcry, so in these first moments of alarm and confusion, the general reaction wasn't charitable. Yes, Tracy sounded

terrified. So what else was new? That was why her room
was sound proofed. That was also why Kitty was her
roommate; her own phasing power gave her a measure
of protection against Siryn's sonic powers.

As for the assault force, they knew then they'd lost the
element of surprise. No more time for subtlety. Time to
shift into overdrive and apply brute force, to take down
the kids before they could muster sufficient wits to resist.
The problem for them was, even with ear protectors,
they found themselves almost as incapacitated by Siryn's
outburst as their targets.

The difference was only a matter of moments here,
moments there. But that difference proved critical.

As suddenly as the sound began, it stopped—Siryn
had run out of breath.

Before she could draw another, one of the commandos
snap-fired his dart gun. The drug's effect was instantaneous; she was out cold before her body even began its
collapse back onto her bed.

Both men turned as one to Kitty, who pitched herself
right through her bed in a clumsy dive that sent her stag-
gering toward and then through the floor and nearest
wall. They had no shot against a target who'd turned intangible, and then, just like that, it didn't matter, as the
door to the room burst open to reveal the bare-chested
Peter Rasputin.

Peter's big brother was Russian Air Force, part of the
Federation space program, and more than a few neigh-
bors' sons had served their tour in Afghanistan; he knew
soldiers, and he knew how to handle himself when there
was trouble.

The moment he registered the armed intruders in Tracy's room, even as the two commandos raised and fired their weapons, he triggered his own power. In the doorway, before their shocked and disbelieving eyes, he grew, quickly becoming too big for the opening. His pajama shorts, which he wore loose and extrasized for this very reason, stretched to the breaking point. Beneath his feet, the floorboards groaned as his mass increased to match his new size. His skin changed in color and texture, acquiring the sheen of polished chrome. More importantly, however, his flesh took on the actual density of metal, until it was transformed completely into a kind of organic armor that possessed the tensile strength of steel.

For all the good they did, the darts that struck his chest might have been spitballs.

With gleaming gunmetal eyes he looked to where Siryn lay sprawled on her bed. He looked back at the two commandos as they grabbed for their submachine guns.

No one heard the sound of firing, and thanks as well to the soundproofing and thickened walls, none of the bullets left the confines of the room. That couldn't be said for the commandos themselves. Peter's code name was Colossus, and with strength to rival his classical namesake, he put both men right through the wall and into the hallway outside.

A moment later Colossus himself emerged, Siryn cradled protectively in his arms so that they formed a steel shell around her. He heard voices and commotion, registered bare feet instead of boots, and turned a corner to find a couple of the younger students huddled in an alcove. A brilliant light speared through the windows just beyond them, and the glass panes shuddered under

the force of the downdraft from the rotors of a Sikorsky
AH-64 Apache attack helicopter as it muscled into position right outside.

For a moment, Colossus and the kids just stood there,
striking a classic deer-in-the-headlights pose, none of
them sure whether the spotlight would be followed by
gunfire, all of them fearing the worst. Colossus reacted
first, leaping forward to put his body between the gun-
ship and the youngsters, wondering as he did so if even
his armored form could withstand the impact of depleted-
uranium "tank buster" shells from the Apache's fearsome
30mm chain gun. That cannon could shoot right through
the mansion, punching holes as big as he was as easily as
through rice paper.

*"This way!"* he bellowed, cursing himself royally as
the kids looked at him, uncomprehending. In all the excitement, he'd spoken in Russian. "This way," he repeated in English, gesturing for the nearest set of stairs.
"Go, go, *go!*"

The light behind him didn't move, but that provided
little solace. He'd already marked at least three more
from directions that told him the mansion was surrounded. Common sense told him there had to be more
troops. There was no safety above ground. And, he
feared, precious little chance of reaching the escape tunnels below. But he had to try.

In the kitchen, Bobby Drake refused to move, refused
to breathe, refused to think. If he didn't do the first,
maybe Logan wouldn't remember he was here. If he
didn't do the last, he wouldn't have to face what he'd just
seen.

He heard the *snakt* of claws being retracted, watched

Logan lower the man's body to the floor. The claws had left their bloody mark on the refrigerator door, and the body left a trail before forming a puddle on the floor.

He'd never seen this in real life, only in movies or on the tube. Even when he was watching the news, it didn't seem real. They were just images, without any tangible impact.

But he'd heard the *huff* of the man's breath as Logan struck and knew with awful finality that the man would never draw another. He'd watch the tension flow out of the man's body until he had no more substance than a rag doll and, worse, had watched Logan's face while it happened. He saw no mercy there at all, and suddenly what he wanted more than anything was to be in his bed at home, cradled in the eternal security of his mother's arms while she sang him to sleep with a tune she'd made up for him alone.

He was crying, ashamed to show such weakness, yet strangely thankful that this was his body's only instinctive reaction. The tears blurred his vision, and when he wiped his eyes, crumbling the frozen water off his cheeks as they formed an icicle mustache, he saw only the body of the soldier. Logan had gone.

He didn't jump when Logan placed his hand on his shoulder, but the face he turned to the older man had lost any pretense of adulthood. It was a child's face, desperately scared.

"We've gotta go," Logan said simply.

Again without a thought, never knowing how high his stock was rising in Logan's opinion, Bobby pulled himself out from under the table and fell into step behind his companion.

Without running, they moved quickly through the

ground floor. Bobby had no idea whether they were simply trying to escape or rescue the others. Logan didn't offer any enlightenment, and Bobby understood that his job right now was to follow Logan's lead and do as he was told. End of story. He heard the sounds of booted feet all around them, men shouting orders counterpointed by the higher-pitched cries of kids in a panic. He thought he heard shooting, he knew he heard a crash that sounded to him like a wrecking ball making contact. Then suddenly, at the short hallway leading to the servants' back stairs, Logan slapped him to a dead stop with an arm like steel rebar across his chest.

"Stay here," Logan snapped, and then he charged.

Bobby couldn't resist a peek, and yielding to that temptation made him more scared than ever.

Two troopers were carrying Jones down the stairway. Another few waited below in the hallway.

Logan turned the scene into a demolition derby. A fist backed by adamantium bones smashed one man's face and hurled the man aside, blinded and broken and bloody. Momentum carried him into the main body of the group, and a piercing shriek of surprise and pain told Bobby that Logan was using his claws.

There was nothing he could do to help Logan, not here, not in this kind of scrap, short of maybe freezing everybody in place. But then what would he do if more bad guys showed up, with Logan occupied?

At the same time, he wasn't prepared to hide anymore, the way he had before in the kitchen. One of the school's rules—written and unwritten—was that the older kids looked out for the youngsters.

He didn't think about what he was going to do; that would have iced him in place more effectively than his power. He lunged across the hallway, straight for the servants' elevator, expecting with every one of the three steps it took him to feel the shock of a bullet to the back. He was so totally out of breath when he made it, and squeezed so deeply into the recessed alcove, that when the door slid open behind him he tumbled flat on the floor and almost couldn't get up.

At the other end of the hall, Logan was peppered with anesthetic darts. They didn't even slow him down. From above on the stairs, one of the men carrying Jones opened up with his sidearm, a 10mm automatic, but only managed to fire a couple of rounds before Logan took off the barrel and his forearm with a single sweep of his claws.

Logan never stopped moving, shifting from one adversary to the next with quick and deadly efficiency. He was a born scrapper, and in a crowd like this the advantage was all his. Everyone he faced was an enemy, whereas the soldiers had to be careful lest they cut down some of their own. The smart play for them would have been to withdraw and try to cut him down with automatic weapons or explosives, but they were boxed in by the tight confines of the hallway and there was no time for them to do more than react purely on reflex and training.

His reflexes were better by far, and their training didn't begin to prepare them for what they faced tonight.

He didn't care if they cut him, if they shot him; he'd bleed a while and then get better. By contrast, the blades that were part of his hands cut body armor and flesh and bone with equal facility, and if he chose not to use the blades, his unbreakable bones would do almost as much damage.

The fight didn't last a minute longer. When it was

done, Logan was the only one left standing, one of a precious few left breathing.

He saw a dart sticking from his arm and pulled it out, flexing his fist and clenching it to make sure there were no ill effects. He found another in Jones and plucked it free as well. He pressed his fingertips to the boy's neck to confirm what his other enhanced senses had already told him. The pulse was slow, but strong and regular. The boy was asleep, otherwise unharmed.

He didn't bother looking back to where he'd left Bobby; he knew the older boy was gone. Hearing told him the elevator was engaged, scent told him which floor he'd gone to.

Logan hauled Jones off the stairs by an arm and pitched him across his shoulders in a fireman's carry. Before the boy was settled in place, Logan was moving up the stairs, two and three at a time. His senses had also given him a pretty decent picture of the opposition's numbers and general location. There was no time to waste, no margin for mistakes.

On the third floor, Bobby stepped out into chaos. The youngest kids, and some of the older ones, were panicking as wind pounded the roof and windows around them. Someone was screaming that the glass was going to shatter; another collapsed to his knees on the floor, face upraised and howling, certain a plane was going to crash right through the wall and bring the building down on their heads. The helicopters were perched outside the windows, using their million-plus candlepower spot lamps to light up the interior of the house in absolutes of black and white. The glare was so intensely bright that everyone was forced to close their eyes, just to keep from being permanently blinded.

Bobby grabbed for the first figure within reach. It turned out to be John Allardyce.

"What the hell's happening?" John demanded between racking coughs that doubled him over. Somewhere he'd swallowed a lot of smoke, and he didn't much like it. Smoke was useless to John without a flame.

"Guys with guns," Bobby said, because that was all he knew for sure and trusted himself to say.

"No shit, Sherlock. We got a war here, we're being invaded!"

"We're a *school*!" Bobby protested.

"Try telling them!"

"We've got to help the kids!"

"Peter's up ahead. They're gathering around him."

"John, where's Rogue? Have you seen her?"

"I don't know. Man, I didn't see *you* till you grabbed me!"

"I'm going to find her."

John opened his mouth to protest, but Bobby was already two rooms down the hall. He didn't want to follow. He saw no percentage in being a *stupid* hero, especially under these circumstances, but he liked even less the idea that Bobby might think him a coward. The fact that Bobby would never conceive of such a thing didn't enter John's head.

Muttering and grumbling, he set out after his roommate, bulling his way against the tide of frightened schoolchildren.

The floor was trembling under the approach outside of a Sikorsky Blackhawk. It took station a dozen feet above the roof, and another assault team rappelled to the target. They weren't playing nice anymore. They used shotguns and shaped-charge grenades to blast skylight windows from their frames, and shock-wave charges to stun everyone in the rooms below.

The troopers burst into the hall like sharks attacking a school of baitfish. One triggered a taser at the closest student, a young Asian girl, and sent a burst of electricity down the double wires into her back. To his surprise, Jubilation Lee didn't fall. She pivoted on one foot, dropping into a shooting crouch of her own with her right arm outstretched, and shot that jolt of electricity through the air right back at him. The blast hit the trooper like the impact of a semi, throwing him back against the wall so hard he left an indent of his body deep enough to hold him upright. Out of the darkness nearby came the sound of a dart gun as another trooper returned fire from cover, and Jubilee dropped, unconscious.

In the neighboring wing, Peter Rasputin opened a hidden panel in the hallway wainscoting, revealing a passage and stairwell lit at intervals by emergency glow globes. Handing off Siryn to one of the older students, he began ushering his charges inside. Speed was the essence here. He had to clear the corridor before they were discovered by any of the intruders.

"Hey, shorty!" he heard from behind him. He thought at first it was one of the enemy and turned, ready to fight, only to find himself facing a figure barely half his size. Without another word, Logan handed over Jones.

"I can help you," Colossus called after him.

"Help them!" came the reply. "You got your responsibilities, bub."

Logan paused at a junction of the hallway. The beams

of two flashlights and a set of green targeting lasers splayed across the wall. He waited a moment, then stepped out of sight around the corner. The lasers went out, and Peter heard a couple of grunts, plus the sound of falling bodies. One flashlight beam vanished as well, and the other skewed wildly sideways before rolling into view along the floor.

"I have mine," Logan finished quietly, stepping briefly into view. "Get going."

Peter didn't need to be told twice. There were no other students in sight. He'd been running a head count of the kids he was shepherding into the escape passage, and he knew he was well short of the total. Who was just missing, who'd been captured, he had no idea. He also knew, although this left him sick and angry at heart, that he couldn't go looking for them. As Logan said, he had his responsibilities, and he would not abandon them.

He stepped through the doorway and locked it closed behind him.

Kitty Pryde didn't bother with doors. She didn't need them. Intangible as a ghost, she raced through the mansion, down to the main floor, where she found soldiers . . .

. . . through one of the classrooms, more soldiers . . .

. . . through the arboretum, more soldiers . . .

. . . through the billiard room where Cyclops would shoot nine ball using his optic blasts instead of a pool cue, more soldiers . . .

. . . through the hallway beyond, and right through the body of one of the invaders before either of them knew quite what was happening.

Kitty's power allowed her to slip the molecules of her own body through the valences of other physical objects.

The process was so quick that it had virtually no effect on the molecular cohesion of those nonorganic solids, any more than the passage of baseline human bodies would affect the air through which they travel. Or, more accurately in her case, the vast emptiness of open space.

That wasn't the case with electrical fields. Any transit by Kitty created a momentary skitz in a power circuit, causing a blink when it came to household wiring, leading to the occasional disaster when she interfaced with higher-order electronics. She was death to hard drives.

There was one other by-product, which her studies with Xavier had only recently begun to explore, and that related to the fact that the human body's central nervous system is one huge electrical network, linked to a supremely powerful biological computer. Whenever she ghosted through a person, she caused much the same shock with them that she did to a power circuit. The consequences depended on how quickly she was moving and where the contact took place.

For the trooper, it was like being momentarily jammed into a light socket. His world went white, just the way he'd read about folks who'd survived lightning strikes, and for an instant after it was over he thought that was what had happened. As a matter of fact, he wasn't altogether sure what *had* just happened. He had a vague sense of a girl popping out of a wall, then diving right through him.

His own reaction was automatic. Even as shock threw him into a vertiginous spin toward the floor, he managed to snap off a taser round after the girl. It was a spectacular shot, especially considering the circumstances. He caught her dead center between the shoulder blades—only the prongs at the end of the taser wires didn't strike living flesh at all. Instead they buried themselves in the wall of the house, at the very instant the girl herself vanished inside.

Upstairs, Rogue had found another girl to add to her collection. Terrified, of course, huddled in a heap, face gleaming with silent tears in the random splashes of brilliance thrown by the circling helicopters and their damn spot lamps. Marie found herself wishing, fervently, for some powers more appropriate to the name she'd chosen for herself, Rogue—something akin to Cyclops' eye beams, or Jean's telekinesis, or Storm's command of the weather. She wasn't feeling picky; she just wanted something to even the odds and maybe tear those gunships from the sky.

"Come on, honey," she said instead, in her best babysitter voice, projecting a strength and calm she didn't have as she gathered the girl to her breast, taking care to always keep a layer of clothes between her own skin and the girl's.

She was glad now that one of the first things she had done on arrival at Xavier's School was memorize the network of hidden passages that honeycombed both the mansion itself and the grounds. At the time she was just staying in character; after all, a girl has to know how to slip away unnoticed for a night of private fun, even if she never found the opportunity to try. Now that work was paying off with interest, the passages enabling her to elude pursuit and scoot her share of students to safety.

"In you go, girls," she told them, "just like Storm taught us, 'kay?"

The girl in her arms was clinging like a limpet, whimpering now along with her tears. Rogue was her lifeline, and she couldn't bear to be parted. Rogue didn't have time for this. They were too close to one of the upper floor's big bay windows. The longer they stayed, the greater the chance of being spotted when one of the helicopters did a flyby and trained its million-candlepower lamp into the house.

"Aren't you coming?" the other girl asked. She was a Scots redhead of barely thirteen named Rahne Sinclair.

"I have to find someone first," Rogue told her. With a winning Highlander grin, Rahne pried the other girl's hands loose from Rogue's neck, offering reassurances of her own as she led the way into the passage.

"When you come out of the tunnels," Rogue told them both, "run straight to the first house you find. Tell them there was a fire. Tell them to contact your folks. Whatever you do, though, you don't tell anyone you're a mutant. Okay?"

The girl nodded uncomprehendingly, but Rahne knew the score. She'd take care of her classmate just fine. Rogue leaned forward to brush a wisp of hair from the younger girl's face. In return, she got a brave attempt at a smile.

"Okay," the girl said.

"You'll be fine," Rogue told her, and closed the secret panel behind them.

Quickly she scooted the length of the hallway. The walls and floor, the very air, were trembling again as the helicopters made another run on the mansion. She had to find cover before she was nailed herself.

Through the infernal din, suddenly, unexpectedly, she heard a familiar voice, someone she thought would be long gone from the mansion by now.

"Rogue," called John Allardyce.

"Rogue!" bellowed Bobby Drake, determined to make himself heard.

"Bobby," she cried, startled to realize how out-and-out delighted she sounded to see him safe and free. John had to make do with just a nod of greeting.

"There anyone else?" she asked.

"I'm not sure," Bobby replied.

"Petey Pureheart was looking after a crowd of kids," John said. "Outside of them, nada. Bad guys galore."

"Where's Logan?" Rogue demanded. "He was s'posed to be looking after us!"

Bobby's face twisted. She knew the look. It echoed her own reaction to some of the things she'd seen Logan do in a fight.

"What's happened?" she said, grabbing Bobby by the shirtfront. To save her life, Logan had let her imprint him and his healing factor. Most of the memories that came with his powers had thankfully faded over time, but under stress she still manifested occasional residual flashes of his personality. "Where is he?"

Bobby didn't need to be asked twice. "He was downstairs," he told her.

"This way," she told them, intending to lead them back toward the secret passage.

Before she could move, an exterior lamp turned the hall brighter than noonday. They saw two shapes vaguely outlined in the glare, hanging outside the window. Immediately Rogue grabbed John, Bobby grabbed Rogue, and they all tumbled around the corner in a heap as an explosion shattered the leaded glass to bits, spraying the corridor with splinters and debris. Right behind the blast came the soldiers, targeting lasers tracing lines through the smoke, fingers ready on the triggers. Each door they passed got the same treatment: shotgun blasts to the hinges followed by a shot from a battering ram to punch it open, a couple of stun grenades to incapacitate anyone inside, sustained bursts from submachine guns to finish the job. Each room took only seconds to clear, and they did the job with murderous, methodical precision.

Without a word, the three young mutants decided that they didn't want to find out what would happen if they were found. When the soldiers reached the corner, the kids were long gone.

Up aboard the Hercules, the technicians staffing the sensor consoles were not happy. At the start of the incursion, they'd had a clear picture of the mansion's interior. They knew precisely where the kids were.

Now, after a span of too few minutes, nothing was certain anymore.

They had troopers down all across the board, with varying degrees of injury, and more than a few deaths. Worse for them, they had gradually lost contact with a significant number of potential targets. It didn't take a rocket scientist to determine the reason: the mansion must possess a number of sections that were comprehensively shielded against remote sensing and imagery. The only way to be sure of cleaning out the place would mean finding the access points and sending teams into the tunnels. Trouble was, given mission parameters, that wasn't an option.

The only alternative would be to widen the search parameters and try to pick the mutants up when they emerged onto the surface. But that would mean significantly degrading the resources available to monitor the prime target, Xavier's mansion. Again, given mission parameters, not an option.

Barring a miracle, any kids who'd escaped into the tunnels were pretty much free and clear.

Unaware of this, Peter Rasputin led his party into one of the long tunnels burrowed deep beneath the estate. Its terminus was a thick stand of woods outside Xavier's holdings, a nature preserve. He had no idea what would happen after that, or what would become of a score of terrified, bedraggled children in their nightclothes, with no money between them and no one close at hand they could trust.

Right now, though, for Peter, that didn't seem so important. He just wanted to get them, and himself, out of danger, to a place where no one would chase them or threaten them with guns. He wanted a breather, time enough to gather his wits and take stock of both the situation and his resources. Of the ultimate outcome, though, he had no doubt.

Awful as things seemed now, in the end he was sure they'd work out all right.

In that regard, Bobby and John would give him the argument of a lifetime. For them, as they hurried with Rogue down the nearest flight of stairs, the order of the evening was that things that were bad were constantly getting worse.

The mansion was crawling with troops, and from the sounds they heard all around, they quickly realized that nobody was using tranquilizer guns anymore. The bad guys were shooting bullets now, and they weren't being stingy with their ammunition.

Abruptly, Rogue stopped in her tracks, so suddenly the others slammed into her from behind. Harsh words were formed, but none were spoken. The sight before them wouldn't allow it.

Rogue was standing amid a pile of bodies, all soldiers.

"Logan was here," John commented unnecessarily, but even he felt small and vulnerable in the face of this carnage.

"This is old news," Bobby said, reaching for Rogue's gloved hand. "We can't stay here, Rogue, we're sitting ducks. We keep running after him like this, we'll just get ourselves in trouble."

She didn't reply, she didn't move a muscle, so Bobby edged forward to look her in the face.

She was staring down at her chest. It was covered in green dots. He looked up, following the beams of light to their source, and found a team of soldiers in the far doorway, weapons leveled.

They never got a chance to fire. Logan saw to that.

He was on the gallery above them, and with a primal scream that was so much more animal than human, he dropped on them like the wrath of God unleashed, arms held wide, claws extended.

The soldiers didn't stand a chance. Bobby couldn't watch this time any more than the last. Rogue wouldn't turn away. Logan was a part of her now, and would be forever, the same as with everyone else she imprinted. She felt her own fists flex just a little and felt an echo of the wild and untamable creature she saw before her.

Something tweaked her attention. Her eyes flicked to the side, and she caught a glimpse of a smile on John's face and a look to his eye that made her sad and scared all at the same time. John was enjoying this. He wanted a piece of it for himself. It would be fun.

A brace of lights hit the entrance from outside and above, pinning Logan in their beams as the helicopters responded to frantic calls for help down below. They didn't wait for orders, they wouldn't have cared anyway; the moment their guns came to bear, they opened fire, pockmarking the lawn with craters and shattering the stone entrance to the mansion to powder. But their target wasn't there anymore.

"Go," Logan told the kids, pushing them deep into the house. *"Go, go, go!"*

John found the nearest escape passage, opened the door, then he and Bobby went leaping through at once. Rogue held back. Imprinting Logan had left her own senses with a faint residue of what Logan himself possessed, and she could hear soldiers closing on their position from every side.

She called his name.

"Keep going," he told her, and shunted her none too gently over the threshold.

"Logan," she pleaded.

He shut the door in her face. And she was glad.

He figured at least twenty close at hand as he put his back to the wall, but only a dozen of them lit him up with their lasers. They didn't fire right away, he didn't care.

He popped both sets of claws, but their fire discipline held. Nobody pulled a trigger.

"You want a piece of me," Logan raged, his face twisted with a wild, untamable grin. "C'mon, boys, take your best shot. You know you want to. Shoot me! And see who gets to walk out of here alive!"

"No," said someone new, with quiet authority.

"Not yet," the figure finished, approaching through the darkness. The voice was familiar, Logan recognized that at the start, but he couldn't find a name or face to match it.

"Wolverine? Is that you?" the man said, closer still, the soldiers reluctantly moving apart to allow him past. He was important to them, but also, and just as obviously, the man in charge. They couldn't refuse. Kill him, Logan sensed instinctively, and this fight could well be won. "How long has it been?"

The man paused, as if expecting an answer to his greeting, his voice showing some good humor as he continued: "Fifteen years? And you haven't changed a bit. Me, on the other hand . . ."

With that, William Stryker stepped into view. He wore combat gear, just like his men, and in that attire his true calling was more than plain.

"Nature." He made a deprecating gesture. "It takes its toll."

The scent rang bells, far more so than the face, yet try as he might Logan couldn't find the labels that would give these random flashes of remembrance proper meaning.

The claws withdrew into their housings.

"What do you want?" Logan asked of him.

Stryker replied with a smile that would have done the Cheshire cat proud.

On the other side of the wall, Rogue stood unmoving in the entrance to the secret passage, bitterly ashamed of the surge of emotion that had swept through her as Logan closed the door. He'd been a stand-up guy for her from the start, and this was how she repaid him, by being happy that he stayed behind—because she felt an echo in her own soul of the berserker rage and madness that possessed his. It made her want to run away from him, more powerfully than any impulse she'd ever felt. But being his friend, being true to her name, she defied those expectations. She spit in their eye. Logan would have done the same, but this response was purely hers, and that, too, was why she chose to stay. They were alike, but they weren't the same.

Hands grabbed her arms. She shook them off.

"Wait," she told the boys, who couldn't believe their ears. "You've got to do something."

"Damn straight," John said hurriedly. "Run like hell while we've got the chance!"

"They're going to kill him!"

That argument fell on totally deaf ears. Both boys had seen Logan in action. Neither believed such an outcome remotely possible.

"Yeah, right." John scoffed for emphasis. "He can handle himself, Rogue. Let's book!"

"Bobby," she pleaded, *"please!"* She was desperate now, determined, because when she said, "They're going to kill him," the part of her that resonated with him suggested that was something he desired.

All Bobby knew was that Logan was the scariest creature he'd ever encountered. He was every nightmare that had ever had come to life, and if he never met Logan again, he'd be haunted by these memories for as long as he drew breath. In a way, he blamed Logan for all that was happening tonight. The first time he came to the mansion was when they were attacked by Magneto; now, the night of his return, the Army. He was a walking invitation to disaster, and nothing good would come of hanging with him. He also saw the way Rogue looked at him, spoke of him, cared for him, and he hated him for holding the place in her heart he wanted for himself.

Leave him. Let him find his own fate. That was the smart play. It was what he'd told them to do.

Stryker took a step closer to Logan, the men behind him making adjustments to their stance and position so that he didn't block any shooter's line of sight. One twitch from him, that would be their cue to cut loose on full auto, with enough firepower to turn anyone alive into hamburger. Another man, whose manner and bearing marked him as an officer, put aside his rifle and set himself to make a grab for Stryker and try to yank him clear if things went sour. Given all Lyman had seen tonight of Logan's handiwork, he suspected that was a forlorn hope. He'd try regardless. That was his job, to look after Stryker, and most likely die with him.

Logan saw the action. Loyalty like that couldn't be bought, he knew. His estimation of the other man went up a serious notch.

If Stryker was a fraction of the man Logan judged him to be, he had to know the danger, but he made no acknowledgment of it. He played the scene as if they were two old companions, possibly even friends, reuniting after a long and enforced separation. No denying his courage, that was sure, and Logan's assessment of him went up another notch as well.

"I must admit," Stryker continued, carrying on this eerily incongruous conversation, "this is the last place I thought I'd ever see you, Wolverine. I didn't realize Xavier was taking in animals." A pause to let the barb sink in. Logan didn't react. "Even animals as . . . unique as you."

"Who are you?"

"Don't you remember?"

Logan blinked, wondering what was wrong with the air. A mist was forming between him and Stryker, the temperature plunging so rapidly that one breath was normal, the next gusting a cloud of icy condensation.

On the other side of the mist, Stryker reached out a hand to encounter a wall of gleaming ice that divided the hallway from floor to ceiling, wall to wall, forming a protective bulwark between the mutant and Stryker. The men around him stirred, suddenly anxious that they might become entrapped in ice themselves. But nobody broke ranks.

Logan considered using his claws. No matter how thick the wall, he could speedily turn it into ice cubes. But first he had to deal with the damn kids.

The look on his face caused John to take a reflexive, cautionary step backward and made Bobby thankful he was inside the passage, his hands held flat against the wall to generate and sustain his ice field. Rogue didn't flinch, didn't fade. She met him eye to eye with a will as stubborn as his own.

"Logan," she said. "Come on."

"Do as you're told, girl. Get outta here. I'll be fine." He used a tone and manner that had always gotten instant results. She returned both in equal measure.

"But we won't." Then, more quietly, "Please!"

Stryker wasn't sure what was happening. The wall was translucent enough to suggest to him that Logan was no longer alone, but it didn't allow him to see how many others had joined him or who they were. With swift, decisive movements, he plucked a penetrator grenade from Lyman's harness and jammed it into the ice. Lyman immediately pulled him back and around, to shield his commander's body with his own. The other troopers shielded themselves and scrambled for cover as best they could in the seven seconds that passed between Stryker pulling the pin and the bomb detonating. The shock resounded through the confined space, leaving those closest to the blast partially deafened, their bodies feeling like they'd just been pummeled by jackhammers. The force of the shaped charge went straight into the ice, filling the air with frozen splinters as it punched through the wall like a spear.

When the mist cleared, the wall lay in broken chunks, filling the hallway and partially covering some of the men.

On the other side, though, was empty floor. Of Wolverine, and the others Stryker had seen, there was no sign.

John led the way, even though Logan could see a lot better in the dark. The boys wouldn't admit it aloud, but both of them preferred having him between them and the bad guys.

At the first junction, John went left.

"John, no," Bobby called after him.

"This is where Petey and the others went."

"I've got a better idea. This way."

The other direction ended at the garage. Like everything else about the mansion, there was a public space and a private one. Upstairs, in a carriage house set a little apart from the main buildings, was the usual group of suvs and vans, plus the professor's vintage Rolls-Royce. The basement held a far more eclectic and personal assortment of vehicles, including Scott's collection of bikes. Some looked normal, others were as wildly modified and revolutionary in conception and design as the *Blackbird*.

The choice for tonight was a sports car, blindingly quick but so well crafted and balanced that it could handle the local roads—which were narrow and wickedly winding—as though it were traveling on rails. The confines would be cramped, but it would carry them all.

John dropped into the driver's seat with the announcement, "I'm driving."

Logan yanked him clear as though he weighed nothing. "In your dreams, smart-ass," he growled. "Boys in the back."

Rogue rode shotgun, Bobby making sure to sit behind her.

"This is Scott's car," he said.

"Oh, yeah?" Logan didn't sound impressed, but actually he was.

"We'll need keys."

Logan's reply was the *snikt* of a single claw extending. He stabbed it through the ignition, twisted some wires together, got a spark, got a start, and they were on their way.

There was an evacuation tunnel for vehicles as well, giving them access directly to Graymalkin Lane, the road that ran along the estate's border. A left turn would take them to the neighboring town of Purdy's Station and the interstate, 684, that linked New York City with the main east-west highway—I-84—that bisected Connecticut and the southern tier of New York State. Turning right put them into the heart of Fairfield County, lots of woodland roads so gnarly and poorly signed that even the locals got lost occasionally. It was hilly country, constantly dropping into little ravines and hollows, which made it difficult to establish sustained radio or cellular communication.

Logan went for it like a shot, taking the turns at speeds that made the three passengers grab for their seat belts and then hold them tight. He drove without lights.

"Uhh," Bobby tried, swallowed, tried again. "You could maybe slow down, you know."

"Like hell," John retorted. "Go faster, dude, get us the hell away from here, *please!*" He finished in savage mimicry of Rogue's plea, both to Bobby and to Logan himself. "Jesus wept," he said, more to himself than anyone else, "what the hell *was* that back there?"

Rogue caught a flicker from Logan's eyes, his fingers working the leather-wrapped steering wheel and making it creak with tension.

"Stryker," he said after a while, as at least one penny dropped in memory. "His name is Stryker."

"Who's he?" Rogue asked.

His mouth stretched ever so slightly into a wry grimace, his head shook the smallest fraction.

"I don't know," he confessed, to her alone. "I don't remember."

She huddled deep in her seat, and he noticed that she was playing with something on her wrist: his old dog tags. He'd given them to her as a keepsake before leaving for Alkali Lake.

Seeing his look, following it to her hand, she unwrapped them from her wrist and held them out to him.

He took them, rubbing his thumb over the embossed letters like Aladdin did his lamp, hoping for his own kind of genie and three wishes to unlock all the secrets of his life, never considering—now or ever—that perhaps those secrets weren't something he should see.

He shifted gears and heard a yelp of shock and protest from John as his elbow clipped the boy in the cheek.

"What's your problem, kid?" he growled as John wriggled his head and an arm between the front seats, reaching for the center console.

"What are you doing, John?" Rogue demanded in that clippy voice that meant she'd been pushed too far and was ready to do some real damage.

"Too much silence, dudes. Majorly uncomfortable. Don't like it."

He pressed a button and the speakers erupted with what passed for music from a techno band that none of them had ever heard of and, after the first few seconds, didn't want to. The car's sound system was as superb as its engine and handling, the choice of CDs was truly deranged, inspiring impassioned and derogatory comments galore from the kids. Logan didn't say a word. His own tastes ran mainly toward roadhouse R&B and classic jazz, with one exception that he'd never been able to figure out, an affinity that went back as far as his memory for the Japanese *koto*.

Of course, being the ultimate gearhead, Scott had built himself a system only he could understand. The damn controls weren't even marked. Probably had an operator's manual the size of the Manhattan phone book. The more John tried to kill the music, the louder it became. Finally, when Logan was on the verge of ending their torment with a swipe of his claws, the boy managed to find the eject button. Only this switch had nothing whatsoever to do with the music. Instead, a tray popped into view, revealing an oval-shaped disk about as small as your basic computer mouse.

With a grumble of righteous exasperation Rogue pressed another switch on the console . . .

. . . and they heard only road noise once more, and the wind rushing past.

She and Logan exchanged looks, he offering silent thanks for her saving the day, while she thanked him in return for his forbearance. Her fist, the arm that had worn Logan's dog tags, was tightly clenched, the same way he held it when he popped his claws. If she'd had claws to go with the residue of Logan's personality and powers she still possessed, John would have been shish kebab ages ago.

John noticed none of this. He was too engrossed in his new toy. He found another button and when he pressed it found himself holding a two-way communication device.

"Guys," he announced, "I don't think this has anything to do with the CD player."

Logan plucked it from the boy's hand. John's survival instincts were working overtime. For once he didn't protest as Logan examined the device. Whatever the infuriating idiosyncrasies of the car's sound system, this at least made some sense to him.

"Where are we going?" John asked after awhile, totally lost.

"Storm and Jean are in Boston" was Logan's terse reply. "We'll head that way."

"My folks live in Boston," Bobby said.

"Good," said Logan.

Rogue heard him, but she wasn't really paying attention. She was looking at Logan's hands, skin covered past both wrists with what could easily be mistaken for dried paint, caked a layer or two more thickly between the knuckles, where the claws went into their housings. Her eyes saw more than she wanted, her sense of smell revealed more than she could bear, and she looked down at her own hands, wondering suddenly how her sleeping gloves had gotten so badly shredded. *Too much skin showing,* she thought, *I have to be really careful about touching anyone.* Her hands were trembling with the memory of what she'd seen him do.

"Don't worry, darlin'," she heard him say, again in that quiet, private voice that was for her alone, "it's not mine."

When their eyes met, she gave a start of surprise, her mouth forming a tiny O of amazement. She was so used to feeling residues of his own ferocious—and murderous—passions, she found it hard to believe when she saw reflected in his eyes an echo of the pain and misery she felt. And strangely, she found that reassuring. It made her feel better—to know that he wasn't a monster after all. That man Stryker had called him an animal, had called him Wolverine instead of by name, but Rogue knew different.

His name was Logan. And he was human to the core.

# Chapter Eight

The mansion itself was the tip of the proverbial iceberg. The bulk of Xavier's School was hidden below ground, in a complex that stretched deep into the earth and sprawled every which way beneath the estate, employing technology as revolutionary as the design of the *Blackbird*. The schematics of the power source alone made the physicists on Stryker's analysis team weep with frustration. More than anything, they wanted to get their hands on this equipment, and none of them was happy to discover that their employer had other priorities.

A significant amount of space directly beneath the mansion was devoted to something Magneto referred to as the Danger Room. It was here that Xavier conducted the bulk of his explorations into the practical dynamics and limitations of the powers possessed by his students. Of equal significance, it was also where he trained his personal assault force, the X-Men.

Technicians began swarming through the building as soon as Lyman's troops reported it secure, but they quickly found themselves frustrated by command protocols keyed to retinal and voice prints they didn't possess and computer codes so deviously encrypted they couldn't begin to make sense of them.

Stryker didn't much care. To him, all that was of peripheral interest. As far as he was concerned, once his plan reached fruition, they could deconstruct the school and all of its tech at their leisure.

Under escort, he made his way down the main elevator to the uppermost level of the underground complex. Troopers with digital cameras recorded everything, to be downloaded into the main database once they returned to headquarters—more grist for the analysts' mill. Chances were, this would leave them in pig heaven for years to come.

They passed a locker room, and Stryker paused a moment to finger one of the uniforms hanging there. Another marvel of structural engineering. The material looked and felt like leather; it fit like a biker's speed suit, almost a second skin. But it was extraordinarily resilient, protecting the wearer from extremes of temperature and environment—snug in winter, cool in summer, dry in a monsoon—and, most practical of all in Stryker's opinion, better than Kevlar as body armor. Projections suggested it could survive a point-blank round from a Barrett .50-caliber sniper gun, the most powerful rifle made, one small step below an actual cannon.

He turned away from the uniform as Lyman hurried up to join him, calling his name.

"Tunnels," he reported to Stryker, standing briefly to attention and giving the older man a salute. "That's where all the kids went. And damn well shielded, too, better than this!" He indicated the circular corridor around them, with its ergonomically cool colors and lighting, the epitome of sensible industrial engineering. "From the way targets kept popping off our scopes, the house must be riddled with them, the entire compound, too! We used a sonic imager to find some of the entrances, but there were deadfalls right inside, sealing the escape routes tight. From the way they booked out of here, they had to have practiced escape and evasion techniques. I don't know if we can catch them at the exit points."

"Very prudent of them. How many did you get, then?"

"Six, sir. What should we do with them?"

"Pack them up. We'll decide later."

As the two men spoke, they approached Stryker's true destination, right at the end of this main hallway. It was a circular door that intentionally resembled the entrance to a bank vault, or to NORAD's command center deep inside Cheyenne Mountain, built to protect the chamber within against any form of hostile incursion. Stryker doubted he had any tools in his arsenal, short of perhaps a baby nuke, capable of breaching this barrier. Fortunately, none were needed.

At his command, a pair of troopers stepped forward and set up the device they were carrying, placing it on a tripod in front of the doorway. To the right side of the door itself was a scanning plate, in which was embedded a multifaceted blue crystal, as pure a sapphire as any had ever seen. They set the lasing crosshairs dead center on the crystal, at the height of a tall man seated in a wheelchair.

The device was activated, the laser immediately refracting into a score of lesser beams that struck the crystal, replicating the retinal pattern they had recorded from Xavier's own eye.

It only took a moment.

"Welcome, Professor," said a gentle feminine voice

with a hint of a highland Scots brogue. Stryker recognized it from Xavier's primary dossier; it was his collaborator, fellow geneticist and onetime lover, Moira MacTaggart of Edinburgh University.

Without hesitation Stryker strode along the platform to Xavier's console in the center of the great globe of a room. The others held back, just a little. To them, this was the heart of the darkness that was their enemy, the place where Xavier supposedly honed and worked his incredible powers. From here, so Magneto said, he could reach out to every mind on the planet. Stryker hoped that was true, hoped the old mutant wasn't exaggerating. Because that made this room the key to his ultimate victory.

He reached out to the gleaming chrome helmet on its stand but couldn't quite bring himself to touch it. This was Xavier's toy; let the mutant mental play with it. Stryker would watch. "Take what you need, gentlemen," he said as the soldiers entered Cerebro.

Saturday night. And Mitchell Laurio, creature of habit, was where he could be found every Saturday night he wasn't working. Fourth stool from the end at the Dew Drop Inn. It wasn't a great bar, but then he wasn't a picky guy. It had televisions to spare and, if the cash was right, a fella could persuade one of the waitresses to join him in a booth and provide a semiprivate show. Most nights, the video choice was sports or sex, but for some reason the bartender had switched the TVs over to some damn news show where two mooks were blathering on about mutants, as if anyone in the world actually gave a rat's ass about their opinion.

Laurio wasn't aware he was speaking those sentiments aloud but wouldn't have cared if he had realized it.

". . . the Mutant Registration Act provides a sense of security similar to Megan's Law," said a middle-aged guy whose title card identified him as Sebastian Shaw, the latest tycoon turned politico. "A list of potentially dangerous mutants living in our communities."

His counterpart was half his age and twice his size, and Laurio remembered him from college ball. An All-American who passed on a pro contract to go to Stanford for a doctorate, the first of a whole bunch, it turned out. His name was Henry McCoy. *People* magazine said he preferred Hank.

"Megan's Law is a database of known felons, Mr. Shaw," he responded heatedly, "not innocent people who haven't committed any crime and may not even be likely to. It's akin to registering every member of a religious or ethnic group in the nation, on the presumption that *some* of them may be terrorists."

"Some might not consider that so bad an idea, McCoy."

"*Some,* Sebastian," McCoy shot back, "might consider America a better place than that."

"A damn mutant almost killed the President!"

"A *person,* who happened to be a mutant, made the attempt, yes. If he was a Lutheran, would you automatically condemn every Lutheran in the land?"

"If the knife had said 'Lutheran Rights Now,' I'd damn sure consider it."

"What people seem to forget is that mutation is evolution in action. In a sense, we're *all* mutants. If not for past mutations, for past evolution, chances are we'd all be sitting in trees, picking bugs from one another's hair!"

"Goddamn it, Lou," Laurio snarled, "turn that shit off. Bad enough I got the godfather of muties in my face the whole damn day long without I got this raining on my head after!"

"I'm sorry," he heard a woman say behind him, in a voice that went down his spine like a shock, "it's my fault. I asked Lou to turn the channel."

He rolled his stool around and found himself facing a woman who put the dogs who usually haunted this place to shame. She was no stick-figure woman, he had no taste for that, she had curves on her and then some, big rack, cute butt, and a waist that made his hands ache to enfold her. She had some mileage to her, but she had a look to the eye, a quirk to the mouth, and a way of looking him up and down that told him she knew how to use it. Her lips were liquid scarlet, sassy, her eyes so deeply shadowed that all he could see were some glints reflecting the neon behind the bar, which gave them a weird yellow cast. She was blond, and taller than he usually liked, but he figured that was due to her stilt stilettos, and as she strode closer he had to admit he loved what those shoes did for her walk.

"You sound like a man with a lot on his mind"—she paused to sneak a peek at his badge—"Mr. Laurio."

He smelled scotch on her breath and noted the half-full tumbler in her hand.

"I'm Grace," she said.

He didn't know what to say. Really, all he wanted to do was sit and stare. She let him. It was obvious that she enjoyed the attention.

"Want another beer, Mr. Laurio?" She didn't wait for him to answer. "Course you do."

"Mitch," he said. "My name's Mitch."

She gave him that dazzling smile again, shifting position beside him so that her skirt rode high enough on her thigh to flash some skin above the top of her stocking and her breasts brushed against his chest. She seemed to lose her balance just a little, forcing him to catch her with his arm suddenly tight around her waist, and she giggled like it was all a big joke and he laughed, too, because this was the kind of moment he only dreamed about.

He didn't see what her free hand was doing behind him as she gathered the beer mug close, dropping a pair of white pills into the foam, where they quickly dissolved.

After a couple more beers, it took only the vaguest hint to propel him off his stool and into the ladies' room. It wasn't much different from the men's room in layout and wasn't much cleaner besides. As they stumbled over the threshold, Laurio tried to take a swallow of beer and grab a kiss on her lips all at the same time and failed in both. That made them both laugh, especially since most of the beer had landed on him. He was stinko, a lot more than was usual after a few beers, but he didn't give it any thought.

"I never hooked up with anyone like you before," he told her, making like the guys on TV.

"I know," she said. "Your lucky night."

She gave a little push, and he dropped onto a toilet seat.

"Kinda dirty, ain't it," he said.

"That's the idea," she replied, leaning forward to tease him with a glimpse of her breasts before squatting down in front of him. Her legs were splayed wide apart, but there were too many shadows, his eyes wouldn't focus right, he couldn't see enough to make it worthwhile. Then, as she unbuckled his belt, he gave up trying to look. Tonight was getting better and better.

"Velcro," Grace muttered as she opened his pants. "Nice."

"Bottoms up," he toasted her, raising his beer high.

"I certainly hope so."

She smiled one last time, and the last of his beer cascaded out of the mug and across his face and chest. His mouth was open, but he made no attempt to drink. He was way beyond that. As his head lolled back against the tile behind him, his pupils dilating to their limits, his suddenly nerveless arm dropped, the mug falling from useless fingers to shatter on the floor.

Grace pressed two fingers to his carotid pulse, satisfying herself it was firm and regular, then used the tips of her fingers to close his mouth and stop the beginnings of a snore. There was no sloppiness any longer to either manner or movement as she snapped the lock shut on the door behind her, then reached down to grab Laurio around the waist and flip the big man over so that his head was somewhere behind the bowl and his butt poked up in the air.

She opened her purse and removed a syringe, tapping the barrel with a lacquered forefinger to clear any air bubbles. It wouldn't do to give the slug an embolism. She pulled down his boxers and pressed the plunger. As she did, the skin on her hand darkened to the same indigo shade as her nail polish. The transformation raced up her arm, across her body, which became longer and leaner, much less the kind of blowsy Reubens woman that Mitchell Laurio dreamed of in favor of someone much stronger and more sleekly muscular. Her hair became a dark autumnal russet shot through with midnight. Mystique bared teeth that were startlingly white against her blue-black skin and patted Laurio where she'd made the injection.

"Bottoms up, darling." And then she was gone.

Lyman met Stryker en route from the landing pad.

"The men are nearly finished, sir," he reported.

Stryker nodded approvingly. "Ahead of schedule," he noted approvingly. "Strip down at source, transport, and reconstruction. I am very impressed, Mr. Lyman. The crews are to be commended."

"You trained 'em, sir. They're just following your lead."

Stryker continued to nod. This was going better than he'd hoped. A good omen for what was to come, perhaps.

"How does it look?" he wondered.

"Flawless."

They passed a reception cubicle where Lyman saw one of the troopers tending to the prisoner Cyclops, fastening a metal band over the mutant's eyes.

"Good," Stryker said, meaning both what Lyman had just told him and what he saw in the cubicle. "Now for the main event."

When he woke, groggy and pummeled, as though every cell in his brain had been given its own personal, enthusiastic beating, Charles Xavier had no idea where he was. Far worse, he had no sense whatsoever of the thoughts around him. He couldn't help a moment's panic, finding himself imprisoned for the first time within the walls of his own skull. As a clinician he'd often used the term "headblind" to describe nontelepaths and had even fantasized about the sensation. Unfortunately it was like trying to imagine being dead; the act of imagination itself effectively invalidated the concept.

This was so much worse. He felt hollow and . . . alone. The background noise, the susurrus of other thoughts that was a constant presence and an occasional annoyance, was gone. His inner cries couldn't even provoke an echo. He could only perceive the world from a single perspective, his own, and it was unbearable.

He was bound into his chair, his wrists tied with duct tape to the armrests. He felt a dull burning pressure around his head and thought of the torture instruments of the Inquisition. One—particularly nasty—was strapped around the skull and gradually tightened until the bone shattered. From how he felt, Xavier assumed that had long since happened. If he let his head loll forward, perhaps he'd see his brain flop out onto the floor. At least that final oblivion would be better—*anything* would be better—than the gnawing emptiness that was consuming him.

He tried to take refuge from his misery by taking inventory of the purely physical. He wasn't in Mount Haven, that was a sure bet. The room was dark, as were some in the prison, but the walls were dank and pockmarked with age. The prison environment was strictly maintained; this was so chilly he was already starting to shiver, a damp cold that ate into his bones. This place had been abandoned long ago, and even though he could hear faint sounds of activity, it was clear to him that no one was planning a lengthy stay.

Reflexively, he stretched his thoughts toward the sounds outside. Big mistake. The Inquisition analogy suddenly took on an agonizing relevance as he felt as if barbed spikes were being driven into him. The sleet storm of pain doubled him over, pulling a hoarse grunt from the pit of his belly. Worse had happened; he could smell and feel the consequences as his body lost all control, and the beginnings of tears burned his eyes at the loss of his dignity.

"I just had to see that work for myself," said Stryker as he entered the room.

Xavier didn't bother to respond at first. Better to take as much time as possible, to gather what few resources remained to him before facing his adversary. He worked his tongue around his mouth, tasting the familiar gunmetal taste of adrenaline, remembering another time and place where his telepathy had been no use to him. A wayward step on a jungle trail, the shock of a land mine that, fortunately, was on the other side of a tree. The encounter had won him a Purple Heart and taught him a valuable lesson: Just because it doesn't have a brain doesn't mean it can't kill you.

Stryker was a patient man, especially when he was winning. He waited until Xavier was ready before continuing.

He hadn't come alone. Standing in the doorway, obviously a bodyguard, was a lovely young woman of Asian extraction. Something about her gaze caught Xavier's attention; there was animation in her eyes, but no sense of real life. She seemed awake, yet totally asleep.

"I call it the neural inhibitor," Stryker continued. "The more you think, the more you hurt. And"—he tapped his own forehead—"it keeps you out of *here*."

"William," Xavier said, and he wasn't surprised to how hard it was to speak even that single word. The inhibitor not only crippled his psychic functions but a degree of his basic cognitive ones as well.

"I'm sorry we couldn't find you more . . . comfortable

quarters," Stryker said. "My old home here is about to undergo some rather major renovations. Much like yours."

Xavier felt stupid, which made him feel angry. He couldn't make the connections, couldn't see the implications of what Stryker was saying, even though the other man was acting like they were blindingly obvious. He fastened on to the only one that came to mind.

"What have you done with Scott?"

"Don't worry, you'll be seeing him soon. I'm just giving the boy a little reeducation." He paused. "But you know all about that, don't you? Altering thoughts and perceptions must be as easy for you as rewriting codes of software."

"There's no need to involve anyone else!" Xavier protested desperately, with more vehemence than Stryker expected.

"No need to involve anyone else?" Stryker sounded genuinely incredulous. "You run a *school for mutants*, Professor! What on Earth do you teach those creatures?"

A question requiring a conceptual answer. That took effort, which brought him pain, but Xavier persevered nonetheless, calling on the same focus and discipline that had enabled him, self-taught, to master his burgeoning telepathy.

"To survive," he hissed through gritted teeth. "To coexist peacefully in a world that fears them."

"I've seen what's buried beneath your house, Xavier. It doesn't look very peaceful to me. I also know—firsthand—the kind of creatures you've gathered to live there. Some species can never coexist. I learned that from you," he finished offhandedly, turning away.

"You wanted me to *cure* your son. But, William, mutation is not a disease."

"Liar," he snapped. When Stryker looked around, his mask of affability was gone. The pain was real, the grief, the rage, and he used his words on his prisoner like a lash.

"You're lying, Xavier," Stryker said more slowly, more forcefully. "You were more afraid of him than *I* was! He was too powerful, and you couldn't control him."

The Asian woman laced her fingers together, cracked her knuckles. Stryker noticed more than Xavier did. The gesture amused him, but only for a moment that quickly passed, the feeling subsumed as always by his relentless fury.

"You know, just a year after Jason returned from your school, my wife . . ." Stryker's voice trailed off, and he stood up. His own right hand was clenched into so tight a fist the knuckles were white, and Xavier guessed from his posture that he wanted to use that fist, on Xavier himself. "He resented us, you see, he blamed us for his . . . condition. He was my *son*. I loved him more than my own life, we both did. How could he feel such things about us? How could he . . . *do* . . . such things?

"He would . . . toy with our minds, you see. He would project images and scenarios into our brains."

As he spoke, the woman's breathing became erratic. Her hands began to tremble enough to finally catch Xavier's notice. There was a gradual but growing look of confusion to her features, a distinct change to the quality of the animation he'd seen in her gaze. She was no longer placid; she was waking up.

Stryker paid her no attention. His focus remained entirely on Xavier.

"Unfortunately," he said, making an effort to hammer the emotion from his voice and thereby revealing the terrible, haunting depth of those feelings, "I had my work. I was overseas, serving my country." His subtext was plain. He hadn't been there to share his wife's ordeal; he couldn't do for her what he felt his job required him to do for the nation—save the day. He had survived and was glad and guilty of it.

"My wife couldn't escape. She was around him all the time. We had to keep him at home, you see. After you sent him away, we didn't dare risk allowing him to attend a school. Can you imagine what he'd have done to all those impressionable minds?"

"I . . . didn't know."

"How convenient for you. My wife, over time, she became easily influenced . . . unable to tell the difference between what was real and what was a part of his warped imagination. In the end . . ." he paused, confronting the memory like a warrior facing down an adversary. "She took a power drill to her left temple, in an attempt to bore the images out of her mind."

The woman swayed, shaking her head once or twice to clear it, reaching up with one hand to steady herself. Absently, Stryker stopped the gesture and lowered the arm back to her side. He was aware of what was happening to her and wasn't bothered in the slightest. Everything was under control.

"My . . . boy," and in that one word were all the dreams and heartbreak of a father's life. "The great illusionist."

"For someone who hates mutants, William, you certainly keep strange company."

"It has its uses," Stryker replied. "It serves a purpose. As do you."

In his hand he held an ampoule of yellow liquid. With the same gentle gesture, which reminded Xavier of the way a trainer might move a horse, he bent the woman forward from the waist until her head was on the same level as Xavier's. He swept her hair aside to bare the back of her neck, revealing a scar identical to the one Xavier had seen on Magneto.

With practiced ease, Stryker applied two drops. The effect was instantaneous. Her breathing returned to normal, she stopped trembling, and when she straightened once more to her full height, Xavier saw no more sign in her eyes of an independent personality.

Stryker whispered something in her ear. She nodded and left the room.

"It was you," Xavier said suddenly, in a burst of intuition that left him shocked. "You arranged the attack on the President!"

Stryker actually laughed out loud. "And you didn't even have to read my mind," he said approvingly.

"You know," he continued, "I believe I've been working with mutants almost as long as you have, but the final solution to the problem continued to evade me. So I guess I'm in your debt. I have to thank *you*, Xavier, because you gave me Magneto. And Magneto gave me the answer."

"You can't eradicate us, William. New mutants are born every day."

"And once I'm finished, they'll be born into a very different world. What are you thinking, that I'll end up like Rameses or Herod or poor old Heydrich? Nice try at genocide, but no cigar?

"Guess again. You see, in all my years of . . . research,

the most frustrating thing I learned is that nobody really knows how many mutants exist in the world, or how to find them."

He leaned close, putting his face directly in front of Xavier's. "Except you."

He held up the vial of yellow liquid and waggled it before Xavier's eyes.

"Sadly, this little potion won't work on you, will it?"

He straightened himself, backed up a step, and returned the drug to his jacket pocket.

"Nope, you're *far* too powerful for that. Instead, we'll go right to the source."

With crisp, military moves that were almost a flourish in themselves, Stryker opened the door.

"Allow me to introduce Mutant 143."

Beyond was a chair, and in that chair sat something that could only charitably be called human. At first glance, because the body was so shriveled and emaciated, the presumption was that it was someone extremely old. The limbs were arranged so neatly that Xavier knew at once they couldn't move of their own volition; the way the head lolled to the side was further evidence of the lack of any effective musculature. There was a water tube close by his mouth, which he constantly licked, but that was just so he could keep tongue and lips from going dry. Fluids and nutrients flowed into him intravenously, through permanent junctions in the major blood vessels of the leg up close to his groin. The site was mercifully hidden beneath a blanket, but Xavier assumed that permanent catheters were likewise employed to deal with all his waste products.

The man's head itself was macrocephalic, swollen to half again normal dimensions, and marked with a cruel scar across the temple as though the skull itself had cracked apart under the pressure of the growing mass within. A grotesque array of tubes and connections sprouted from implants in the back and base of the skull, draining a continuous volume of what had to be cerebrospinal fluid into clear containers mounted on the back of the chair. The fluid was an electric chrome yellow, and Xavier knew at once it was the substance Stryker used to control the woman, and Magneto, and Lord knows who else.

The man in the chair had one eye of a brilliant robin's-egg blue, the other an equally rich shade of green, Xavier noted, as the Asian woman and another trooper wheeled the chair directly in front of him. It was what Xavier saw *in* those eyes that struck him like a body blow: a look of cruel and feral cunning, representing an intelligence worthy of respect. The man knew exactly what he was, and he hated it beyond all levels of sane comprehension.

Xavier, who thanks to his own gifts forgot nothing, knew the man at once, from the shape of the jaw and especially those unique eyes.

"Jason . . ." he breathed in a voice that barely registered as a whisper. And then, in that same hushed, horror-struck tone, to the father: "My God, William—what have you done to him? This is your *son*!"

"No, Charles. My son is dead."

The look Xavier received from Stryker's blue eyes was a match for the emotions that emanated from the young man.

"Just like the rest of you."

# Chapter
# Nine

Past Hartford, Logan abandoned the back roads for the interstate, figuring a sports car in the middle of nowhere would draw a lot more curiosity than one more amid the many that cruised between Boston and New York. For him, the perfect place to hide now was in plain sight. He timed it perfectly, joining the morning rush-hour crowd as it crawled through Connecticut's capital, thankful that Scott hadn't indulged in a stand-out color like canary yellow or Ferrari scarlet. To the casual eye, this seemed like just another generic speedster. Stay with the flow of traffic, stay close to the speed limit, there shouldn't be any trouble.

They made decent time and rolled into the Boston suburb of Quincy just past noon. Nice streets, respectable houses, the sidewalks shaded by trees that had been here since before the Revolution.

They'd left the mansion with a full tank of gas, and Logan hadn't made a stop anywhere along the way. He was too much of a mess and the kids were all in pajamas, it was asking for trouble. The downside was, they were all pretty hungry and in desperate need of a bathroom and, being teenagers, weren't at all shy about letting him know how cranky they were becoming

Bobby gave directions, and Logan eased the car up the drive of a lovely two-story home. The garage was locked, so they had to leave the car exposed in the driveway.

Same went for the house itself. They were on the porch only a moment before Bobby found the key and let them inside.

"Mom?" he called. "Dad? Ronny? Anybody home?"

Logan could have told him the house was empty, his senses had reported that while they were all still outside, but he decided it was better to let the boy establish it for himself. He was itching to move on, instinct telling him that staying put anywhere guaranteed trouble, but he shoved those feelings aside. By nature he was a loner, but also by nature he understood the concept of responsibility and obligation—although for the life of him he couldn't have told anyone where he'd learned them. These kids had been placed in his care, and he wouldn't abandon them.

"We've got the place to ourselves," Bobby said. He looked to the phone and started to reach for it. "Maybe I should call—"

Logan covered the phone with his hand and shook his head.

"Leave it for now," he said. "You never know who might be listening."

"What, you saying those guys tapped my parents' phones?"

"I'm saying we need to be careful. This isn't a game, Bobby." Logan swung his head around to allow his gaze to encompass them all. "Those troops were serious, and they were good. If we want to have a chance of coming out of this clean, we have to deal with 'em on that level, clear?"

Bobby nodded, his lower lip between his teeth a sure

sign of how worried he was. Still, when he turned to the others, his voice was under control.

"I'll try to find you some clothes," he said to Rogue, and then, to John: "And you, don't burn anything."

Being guys, they immediately traded gestures—a finger from John, a retorting smirk from Bobby.

Upstairs, Bobby gave Rogue use of his own room and first crack at the shower. She turned the water as hot as she could bear and let the spray pound her like a monsoon, standing with her eyes closed in the vain hope that when she opened them once more this would all turn out to be some dream or another bogus training scenario.

Wrapped in a bath towel, she swept her hair back from her face and tied it in a loose ponytail. The decor here echoed his room at school—emphasis on snowboarding posters and the obligatory Red Sox pennant. One surprise, an autographed football that made her eyes widen when she realized that it was from the 2001 Super Bowl that the New England Patriots had won.

She was flipping through his CDs, singularly unimpressed by his choice in music—was she the only person in the school with any taste?—when he backed in carrying some clothes. He must have thought she was still in the shower, because he went as pale as the blouse in his arms when he saw her. Suddenly she was conscious of how small the towel felt, of how much skin was showing. At the same time, though, she found herself wondering what he thought: Did he like her legs? Her figure wasn't much compared to some of the other girls, especially Siryn, but his eyes kept coming back to her, so there had to be something in the package that he liked.

Was his mouth as dry as hers? Was his heart pounding

the same fandango? Usually he was easy to read. Now he looked as cool as the ice he generated.

"Hey," he said in greeting.

"Hey," she responded in kind.

"I hope these fit."

"Thanks."

"They're my mom's. From before I was born. But I think they'll fit."

"Groovy," she replied lightly, grabbing at a similarly ancient word.

He handed her the clothes but made no other move until she motioned for him to do a U-turn and scoot. All at once, his composure vanished, so much so that he collided twice with the door trying to make his exit. He didn't close it all the way, though, and took up station just outside while she got dressed.

Downside was, the blouse he found was short-sleeved. He had a solution.

"These were my grandmother's," he explained, holding out a pair of pristine opera gloves. The cloth would cover her almost all the way to the sleeves. Not a perfect answer, but one that touched her.

But when she reached for them, he tried to catch her hand, almost making contact before she snatched hers back as though she'd been scalded. She stepped back, a gasp rising in her throat, her other hand held defensively, palm toward him.

"You know I'd never hurt you," he said, inching closer.

"I know," so quietly she was just mouthing the words. She ached to take him in her arms, it had been so long since she'd felt anything as simple, as basic, as the stroke of someone else's skin on hers. She'd told him about her power right from the start—everyone knew the prohibition about touching her, that came from Xavier himself—but she suspected nobody really believed it.

Right now, she didn't want to.

He moved his hand close to her face, and tears sprang from her eyes as static electricity made the fine hairs of her cheek stir. She clenched her fists, feeling her body tighten from head to toe as though she were being stretched on a medieval rack. His breath touched her mouth—first warm and tempting, then chill enough for her own breath to leave a cloud of condensation in the air between them, then warm again, so inviting that she couldn't hold back any longer.

She pressed her lips to his, arms around his neck as his went around her body, and felt a sweet spark of contact as their tongues touched, and she giggled as a burst of frost rolled across her.

For a moment, it was bliss.

Then she imprinted.

The warmth between them became fire, a torrent of raw lava coursing along her nervous system, agony for him, ecstasy for her. The shock of contact made the veins bulge and pulse on his forehead, across his chest, eyes going cloudy and rolling up in their sockets. He spasmed once, twice, pinned on the verge of a grand mal seizure as she pushed against him with all her might to separate them before it got any worse. The initial stage of imprinting was physical, the equivalent of giving a car a jump-start or throwing a jet engine into afterburners. It delivered a jolt of energy to her system that would keep her going at peak levels for days. Break contact then, that was it.

Hold longer, the second stage kicked in, where she

absorbed the parahuman abilities of the person she was
touching. Months earlier, on Liberty Island, Magneto
had used her as the power source for his great machine,
even though he'd known the process would kill her. He'd
considered it a necessary sacrifice. Logan had destroyed
the machine, but not before its infernal energies had inflicted mortal injuries on her. He'd initiated contact himself, trusting her power to kick in automatically and do
the rest. She'd imprinted him completely, and his healing
factor had literally brought her back from the dead. That
was where she'd gotten the skunk-stripe forelock on her
hair. That was also why she never tried to hide it. It was
her personal badge of honor—acknowledging what he'd
done for her and reminding her of what she'd done to
him in turn.

Because there was a third component to her power,
one that wasn't temporary. The energy boost faded with
time, and so did the powers she absorbed—but if contact
lasted long enough, she took into herself the mind and
memories of her imprintee. A residue of the other's personality moved into her own psyche and, she thought,
she feared, maybe she gave up a portion of herself to the
other as well.

They'd made jokes about it after the fact, about how
she'd taken on some of the more salty aspects of Logan's
personality while she was healing. In time, as she got a
handle on this new part of herself, it seemingly went
away. She returned to what passed for her as normal.
Only she knew the truth, that Logan would be a part of
her forever.

And if she held on to Bobby for much longer, so
would he.

With a cry, she pushed him away, collapsing onto the

bed as he reeled back into the corner formed between the open door and the wall. She couldn't bear to look at him. The glimpse of pain and terror on his face while he was in her grasp was haunting enough.

"I'm sorry," she sobbed, feeling a different kind of ache through her body at how inadequate her words sounded.

"It's—okay," he said.

She heard him shuffle around the door with the moves of an old man. She stared at her hands, hating what she could do, hating how glorious it made her feel, hating most of all the fact that she couldn't control it, that she couldn't put back what she'd stolen. She sat there with the gloves on her lap, smoothing her palms across the sleek fabric over and over and over again, like she was ironing, desperately seeking something she could put right.

John heard Bobby stumble downstairs but didn't bother to see if he needed any help. He was in the family room, flicking the lid on his lighter, staring at the crowd of pictures on the wall, on shelves, on the big TV. A happy family, just what you'd expect to find in any part of America.

He hated it.

In the kitchen, Logan knew everything that had transpired upstairs. Too late, he'd sensed what was about to happen, had been on his way to the stairs when he heard Rogue's faint outcry and the thump of Bobby's body against the wall. He held position for the few moments necessary to reassure himself they'd done each other no lasting physical damage, then turned away. He hadn't a clue how to help either of them, and the only advice his own instincts and experience could offer was to give them space. Let them lick their wounds and regain their inner equilibrium in private, as he would.

What he needed, he knew, was a trained professional. What they needed was a real teacher.

He slid open the communicator he'd taken from John Allardyce in the car.

"Hello," he said into its tiny grille, feeling like twelve kinds of idiot. "Hello? C'mon, Jean, pick up the damn phone! Where the hell are you, woman? You're s'posed to be a telepath—if you can't hear my call, what about my thoughts? Where *are* you?"

Nothing but static from the radio, silence within the confines of his head.

He found a beer in the fridge, that was good. Miller Genuine Draft, which was acceptable. He drained half the bottle in one extended swallow that brought forth a comforting burp.

He crossed to the sink and turned on the water, hot and hard, using dishwashing liquid to clean the blood off his arms and hands. He flexed his right hand and popped the claws to see if they needed any cleaning. At the same time, a house cat leaped up on the counter to see if he was offering any food. A big marmalade tabby, whose relaxed manner told him she ruled this roost. He held his hand still while she approached to give him an assessing sniff. She must have liked what she found, because she started licking up across his knuckles, cleaning him the way she would herself after a scrap. Her ridged tongue rubbed across his skin like a rasp, with the same kind of sound. This was why he liked animals, preferred the wild to civilization. Life was a lot less complicated; the animals either trusted you or they didn't. If they didn't, they either attacked or ran away. People could come at you every which way, whenever they pleased, for no reason whatsoever. They created entanglements, which wrapped you up so tight you couldn't think straight or found yourself thinking about the wrong thing.

Case in point, as he realized with a start that another car had pulled into the driveway and three scents that carried common elements with Bobby Drake's were approaching the front door.

He retracted the claws, which made the cat yowl in surprise and hiss as she sprang clear. A moment later, William Drake stormed over the threshold, followed by his wife, Madeline, and Bobby's younger brother, Ronny.

"Who the hell are you?" Drake demanded.

Logan had no answer right away that would improve the situation. so he bought himself a moment by finishing his beer. Clattering feet from upstairs and the other rooms diverted Drake's attention before any more angry words could be said, and Bobby led the three Xavier kids into the kitchen.

"Dad!" he said brightly. "Mom! You guys are home!"

His father looked from Bobby to Logan, and Logan knew at once the situation was more serious than ever. Drake had seen the circles under his son's eyes and assumed that Logan was responsible.

"Honey," said Madeline, "aren't you supposed to be at school?"

"Bobby, who is this guy?" Drake demanded of the boy, indicating Logan.

"Professor Logan" was the reply. His dad didn't believe a word.

Madeline wasn't interested in Logan. She was glaring

at Rogue, and especially at the white opera gloves that covered almost the whole of her arms.

"What is that girl doing wearing my clothes?" she asked. "And—are those *Nana's* gloves?"

Bobby stammered a reply: "Mom, uh, guys, can I talk to you about something?"

Mitchell Laurio was whistling as he came on shift. He couldn't remember many of the details of what had happened in the ladies' can, but he'd never felt better in his life than he had after it was done. Just the memory of Grace's farewell kisses was enough to stir his blood and put a spring in his step, and the fact that she'd left a whispered promise to meet him again tonight made him wish as he never had before for the day to end.

The guard at the final checkpoint was the latest to offer comment: "Mitchell Laurio, what *is* that on your face, man?

"Sa-tis-*fac*-tion!"

He'd heard the story and didn't believe it any more than had the man who'd told it to him. Lard-ass Laurio actually scoring on a dame with a pulse? His trysts were few and far between—the man was such a piece of work the pros charged double for a quickie. He wanted more, they got a headache. And by all accounts, the broad had halfway decent looks, which made the whole thing even more incredible. Had to be drugs, was the general consensus, or somebody with a major twist to her psyche.

The only thing that couldn't be denied was that it had actually happened. The bartender was a witness, his oath to God.

Now of course Laurio had to provide his own chapter and verse of the evening. It wasn't a bad story, even the way he told it, which was why neither man noticed a blip on the scanner that indicated the presence of metal. It wasn't a significant glitch; it barely lasted a fraction of a second before the system registered clear. If the guard had been paying attention, he probably wouldn't have noticed. But he wasn't, and from that moment Mitchell Laurio's fate was sealed.

"You're clear," the guard said, and cycled the umbilical out to the cell in the center of the room.

Eric Lehnsherr was asleep until Laurio stepped over the threshold. Then, just like that, he came completely awake with a rush he hadn't felt since his capture.

"Sweet dreams, Lehnsherr?" asked Laurio, his mockery plain. Just because he'd had the best night of his life didn't mean he was going to pass on the morning beating. The one gave him just as much pleasure as the other.

Laurio set the tray on the table. Lehnsherr hadn't moved, beyond sitting up on the bed. There was something different about his expression, though, like there was a big joke being played here that only he was privy to. But at the same time, there was a predatory cast to his eyes that made Laurio suddenly wish the internal monitors were active and that he were somewhere else.

As was usual for him when he felt ill at ease or threatened, Laurio got aggressive. This time, he decided, he wasn't going to stop until the old man begged him.

"There's something different about you, Mr. Laurio," Lehnsherr said with a slight question to his voice, as if he couldn't quite credit what he saw.

There was something different about the old man, too. They'd done variations on this dance before; Lehnsherr had to know what was coming. Before, he'd faced it with a stoic resignation. Today, though, he was alert, watchful—

almost amused. Where his strength had presented itself in his passive endurance of Laurio's beatings, now it was active, a coiled spring tensing inside his body. It occurred to Laurio that maybe this time the old man intended to fight back. That would give Laurio sanction to do pretty near anything in retaliation, which would make his day.

He said as much in reply: "Yeah, I think I'm havin' a pretty damn good day."

Lehnsherr came to his feet with a grace and ease he hadn't shown in months, that belied the age apparent on his face.

"No," he said, "no, it's not that."

"Sit down," Laurio told him. He didn't like the way this was going, that he and his prisoner seemed to be reading from two different scripts. He made a show of putting his hand on his billy club. Lehnsherr knew first-hand how quick he was with it and how formidable. One snap of the wrist to the gut would have a prisoner doubled over, gasping desperately for breath; after that, it would be Laurio's choice, his pleasure, where to administer the follow-up hits for maximum impact. Every word, every gesture from Lehnsherr would only make matters worse, yet the old man clearly didn't care. He wasn't afraid of Laurio. He'd never been afraid of Laurio.

They'd put the tiger in a cage, but they hadn't broken him. They hadn't even come close.

"No," Lehnsherr said.

Laurio started to move. . . .

"Sit your ass down, or I'll—"

And then he couldn't.

"Well, well, well," Lehnsherr said in a tone of detached bemusement, a professor considering a problem.

He flicked his fingers, and the billy club dropped from a numb and nerveless hand.

"What could it be?"

Laurio wanted to call for help, but his jaw wouldn't work, either. His whole body had become frozen. And with the monitors disengaged, nobody outside had the slightest clue anything was wrong. The guard in the monitor room at the far end of the umbilical wouldn't have a clue; from his perspective, he'd just see the two of them standing across the cell from each other, and he'd be looking at Laurio from the back.

Laurio wanted to beg for mercy. Lehnsherr knew that.

Instead he made another slight upward motion with his fingers, and Laurio rose six inches off the floor.

"Ah." Lehnsherr had found what he was looking for. "There it is."

Like a conductor summoning his orchestra to play, Lehnsherr made a sharp, slashing gesture toward his body, and Laurio arched as much as was possible against his invisible constraints as a fine scarlet mist exploded from every pore of his body.

"Too much iron in your blood."

For Mitchell Laurio, it was as if barbed hooks had been sunk into every square inch of his skin to flay him naked, then salt scattered on the raw and exposed nerves of his body to sear him as fiercely as acid. He wanted to die right then and there, anything to stop the pain, but Lehnsherr wasn't in a forgiving mood.

The mist fell away to form a glittering film on the floor of the cell, leaving a cloud of metallic silver behind in the air.

Lehnsherr made a fist and the particles of iron coalesced into three perfect spheres, each the size of a marble.

The Nazis had taught him to make ball bearings; it seemed only fitting to adopt them as the talisman for his power.

Their size was deceptive as the last few droplets of Laurio's blood were squeezed out of them by pressure. Lehnsherr used his power to bond the atoms together far more tightly than nature would have, so that they massed as much as depleted uranium. Unaided, he doubted a champion weight lifter could pick up even one.

The balls began to move, forming small orbits over his upheld palm.

"A word of advice, Mr. Laurio," Lehnsherr said with a smile, as though their relationship had been a genuine pleasure, "a little something . . . else to remember me by. Never trust a beautiful woman. Especially one who's interested in you."

He cut the ties of power that held Laurio aloft and the big man collapsed, a limp and bloody heap in the corner.

Lehnsherr flung the balls at the plaster wall of his cell and watched it shatter under the impact.

He heard alarms, he knew they'd be trying to track him with the defensive remote-controlled miniguns mounted in the cavern walls, knew they'd be flooding the space with nerve gas. But it was a huge space, and the guards had grown lax over time. They assumed he was no longer a threat. That gave him more than enough time.

The umbilical retracted immediately. He paid it no notice.

He concentrated on one of his spheres, and it obediently flattened itself into a paper-thin silver disk that was easily wide enough for a man to stand on, which he did. Under his direction, it rushed him across the chasm to the main exit. He could see the guard in the monitor room calling for help. One sphere for him, the other for the door itself.

They struck with the force of armor-piercing cannon shells. He stepped over the guard's ruined body into the monitor room and found the hardwire link that led from his computer into the prison's central network. He bared the cable and set his spheres to spinning until they produced an electrical field worthy of a mainline generator, and then, backing it with all the passion and rage and hatred he'd kept ruthlessly in check all these wretched months, he pushed that power into the cable. Sparks galore exploded all around him, and every monitor screen in the room dissolved into static, then went dark. The lights went out as well, although they were replaced at once by the emergency spot lamps.

This place was controlled by computers, and with this surge of energy Lehnsherr had just killed them all. The electronic doors wouldn't work; neither would the electronic sensors, or the defenses. They wouldn't know where he was until he revealed himself, and then they'd have precious few resources to try to stop him.

They liked to mock him with the name he'd chosen for himself. Now he would remind them why Magneto was a force to be reckoned with and an adversary to be respected, and especially feared.

# Chapter
# Ten

Jean Grey wasn't a happy woman.

"Professor Xavier, come in, please?" she spoke aloud, repeating the same call, far more loudly, with her thoughts. "Scott, are you there, are you receiving, over?"

Static.

She tapped a new number on the speed dial, switching functions on her headset from radio to cellular phone, and tried all the lines at the mansion.

Static.

She tried Scott's cell and the phone in Xavier's Rolls-Royce.

Static.

For the hell of it, she ran a full-spectrum diagnostic on the *Blackbird*'s communications array, wondering if a day's immersion in the water of Boston Harbor had somehow degraded the antennae. The computer told her everything was fine, just as it had the previous two times she'd executed the program.

She changed channels and listened a minute to WBUR, changed them again and eavesdropped on local and federal law enforcement frequencies.

End result, they were sending and receiving perfectly.

The problems lay at the other end. Nobody was picking up, not even voice mail.

She covered her face with her hands, then swept them up and over her head, smoothing her thick, occasionally unruly hair into momentary submission before clasping her fingers together behind her neck and bending her head forward to rest her chin on her collarbone. She flexed her shoulders outward and stretched as long as she could up the full length of her spine to ease the aches that tension and worry had planted there.

She caught a wisp of a thought, a sense of movement, that told her Storm had stepped up to the flight deck, and then felt her friend's hand cover hers from behind. Without opening her eyes, Jean clasped Storm's hand in both of hers and held it, smiling as a cool breeze insinuated itself through the collar of her uniform and washed all over her.

"Ohhhh." She groaned in delight. "If you could package that in a bottle!"

"It wouldn't be anywhere near as much fun."

Storm was just as concerned.

"How long has it been?" she asked.

"Too long. No land lines, no cell, no radio, no indication from the news of any disaster in the area."

"Send an e-mail?"

"Too risky. Anyone capable of knocking the mansion so completely off-line could back-trace a computer link. I'm pushing our luck with the com devices."

"No telepathy, either? From the professor?"

"Nope."

"So?"

"I was going to wait till dark before heading home. I'm starting to reconsider."

"This may be the ultimate in stealth aircraft, Jean, but we can still be seen."

"That, Ororo, is where I figure *you* come in."

"I'll see what I can do."

"Thanks. Whatever it is, make it quick, okay?"

"I'll see what I can do."

"By the way, how's our passenger?"

Nightcrawler was praying.

He'd tucked himself into one of the highback chairs in the passenger compartment, legs folded into lotus position, hands clasped in his lap, eyes closed. Storm half expected to find him hanging from the ceiling. He stood six feet tall, but you never noticed because he spent most of the time in a crouch, rarely straightening to his full height. He seemed just as comfortable upside down as not, using his big toes or his tail, or both, to anchor himself in place.

He had a good face, especially now that Storm could see it relaxed, in repose. Much younger than she'd first suspected. Now that she could get a closer look at him, she saw that his indigo skin was covered with a series of tattoos.

"It's an angelic alphabet," he told her, and she raised her blue eyes to meet his yellow ones, "passed on to mankind by the Archangel Gabriel."

"They're beautiful," she told him truthfully, even though the black etchings on blue-black skin were almost invisible, like the man himself when he stepped into shadows.

"How many are there?"

"One for every sin. So"—a quirk of his full lips that might have been a smile—"quite a few."

"That, I don't believe."

He looked at her with a disconcertingly level gaze. "You know, outside of the circus, most people are afraid of me."

"I'm not afraid of you."

He swallowed and looked away, and she could tell by the minute shift in the heat gradient of his cheeks that he was blushing. He took refuge from the moment in an examination of the cabin, his eyes taking in the sleek configuration of the interior hull and furniture while he ran his hands over the material of the chair itself.

"You and Miss Grey—*Doktor* Grey—you're both . . . schoolteachers?"

"Is that so hard to believe?"

He actually chuckled.

"Yes," she told him, "we are. At a school for people . . . like us. Where we can be safe."

"Safe from what?"

"Everyone else."

"You know, outside the circus, most people I met were afraid of me. But I never hated them. I actually felt sorry for them, do you know why?"

Storm shook her head.

"Because most people never know anything beyond what they can see with their own two eyes."

"I gave up on pity a long time ago."

"I'm sorry to hear that."

He reached up and placed his fingers against her cheek with a gentle caress that sent a burst of heat rippling beneath her skin, together with the surprised thought: *He's* flirting *with me*. She didn't move away, because along with that realization came the discovery that she liked it. She liked him. There was a serenity to his soul that was totally at odds with his outward features, as though a demon incarnate might have in him the makings of a saint.

"Someone as beautiful as you shouldn't be so . . . angry," he said, simply as an article of faith.

"Sometimes anger can help you survive."

"So can faith."

"What did you do in the circus?" she asked, remembering the posters from the church. Before leaving, he'd carefully taken them down and packed them away in his single case.

"I was—" he began, and then both of them reacted to a shout from up front.

"Storm!" Jean called. "I think I've found an active com unit!"

Logan would have played things differently, but this was Bobby's house, Bobby's family; he let the kid take point.

The kid then proceeded to tell his parents what he was.

Now they were all gathered in the living room, and the general atmosphere would have put a session of the Spanish Inquisition to shame. The layout of the room put a couch on either side of a coffee table. Mom, Dad, and Ronny Drake sat on one, Bobby and Rogue on the other. John Allardyce hung out behind Rogue, his butt perched on the edge of an antique side table in conscious oblivion to the sharp glances that occasionally came his way from Mom. He had his lighter out and was, as usual, playing with the lid, as if the sound of the ticking clock weren't intrusion enough.

Logan stood in the doorway to the kitchen, nursing a new beer. His casual attitude was a deception. He was covering the room, ready to act if there was trouble of any kind. He'd expected Dad to be the flashpoint, but the man had proved to have a lot more in common with his eldest son than first impressions had suggested.

"So, uh, Bobby," Madeline said, utterly lost, "when did you first know . . . that you were a . . . um . . ."

"A mutant?" John finished for her, flicking his lighter open, then closed, open, then closed, open—

"Could you please stop that?" said Madeline with some asperity. This was her house, and she'd had enough of his insolent behavior.

"You have to understand," William said slowly, "we thought Bobby was going to a school for the gifted."

"He *is* gifted," Rogue interjected, prompting a small smile of gratitude from the boy sitting beside her, who otherwise looked like someone en route to the guillotine.

"We know that," William conceded. "We just didn't realize that he was—" Then, without warning, a flare of anger toward his son that was compounded in equal measures of confusion and a very real pain that bordered on grief. "Why the hell didn't you *tell* us? What were you thinking, Bobby? We're your parents, for God's sake! How could you keep this to yourself, how could you not trust us—how could you *lie*?"

"Dad." Bobby sounded helpless, strangling on his own guilt and shame. "You don't understand!"

"Obviously."

"Dad!"

"You lied, Bobby. Xavier lied. To my face. He kept your secret. What am I supposed to believe about him now, or this precious school of his? Or you? How many other secrets are there?" He turned to Logan. "Just what is it you teach my son, 'Professor'?"

"Art," he said sarcastically. "And it's just Logan."

"You show up without a word of warning or explanation. Apparently without even clothes of your own to wear. What's that supposed to mean?"

"We still love you, Bobby," Madeline said, starting to reach out to him but holding back right at the last, the same way people did around Rogue. She looked at her hand, at her son, at her hand again, as though it had suddenly become some alien part of her. The thought behind the hesitation was plain to the room. *Am I suddenly afraid of my own baby?* She tried to find some explanation, some rationale, in words: "It's just that the mutant problem is very . . ."

"What mutant *problem*?" Logan asked. She didn't pay attention, she hadn't heard him.

". . . complicated."

Rogue tried to lighten the mood.

"You should see what Bobby can do."

Everyone looked. He stretched out his hand to his mother's teacup, ignoring how quickly she snatched her own hand clear, and touched it with a fingertip. Instantly a layer of ice crystals formed around the rim and down the sides.

He turned the cup over and the tea within, frozen completely solid, dropped onto the saucer with a quiet *clink*. The marmalade tabby wound its way around Rogue and him and used his thigh as a springboard to the table, where she proceeded to lick the tea.

"I can do a lot more," he said.

There was a light in William's eyes, a dad's classic and instinctive *My boy did that*! What hurt him about all this was being cut out of the loop.

Mom wasn't anywhere near as amused, and she wasn't proud in the slightest. As for Ronny, he got up from the couch and bulled his way out of the room, deliberately giving John a shoulder check as he passed.

He made a lot of noise pounding up the stairs, and he shut his door with a slam that resounded through the house.

Ronny Drake had a teenager's obsession with privacy and personal space. He'd marked his territory accordingly, with a huge sign on the door that said RONNY'S ROOM. STAY THE F**K OUT! Mom had wanted to tear it down, but Bobby had defused the situation by hijacking a pair of anime panda stickers—so cute they made Powerpuff Girls look hardcore—and using them to cover the middle two letters. Ronny hated him for doing that, Bobby got to play the damn hero as always, but at least he got to keep his sign.

All he could see, though, in the center of his room was a torn and bloody T-shirt. Not his. Not Bobby's, 'cause he had his own room. That meant a stranger had been in here.

The TV monitor caught his attention, turned to Fox News Channel—more proof that his privacy had been violated. This was a channel he had *never* watched, until now. It wasn't the reporter, doing his stand-up from the White House lawn, that caught his attention, but what the man was saying.

". . . in the wake of the assassination attempt on President McKenna, there are unconfirmed reports of a raid on what is believed to be an underground terrorist mutant organization based in Westchester County, New York . . .

"Authorities refuse to comment, but it's believed that

a national manhunt for several fugitives from the facility is now under way . . ."

Watching, listening, looking from the screen to the sodden shirt on the floor, Ronny's expression changed. Bobby was his big brother, but he didn't know anything about the people who were with him, except that they creeped Ronny out, big-time.

He picked up the phone, hoping he was doing the right thing, terrified of what might happen if those other mutants found out. Half expecting his brain to be incinerated at any moment, he pressed 911.

Downstairs, Madeline Drake put her head in her hands. "Oh, God, this is all my fault."

Before Bobby could even try to make things better, John Allardyce jumped in to make them worse.

"Actually," he said, "they've discovered that males are the ones who carry mutant genes and pass them on to the next generation, so I guess that makes it"—he jutted his thumb toward Bobby's dad—"his fault."

William Drake ignored the comment, although his son looked ready to make the other boy eat the words.

Madeline tried again to be the gracious hostess: "And you," she said to Rogue, "you're all gifted?"

Rogue shot daggers at John, who returned them as a grin. "Some of us more than others," she replied tightly. "Others who shouldn't ever be allowed out in public."

"What's that?" William said, reacting to a *beep*.

Logan had the little com unit in his hand. "That's mine," he said. " 'Scuse me." And he slipped through the kitchen to the backyard porch, with Madeline's next line to her son to speed him on his way.

"Bobby," she said, "dearest, have you tried . . . *not* being a mutant?"

Bobby sighed. John laughed out loud.

"Charley," Logan said, and his face lit up at the voice that replied.

"Logan," cried Jean, "thank God it's you! We couldn't reach anyone at the mansion."

"No one's left," he told her bluntly. "Soldiers came."

Aboard the *Blackbird*, Jean sank into her chair. They'd speculated about the possibility of some kind of hostile action, they'd made what they hoped were adequate preparations, but none of them really took it seriously. In a way, they believed too much in their own press: Xavier's was a *school*. How could anyone perceive that as a threat?

But then again, she considered, Islamic *madrasas* were schools as well, and many in the intelligence community believed them to be the spawning ground for terrorists.

"What about the children?" she asked.

"Some escaped," he reported, "but I'm not sure about the rest."

Jean created sparks as she shifted position, and she shot a warning glare at Storm, whose anger was supercharging the air inside the plane with electricity. Not a good thing, generating a bolt of lightning inside a plane loaded with jet fuel and other combustibles.

"We haven't been able to reach the professor or Scott, either," she said. The conclusion was obvious to both of them: In all likelihood, they were lost, too.

Storm spoke into her own headset: "Logan, where are you?"

"Quincy," he said. "Outside Beantown, with Bobby Drake's family."

"Do they—" Jean started to ask, provoking a snort of amusement from the other end.

"Oh, yeah!"

"All right," she said, leaning across to the center console to initiate the engine start-up sequence, "we're on our way."

"Storm?"

"Yes, Logan?"

"Make it fast."

The two women looked at each other, both recognizing the subtle change in Logan's voice.

"Five minutes," Jean told him as she locked her harness closed and mentally told Nightcrawler to grab his chair and do the same.

"Make it fast," he repeated, and signed off active audio, leaving only the carrier signal for them to home in on.

The picture of nonchalance, he patted his pockets for a smoke, sighed loudly when he didn't find one, and reentered the house in two quick steps. Without turning his body, he snapped the lock closed on the door and took the next two steps into the living room.

"We have to go," he said without preamble. "Now." The kids took their cue from him and leaped to their feet.

"What?" William asked.

"Why?" Rogue echoed.

"Now," he said simply, as sound and scent told him they'd run out of time. One assault team at the back, another out front, boxing the house. Bobby's parents jumped, William grabbing his wife into his arms, as Logan extended his right-hand claws.

"Logan," Rogue demanded, "what's going on?"

John mouthed an answer: "What d' you think?"

"Follow my lead," Logan told them.

There were two cops waiting on the front porch, flanking the door with guns drawn. They locked on Logan as the primary threat. A police cruiser was parked on the lawn, another partially blocking the street, its patrol officers taking aim from behind the cover of their car. Sirens closing in from the near distance told them all that more were on the way.

Bobby's face tightened with anger. He knew what had brought them here.

"Ronny!" he fumed under his breath.

Directly upstairs, Ronny watched the officers take position, anxiety quickly giving way to excitement. This was cool, better than TV.

"You," barked the cop to Logan's right, "get down on the ground."

"What's going on here?" Logan inquired calmly.

The kids were scared, and rightly so. This was the second time in a day they'd been threatened by guns, only these didn't fire stun darts. This was the real deal, 9mm, Glocks with fifteen-round magazines, and one of the cops in the street had unlimbered his shotgun. Logan heard the frantic *click, click, click* of John's lighter. The cops heard it, too. They didn't know what to make of it, and that made them even more jumpy.

"Put the knives down slowly," the same cop said. "Slowly. Then down on your knees, cross your ankles, and raise your hands in the air. You kids do the same. *Right now!*"

"Hey, bub, this is just a misunderstanding," Logan replied.

Inside, Bobby's parents were only just starting to comprehend what was happening on the porch when the glass of the kitchen door shattered under the impact of a nightstick. They barely had time to turn their heads before a trio of uniformed officers rushed into the room, guns leveled, all of them yelling at the top of their lungs: "Police!" "Nobody move!" "On the floor, on your knees, keep your hands where I can see 'em!"

Madeline screamed, William tried to protest, Bobby reacted like any son. He turned to help. The cop on the left shifted aim. His partner screamed louder: "Put down the goddamn blades!"

"I can't," said Logan, and raised his hands to show they were a part of him.

The gunshot took them all by surprise.

The left-hand cop had fired, straight to the temple. The point-blank impact blew Logan off his feet, twisting him as he fell so that he landed on his face, partially sprawled down the steps.

Rogue screamed and the three kids all dropped, Bobby trying to shield Rogue's body with his own, yelling as loud as he could for the cops to stop firing. "Don't shoot, don't shoot!"

A crowd had begun to gather on the sidewalk across the street, drawn by the flashing dome lights and the commotion. The sharp report of the officer's gun startled those close enough to see what had happened. They ducked as well. But mostly, folks kept milling about, confused, intrigued, like rubberneckers passing an accident, blissfully oblivious to the danger.

The cops were just as startled, just as scared. The one who'd fired had made himself a statue, his weapon centered on Wolverine like he expected the man to leap up and charge him. Or maybe he was praying for him to do precisely that, to take back the action of the last half minute.

"Easy," his partner yelled, in a voice meant to be heard inside the house as well as out to the street. "Everybody take it easy. Get a grip!" That last was directed mainly at the shooter. His partner knew this was bad, every shooting is for the officer involved, but under his breath he thanked God and all the saints they hadn't popped the kids as well. After that kind of mess, there'd be hell to pay.

"Okay, kids," he told them, "same as before. Stay cool, we'll get out of this just fine."

"We didn't *do* anything!" Rogue shrieked at him.

"On your knees, girl!"

She yelled at him some more, partly to purge her own terror, but most of all to keep attention away from Logan. She knew the adamantium interlaced with his skeletal structure meant that his bones couldn't be broken. All that bullet had likely done, aside from breaking the skin—which was decidedly messy—was give him a royal headache. More importantly, though, his healing factor would be speedily dealing with both the wound and the headache. She didn't know what he could do once he recovered, but it would be one more asset than the kids had right now.

Bobby gave her a hand as they both did as they were told. John had other ideas. He stood up.

"Don't be stupid, kid," the left-hand cop said. "This is no time to flash attitude. We don't want to hurt you!"

John's attitude was plain: *Like I care,* he seemed to be saying. *Like, you* could?

"Hey," he said, "you know all those dangerous mutants you hear about on the news?" He paused a moment to let the implications sink in.

"I'm the worst one."

He popped the lid on his Zippo, but this time, he ignited a flame.

From the wick grew three distinct streamers of flame, which whirled sinuously around him like the fearsome salamanders of medieval tales. One shot right, the other left, the third burned its way through the door to scorch across the main floor of the house.

The cops on the porch dove desperately for cover as flame roared past, close enough to leave their uniform shirts smoldering. Those inside weren't quite so quick, or so lucky. One was struck head-on, with force enough to hurl him into his companions, who had to scramble to save him as his clothes caught fire.

John turned his focus to the cars. It all happened so fast, the attack was so savage and shocking, that the cops on the street didn't know how to react. Those news reports notwithstanding, none of them really believed in mutants; they couldn't believe a kid was doing this.

They'd get over it real quick, John knew, if he gave them the chance.

He had a better idea.

While the two main streamers he'd manifested kept them occupied, he snaked a pair of much thinner strands along the surface of the lawn and underneath the cars to their tailpipes. This would be fun.

He ignited both gas tanks at once, pitching the cars up into the air and flipping them over like they were sandbox toys. A third car had just then rolled onto the scene, and John grinned as he surrounded it with a cataract of fire. The driver threw the gearshift into reverse, but John melted the tires to the street. The cops tried to bail from the unit, only to reel back inside as he turned the flames around them into a wall so thick and hot they'd be crispy critters before they took a decent step. He saw one of them calling frantically for help on the radio.

This would be the best. He'd let 'em cook slowly until the fire department arrived. He'd allow them the illusion of hope. Then—*kaboom!* Instant inspector's funeral, film at eleven.

Logan's eyes fluttered as the shattered remains of the officer's bullet fell from the healing wound. Rogue was right; his head was murder. This was a great power, no argument there. But the downside was that all the sensations of the process of natural healing were compressed into a fraction of the time and, as a consequence, hugely intensified. Yes, he had long ago learned to endure the pain; yes, it passed relatively quickly; but it always remained a brutal experience, to be avoided whenever possible.

Some of the other cops, the mutants on the porch forgotten, tried to save the two who were trapped. John played with them a little, letting them almost break through before generating a flash furnace to force them back.

He never felt Rogue's hand on his shin as she grabbed him from behind. She wasn't holding back this time, as she had with Bobby, trying to control a power that seemed as untamably rebellious as her name. She couldn't have done better if she'd clipped him with an iron bar.

Without any warning or preamble, John's eyes simply rolled up in their sockets, and he dropped to the porch. The lighter skittered from his grasp.

Rogue's mouth twisted with disgust as his psyche rolled over hers like an oily tide. She wanted no part of it, so she called up a burst of flame within her own head to torch the images as they appeared.

At the same time, now that she'd successfully imprinted his power, she held up a hand in a summoning gesture. She was breathing very hard, almost panting, in and out to the same metronomic pattern John established with his lighter. Her visual perceptions skewed far away from normal to embrace the infrared. Her world became defined by the heat it generated; she could actually see the primary states of being on a molecular level, she understood instinctively how to sustain and manipulate fire itself.

The raw passion of it left her breathless, because by playing with this elemental force, she *became* it as well, tasting an insatiable hunger that made her want to ignite the whole world. It would be so easy—so much energy to torch a tree, so much for a vehicle, so much for a person. To her, they were all becoming mere objects, without any value or purpose other than as fuel. It was a temptation, a glory, she'd never known, nor imagined could even exist.

But she had picked her name for a reason. Rogues don't play by anybody's rules unless they choose to, and they never ever do what's expected of them.

She called the fire home—not merely the streamers that John had initially created but all the conflagrations they'd ignited. On the street, the trapped car whose metal surfaces had been glowing red hot became amazingly cool to the touch. The other cars were likewise smoldering wrecks.

For that instant, Rogue herself burned, shrouded in flames from head to foot, so hot—hotter than a blast furnace—that Bobby quickly pushed himself clear in a frenzied crab scuttle, dragging John with him, to keep from being blistered. The fire faded at once, without leaving a mark on the girl, although the porch wasn't as fortunate. The planks beneath her feet were deeply charred, as was the roof overhead.

She swayed a little with fatigue, and Bobby leaped at once to her side. John stirred as well, the shock of her imprinting wearing off. As he shook off the effects, he grabbed reflexively for his lighter and looked sour to find his flames all gone. No doubt he would have said something, done something, very foolish—except that Logan also got to his feet.

The boys had never seen him shot before. They didn't believe it any more than the watching cops did. They were so caught up in the aftermath of the moment they didn't realize their danger.

The cops knew now what they were up against. They were shaken to the bone. As far as they were now concerned, it was their lives or the lives of these . . . monsters. They were ready to shoot and keep shooting until the threat was over.

That's when Jean landed the *Blackbird*, maybe a minute ahead of schedule.

Storm announced their arrival with a clap of thunder that shook the very air and a gust of gale-force wind that forced both cops and onlookers to flee from the scene.

Jean made a combat approach, a vertical descent straight
down to the street in front of the house. Between the wild
weather and the sleek, dangerous-looking aircraft, the
cops didn't know what to think. Maybe the military,
come to the rescue?

As soon as the wheels touched down, Storm dropped
the boarding ramp and beckoned Logan and the kids inside. Nobody needed to be told twice. The kids went
with a rush, Logan more slowly.

A flicker of movement revealed one of the cops from
the porch, the one who hadn't fired, who'd tried to keep
the situation calm. He looked a mess, uniform scorched
and torn, some hair burned off, soot all over his face, but
he held his Glock in an unshaking grip, determined to do
his duty.

Logan looked at him, held his hands open at his sides
to show they were empty, no claws. He didn't want a
fight, never had. But the implication was clear: You
know now what'll happen if one starts. Is that what you
really want?

They held the pose for a few seconds, but to those
watching it seemed an eternity.

Then, with a tremble, the cop shifted his gun barrel
upward.

Logan nodded and made his way up the ramp. Jean gave
him a smile he'd never tire of; he gave her back a wink.
Then, while he was giving the kids a quick once-over to
make sure their harnesses were secure and that Rogue had
come through her ordeal okay, Nightcrawler popped up
from the row behind. Rogue and John yelped—too many
shocks, too little time, they were way over their limit.

*"Guten Morgen,"* Kurt said.

"*Guten Abend,*" Logan corrected. "Who the hell—"

Nightcrawler bowed, with a circus performer's flamboyance. "Kurt Wagner, *mein herr*. But in the Munich Circus I was billed as 'The Incredible Nightcraw—' "

"Whatever. Storm?" he called.

"Ready to roll, Logan," came back from the flight deck.

"Not yet! We're one short!"

Bobby stood in the hatchway. He hadn't boarded yet; he was looking back at his house, thinking of the life he'd lived there, realizing that perhaps he could never go home again, not to the way it was. He'd never considered being a mutant in those terms, never imagined the consequences of possessing these fantastic powers might cost him his family.

He knew at that moment that every memory of this house and his life here would be defined by this scene, the stink of burned rubber and metal and plastic, the groans of the wounded and the cries of the terrified, the sight of scorched wood on the porch where he'd played, the burn hole where the front door had been.

He saw his parents and his brother in the upstairs window and knew their faces would remain to haunt him always. His father, shocked and hurt—not just by what had happened, but by his own sense of responsibility; if his son had come to this, then he had failed as a father. His mother, sobbing, like he wasn't her son anymore but had become, now and forever, a stranger.

He wondered if he could forestall all that by going back. Like that old Cher song said, "If I Could Turn Back Time"! He had to laugh a little at the yearning: Where was a mutant with a truly useful power when you really needed one?

He gave his family a final wave, and closed both ramp and hatch behind him.

Descent to dust-off, maybe a minute. Engines shrieking, the *Blackbird* hovered above the rooftops for a few seconds, then oriented itself and shot up and away at an incredibly steep angle and a speed those watching couldn't believe.

The cop on the lawn holstered his weapon, then thumbed the call button on the walkie-talkie handset clipped to his shoulder to make sure the unit was working.

"Dispatch," he reported when he got them to calm down enough to hear him speak, more than a little amazed himself to discover that he *could* speak, "all units are down. We have casualties. We need fire and rescue units onsite, ASAP. Perps positively identified as mutants and hostile. They're mobile, escaping aboard some kind of high-performance aircraft, heading west and climbing fast. You'd better notify Hanscom Air Force Base. If we want these guys, they'd better scramble some interceptors right now! An' you tell 'em from us, good hunting."

But he had to wonder, as he picked his way across the lawn toward his ruined squad car, against adversaries like this, if the Air Force would have any better chance of success.

# Chapter
# Eleven

Charles Xavier never tired of the view from his office.

The main floor of the mansion was built up a level from the ground, creating a distinct separation between the reception areas of the house and those rooms and areas where the household staff actually did their work. He could turn from his desk and look out through the big bay window, across the tiled expanse of the terrace to the lawn and formal gardens beyond. In summer, the garden caught the eye, with its cavalcade of flowers and shrubs. In autumn, once the flowers faded and the leaves began to turn, the trees beyond took over, painting the distance in a riot of fiery orange, scarlet, and gold. In winter, if he arose early enough after a snow, he was usually assured of about an hour to look on the yard in an unmarked, pristine state, as nature intended. Then, of course, his students—regardless of age—erupted from the house to embark on an endless succession of sled races down the far slopes, the construction of various animals, and the obligatory snowball fights. By sunset of that first day, the snow had become so trampled it resembled a beach under the onslaught of midsummer bathers.

The moments he cherished best, though, came in spring. The air, still crisp with the bite of a winter reluctantly passing, was filled with the promise of new life and new hope. The garden was scattered with dots of brightness and color, teasing the onlooker with hints of the coming glory.

A breeze riffled the treetops, creating that *shushhhing* sound he loved, and stirred his senses as it brought a sharp and heady mix of smells through the open window. The pleasure was acute, but for some reason it brought to his face not a smile, but tears. In the midst of this natural wonder that was so familiar and usually so comforting, he felt an inexplicable and aching sense of loss.

On the windowsill, he saw a chess set, arranged to suggest he was playing someone outside, although the terrace and grounds beyond—indeed, the entire school—were empty. No sound of voice, of movement, when usually the challenge was to create some small semblance of peace amid the constant clatter. Not even a hint of a stray thought.

He'd never known such silence, nor felt so utterly alone. For as long as he could remember, there had always been someone or other's thoughts to reach out to. He rarely did, he liked to be as respectful of the privacy of others as he was protective of his own, yet it was always reassuring to know they were there.

Now, nothing.

He looked again at the chess set. He was white, and he'd lost almost all his pawns. His king was in jeopardy, virtually checkmate, and while his queen remained on the board, she was sufficiently threatened to prevent her coming to his aid. His only effective ally was a knight.

Thinking about the game made his head ache. Rubbing his temple didn't help. Perhaps a walk . . .

That made him pause.

He was standing.

He looked over his shoulder at his office, unwilling yet to make a move that trusted these newly functional limbs. He saw only normal furniture and a desk that made no provision for the presence of a wheelchair.

Xavier closed his eyes, reaching deep into memory for the exercises he'd first learned to help him focus his abilities, the way he'd taught himself to stay afloat against the riptides of outside thoughts crashing against the shores of his own conscious awareness. Gradually, as he gained an increasing measure of control, he had crafted a series of psychic levees to guarantee the integrity of his own personality, no matter how many minds he interfaced with.

Evidently, all those meticulously constructed defenses had been subverted. He didn't like that and liked even less the struggle he went through to keep that anger from showing. Instinctively, he knew the source of his troubles.

"Jason." He spoke aloud, severely. "Stop it."

Jason had other ideas, so Xavier returned once more to his most basic mantras, building upward from that essential psychic foundation. The first thing to change was his own personal perspective. The view out the window lowered somewhat, dropping by more than one-third to the level of a tall man sitting in a chair. Carved stone morphed into Sheetrock, painted in institutional greens and beige and looking very much the worse for wear. Natural sunlight gave way to the passionless radiance of overhead fluorescents. His favorite things went away, to be replaced by his prison cell . . .

. . . and the demented monstrosity that Stryker called Mutant 143 and who Xavier remembered as a quietly frightened little boy.

There'd been only the one consultation. The boy's

DNA contained markers for the mutator gene, and Stryker's contacts within the American intelligence community had led him to Xavier. He had no idea then that Xavier was himself a mutant, only an acknowledged expert in the field. And while Xavier could confirm that the boy possessed the requisite gene matrix and that in all likelihood he would be active, there was no way to determine the type and extent of abilities the boy would manifest. Xavier suggested admitting the boy to the school, but Stryker would hear none of that. He wanted the mutantcy removed. When Xavier told him that wasn't possible, the other man lost his temper. He took away his son, and that was the last Xavier had heard of Jason, even though, in the years following, he made a number of his own discreet inquiries to try to determine what had happened. Finally word came that the boy had died.

Sitting across from him, Xavier couldn't help thinking, *Would that he had.*

The buzzing in Xavier's ears, radiating through his skull with the annoying fury of a bone saw, was murder, leaving his teeth bared and clenched in a perpetual grimace of pain. Stryker's neural inhibitor, doing its job.

The hell with that man, the hell with his toys.

"Jason," he said, speaking with care to avoid triggering further retaliation from the inhibitor, "you must help me."

No response, so he tried again. And again, his eyes meeting the mismatched gaze of the poor creature in the other wheelchair, ignoring the seething cauldron of emotions that were so nakedly displayed.

"You must help me," Xavier repeated, ruthlessly crushing the surge of elation he felt when the boy's mouth began to move in concert to his words. No distractions, not till the job was done.

"You must help me," he said once more, and this time he could hear the words from Jason, a beat behind.

Gradually, with each repetition, Jason caught up with Xavier until their speech was totally in sync.

But at the same time, Jason's withered arms were struggling upward from his lap, his face contorting with effort and with rage as he extended them toward Xavier. His chair moved forward as well, bringing him within reach. Jason's hands came to rest on Xavier's shoulders, those burning eyes, pulsing with inner light, filling his vision. He felt them on his neck, so little strength in them it was more like being grasped by a toddler. Tears burned at the corners of Jason's eyes, sympathetic counterparts squeezing from Xavier's, but he couldn't read the emotions behind them, save that they were powerful and primal.

"Stand," Xavier said simply, putting the full force of his will behind that single injunction.

"Stand," Jason repeated, same tone, same inflection. And they said it again until they were one.

His mouth forming a great O of astonishment and protest, Jason levered his body forward and pushed himself erect. With disturbingly liquid popping sounds, the junctions on all his connectors pulled free of their housings, allowing cerebrospinal fluid to leak from the port in his skull. His legs were as spindly and apparently useless as his arms, but he gained his feet with far more ease. His hands rose with him, up from Xavier's throat, to catch hold of the circlet of sophisticated electronics that rested on his head.

A quick tug, followed by a clatter as the circlet slipped from Jason's fingers to the floor below, and the buzzing was gone, the pain as well.

Xavier exhaled in relief. "Thank you, Jason."

"Thank you, Jason" was the boy's mumbled response.

For Xavier, it was like staring down at the world from some Olympian height and watching all the lights come on. First one thought came to him, and then a multitude, the same way the first few drops of rain in spring herald the approaching monsoon. Most would drown in such an onslaught.

For Charles Xavier, it was a rebirth. Of self, of purpose.

He felt Jason touch him once more, gently, on the cheek, and used that momentary contact as the physical link to release the controls he'd established over the boy. He might as well have thrown a switch. All expression immediately faded from Jason's features. As the boy lowered himself to his own chair, Xavier assumed that the passion he'd seen earlier was merely a reflection of his own.

"This should not have happened," he told Jason. "I don't know what can be done, my boy, but you have my word, I'll find some way to help you."

His mind was on other things, flush with the excitement of his reawakened telepathy. He didn't see the flash in the boy's eyes that belied the quietude of his behavior.

Xavier wheeled himself toward the locked door, making sure to roll across the inhibitor, taking a rude pleasure in the sound of its delicate workings crushing under his wheels.

"Mr. Smith," he called, aloud and with his thoughts, "are you there?"

Of course he was; his mind was as plain to Xavier as the sunrise on a clear day. In short order, the door was unlocked, and Xavier's arms were released from their restraints. His companion guard simply stood where he was, as Xavier told him to, watching disinterestedly.

"I arrived here with a friend," Xavier ordered. "Take me to him."

Scott Summers had a cell all to himself, his optic blasts restrained by a high-tech inhibitor of their own. He was also shackled to the bed, to keep him from getting ideas about unleashing his beams himself.

"Remove his restraints," Xavier told the guards.

While Smith did as he was told, his partner hurried forward with Cyclops' visor. Taking great care to keep his eyes tightly closed and his face turned away from any living targets, Scott donned the visor.

"Thank you," Xavier said to the soldiers, and then to Corporal Smith: "What is the quickest way out of here?"

"The helicopter, sir" was Smith's reply, at attention, as if to a general.

"Take us there, now."

Two-thirds of the way eastward across the continent, in the passenger cabin of the *Blackbird*, on its way to the mansion, Bobby Drake wasn't happy with his roommate. John Allardyce, cheerfully flicking his lighter cap open and shut, open and shut, couldn't care less.

"You think it's funny," Bobby fumed, refusing to let up even though he'd been speaking to deaf ears since they went airborne. "Let's go set fire to *your* house next time!"

"Too late," John said cheerily.

"You almost killed those cops, John," Rogue told him.

"So?" John turned toward her. He spoke with exaggerated patience, as though explaining the most obvious facts of life to the terminally dim-witted. "Logan would have"—he gave a pointed look at the man across the aisle—"if he hadn't gotten shot in the head."

Logan ignored the boy. He wanted no part of this argument, because in this one instance, both sides were right. John was right. Given the circumstances, he would have charged those cops and likely used lethal force. But he also sided foursquare with Rogue. Just because he was prepared to shoulder that karmic burden didn't mean it was right for these kids to do the same. Hell, it probably meant precisely the opposite.

Mercifully, Jean gave him a high sign from the flight deck, and he clambered up the aisle to join her and Storm.

"They'll be all right," she assured him. Unconvinced, he growled, crouching down behind the cockpit seats and occupying himself with an examination of the dials and display screens. Jean was staring at him, first at his reflection in the windscreen, then straight on as she swung around in her chair to look him full in the face. He thought he'd welcome such attention, but her direct gaze made him distinctly uncomfortable.

She must have picked up the cue, from body language or his thoughts, because she reached out and used her thumb to wipe a smudge of blood off his forehead, from where the bullet had struck back in Boston. She didn't move her hand away, though, but stroked him again with her thumb, a quick caress right over the now-healed wound.

More than anything right then, he wanted to take that hand. He wanted to kiss those lips, he wanted to lose himself in the scent of her hair. He wanted—

Too many things.

"So," he said, taking refuge in the proprieties, "any word from the professor?" Seeing a faint quirk at the edge of her mouth when she shook her head, he remembered to add, "Or Scott?"

"Nothing," she told him.

"How far are we?" he asked.

"We're coming up on the mansion now. Once Storm whistles up some cover—"

"I've got two signals," Storm interrupted, "coming in fast."

Accompanying her announcement, a proximity alarm sounded. Warning lights flashed on the main console, and the main display shifted channels to a radar field. Two blips, rising and approaching from behind, identified by the plane's onboard computer as F-16s. They were armed and trying to paint the *Blackbird* with their target acquisition systems.

The *Blackbird* shuddered in wake turbulence as the Falcons shot past to announce their presence, then throttled back to pace the bigger aircraft, taking up flanking positions on either side. Each of the pilots was making a downward gesture, telling them to land at once.

They made the same point over the radio: "Unidentified aircraft, this is Air Force two-one-zero on guard. You are ordered to descend to twenty thousand feet and return with our escort to Hanscom Air Force Base. Failure to comply at once will result in the use of extreme force. Do you acknowledge?"

When there was no reply, the fighter pilot repeated his instructions.

"Somebody's angry," Storm commented.

"I wonder why" was Logan's pointed response, with a glare over his shoulder at John Allardyce.

Logan hung back in the shadows so that the fighter jocks could only see the two women at the controls. Nightcrawler had started mumbling prayers again, and the kids aft were demanding to know what was happening; they weren't shy about sounding scared, either.

Jean looked at Storm, then at Nightcrawler. She'd already come to her decision.

Logan was about to ask, "What now?" when the lead fighter told them.

"We're marked!" Storm cried as the *Blackbird*'s systems confirmed the worst. "They're going to fire! *Seat belts!*"

She slapped the throttles to their firewalls and pointed the big black aircraft toward the stars. The *Blackbird* surged forward as though it had been launched from a catapult, and Logan had his hands full grabbing hold of the back of Jean's chair with one hand and catching Nightcrawler with the other. Strangest damn feeling for Logan, and then some, to find some guy better than a head taller wrapping himself like a monkey around his arm and using it to climb up to his torso.

They felt another minor shudder as the *Blackbird* broke the sound barrier. In their wake, the F-16s went immediately to afterburner and rocketed after them. Alarms and displays on the main panel revealed two minor blips separating themselves from the pursuing fighters and beginning to close the gap at a significantly greater speed.

"Who are these guys?" Bobby yelled from the back. "What the hell is happening? Why won't they leave us alone?"

Nobody up front paid him any attention. They had enough to worry about.

"What's the threat?" Logan demanded.

Jean pointed at the display: "Sidewinders. They're

heat seekers. We give them minimal profile with our exhaust, we can lose 'em."

"Everybody hang on!" Storm yelled, and she and Jean together swung the wheel hard over.

The *Blackbird* peeled off to the left, pitching up and over into a barrel roll that allowed them to reverse direction without needing a wide turn. The missiles, closing on where the plane had been, triggered their own proximity sensors and detonated, creating a minor fireball too far behind the *Blackbird* to do any damage. In response, both pursuing fighters split in opposite directions to come in on them from either side.

Storm jinked them the other direction, turning headlong in the direction of one of the fighters and forcing both of them to maneuver to prevent a collision. Nightcrawler wedged himself into a corner, holding on with hands and feet and tail while praying for all he was worth. Aft, John Allardyce had no smart comments, just a lot of sweat as he grabbed for a barf bag.

"They're not backing off," Storm said. "And they're not giving me a decent opening to outrun them."

"Don't we have any damn weapons in this heap?" Logan demanded as the fighters struggled for position. The women were good, but these guys were trained professionals at the top of their game. No way would they lose a dogfight.

Jean shot a glance at Storm, who released hold of her controls. Jean had the aircraft now.

Storm's eyes burned white, occluding iris and pupil. The air around her became supercharged with electricity, and Jean flicked a line of switches to disengage the systems on her side of the panel. Even so, performance on the main displays began degrading markedly, the screens becoming more and more crowded with static.

Through the canopy, Logan saw clouds darkening the sky ahead as puffy cumulus crashed together and built themselves before his eyes into a towering series of thunderheads. Lightning announced the storm, and he knew down on the ground people would be picking up the pace, cursing the weatherman for getting the forecast wrong yet again, as they hurried toward shelter.

On the radar, despite the electronic interference Storm was creating, he could see the shape of the storm up ahead. To his uneducated eye, it looked nasty. Without hesitation, Jean sent the *Blackbird* rocketing into its heart.

The Falcon drivers couldn't know what to make of the freak weather. They didn't care. They followed.

On radar and to the naked eye, wisps of cloud began to swirl, faster and faster as Storm manipulated pressure gradients and temperature to create air effects within these clouds more common to the great plains than the northeast. Great rams of high-pressure cold bludgeoned hot low-pressure air, generating maelstroms of tremendous force that found expression as airborne tornados.

Aboard the *Blackbird*, despite the best efforts of both Jean and Storm, it was a rough and rocky ride, akin to thundering over potholes the size of New Jersey. Wind smashed at the hull; one minute they were in clear air, the next the canopy was covered with sheets of rain, the next, completely occluded by ice. The only constant was that visibility sucked and maneuverability was worse.

Hard as it was for them, though, Logan didn't want to imagine what it was like for their pursuers. He counted over a dozen whirlwinds, writhing impossibly across the sky both vertically and horizontally, creating an atmospheric gauntlet no aircraft could possibly survive.

Still, they tried, using every ounce of courage and skill to close to the point where they could establish a solid lock.

"We're marked," Jean cried out . . .

. . . and Storm responded by sandwiching the nearer fighter between a pair of tornados.

They literally tore the plane to bits, scattering wreckage across the sky in pieces no larger than a Zip disk. In the blink of an eye, the pilot found himself cast out of his vehicle and into the teeth of weather more ferocious than he could imagine, much less recall. He'd never had a plane disintegrate around him before, prayed never to endure the experience again. But most amazing of all to him was what happened afterward.

He thought for those first awful moments only of his wife and kids, but then it was as if the hand of God had reached out to enfold him. Yes, he was falling from miles in the air, but from the moment he separated from his aircraft, it was as if the storm had lost all interest in him. He might as well have been falling through a clear summer sky on some training exercise. Not a breath of wind touched him, nor rain, either, even though he fell for miles through the darkest and most terrifying pile of cumulo-nimbus thunderheads he'd ever seen. His parachute opened without a hitch, and he descended to a smooth landing somewhere close to Syracuse.

His wingman knew none of this. He only saw his fellow plane disintegrate, heard a final, frantic squawk of shock and terror over the radio before contact was lost. He made the logical assumption, and just like that the fight became personal.

The tornados came looking for him, and he skated around them with a daring and skill that pushed his interceptor well beyond the envelope of its flight and combat dynamics in his determination to nail them. He wouldn't give up, he wouldn't back off, and as the increasingly desperate maneuvers progressed, he gained height on them.

All Jean wanted was to break off the engagement, to use the *Blackbird*'s far superior power plant to put so much distance between them that he couldn't follow. But if she ducked to the side, if she turned tail, the Falcon would have a shot. If she bulled down his throat, he had a shot.

Storm let her temper get the better of her. Logan jumped as small flickers of lightning crackled from her eyes and the interior of the flight deck resounded to the kettledrum riff of thunder. Outside, all the subordinate funnels coalesced into one, that megatornado expanding until its cone engulfed first the *Blackbird*, and then the Falcon on its tail.

Quick as she was, the pilot got tone before she could grab him. This time, before his plane went the way of his wingman, he popped a pair of slammers: AIM-120 AM-RAAM "fire-and-forget" air-to-air missiles. Even as he bailed, even as the storm around him abated to give him an equally smooth and safe descent to the ground, he knew he had the target nailed.

Explosions high in the atmosphere confirmed it. When

he was picked up, over the Canadian border in the woods above Lake Huron, that's what he reported.

Jean kicked the *Blackbird* through the whole regime of missile avoidance maneuvers. She pulled a vertical rolling scissors, snapping back and forth across her base course violently enough and often enough to break the radar lock the slammers had on them. She tried a high-speed, high-G barrel roll to flip up and over the missiles and come in behind them. For all the good she did, the damn missiles might as well have been tied to the *Blackbird* with wire.

Without a word, using a slap to the arm to get the other woman's attention, she handed the controls back to Storm. They were leaving her storm well behind, although the air, and the ride, remained bumpy. The missiles were too small, too close, too fast for Storm's power to do any good. Their survival was Jean's to decide.

One small blessing: As Storm scaled back her power, the radar cleared up. Jean had a clear electronic view of their tormentors. All she had to do now was slide her consciousness down that invisible line connecting the *Blackbird* to the missiles . . .

Storm cleaned up the *Blackbird*'s flight profile, exchanging maneuverability for raw speed as the variable-geometry wings folded close to the hull, creating an airfoil ideal for high-mach hypersonic flight. Given a small fraction of a minute, they could outrun the damn missiles, stretching out the pursuit until the missiles ran out of fuel. But the missiles were already going hell for leather, far faster than the planes that launched them, and the time the *Blackbird* needed to accelerate was time they didn't have.

As the missiles struck the unseen barrier that she threw

up in their flight path, Jean's body reacted to an invisible impact and she gritted her teeth, hurling another telekinetic boulder at them. Again and again they plowed through her obstacles, the impacts psychically translating themselves into physical terms so that each one felt like a heavyweight punch. But this succession of hammer blows only made Jean that much more determined to prevail. She wasn't trying to finesse the intercept by manipulating the missiles' flight-control surfaces or even just grabbing hold of them and throwing them away; there was too much risk of losing her telekinetic grip, and no time to recover if she did.

She vaguely registered a cry of elation from the seat beside her and felt a sudden, pronounced wobble on the trajectory of the nearest missile. She hit it again, and again, and again, cursing it in terms that would impress Logan, furious with herself for not having the raw power necessary to do the job in a single shot.

She felt her body flush with a heat unlike any she'd ever known, not a physical sensation at all so much as a . . . spiritual one. She heard something faint in the distance, like a carillon fanfare, a call to glory that made her ache to answer, a sense of a window opening onto possibilities beyond number. It registered to her as music, but she knew it was so much more. It spoke to her as fulfillment, but of what she did not know.

"Jean," she heard Storm call, from as great a distance one way as the fanfare was the other, and for that moment was torn between which one to answer. "How are you—"

The last shot did the trick, sending the missile straight up so that its proximity fuse, mistaking its fellow missile for the target, detonated. She was aiming for a twofer, a double kill.

Aft, at the rear of the passenger cabin, John Allardyce had long since run out of barf bags, long since ruined his borrowed clothes. Bobby Drake didn't feel much better, although—since his uncle was a Gloucester man who made his living fishing the Grand Banks and enjoyed taking his favorite nephew for the occasional jaunt—he'd acquired a cast-iron stomach long ago.

Rogue, unfortunately, was in real trouble. The *Blackbird* didn't use standard seat belts; all the seats were fitted with four-point military-style restraints. Procedure mandated that passengers lock themselves in at takeoff, but she'd been talking with Bobby, who was really rocked by how wrong things had gone back at his house. He wasn't even sure anymore whether or not he could even go home again. In addition, she'd been so upset—still and probably for a while to come—with John for the stunts he'd pulled during the fight that she never got around to buckling herself in. Once the dogfight started, she found to her increasing dismay that she couldn't.

All the *Blackbird*'s wild and unpredictable moves forced her to spend most of the time just hanging on, to keep from making like a hockey puck against the walls and ceiling. Every time she got hold of a damn buckle, it wouldn't lock into the mechanism. She'd think one was anchored, but then when she tried to close another, the first would pop out. It happened so often—making her so frustrated she was ready to cry—that she believed the plane was doing this to her on purpose.

She knew she was getting upset, so she followed Jean's training. She forced herself to take big, slow, calming breaths. She was still scared but tried not to let that matter so much as, one by one, she gathered the buckles and slugged them into place.

This was going to work. She was going to be okay.

Up front, three pairs of eyes—green, brown, and blue—stared transfixed at the radar screen and the big blotch way less than a mile behind the *Blackbird* that represented the exploding missile. Things were looking good. They were going to be okay.

The panel *beeped* an alarm, and the second missile raced free of the debris field, locked and closing.

They had seconds to save themselves.

Jean threw everything she had into its path, focusing her concentration so tightly that the shape and fabric of the world around her began to fade. She didn't perceive herself anymore as being surrounded by the solid structure of the *Blackbird*; instead, she beheld the glittering atomic and molecular matrices that composed it. The world for her became a panoply of brilliant pinpoint lights and colors, shot through with vistas of unfathomable emptiness, almost as though reality was no more than an illusion, with all the tangible substance of a dream.

She closed her eyes, tasting the harsh gunmetal of blood from her nose.

The proximity *beeps* of the radar were coming closer together as the missile closed the range. She took a final roundhouse swing—and missed.

The missile's course never wavered.

"Oh, God," she breathed.

Inside the hull, it felt as though the *Blackbird* had just had its back broken by a baseball bat. The big plane bucked downward under the impact of the pressure wave. Shrieking metal matched shrieking voices as shrapnel punched a score of holes in the roof.

Decompression did the rest, blowing out a major section, the plane's own velocity wrenching the piece away. Instantly the cabin was swept by winds far greater than any hurricane. Rogue's harness held for all of a heartbeat, and then, to her absolute horror and disbelief, her buckles disengaged and she was swept screaming up and out the hole, into the sky.

Everyone saw what happened, only one was able to act on it.

Nightcrawler vanished in his distinctive *bamf* of imploding air and the faint stench of sulfur.

Rogue didn't know what to do or think. She'd never fallen out of a plane before; this was the kind of thing that only happened in movies. She remembered what she'd seen about skydiving and spread her arms and legs to try to stabilize herself. At the same time, she was laughing hysterically inside, demanding to know what the hell good that would do because she didn't have a parachute and sooner rather than later gravity was going to reintroduce her to the ground, the hard way. She doubted after that happy moment if even Logan's healing power would make much difference.

It was really cold, too. She'd hardly begun falling and already she couldn't breathe and she'd likely pass out and freeze to death before anything serious happened. It was so unfair.

That's when the demon caught her, indigo skin making him hard to see against the darkening sky that was left over from the storm. He rocketed out of nowhere with a grace and skill that told her he knew all about skydiving and wrapped himself around her, arms, legs, and tail. And teleported.

She didn't know where they went for the split instant they were in transit, and for as long as she planned to live she never wanted to find out. There was a cold that chilled her to the marrow, more completely than Bobby could. There was a silence that had nothing to do with the absence of sound. There was a raging disorientation that made her wonder if her insides and outsides had been transposed. There was an awful sense of *nothing*.

And then she was whole once more. And the pair of them were dropping the last couple of feet to the wind-ripped deck of the *Blackbird's* main cabin. Which, in Rogue's estimation, was *not* an improvement, because the plane was falling just as out of control as she had been.

Storm yelled their altitude, diminishing rapidly, as she and Jean fought to pull the plane out of a flat spin. The explosion had crippled the flight controls, they had minimal hydraulics, which made the act of turning the wheel or pulling on the yoke or pressing the rudder pedals akin to bench-pressing a fully loaded semitrailer. They had a flameout on one engine, possible shrapnel damage and a fire-warning light from the other, which they ignored as they rammed its throttle past the firewall in an attempt to stabilize their descent.

Logan braced himself in position and laid his hand beside Jean's on her yoke, using his strength to buttress hers. They were into the breathable atmosphere, that was good. But they were fast running out of sky, that was way bad.

Storm's eyes went white again as she fought to bring a wind into their path, to use it to check their headlong fall. But for all the passion of her indomitable will, she was still constrained by natural forces. She could generate a wind to cushion their landing, but not in the space they had left.

"You can fly," Jean told her. "Grab the kids, get them clear!"

As she spoke, Jean once more turned to her own teke, but that well was too dry to be of use. She had will to spare, but no strength to match the terrible momentum of their descent.

Without thinking, responding solely to a surge of emotion that caught them both by surprise, she placed a hand over Logan's. The look he saw when he met her eyes was a revelation that he knew would break both their hearts. And yet, it was a moment and a memory he'd carry with him to the grave.

Storm cleared her harness and shoved herself past Logan, calling to the kids.

Strangely, it was Nightcrawler, holding tight to Rogue, who responded.

"Uh . . . Storm?" He was pointing to the roof.

She followed his upraised finger and didn't bother hiding her astonishment as the fabric of the hull came alive before her eyes. Dark threads of metal alloy polymer laced their way across the hull spars as though they were being spun from a loom. The spars themselves that had been twisted and broken politely straightened themselves. The roar of wind through the hull gradually lessened to a whisper, then to silence.

Around them, the hull righted itself, returning to level flight.

Logan looked questioningly at Jean, wondering if this was her doing. As mystified as he, she shook her head, but she also didn't move her hand. Indeed, she tightened her grip, interlacing her fingers with his.

They were a couple of hundred feet in the air, but their velocity had dropped to less than a hundred knots. With each ten feet or so they lost another ten knots until, ten feet off the ground, they stopped.

They sat there, floating just above the ground, for maybe a minute before anyone had the presence of mind to mention the landing gear. That provoked more than a fair share of nervous chuckles as Jean broke contact with Logan to slap the big landing lever from the top to the bottom of its cradle. A quiet whine and a dull *thunk* told them what the status lights confirmed: gear down and locked.

The next sensation was an equally understated *thump* that told them they were once more on the ground.

The kids in the back, being kids, let out a cheer.

On the flight deck, the first flush of relief had been cast aside by the sight of what was waiting for them. They had descended into a forest clearing not much bigger than the *Blackbird* itself. On the edge of the clearing, parked under the sheltering evergreens, was a black limousine, not the sort of wheels normally used for a camping trip. But then, the couple using it wasn't the sort you'd expect to find out here roughing it, either.

Mystique gave Jean and Logan a wave from where they stood midway between the nose of the *Blackbird* and their car. Magneto, once again properly clothed in his signature black and gray, held out his hand in welcome. Mystique stood at his side.

"If I set you down gently," he offered in a pleasantly companionable voice, the kind you'd want in a favorite old-country uncle, "will you hear me out?"

# Chapter
# Twelve

It was a good place to hide, even without the stealth netting that Storm and Logan quickly spread across the hull. Jean wanted to help, but her psychic exertions in the air had taken a physical toll—which she'd discovered when she tried to climb out of her pilot's chair. The spirit was willing, the flesh had other ideas. She didn't have strength to move, and Logan had to carry her out.

Magneto had set the *Blackbird* down hard against a nice-sized escarpment, part of a line of large hills—baby mountains, really—that formed a valley with a mainly north-south orientation. It had been carved out of the landscape by the great ice ages, when the advancing glaciers had plowed troughs in the earth like a plow. This was still technically wilderness, with no roads to speak of for fifty miles in any direction, pretty rough going on foot through the forest. Magneto had brought his limo in the same way he saved the *Blackbird*, with his power.

For Storm and Jean, that had proved a daunting revelation. The plane had been designed with Magneto's abilities in mind, to make it as impervious to him as possible, and yet he'd grabbed hold of it and repaired it with frightening ease.

The cliff formed a wall at their back. Every other direction, they saw only trees. Old-growth forest, timber that had never been cut, thick stands of fir that towered thirty meters and more in height. This was rugged country that made no concession to modern man or the amenities of modern society, as the kids learned when they decided to go exploring and almost immediately got themselves lost. Logan found them without any trouble but wasn't happy about it, and he made it clear to them that next time they were on their own.

"Think they listened?" Jean asked him.

He snorted derisively. "That'll be the damn day. Especially John. He'll do it again just to spit in my eye." His expression sobered. "How you doin'?" he asked her.

"Pretty much fine, thank you," she replied, interlacing her fingers and stretching her arms till the joints cracked. "Just being lazy."

"You're entitled."

"Absent the circumstances, and the company," she added, with a pointed flick of the eyes toward the limo, "I'd agree with you. I've been monitoring GUARD." She meant the military command frequencies. "Both pilots are okay." Logan made a face. He understood her impulse to save the two men, but frankly he couldn't have cared less. Guy tries to kill him, the guy takes his chances. No bitching, no tears.

"The second pilot's reporting us as a probable kill," Jean finished.

"They buying it, the brass?"

"Well, Ororo didn't entirely disperse her storm. It's raining pretty hard over the probable crash site, zero-zero visibility, no hope of flight operations until it clears, which she assures me"—ghost of a grin—"won't be for a while. System seems to have stalled. Meteorologists are baffled."

"I'd keep looking if it was me, till I knew for sure."

"Hence our precautions," and she indicated the netting, shrouding the plane and the car. "Even enhanced imagery won't spot the plane, and our heat and electronic emissions are close to zero. By the time we finish setting up, we'll look like a camping party, nothing more. There should be nothing here to merit a second glance."

"Except for him," Logan noted, jutting his jaw in the general direction of Nightcrawler, who was carrying a tent pack over to where Mystique had begun to lay out their campsite.

"Whatever happens, Logan, we'll deal."

"So tell me, Jean, just how many people *are* there in the world with that color skin and those color eyes?"

She shrugged. "How many are blond and blue, or red-headed with green eyes?"

"I don't believe in coincidence."

Her tone sharpened. "And I don't believe in judging someone without giving them a fair chance. You of all people might appreciate that."

With a grunt of effort, deliberately ignoring, then waving away, his offer of help, Jean pushed herself to her feet and strode toward the open hatch of the *Blackbird*. Logan fumed as he watched her go, but he was mostly angry at himself. He had nothing against the German, couldn't help liking him in some ways. But the attack on the mansion, and now finding himself in close proximity with a man he'd cheerfully slaughter, had put all his combat instincts on high alert. Jean was too much like Xavier, always determined to see the brighter angles of human nature. Logan had walked too long, too far, with killers. Trust came hard for him because he knew, deep down to his soul, the cost of betrayal.

He felt as if he'd already failed once, by being caught by surprise at the mansion. He wasn't going to let that happen again.

Mystique was supervising the layout of the camp, and Logan had to admit the woman knew her stuff. She knew he was watching and if that bothered her, she didn't let it show. Quite the opposite, in fact; she seemed amused by his attention.

Logan smelled a faint acrid wisp on the wind, the detritus of a striker generating a spark, over and over, in an unsuccessful attempt to ignite a flame.

That made him grin. The kids were going all Boy Scout. How cute.

Bobby Drake didn't share that amusement as repeated attempts to use John's lighter to torch some kindling led to a huge amount of frustration. He tried paper, he tried twigs, he tried dry leaves, but nothing would catch. All the time he was conscious of John, sitting behind him with his back to a tree trunk, silently laughing at his failure.

"You could help, you know," Rogue snapped to John. There was no expression on the boy's face as he looked up at her. His eyes were cold and unreadable.

Forcing himself to ignore everything but the need to generate some fire, Bobby followed a couple of sparks as they landed on a leaf, pursing his lips and giving them a gentle puff of air to excite them into a true flame as they burned through the leaf and left a glowing boundary that quickly expanded outward in their wake. The more Bobby breathed, the brighter the embers glowed, until he saw the ghost of a flame. Stifling a cheer, he grabbed for some more tinder to feed the baby fire.

Then, with a speed that surprised and saved him, Rogue's hand caught him by the scruff of the neck and yanked him clear, his own muscles engaging that very same moment in kinetic response to a threat his conscious mind wasn't yet even aware of. In that selfsame instant, the tiny flicker of flame exploded into a pillar of raw fire, hot as a blast furnace, that reared up better than ten meters before fading to a happy little campfire.

Bobby scrambled around to confront the boy behind him, but he lost his balance as he did so and sprawled awkwardly on the grass, which kept John from being on the receiving end of a roundhouse punch to the face. He glared at John, so did Rogue, but all they got in return was the most innocent of smiles.

John held out his hand, gesturing for the borrowed lighter. Bobby wanted to throw it away or, better yet, encase it in a block of ice that would last as long as a glacier. Instead, remembering all he'd been taught at home and at Xavier's, he mastered his rage and dropped the lighter into John's open palm. Then he and Rogue turned their backs on him and walked away. Once they were back at the school, assuming there was a school to go back to, Bobby determined to insist on a new roommate. John had crossed too many lines. Bobby wanted no more to do with him.

After the fire came dinner. Nothing fancy, nothing that needed cooking. The campfire was mainly for psychological comfort, to give the scene an air of companionability that was lacking on the faces of most everyone present.

It was an adversarial setting, Magneto and Mystique on one side of the fire, Jean, Storm, and Logan on the other. Everyone but Logan was seated. He stood behind the women and a little to their side, with a clear shot at Magneto. His stance appeared casual, but nobody was fooled. The question that lingered unspoken between them all was whether or not he could reach the older man and deal with him before Magneto could bring his own powers to bear.

Magneto sat in a camp chair, with a presence that made it seem more like a throne. Mystique hunkered down beside him in a crouch, her movements so fluid it was hard to believe she had a skeleton beneath her indigo skin. There was a snap to the air, a harbinger of the fast-approaching winter, that made the heat of the fire welcome. Magneto had hated the cold since Auschwitz and had bundled himself inside an open greatcoat to keep it at bay. Mystique, by contrast, didn't seem to mind a bit. She walked naked, using a decorative scattering of bony ridges across the chest and hips as a minimal acknowledgment of propriety, and dared the world to make a comment.

Jean sat on knees and heels, a very Japanese stance that amply demonstrated her natural grace. She, too, was playing a role, presenting herself in an apparently submissive posture that was in fact anything but. Like a samurai, she could stay this way for hours, yet remain constantly ready to spring to her feet faster than anyone might have guessed. She rarely looked at Magneto, yet

Logan knew her focus on the man was as intent as his own.

Of them all, Storm looked the most natural as she tended the fire, feeding it the occasional length of wood while using her control of the winds to channel a constant breeze through the base of the blaze, keeping it hot. She sat cross-legged, in a position she'd learned as a child out on the Great Rift Valley, wandering with the Masai.

The kids, showing more sense than Logan expected, were keeping their distance, as was Nightcrawler.

Logan told the story of what had happened at the mansion. Magneto told them of Xavier's and Scott's capture.

"Our adversary," Magneto said at the end, "his name is William Stryker. He is very highly placed in the national intelligence community. Specializing in clandestine operations. Ostensibly accountable to the President, but it's clear now he has an agenda all his own."

"What does he want?" Jean asked.

The look Magneto gave her made his feeling plain: *Shouldn't that be obvious, child?* But Logan spoke before he could repeat those sentiments aloud.

"That's the question we should be asking Magneto," Logan challenged.

Magneto inclined his head, very much the monarch holding court, the civilized man confronting a band of barbarians. Or worse, children.

Storm had as little tolerance for being patronized as Logan did. "So," she demanded curtly of the older man. "What is it, Eric? What do *you* want?"

Magneto's expression tightened so fractionally only Logan caught the change. He wasn't used to being spoken to like this, and he didn't like it. He knew his priorities, though. He'd leave any response for later.

"When Stryker invaded your mansion, he stole an essential piece of its hardware."

"Cerebro?" Jean asked, shaking her head in denial. She didn't want to believe that that was what had happened. "Stryker would need the professor to operate the system," she said.

"Precisely," Magneto agreed. "Which is the only reason I believe Charles is still alive."

"What's the deal?" Logan asked sharply. "Why are you all so scared?"

Magneto answered him. "While Cerebro is working, Charles' mind—amplified by its power—has the potential to connect with every living person on the planet. If he were to concentrate hard enough on a particular group of people—let's say mutants, for example—he could kill us all."

"You've gotta be kidding," Logan said.

"Charles and I built Cerebro as a tool," Magneto continued, "one I believed, we both believed, would unite the world."

Flatly, a statement of fact, like announcing there are stars in the sky, Storm said, "Liar!"

Magneto met her gaze and saw in her eyes the character of a woman who had faced down lions bare-handed.

"You wanted to use Cerebro as a weapon against nonmutants," she continued in that same calm, devastating reportorial tone. "Only the professor wouldn't let you."

He didn't try to defend himself. "Now, I fear, he has no more choice in the matter."

"Can you hear anything?" Bobby asked Rogue from the opposite end of the campsite.

"Excuse me?" she asked him back, with a look that said she thought he was nuts.

"I dunno, I thought, y'know, since you imprinted Wolverine—"

"His name's *Logan*," she retorted in a fierce whisper. Even though she couldn't hear what the adults were saying, she knew Logan could hear the kids just fine if he wanted, and suspected Jean could pick up their thoughts just as easily. "And I can't, okay?"

"Okay," he said hurriedly in a placating tone. "Sorry I asked."

John, busy staring at their campfire, snorted.

"I beg your pardon," said Nightcrawler, his yellow eyes the only part of him that could readily be seen against the background shadows, "but I can get a closer look."

Bobby and Rogue nodded in tandem, and the yellow eyes vanished, leaving behind a faint *bamf* of imploding air and his distinctive scent of smoke and brimstone.

"Nice," Bobby said in admiration.

John waved his hand in front of his face. "Oh, yeah. Mutant teleport farts. Real nice."

Nightcrawler didn't catch the last remark, but if he had, he wouldn't have thought anything of it. There wasn't a joke or comment that could be made about the by-products of his power that he hadn't heard already. Some of them actually made him laugh. Regardless, he always made it a point to smile. Grace in adversity was an article of faith with him.

His destination was a fir tree just beyond the adults' campfire. The challenge was getting close enough to reach a branch—without materializing impaled on one—and to avoid making so much noise when he grabbed hold that it would draw the attention of anyone down below.

Using hands and feet and tail, he clambered silently down the trunk until he found a vantage point that kept him hidden but afforded a decent view of the others. Then he simply wrapped his tail around a branch, hung upside down, and listened.

Storm was speaking to Magneto with an almost prosecutorial manner: "How would Stryker know what Cerebro is—or where to find it?"

Magneto didn't answer right away. He laid his right hand for a moment on the inside of his left forearm, where he'd received his identification tattoo from the SS guards at Auschwitz, rubbing his thumb absently back and forth across his sleeve as though he could feel the marks left in his skin through the thick, heavy cloth. Then, his expression strangely unreadable, he lifted his hand to the back of his neck, to the scar left by Stryker's injections. He'd now been branded twice in his life. As a boy, there had been no way he could fight back. As a man, he'd thought there was no way he would allow such a thing to happen again.

*Vanity,* he thought, remembering the ancient Roman injunction to their Caesars: *All is Vanity.*

"*I* told him," he said at last, an admission dragged from the depths of his soul.

He looked from Storm to Jean, both women in the eyes, not bothering to hide the rage and shame that roiled within him like magma beneath the caldera of a dormant volcano, and was impressed that neither flinched. "I helped design the system, remember? I helped Charles build it.

"Stryker has undeniable methods of . . . persuasion. Effective against me. Effective even against a mutant as strong as Charles. Believe this, if Stryker has Charles, he will find a way to break him. And suborn him to his purposes. If he weren't absolutely certain of that fact, he wouldn't have acted."

"Who the hell is this Stryker?" Jean asked.

"He's a military scientist with considerable ties to the clandestine intelligence community. He has spent his professional life looking for a solution to what he considers the mutant problem. But if you require a more . . . intimate perspective, why don't you ask the Wolverine?"

"His name is Logan," Jean said, coming too quickly, too sharply to Logan's defense, in a way that made Magneto smile very thoughtfully as he turned his attention back and forth between them.

"Of course it is," he said. "But what's in a name?"

"William Stryker," he continued, "is the only other man I know who can manipulate adamantium. The metal laced through the Wolverine's bones, it bears *his* signature.

"Are you sure you don't remember—Logan?" In return, he got a blank look. "What a pity."

"The professor—"

"The professor trusted you were smart enough to discover this on your own. He gives you more credit than I do." Logan's eyes flashed, but beyond a subvocalized growl, he offered no other reaction to Magneto's insult.

"So Charley knew," he said.

" 'Charley' has always known."

Jean looked sharply at Logan, but his face was as still as his thoughts.

Logan didn't react.

"Charles has always known."

"Please understand," Storm spoke calmly from the fireside, "if we don't take this all purely on good faith. You went to some trouble to save us—for which we're all quite appropriately grateful. The question is, why? What do you want, Magneto? Why do you need us?"

"Mystique discovered plans of a base where Stryker's had his operations for decades. Unfortunately," he shrugged, "we don't know where it is.

"However, I suspect one of *you* might."

"The professor already tried," said Logan.

Magneto sighed. "Once again, you think it's all about *you*."

Then his eyes lifted to the branches above.

Nightcrawler's first impulse was to flee, but he took strength and comfort from the smile of greeting that Storm gave him, the wave of invitation that followed to join her at her side. He came down as a circus acrobat, swinging lithely from branch to branch, ending with a triple somersault that landed him right where Storm had indicated. He held the pose for a moment, out of habit, before reminding himself that this wasn't an occasion, nor this an audience, for applause, and he squatted close beside her.

Her hand across his shoulders was reassuring.

"I didn't mean to snoop," he apologized.

Storm gave him a squeeze that told him it was all right, and Jean said, "Relax."

She rose to her feet, with a smooth grace that almost matched Mystique, and took position in front of Nightcrawler.

Jean spoke aloud again, but also with her thoughts, telling him again, "Relax." He heard far more than the simple word, however. She used telepathy to enfold him in a great psychic quilt that left him all warm and snuggly and safe in ways he should be able to recall from childhood, if he had the happy memories for it. She gave him a window into her own soul to reassure him that these sensations were true, that she meant him no harm, that she genuinely liked him and cared for him. In turn, she found a soul that had weathered the tempests of life with remarkable success.

Her mouth made a small O of astonishment. Strangely, Nightcrawler represented something she'd never considered, a purely physical mutation that manifested at birth. Herself, Scott, Storm, virtually all the mutants who'd been gathered at the mansion, they were outwardly indistinguishable from their nonpowered brethren. Their powers had manifested at puberty, that's when their lives had changed; but before then everything had been wonderfully normal.

Not so with Kurt. He'd never been able to hide. That was why he'd ultimately taken refuge in the circus, even though he'd spent his earliest days there as part of the freak show. Soon, though, with the natural exuberance of childhood, he'd discovered that he could climb faster and better than anyone else he knew, and that his tail provided opportunities for performance that left the others gasping. He was more at home in the air than on the ground, and he quickly became one of the arena's chief attractions. Despite the evident skill, despite the tumultuous cheers from every audience that ever saw him, he was never invited to join the great world-class circuses. A scout from Ringling Bros. came once and quickly conceded that he'd never seen anything like Nightcrawler. He brought Kurt to the States for an audition. The bosses reacted the same as their scout: Nightcrawler was unique. Unfortunately, that was the point. No one at their level had ever knowingly hired a mutant, no one was willing to take the risk of a backlash. Better he should stay in a regional show.

Truthfully, Kurt himself didn't mind. He liked the smaller scale of his own shows, the more intimate relationship with his audience. In the far brighter lights of the big cities where the big shows toured, he wouldn't be able to continue his own personal quest for meaning, for enlightenment. He found a measure of release, and comfort, on the trapeze, but no answers to the questions that had haunted him since he was old enough, aware enough, to frame them: Who am I? What am I? *Why* am I? What kind of God would create a creature like me? What purpose would it serve?

Jean expected to find a person bludgeoned and tormented by his appearance. In stark contrast, she embraced one of the most gentle and secure and stable beings she had ever encountered, who was surprisingly at peace with himself—even if he was still working on his place in the scheme of things.

He trusted her, wholly and unreservedly, and in the face of that innate nobility she felt humble. It was a faith she would cherish, and it made her absolutely determined to keep him safe as she stepped into the vaults of his memory.

The images were broken and scattered: flashes from every direction, strobes without number as every camera in the circus tried to take his picture. He was used to it.

The scout and his bosses gave him a ticket home, but he decided to stay a while, to visit in person this country he knew only from the movies.

He found himself the abandoned church in Boston to use as his home. He did most of his sightseeing at night. He had no thought of danger. What would anyone want with a circus aerialist?

Ambush. Bodies slamming into him from every direction, men in uniform, hitting him first with a shot of pepper spray, then mace, screwing with his concentration so he couldn't teleport, covering his mouth so he couldn't yell for help. . . .

A spray hypo . . .

Oblivion . . .

Vague recollections of soaring high above the ground, wind in his face, a *whuppawhuppa* noise that he belatedly identified as a helicopter . . .

He saw trees and a wall of gray concrete that filled his vision to the horizon on either side and up to the very top of the sky, which vanished as he was rolled on a gurney into a long tunnel, plunging as deep into the bowels of the earth as he'd been carried above it in the aircraft flying here. . . .

An annoying itch on his neck, where he wore a sedative patch to keep him tractable, no energy to do anything about it, a room, a man holding a syringe . . .

Soldiers held him down, and he felt acid fire at the base of his skull. He wanted to scream, to curse, to plead, to die, but he'd forgotten how. He was empty, and only the man's voice could fill him. . . .

He remembered the White House, the Oval Office, the gunshot, running for his life, teleporting until he couldn't go any farther. . . .

He found his church, claimed it now as his sanctuary. . . .

And Jean found him. . . .

She broke contact, cradling his upturned face in both her palms, wishing she could borrow some of the peace and tranquillity she saw within him for herself. She gave him a kiss of thanks. She'd never felt so drained, not even after the aerial dogfight aboard the *Blackbird*.

"Stryker's at Alkali Lake," she told the others without looking at any of them.

"I've been there," Logan said. "That's where Charley sent me. Nothing's left."

"There's nothing left on the surface, Logan. The base is underground."

They talked a while longer, with Magneto leading the debriefing, delicately mining Jean's memory for every possible nugget of information before turning his attention to Logan. He proved a surprisingly skilled and patient interrogator, turning the smallest nuance of dialogue or gesture into a means of extracting even more data than the subject, more often than not, was even aware he (or she) knew. Watching him, listening, Jean beheld the man that Charles Xavier had befriended, a vision of what might have been had Magneto not embraced the inner demons of his childhood. He was just as inspiring a leader, just as intuitive a teacher. He recognized her interest and her nascent insights and for a moment between them there were no barriers.

The tragedy she saw then was that he knew it, too. All that could have been, perhaps even should have been. All that might yet be. Knew it, and rejected it. Charles Xavier was a man energized by humanity's potential; his life, his purpose, had always been defined by hope. Magneto refused hope. His heart had been broken too many times. Long ago, his spirit had been pared down to its essence, brought to white heat in the most awful of crucibles and then pounded by adversity into the shape of a weapon. The metal of his being had been folded a thousand thousand times, as the classical sword smiths of ancient Japan forged their samurai blades. Thanks to that cruel tempering, he could bend without breaking. But regardless of what happened, he would never lose his edge, would never be anything other than what he was. There was a greatness in him, that was undeniable. He was the living embodiment of the primal forces that formed the foundation of the universe. And as a consequence, he was just as terrible as he was glorious.

She found she couldn't bear to be near him anymore. The bleak hollow at the center of his soul was like a whirlpool; to wander closer was to be dragged to a similar oblivion.

She broke from the campfire and took refuge in the *Blackbird*, returning to the purely mechanical tasks that had filled the afternoon and evening,

Watching her leave, Logan decided he was done with Magneto's Q&A. Brusquely excusing himself, he strode after her through the campsite to find her standing underneath the wing of the *Blackbird*, with her head and shoulders hidden inside an open belly hatch. She was muttering to herself, in a tone and using words he didn't expect from her. It made him suspect she'd been hanging around him too much; Xavier and Scott would accuse him of being a bad influence. *Outstanding!*

"How bad is it?" he asked her.

"I'm running fluid through the hydraulics. If the test passes, it'll still take four to five hours to get off the ground. Like it or not, we're stuck here for the night.

Fortunately," she continued in a rush, "our stealth netting should hide the *Blackbird* pretty well from any casual reconnaissance. As for the rest, the passive scanning array says we've got clean sky to the horizon, and according to the infodump on the main computer, there shouldn't be any surveillance satellites overhead, either. That means minimal risk of detection."

"That isn't what I meant."

"I know what you meant, Logan. This is how I choose to answer. Okay?"

He said nothing. He had a hankering for a beer, but he knew there was none aboard the *Blackbird*, and Magneto struck him as more of a wine guy. A case of five-star *premier cru*, not a problem; God forbid the man even consider a can of Molson's.

From Mystique he expected nothing less than poison. It didn't matter to her that his healing factor made him immune. Quite the contrary. It struck him that the fun for her would be in seeing how much it would hurt him to recover and how long it would take.

After a while, conceding to herself that Logan wasn't going to go away, Jean allowed herself a sigh.

"I'm worried," she confessed. "About the professor. About . . . Scott."

"I know," he said.

He stepped under the shadow of the aircraft and reached out his arm to her. In flats, she was his height, but her uniform heels gave her an edge. It amused him to have to look a little bit up to her. At his touch, she folded against him to rest her head on his shoulder, allowing him to take the full weight of her body, which he did without any effort. There was no separation between them, physical or emotional, and his nostrils flared as he realized the implications.

"I'm worried about *you*," he told her softly. "That was some display of power up there."

She snorted dismissively. "It obviously wasn't enough."

He turned his head to look her in the eyes. She kept hers downcast, using her lids to shroud them, to keep him at a distance. But he didn't need eyes to see what was so obvious, or to sense the depth of the attraction between them. He'd known it from the start, that first moment when he'd awakened in the mansion infirmary to find himself staring up at a face that would haunt him forever.

He was barely breathing; he didn't want to do anything to break the moment. She felt the faint touch of air across her face, and her mouth opened in response, as if it were life itself to her, her head tilting just so against him to give him freer access.

The kiss was there for the taking.

Any other time, he wouldn't have hesitated. Any other time, he wouldn't have cared about the consequences. Now, consequences were everything.

"I love him," Jean said, mostly to herself, because she still wouldn't look at Logan. He knew she believed that with all her heart, so why didn't she sound convinced?

"Do you?"

She looked confused, as if she didn't understand the question. For those few seconds it took to answer, he saw her throw off replies the way a pitcher would reject signs he didn't like from the catcher. The one she settled on satisfied nobody, least of all her.

Now she looked at him. "People flirt with the bad guy,

Logan. But they don't take him home." She pulled her hand away. "They marry the good guy."

"Is that enough?" he asked quietly. And then, in response to her silence: "I could be the good guy, Jean."

"Logan, the good guy sticks around."

He threw caution to the winds.

He laid a palm lightly against the slim column of her throat, fingertips tucked behind the knob of her jaw while his thumb caressed her chin. Her skin was the softest, smoothest surface he could remember touching, and the contact between them was electric. He felt a flush of heat against his hand, saw color rise beneath her skin to give it a roseate glow that was a pale echo of the fire of her hair. Her breathing quickened in concert with her pulse, her heart pounding so strongly he could feel it against his own chest, even through the armored fabric of her uniform.

She trembled as if her body were being swept by a succession of microquakes. And he held back a smile at realization that her skin was puckering all over with goose bumps.

They were balancing on edges of passion and emotion that put the keenness of his adamantium claws to shame. And yet, because both of them recognized the seriousness of the moment, they both felt perfectly in control. They were poised on the crest of the perfect wave—for him, one of snow, part of an avalanche; for her, one of surf. No effort at all would be required to bring it to an end, to call this quits before they went too far. She didn't need to say a word, to make a gesture; he'd take his cue from the primal signals that weren't under her volitive control.

She caught him by surprise, covering his hand with hers, reaching out at the same time with her telekinetic power to close the miniscule gap that remained between them.

Now it was his breath that was caught up by a sudden gasp, his own heart that skipped a beat amid its own increasing trip-hammer riff, as her lips brushed his.

That first contact was fleeting, tantalizing with possibilities, but he didn't give her a chance to pull away as he opened to her, meeting her mental strength with that of his body. He heard a small noise that mingled desire and satisfaction, but couldn't tell whether it came from him or her as they pulled each other closer, and he came to understand the incredible strength that lay hidden within this lean, whipcord figure.

He lifted her off her feet, shifting his own stance just enough so that he supported her against the whole hard length of him, and now there was no question. *He* was the one who moaned as barriers collapsed between them and Jean gave him access to her own mind, her own sensations, her own emotions.

His nostrils filled with a rich woodland scent, and he knew this was how he presented himself to her.

The world blurred around them, took on a new shape as her desire caught up both of them, laying them bare to their souls. As their thoughts merged, it struck him that he should be afraid. There were memories here that he fought to keep hidden from Xavier, two volumes to the book of his life. The first, which he believed had been stolen from him, which Magneto now suggested was intimately involved with William Stryker, and which Xavier apparently had known about from the start. But the second, everything that had happened to him since, had more than a few moments that weren't pretty.

Yet he didn't even try to hide any of them; she was too important. He wanted her to see the whole of him; he wanted to give her every excuse to run away, because if she chose to stay, if she accepted what he was, then this was real. It would last.

What surprised him was the discovery that she was just as scared, just as determined.

He saw her playing in a yard, a fragment of her thoughts providing the date and setting: her parents' home at Bard College, an hour upstate from Xavier's, where her dad taught. Jean was eight and hanging with her best friend, Annie Malcolm. Annie tossed a Frisbee for her dog, but a wayward puff of breeze hooked the plastic saucer off over the fence. The dog bolted through the gate, Annie chasing after, heedless of the danger posed by this stretch of River Road.

Jean saw what Annie hadn't, a car speeding around the blind curve. There wasn't even a screech of brakes, before or after, just a sickening *thud* and the sound of tires skidding on asphalt as the driver struggled to regain control before he sped away.

She found Annie against the stone wall by the gate, her body folded at impossible angles, blood—so much blood, too much blood—splashed everywhere. Jean wanted to scream, to shriek, to howl, but some part of her that refused to relinquish control forced her lips to form proper words, forced her lungs to provide air for sufficient volume to make this a proper shout as she called for her mother.

Annie couldn't speak, the only thing moving about her was her chest, desperately striving—broken as it was—to draw another breath. As well there were her eyes, bright with confusion as her brain struggled to make sense of what had just happened. Jean couldn't stop her own tears. They poured silently from her eyes as she knelt beside Annie and wrapped her arms around her friend.

She found herself in a vast space of light, filled with sparkling clusters of energy. She touched the closest and was filled with an awareness of a specific time and place, together with a torrent of associated emotions, and in a sudden burst of insight realized that each of these clusters represented one of Annie's memories. With a directness only a child can muster, she concluded at once that she was inside Annie's head.

But her delight at this new adventure was short-lived. Even as she watched, she became aware that the brilliance of the individual clusters was fading, along with their background radiance, which suffused this apparently infinite space. It was like looking at the daylight sky, only in this case it was chockablock with stars of every conceivable color and magnitude, and realizing the gradually encroaching presence of night.

To her horror, Jean saw that the clusters closest to the darkness exploded apart in a fireworks shower of sparkles, and just like fireworks, these flaring embers vanished before they reached what she thought of as the ground. But unlike sunset, where the night came from a single horizon, this darkness closed on her from every side, not simply along a horizontal plane but lowering from above and rising from below. She tried to catch hold of the memory clusters, to carry them to some place of safety, but couldn't find one. With each that vanished, she found that less and less of a cohesive sense of Annie herself remained.

She called her friend's name, but the word echoed through a space where it had no more meaning. Annie was going, and there was no way Jean could call her back.

Jean embraced the final cluster, her own heart so full of grief she thought it would explode while her noncorporeal cheeks burned with tears. She thought if she could push her own strength, the essence of her own will and soul, into this last fleeting scrap of her friend, she'd still be able to save her.

The last of the light went out. All around her, save this last scrap of Annie's self, was darkness.

But paradoxically, as this final night fell, the cluster that Jean embraced blazed more brightly than before, more brightly than any radiance Jean had ever seen, so bright it put the sun to shame. She beheld colors she had no name for, that reached out to all her senses, manifesting themselves as tastes and scents and textures. It was a warm and welcoming light, pure in a way that poets strive for and only lovers attain, and that, rarely.

The last cluster, the last scraps of Annie, broke apart in Jean's grasp and slipped through her fingers, rushing away into the core of this new light. There was such peace and such beauty that Jean's first impulse was to follow so that her friend would not face this new place by herself.

That would be so easy. No more pain, no more fear. She could avoid the crushing weight of grief that awaited her the moment she opened her eyes for real, the memory of her friend, the awareness of the bloody rag doll she'd become.

Someone was yelling, in a voice raw with horror and with fear, and Jean was a little bit shocked to realize that she wasn't simply hearing the words her mother spoke as she cradle-crushed Jean in her own arms as Jean had done Annie, as heedlessly as her daughter had been of the blood that soaked them both. She could feel her mother's emotions as well, and her thoughts, relief that it was Annie lying there and not Jean, shame at that acknowledgment, fury that either girl had been so careless, a terrible and welling rage at the driver for not stopping.

*It's okay, Mommy,* she remembered saying, sure for years afterward that she'd spoken aloud, which was why she was so startled when her mother fell backward in stark and visible shock. *There's no need to cry, I'm okay.* Only much later did the understanding come that she hadn't said a word with her voice but had spoken directly, mind to mind.

And much later after that, the comprehension that she'd been quite wrong in what she'd told her mom: Nothing for Jean after that fateful moment when her psi catalyzed into being, years before it was supposed to, would ever be truly "okay" again.

"It's okay, darlin'," Logan said softly, brushing tears from her cheek. "There's no need to cry. You're okay."

She shuddered again, as though the surface temblers had given way to a deep and lasting tectonic shift, from the kind of quakes that level buildings to the ones that reshape the face of continents and raise mountains to the heavens.

She kissed him on the lips, on the cheeks, and he stifled a smile at the realization that he was crying, too.

She took a deep, calming breath but said not a word. Logan followed her lead. There was nothing that needed saying between them, not now, perhaps never again. It would be easy if her heart told her one thing and her head another; scientist though she was, empiricist to the core, she knew she'd follow her heart.

But her heart felt equally, passionately torn between them, and she couldn't see any way yet to heal the rift.

It made her head hurt and her soul ache, and she knew she wasn't likely to feel better anytime soon. Logan wanted to kiss her again, so much and so hard it was an ache within him. He wanted her more than his life, more than his past.

But she shook her head and pulled away.

"Logan, please—don't."

Against every instinct and every desire, he nodded assent and did nothing but watch as she strode away. That wasn't like him at all. His solution to every problem was direct and invariably physical. No hesitation, less regrets.

Until now. Until her. Somehow she brought out the best in him. Even more, she fanned in him a desire to be better, to transcend the person and life he was accustomed to. That would be a lot easier if he knew that at the end he'd have a shot, a chance to gain her as the prize. What made him smile at the wicked joke fate was playing was the realization that winning her *wasn't* guaranteed. It might not even be possible, no matter how he proved himself. Whatever they felt for each other, her love for Scott was just as strong and could not be denied.

Knowing that, why make the effort?

Knowing that, he found himself wanting to try anyway. Because, even though it made him crazy, he liked the way it made him feel.

Nightcrawler couldn't take his eyes off her, but how she reacted to his interest Logan couldn't tell.

"They say you can imitate anybody," Nightcrawler said to Mystique as the shape-shifter's gaze followed Logan across the campsite. "Even their voice?"

She looked over her shoulder at him and replied, in perfect mimicry, "Even their voice."

Nightcrawler couldn't help a grin of delight that stretched from ear to ear, and he clapped his hands together in one performer's appreciation of another.

"In your case," she told him, speaking as herself now, "the voice is easy. The tail, now, that might take some work."

"It would be like mine—*ach,* what is the word—"

"Prehensile," Logan said.

"*Ja, ja, ja,* that's it, like a monkey!"

Mystique searched once more for Logan and thought back briefly to their battle on Liberty Island. Her morphing ability had allowed her to generate a set of facsimile claws that were almost as good as the real thing. As well, it had enabled her to survive three of his own adamantium blades that had gone right to her heart.

"It isn't polite to ask a woman's secrets, *mein herr,*" she said gently. "Or expect the woman to give them up, just for the asking."

"Forgive me," Nightcrawler said hurriedly, recognizing the undercurrent of emotion flossing through the other mutant without knowing quite what it represented, "I did not mean to offend."

"Not even close," she assured him.

"I was wondering, though," he continued, "with such an ability, why not stay disguised all the time? You know . . . look like . . . everyone else." What he meant, and it was heartbreakingly plain to see, was "like *normal* people."

Her answer was direct: "Because we shouldn't have to."

His expression showed that he liked that. He just as obviously liked her, for reasons that had nothing to do with her appearance.

Logan should have been sleeping, but he didn't even try. From the moment he crawled into his tent, he'd been fingering and staring at his dog tags, as though physical contact—or glaring at them—might inspire some miraculous revelation. Charley had told him to be patient about his past, that his mind demanded the same opportunity and time to heal as his body would. Clear implication: This was a journey they'd take together. Now Magneto comes along to imply that Charley knows more—a lot more—than he's let on. Truth? Or was the bad guy just screwing with Logan's head?

The faint scent of Folavril—her perfume—announced her presence a moment before Jean opened the tent flap and crouched inside. Suddenly, his heart rate kicked into high gear, and he could see from the pulse on her throat, the faint flush to her skin, that the attraction was as undeniably mutual.

He started to speak, without the slightest idea of what he wanted to say, but she stopped him with a finger against his lips. Her eyes were laughing with anticipation and delight as she crawled closer across his sleeping bag. His own eyes couldn't help but follow the line of her shirt, more open than she usually wore it, to the shadows between her breasts. She straddled him and settled her weight on his hips. The touch of her was electric, the scent intoxicating, as she slid her hands across his chest, up the thick column of his throat to take hold of him along the line of his jaw and bring his lips to hers.

There was no hesitation this time. The kiss was dynamite, fulfilling all the promise of the first, and he returned better than he got, moving his left hand up to cup her neck and his right beneath her shirt to caress her across the ribs and belly. She trembled against him, catching her breath with the sparkling overload of physical sensation.

That's when he popped his claws. The outsiders from his left hand, to bracket her throat right beneath her chin, forcing her to hold her head erect and at attention, or risk slicing skin—and likely bone—on the razor-keen adamantium blades. The middle claw was the kicker, the final incentive to behave: One false move, she'd be done.

At the same time, he tore open her shirt to reveal three scars right below her left breast, the indelible legacy of his claws stabbing through her rib cage to her heart.

"Busted," Mystique said, sounding not at all dismayed. If anything, her smile was broader and livelier than ever, as was the light in her eyes. She danced with danger, it gave life spice and meaning. As he watched, green eyes turned chrome yellow, that color expanding to subsume the entire eyeball. Then, in the kind of dissolve animators love to use, the transformation spread outward from her eyes. Her hair shortened and turned a darker, more angry shade of red; her clothes faded into her skin, which in turn morphed from pale to indigo blue.

As an acrobat, she was in Nightcrawler's league. Logan knew from experience she could give and take a serious punch. Whatever her appearance, her strength demanded respect. Now she used that strength to gently but firmly push his blades clear of her neck. She did a good job; with barely a millimeter to spare, the edges never touched her skin.

At the same time, she melted against him, as Jean had beneath the *Blackbird*, kissing her way from mouth to ear.

"No one ever left a scar quite like you," she said.

"You want an apology?"

She chuckled, much as he might. "You know what *I* want."

She bit him, on the lobe, hard and sexy, and when she sat straight up before him she shifted position just that little bit needed to make her intentions and desires unmistakable.

"But what is it," she continued, her voice going as sultry as her manner, "*you* want?"

She changed in his arms, skin turning brown, hair turning silver, eyes turning blue, gaining height and majesty until it was Storm sitting there, spectacularly naked. She lifted her arms to spread her hair wide across her shoulders, allowing him an unobstructed view . . .

. . . and then she changed again—shrinking in size and stature, skin paling, eyes turning green, hair going brown with its distinctive skunk stripe down front, covering her nakedness demurely with crossed hands as she presented herself as Rogue . . .

. . . and then she was Jean again.

He'd had enough. He hit her, palm of the hand, flat to her chest, with force enough to pop her off his lap and almost to the opposite wall of the tent. He'd caught her off guard, and there wasn't time for her to recover. She landed in an inelegant sprawl, which only made her more amused than ever as she rolled over onto her belly and levered herself up on her hands.

By the time her arms were at full extension, Logan was staring at William Stryker.

"What do you *really* want?" Mystique asked him in Stryker's voice.

Face and body carved from stone, claws held in a defensive fist between him and the shape-shifter, Logan replied, "Get out."

She shook her head with a sneer and did as she was told.

Only when he was alone did Logan withdraw his claws. He hadn't been fooled from the very start—there was more to Jean's scent than her perfume, and elements of Mystique's that couldn't be hidden, more differences between them now than the other woman could possibly suspect. He told himself there were all manner of sensible reasons for indulging in the fantasy, but he knew they were lies. It was a glimpse of what might have been, if life were more fair.

Problem was, he'd already made a commitment and he would be true to it, no matter what, to the end. He'd been betrayed many times in his life. He swore he'd never be party to betraying another.

He rubbed his left hand with his right, over the space between the knuckles where the claws extended, while the pain of their use faded away. There was never any visible scar, his healing factor saw to that, but each time the claws came out the pain was as fresh, as shocking, as the first. On one level they were as much a part of him as his natural senses. He accepted their presence whole-heartedly. But on another, they were close to the ultimate violation. Someone had put them inside his body, someone had stripped him of even the pretense of humanity by making him a hybrid cyborg construct. A literal machine.

From a man like Stryker, if he was indeed responsible, it was no less than Logan expected. But if what Magneto said was true, if Xavier knew the truth and kept it from him, how could Logan trust the man ever again? Because the answer to that question begged an even darker one—was Xavier somehow involved in the process? Was he somehow responsible?

What then, he wondered. And with a thought, triggered his claws once more.

*Snikt!*

What then, indeed?

# Chapter
# Thirteen

The ladies worked straight through the night, and by morning the *Blackbird* was ready to go. As Logan finished zipping his uniform closed, he caught Rogue and Bobby eyeing him discreetly. They'd spent the night together, tangled up with each other in a pose that managed to be incredibly intimate while remaining wholly innocent. Rogue had taken great care to make sure no stray skin showed, other than her face, and she pulled her hood close around her head to minimize the risk of contact. Bobby wore his own gloves. Nightcrawler hung batlike from a branch above, as though he were the kids' very own swashbuckler gargoyle saint.

Only John Allardyce remained awake the whole night, sitting opposite Bobby and Rogue, staring at them across the campfire, continually flicking his lighter open and closed, open and closed.

The kids weren't interested in their classmate, though, which Logan knew was part of John's problem. It was the uniforms they wanted.

"Where're ours?" Bobby demanded.

Logan responded with a gruff snort that was echoed (in his ears or in his thoughts, he couldn't tell) from up front by Jean.

"On order," he told them. "Should arrive in a few years."

Logan supervised the breakdown of the campsite, mainly to keep tabs on Magneto and Mystique. Magneto boarded the plane as if he owned it, but Mystique paused just a moment in passing and flashed Logan a secret little smile to remind him of what had happened during the night. As Logan closed the hatch, she made sure he caught her flashing the same smile at Jean, most likely to make him wonder if she'd pulled the same trick with her. And, of course, to imply that Jean had fallen for the masquerade.

Even as their allies, she and Magneto were always trying to play the X-Men, to find the edge that would give them a tactical advantage. You could never let down your guard with them, on any level, because every encounter had to be some kind of challenge—and they always had to win.

That's what Rogue discovered right after takeoff, as she made her way back to her seat from the bathroom. Magneto was sitting across from John Allardyce, and he smiled at her as she passed. It was a genial smile, the kind you'd expect from family.

"Rogue," he said, by way of greeting, but when she didn't respond, when she tried totally to ignore him, he continued without missing a beat, "we love what you've done with your hair."

Her lips, her whole body, went tight as a drawn bow, but she kept walking. She wouldn't look back, she wouldn't give him the satisfaction. The device he'd intended to use months ago on the United Nations delegates had required his specific power to activate it. But doing so would have killed him, so he came up with what he felt was a far better idea: Allow Rogue to imprint his abilities, thereby enabling her to wield magnetism and take his place as the catalyst. Regrettably, she would have to die in the process. A tragic but necessary sacrifice for a noble cause.

She didn't see it that way. He didn't care.

Logan had saved her, first by destroying Magneto's device and then by allowing her to imprint his healing factor. But the energies that had burned so fiercely through her system had left a lasting mark, her skunk stripe, the distinctive widow's peak of silver hair springing from her forehead.

John watched her strap herself into her chair, realized that Logan was glaring back at Magneto from the flight deck, and turned to observe that Magneto wasn't bothered in the slightest by Logan's fury. Indeed, he seemed to enjoy it.

John was impressed, though he made sure not to show it. He sounded almost bored as he noted, "They say you're the bad guy."

That amused Magneto, who kept his gaze on Logan.

"Is that what they say?"

John started flicking his lighter, the reassuring *click* going almost unheard against the sound of the *Blackbird*'s swift passage through the morning sky.

"That's a dorky-looking helmet," he said. "What's it for?"

At last he'd caught Magneto's attention—an interest, though John didn't know it, that he'd had from the start—and as that noble head turned toward him, he suddenly wished he hadn't.

"This helmet," Magneto informed him quietly, "is the only thing that's going to protect me from the *real* bad guys."

He snapped his fingers, and the lighter flew from John's hands to his. With a practiced flip, Magneto ignited a flame.

"What's your name?" he asked.

"John."

"What's your *name*, John?" he asked again. John almost made the mistake of thinking the old git was deaf or senile, or stupid, asking the same question twice, until a flash of intuition told him it was some kind of test.

John reached across the aisle, extending the tip of his forefinger to touch the small flame and lift it from its cradle. Fire never burned him; the most he ever felt from the flames he manipulated was a warmth that reached deep inside his body. In his imagination he'd tell himself that it was the same kind of glow the sun felt high in the heavens. It was his secret, his special pleasure, and he'd always resented the fact that Charles Xavier's telepathy might have pried it from him without his knowing.

"Pyro," he said, absently rolling the flame between his fingers like a coin.

"That's quite a talent you have, Pyro," Magneto said. The way he said John's code name gave the boy a thrill of pleasure, like it was a title of some kind. But outwardly, his mouth twisted downward in irritation.

"I can only manipulate the fire," he confessed. "I can't make it."

He closed his hand around the flame, and it was gone.

"You are a god among insects," Magneto said. "Don't let anyone tell you different."

With that, he opened his own hand and used his magnetic power to float the lighter back to its owner.

John didn't flick the cap anymore, he just held the lighter and stared at his blurred reflection in the stainless-steel surface. Xavier had never said such things to him. At the school, the endless official mantras were "responsibility" and "control." He was almost a grown man, yet when it came to his mutant powers it was just like being in kindergarten. The teachers weren't impressed with the things he could already do with fire, they were more concerned with ethics and behavior. They were afraid of what they were, they wanted to hide.

He snorted—helluva lot of good that did. Maybe, if the soldiers had known what he could do, what Bobby could do if he weren't such a terminal wuss, what any of the kids could do, they'd have backed off and left them alone.

Magneto wasn't scared. That was obvious. He was ready to fight for what he believed in. Even though Charles Xavier was responsible for his capture and imprisonment, he was flying with the X-Men to the rescue. How, John wondered, *Pyro* wondered, could that possibly make him one of the "bad guys"?

And if Xavier were wrong about him, maybe the kids were wrong in their assessment of Xavier.

At Alkali Lake, William Stryker reviewed the security procedures from the control room. He wanted nothing left to chance. Electronic sensors were on line, video surveillance active and tracking, sentries posted, fast-reaction combat teams armed and ready.

He couldn't employ an AWACS here as he had over Westchester, but he had sufficient ground radar capability in place to create a secure airspace better than a hundred miles in diameter, backed up by Doppler imaging systems that would detect the heat signatures of any jet engine or the ripples in the air caused by its wake. He was confident nothing could approach them undetected, even so advanced a stealth airframe as Xavier's.

He didn't acknowledge it as the door opened behind him. He didn't have to. As Lyman and his escort entered the room, Yuriko Oyama stepped out of the background shadows to put herself between them and Stryker, poised on the balls of her feet, her fists clenched.

"Sir?" Lyman called to announce himself. Stryker shook his head ever so slightly at the faint tremolo to the man's voice. Yuriko had that effect on people when she was at ready to fight. They didn't know what to make of her, only that she was supremely dangerous.

Stryker spared a glance at their reflections in the inactive display screens mounted on the wall before him. He didn't reply at once, while he and Wilkins, the duty officer, continued through the checklist, and when he did his tone was curt and dismissive.

"Your men can wait outside, Mr. Lyman."

"Sir," Lyman acknowledged, and the others took up station outside. At a cue from Stryker, Yuriko stood down as well.

"The machine has been completed to your specifications," Lyman reported.

"Good."

"If I may ask, sir . . ." Lyman paused as though he'd come to a kind of inner crossroads. "Why are we keeping the children?"

In quick succession, Stryker activated the monitors. Six screens, six holding cells, six mutants, none of them very happy to be where they were. By contrast, Stryker was almost jubilant.

"I'm a scientist, Mr. Lyman," he replied. "When I build a machine, I want to know that it's working."

Lyman didn't understand.

"Consider them a . . . control group. Our living benchmarks. What happens to them shows us what's happening outside. If necessary we can adapt settings and protocols according to their reactions, for greater efficiency, greater potency."

"Sir, they're children," Lyman blurted out, a reflex that was more surprise than actual protest, and the instant Stryker met his eyes he regretted every word.

"They're mutants, Mr. Lyman," said the older man. "And this is war."

At that moment, the plane Stryker was so concerned about was sitting within a few miles of where he stood, in a patch of snowy woods. Yes, he'd modified his systems to compensate for the *Blackbird*'s stealth capabilities, but he hadn't taken into account the fact that Magneto's power deflected the radar pulses long before they reached the aircraft. Or Storm's control over the weather, which allowed her to smooth the air behind them and counteract the heat of the jet's exhaust.

They'd come in low and slow, taking the notion of nap-of-the-Earth flying to its extremes as they skimmed treetops when they had to and dropped beneath their branches when they could. Helicopter pilots would have thought twice about some of the maneuvers they employed. Jean spent most of their approach with her teeth gritted with determination—and her fair share of delight—because they were in violation of so many fundamental flight safety protocols that the computers refused to handle the approach. She was forced to fly the plane manually. At the same time, she'd cast her telepathy ahead of them, much like her own personal form of radar, to prevent them from stumbling over some stray sentry or other.

Once they were down, the stealth netting was once again deployed to cover the plane, to hide them from both visual and electronic detection. Internal systems were kept to a minimum to guard against any stray emissions. Given the terrain, the likelihood of them being spotted was minimal, but recent experience had inspired them all to be prudent.

Aboard, they integrated the data stolen from Stryker's offices by Mystique with the information Logan had brought back from his visit to construct a three-dimensional map of the installation, then projected it as a hologram for all to see.

There was nothing aesthetic about the dam, no attempt at the grandeur of Grand Coulee or Glen Canyon or Hoover. Engineers had thrown a massive wall across the valley, and that was that, although they'd constructed the dam in the shape of a shallow L. There were two active spillways along the long face of the dam, and another on the short leg, pouring a continual flow of water downriver. As well, two huge concrete trenches had been dug on each bank. One was dedicated to the hydroelectric generators that had originally provided power to the base; the other, which began where the short leg of the dam ended, was for safety, to allow for a controlled release in the event of a significant snowmelt.

The X-Men turned some of the government's technology to their own purposes by tapping into one of the same keyhole surveillance satellites that had spied on the mansion and downloading current pictures of Alkali

Lake. Presumably, when the complex had been abandoned, the emergency spillway had been intended to bleed off the excess capacity of the lake behind the dam. However, over time, it had become blocked by an accretion of broken timber and boulders from a succession of rock falls. Water hadn't flowed down that trench in a long time, and as a consequence, Alkali Lake itself had risen to dangerous levels.

The power trench looked clear, but the depth of snow that was visible made it plain that nobody had opened those gates in quite a while, either. Beyond, in an oval of land that had been stripped bare of trees, lay the surface structures of the Alkali base that Logan had explored only days before. As with every other aspect of the valley, there was an obvious air of abandonment.

"Surface scans are cold," Storm reported. "No electronics emissions, no power, no heat signatures. As far as the keyhole is concerned, this place is dead. Apparently for years."

"We're shielded," Jean pointed out.

Storm shrugged, tapped the control keypad, and the scene before them changed, presenting a different perspective of the base.

"The first image was a topographic representation of the area. This one"—she indicated various points on the display—"shows the density changes in the terrain. The lighter the coloration, the heavier the repetitive activity." To the naked eye, the right-hand spillway, the power trench, was covered with virgin snow. Under the enhanced imagery of the spy satellite, however, a vastly different picture emerged. The trench was covered with literally hundreds of colored lines, running the length of the spillway and up a ramp to the single road that terminated at the Alkali base. It didn't need a glance at the legend for everyone to realize that this was extraordinarily heavy activity, not simply in terms of raw numbers of vehicles but of their weight as well.

"Somebody's been very busy," murmured Jean.

"And it's fresh," Storm echoed.

"That's the entrance," Logan told them. When both women looked at him in curiosity, he shook his head. "I remember, okay? Sue me." Instead, they chuckled along with him.

Once more, Storm switched perspectives and focused on the spillway. Below the dam, the trench was displayed in varying shades of blue, whereas the surrounding landscape appeared in those of white.

"The legend tells us the depth of snow and ice that cover the ground," she said. "There's been recent water activity."

Jean sounded worried as she leaned close to the image. "If we go in there, Stryker could flood the spillway."

Storm looked to Nightcrawler. "Kurt, could you teleport inside?"

He shook his head. "I have to be able to see where I'm going. Otherwise, I might materialize inside a wall."

Logan stretched, cracking his joints in sequence. "I'll go," he said as casually as anyone else might announce they were going out for a carton of milk. "I have a hunch Billy will want me alive."

At last Magneto strolled into the cone of light thrown out by Storm's holograms.

"Logan," he said with so natural an air of command that all present automatically gave him their full attention, "whoever goes inside that dam needs to be able to operate the spillway mechanism and neutralize any other defenses. What do you intend to do, even if you knew what to look for and where to find it? Scratch the box with your claws?"

Logan almost told him—he almost gave the man a practical demonstration—but decided against both, contenting himself instead with hunching his shoulders and glowering, precisely the wounded response Magneto would expect from him. Magneto's game, he knew, was chess. Logan preferred poker, and he'd yet to meet anyone he considered his equal. He knew when to play a hand and when to keep his cards well hidden and needed no thought at all to decide which choice fit this moment best.

He glared defiant fury and growled, "I'll take my chances."

"But I," Magneto told him in a tone that brooked no argument, "won't."

This time Logan didn't try to hide as he made his approach to the base. He took a leaf from Magneto's book and walked up to the ruined and broken gates like he was monarch of all he surveyed, without a care in the world and with even less fear. He followed the ramp down to the base of the spillway and headed for the mouth of the tunnel they'd seen on Storm's hologram. The spillway followed the same brutally practical design scheme as the dam itself. There was no consideration of the surrounding environment: this was man imposing his rule on nature without regard for any consequences, only for the fulfillment of his desires. The spillway itself was as wide as a four-lane highway; you could drive a quartet of semis side by side with room to spare. The walls themselves rose as high as a small skyscraper, better than thirty meters, a hundred feet, and their appearance was more in keeping with a fortress than any dam Logan had ever seen. He'd never seen a more perfect killing ground.

He saw no sign of any cameras.

"Stryker," he called at the huge entrance to one of the tunnels. It reminded him of the Jersey entrance to the Lincoln Tunnel as his voice echoed and reechoed into the darkness.

He called Stryker's name again and added, "It's me, *Wolverine!*"

In the control room, Wilkins dialed up the speaker volume in time to catch the name and played with the controls on the panel in front of him to bring the intruder into focus. He turned two additional cameras to catch alternate views of the X-Man, and immediately started a diagnostic sweep of the external monitors to make sure he hadn't brought any friends.

"Look who's come home," Stryker murmured from above and behind Wilkins' chair. "The prodigal son returns—what is he doing?"

Apparently, from the evidence of the cameras, he was strolling down the entry tunnel.

"Is he alone?" Stryker demanded.

"Appears to be," Lyman replied. "All our scanners are clean, camera fields, too."

"Keep looking," Stryker told him, and then, "Send your team to collect him." He rounded on Lyman, poking him with a knuckle to the chest for emphasis. "Don't allow him inside until he's shackled—knuckles to chin! Once he's secure, bring him to me in the loading bay. Carefully, Mr. Lyman," he added, stopping his subordinate before Lyman had taken more than a step. "Very carefully."

Lyman nodded, remembering what had happened at the mansion. He'd do as he was told, he was too good, too well trained, a soldier to do otherwise, but if it was his call, he wouldn't have gone near the little man in the tunnel until his troops had shot him to pieces.

Ten meters ahead of Logan, a section of the tunnel wall suddenly opened and three troopers broke into view, leveling two HK MP5s with laser sights and a Smith & Wesson automatic assault shotgun with the big thirty-round box. He heard more movement behind him as another fire team took position, the troopers setting themselves in a triangular formation, with him in the center, allowing them clear fields of fire. Less danger of shooting their own guys. The shotguns were there to knock him off his feet, with a rate of fire comparable to a low-end submachine gun. Once he was down, their tactics told him, the others could finish him at their convenience.

He smiled. These guys were good, they'd learned from their last encounter with him.

"Don't move," yelled one of the troopers in front of him. "Stand where you are, hands in the air!"

Logan was impressed by their fire discipline and what that told him about their commander. Tone and body language made clear to Logan these troopers did indeed remember the fight at the mansion, the comrades and buddies they'd lost to his claws. They were itching to pull the trigger. All they lacked was the slightest excuse to justify it.

Instead, to their surprise—and disappointment—he did as he was told.

The troopers weren't gentle with him. Even though he offered no resistance, he collected a share of surreptitious punches and kicks as his hands were shackled together with his knuckles pressed up tight to both sides of his neck. The idea here was that any use of his claws would essentially cause him to decapitate himself. Stryker's curiosity was leavened by his malicious sense of humor—could Logan's claws, forged of pure adamantium, cut through his own skeleton, which was an amalgam of adamantium and bone? Could they slice through his vertebrae? He actually found that amusing, the tradition that worked for vampires possibly doing the same for this otherwise unkillable mutant.

The vehicular entrance to the loading bay was blocked by a set of sliding blast doors more appropriate to a bank vault, armored steel better than a foot thick. That's what Logan had noted during his initial reconnaissance, that the base had been designed as the ultimate prison. And that whatever had been incarcerated here during its heyday represented a serious threat. Couldn't have been Magneto, though, way too much metal. Or anyone like Cyclops, who could project beams of force. This place dealt with purely physical strength or—and here Logan's eyes flicked sideways to his imprisoned hands—weapons. That was the constant with these doors, they were all thicker than the length of his claws. He might be able to cut them, but not easily cut *through* them.

Custom built, perhaps, for one specific class of mutant—and then abandoned when the manifestation of other kinds of powers had rendered it obsolete?

The floor of the loading bay continued the same over-sized scale of the rest of the installation, with room to spare for a convoy of full-sized semitrailers. A dock ran across the length of the wall opposite the entrance, allowing access to the interior corridors of the base. A couple of military-painted Humvees were parked flanking Logan and his escort. Both vehicles carried powered miniguns, whose six-barrel Gatling configuration allowed them to unleash five thousand rounds per minute. They were manned, and the tension on the gunners was obvious. One false move, they'd fire until the barrels melted.

Their laser sights were aimed right at him.

Waiting on the dock were Stryker, Yuriko, and Lyman, whose hand rested on the butt of his holstered Beretta. He wasn't taking any chances, either.

Stryker was grinning broadly as he approached the prisoner, but with each stride his expression changed, triumph gradually giving way to confusion. His eyes narrowed as he began to examine Logan more and more intently.

He nodded, then asked, "Who do you think you're looking at?"

The troopers had no idea what he meant. The answer was obvious to them.

"Sir?" asked Lyman.

Stryker shook his head. "The one thing I know better than anyone else . . . is my own work."

He turned his back and said, "Shoot it."

By rights, the troopers with the miniguns should have opened fire—but their buddies were in the kill zone! Logan's escort started to respond, backing up to give themselves a better shot. In each case, though, there was a

moment's hesitation, born of surprise, as the soldiers
processed the unexpected order.

By the time they reacted, Logan was way ahead of
them. Before their disbelieving eyes, the prisoner's features blurred like watercolors in the rain. He grew taller,
slimmer, changed color, changed gender. With blinding
speed, the prisoner—a woman—*Mystique*—lashed out
to either side, kick to the chest, kick to the head, to deal
with the flanking guards. Hands slipped free of shackles
configured to wrists twice their size, and while she was
still in midair from the second kick, she hurled the cuffs
into the face of the guard behind her with force enough
to turn his features bloody and smash him to the ground.
As he fell, his finger spasmed on the trigger of his automatic shotgun, spraying the ceiling with round after
round of magnum buckshot. His shells hit some lights as
he fell, and apparently some power cables, too, because
the remaining lights started flickering like strobes.

Mystique was far faster than the troopers expected,
and incredibly agile—the gunners couldn't keep up with
her. With Stryker in the room, they dared not open indis-
criminate fire. She knew that, she used it, landing in a
spider crouch before leaping for the dock. Take him prisoner, the whole game changes. Kill him, it might even be
over.

She never even came close. Yuriko intercepted her in
midair with a speed and agility to match, and a strength
that left Mystique breathless. She caught Mystique by
the arm, twisted, and the moment her feet touched the
floor she hurled the blue-skinned invader all the way to
one of the parked Humvees.

Mystique heard yelling behind her, Stryker ordering
everyone present to start shooting. The gunner on the

Humvee, realizing his own danger, abandoned his post and dove frantically for cover. Yuriko's intention had been to bounce Mystique off the vehicle hard enough to leave her stunned. Even if it was just for a moment, that would be enough to give the others a target.

But just as Mystique had underestimated Yuriko, so, too, had Stryker's bodyguard made the same mistake.

Mystique pivoted in midflight so that she landed on her feet, touching down just long enough to use the hood of the Humvee as a launch point to hurl herself back onto the dock. Before a single trigger could be pulled, she disappeared down the adjoining tunnel.

Throughout the complex, alarms sounded; the halls and tunnels resounded with running feet and shouted commands as Stryker's men rushed to their stations. The airwaves filled with queries and orders, everyone demanding a fix on the intruder's position.

In the control room, Wilkins was trying his best to comply, using the computer to handle the search through one set of monitors while he controlled the second set manually along the tunnel Mystique had used to escape from the loading bay.

He caught sight of a familiar—and now very welcome—figure coming down the corridor and spun his chair around to face Stryker as the commander entered with an escort.

"Sir," Wilkins asked anxiously, "what's happening?"

Stryker glared hawklike at the monitors. "We have a metamorph loose," he said with a growl of barely suppressed rage. "She could be anybody."

"Anybody?" Wilkins found that hard to accept. And then his eyes widened as a second Stryker appeared on screen, accompanied by Lyman and Yuriko and a trio of troopers.

The Stryker standing beside him elbowed his escort in the belly. A second shot—a palm thrust to the face—put him down hard even as Stryker wrenched his MP5 off his shoulder. Wilkins was just starting to react, rising from his chair, grabbing for his sidearm, when the butt of the submachine gun snapped toward him at the full extension of "Stryker's" arm, connecting like a baseball bat with force enough to upend the chair. Like the guard, Wilkins was unconscious before he hit the floor.

Approaching the control room from outside, the real William Stryker watched in futility as his double blew him a kiss. Then the doors slammed shut in his face.

Inside, Mystique reverted to her baseline physiognomy and took a seat at the main console. Above her on the wall display were images of the captured children from Xavier's.

She paused a moment, looking at them one by one, as if to imprint their faces on her memory. That done, all business once more, she donned a communications headset and tapped a set of commands into the keyboard. The children vanished from view, replaced by a three-dimensional schematic of the base.

Then she made a call.

Ever since she'd left the *Blackbird*, all the others had heard over her com channel was a carrier wave of static, telling them she was off-line. Ever since she'd left, Logan had paced the length of the aisle, back and forth like a caged tiger. No one said a word to him, no one got in his way. He was convinced from the start this was a mistake, and each additional minute of silence made him that much more certain.

Until Mystique's cheery voice stopped him in his tracks.

"I'm in," she reported.

Magneto smiled proudly, and even Logan had to admit he had reason.

"She's good," he conceded.

"You have no idea," Magneto replied.

While the three X-Men finished their preparations, John Allardyce stood up.

"Let us help," he said. Behind him, Bobby and Rogue nodded assent.

Storm put a stop to that notion.

"You're not helping with anything," she told them.

John started to protest but said nothing as Storm held up her hand.

"If something . . . happens to us," she continued, speaking to them all, "activate the escape-and-evade flight sequence that's programmed into the autopilot, just the way we briefed you. Don't touch any of the controls, on the ground or in the air. The *Blackbird* will take care of you just fine. The autopilot will fly you home."

"Then what?" Bobby demanded. He didn't hide his thoughts. *Like any of us have a home to go to anymore. Or a school!*

"You've all got superpowers," Logan told him. "Figure it out."

# Chapter
# Fourteen

Outside the control room, Stryker wasn't a happy man. He tried his key card on the electronic lock; no joy. Same for the manual combination, punched into the keypad. Same for the override. He tried the backdoor codes that only he knew, that were hardwired into the system and guaranteed unbreakable.

The door didn't budge, and as he pounded his fist on its steel face in righteous frustration, he swore he could hear that blue-skinned shape-shifting mutant bitch laughing at him with every failed try.

"It's . . . a very thick door, sir," Lyman said, and Stryker stared at him incredulously, wondering if this was some lame attempt at humor or if the man was a total idiot.

"Yes," Stryker told him, giving vent to his rage with such vehemence that his men backed off a step. Even Yuriko looked anxious. "But she's in there—and *I'm out here!*"

He took a breath, then another, forcing himself to calm down.

"Isolate the systems and transfer operations to the backup command center," he ordered. "Chances are she's locked you out, same as she did with the door, but you never know. We might get lucky. Meanwhile, she's locked in. Get some charges, and blow the damn doors! Do it quickly, Mr. Lyman, and kill whoever's inside. No questions, no hesitation, no mercy. I want them dead, I don't care who they look like."

Inside, Mystique had indeed locked out all the secondary command nodes. For what it was worth, the computers and systems controlling the physical plant of the base were hers to control. Pity the intruder net wasn't operational anymore; life would have been so much simpler if she could just flood the tunnels with knockout gas. As well, time and neglect had taken their toll. There were entire sections of the complex she couldn't access.

Fortunately, that didn't apply to the external doors. She called up the loading bay on the menu and pressed the appropriate button. Obligingly, the monitor flashed the legend SPILLWAY DOOR OPEN.

There were still a handful of troops in the loading bay, and they reacted with surprise as the double doors separated and slid apart. Seeing who was standing on the other side, they went for their weapons. Mystique, watching on the monitor, shook her head: They had a lot more courage than brains.

Any one of the intruders could have dealt with the situation. Between Logan, Jean Grey, Storm, Nightcrawler, and Magneto, the troopers didn't have a chance. Not one got more than a step, did more than begin to move, before he was rendered unconscious.

In passing, Magneto looked up at the ceiling-mounted camera—his awareness of magnetic fields allowed him to sense the location of any power conduit or video link—and smiled. Mystique smiled back. This was going to be fun.

Payback was a bitch, and so was she.

She had no view of the hallway outside her door. One of Stryker's first orders must have been to disable all the external cameras covering the approaches to the control room. She could guess what was happening now.

A team of demolition experts were in the process of attaching C4 plastic explosives to the doorway, spiraling them outward from the central locking mechanism.

There was a crackle from one of the walkie-talkies, the faint sound of gunfire, and screams.

Lyman raised his own radio and said, "Post five, report."

He looked at Stryker, who nodded. They both knew what this meant.

Guns were leveled at the sound of running feet, forcing the two troopers racing around the closest corner to come to a quick stop, their hands raised clear of their weapons. Everyone was jumpy, but Stryker had trained them well. Discipline held.

"Sir," one of them reported, "someone's opened the loading bay doors. More mutants have entered the base."

"How many?" Stryker demanded.

"We don't know."

"Who are they?"

Both soldiers shook their heads. Anyone close enough to discover that crucial information hadn't been allowed to escape to report it.

"Should we engage them, sir?" Lyman asked

Stryker looked thoughtful.

"No," he said. "Have the rest of your troops meet us

outside the machine, with all the heavy ordnance they can carry.

"Keep working on the doorway," he told the demo team, and then, to the new arrivals, "You two are with me." He motioned for Lyman and Yuriko to accompany him as well as he strode briskly down the hall. "They can't stop anything," he said as an absolute statement of fact. "In fifteen minutes, they'll all be on their knees."

It was a morning to write home about, the sun still hidden below the horizon as the helicopter skated along the crest of the fog layer that shrouded the hills and hollows of the Hudson Valley. To anyone watching, this was just another corporate helo, taking care of one of the many moguls and high-ranking politicos who made their home in this part of Westchester County and neighboring Connecticut.

They'd made a quick and uneventful flight from Alkali Lake to the coast, but the closer they came to their destination, the harder it was for Charles Xavier to mask his impatience. Or keep tight rein on the niggling sense of dread that wandered the outermost regions of his awareness, where he rarely went.

At Xavier's mental direction, the pilot made a combat approach to the back lawn, swift and certain, popping over the surrounding trees and down to a safe landing in a matter of heartbeats.

Just as quickly, Cyclops helped Xavier from his seat and into his wheelchair. As Scott pushed him up the ramp to the terrace, Xavier had the pilot shut down the engines and then fall asleep.

Using telepathy, he'd been calling out to his students since they departed Alkali Lake, expanding his mental awareness as widely as possible in hopes of hearing an answer, no matter how faint. From Jean, at the very least, he should have received some response.

Now, at the mansion, he again felt that disquieting absence of contact.

"I don't like this, Professor," Scott said as they entered the foyer. He called out as loudly as he could, but all either man heard was the fading echo of their voices through the empty rooms and hallways. "Where is everyone?"

"See if you can locate the *Blackbird*, Scott," Xavier told him. "Use the transponder, try to raise the onboard computer. Find some way to contact Jean and Storm. I'll use Cerebro."

With a nod, Scott took off down the corridor, while Xavier turned his chair toward the elevators that gave access to the mansion's underground complex. It never occurred to him that Scott was violating protocol, not to mention common sense, by leaving him alone in a potentially hostile environment. And since he was resolutely ignoring that pernicious sense of dread that just wouldn't quit, he never turned his head to see Scott vanish behind him into thin air.

The hallways underground were as empty as those above as the elevator doors opened and he rolled out onto the polished floor. Until his ears caught the sound of crying.

He did a slow pivot at the main junction, where the two sets of corridors came together in front of the elevator to form yet another of the ubiquitous Xs that popped up throughout the complex.

"It's all right," he called, wondering why he couldn't pinpoint her location, either by sound or thought. "You can come out now."

He found her hiding in a corner of the computer room on the main floor of the mansion. She was far younger than any mutant of his experience, not yet of middle-school age, with blond hair and blue eyes and a classic peaches-and-cream complexion. Her eyes were very large and wounded and brimming with tears, and she wore a nightgown.

"Are they gone?" she asked tremulously, and Xavier knew she meant Stryker's invasion force. It didn't bother him in the slightest that a violent invasion of his school had left it in pristine condition. That wasn't important. Only this girl mattered, and his lost students.

"Yes," he replied. "Where are all the others?"

She shrugged.

"Then I guess we'll have to find them, won't we?"

He held out his hand. She took it. Together, they moved down the hallway toward the vaultlike door that was the entrance to Cerebro.

Xavier stopped in front of the retinal scanner, and once it had confirmed his identity, Cerebro greeted him politely. "Welcome, Professor."

The door cycled open, revealing the great spherical chamber beyond.

He smiled at the girl, she smiled back, but when he turned to wheel himself inside, she called out in a panic.

*"Please don't leave me!"*

Her cry went through him like a knife! How could he be so unthinking, uncaring? What sort of teacher was he, to abandon a child—especially after the traumas she must have suffered?

"Don't leave me," she begged. "Please!"

"All right," he said, projecting comfort and reassurance

with his thoughts to complement the smile on his face, the gentle tone of his voice. "You can come inside."

With a grateful smile of her own, so radiant it made Xavier's heart sing, she followed close behind him.

He never looked back. He never saw the polished floor of home fade to cracked and filthy concrete, never saw the twisted nightmare shape of Mutant 143 keeping pace with the girl whose image he was projecting into Xavier's mind or the pair of armed troopers standing with guns ready at the doorway, just in case.

Xavier thought he was free, but in truth he'd never left Alkali Lake. He was more a prisoner than ever, and for Jason Stryker, he was the best toy he'd ever have to play with. A mind of sublime grace, of infinite possibilities, that when he was done with it would be a wasteland.

This would be such fun.

Stryker had just reached Xavier's location when he got a call from the demo team. They were ready. He was curt with them—they had their orders, what were they waiting for? Blow the door and slaughter that shape-changing bitch before she caused any more trouble.

The hallway was crowded with Lyman's fire team, a reinforced squad of a dozen men, carrying automatic and heavy weapons. Given their equipment and position, they were a match for ten times their number and more.

"Mr. Lyman," Stryker told his subordinate, "position your men."

Leaving Lyman to do that job, trusting him to do it right, Stryker followed Xavier's path into the hollow chamber, along the gantry extension to the circular platform at the end, which was a makeshift replica of the original back at Xavier's.

The control console wasn't pretty to look at, none of this was, but what mattered was that the stolen components all worked here precisely as they did in the true Cerebro chamber. Xavier sat in his proper place before the console, with 143 behind him and a little to the side. Neither mutant responded to Stryker's presence, and that made the older man smile. The greatest mutant mind on earth was aware of nothing beyond what Stryker allowed. Charles Xavier, reduced to the level of a performing seal. It almost made Stryker laugh.

That would wait till later. He was here on business.

He leaned close to his son's ear and whispered his instructions.

Xavier thought he heard something—*damn* that buzz in the back of his head, why wouldn't it go away?—but thought nothing more of it as the girl touched his arm and whispered in his ear.

"Is it time to find our friends?"

Xavier's heart leaped as though he had been empty and now had purpose. He'd never felt such glory, it was almost rhapsodic.

"Yes," he said, and meant it with all his heart.

Stryker whispered to his son . . .

. . . and Mutant 143, through the image of the girl . . .

. . . whispered to Xavier.

"All of the mutants," she asked. "Everywhere?"

"Oh, *yes,*" Xavier replied. Before him the path to fulfillment was laid out, as straight and clear as a highway. And yet . . .

Always "and yet." Try as he might to embrace this wonderful moment, something kept holding him back, trying with ferocious persistence to pull him away. It refused to be ignored, it wouldn't be denied.

Fortunately, the girl's voice was stronger.

"Good," she said.

"Good," said Stryker, all to himself. He started to lay his hand on 143's shoulder, came so close they almost touched—then pulled himself away and curled his fingers into a protective fist. For that moment, he had seen 143 not as a tool, a weapon in the fight to defend humanity, but as his son.

That was uncharacteristic of him. It was weak. Now, more than ever, that was an emotion he could not afford and would not countenance.

With military bearing and precision, Stryker turned on his heel and strode from the chamber. He didn't look back. He would never have to see Mutant 143 again. The images of his son that he would keep with him would be from before, the mahogany-haired boy with round cheeks and a ready giggle who loved to ride on Daddy's shoulders and who Stryker loved more than his own life.

The world that was, the world that should have been, but for Xavier and those like him. The world he would pay any price to restore.

If Jason knew any of this, he didn't seem to care. What fascinated him was his new toy, and his mismatched eyes began to dilate and glow as he began to play.

Xavier finished his preparations and smiled at his companion.

"Just don't move," he warned the girl, speaking gently so as not to frighten her.

He donned the helmet, settling it comfortably on his head and himself comfortably in his chair.

The walls around him fell away, and just for a moment, as his perspective and perceptions expanded outward to encompass the chamber, he jumped. Because on the platform with him wasn't a girl at all but the twisted horror that was Jason Stryker.

No, he was wrong. It was only the girl. Strange how he never noticed her eyes before. One green, the other blue. Almost hypnotic in their brilliance.

Around him appeared a holographic representation of the globe, just as he'd manifested for Logan only days before. He and the girl floated in its center, at the heart and core of the world.

He exhaled, and as his breath rushed from his body it was as if he'd separated into a million million versions of himself, racing through fire and stone and steel and concrete, through earth and water and air, to every point on the planet where a mutant could be found. And not just the active ones, the comparative few who had manifested their unique abilities or were on the cusp of doing so, but the latents as well. Every person who possessed the mutator pairings in their genome, even if it was only potential and unlikely to be activated for one or two generations yet to come, was revealed to him. He'd never dreamed there could be so many.

He found one sitting in a poker game in New Orleans, another wandering the Scots highlands picking heather to serve as a decoration at Moira MacTaggart's dinner table; he found a spectacularly beautiful woman serving as a lifeguard on Bondi Beach and an ancient aborigine sitting cross-legged at the summit of Uluru, the sacred rock of his people. He found a young boy who looked like a bird and a quintet of ash-blond psychics who were perfect copies of one another yet wholly unrelated. He found telepaths and telekines, he found energy casters and others who absorbed energy as sustenance. He found mutants with strength, and mutants with skill, some who could fly or run like the wind or who made their home in the ocean. He found one who could fold herself flat as paper and another who could transform into any substance in the periodic table simply by tearing off her skin. He found some born to be predators, others who were prey, and a vast majority who hadn't yet come to that crossroads.

He saw a world ready to tear itself apart, poised on the cusp of what was and what might yet be—and knew in that blinding flash of insight that in his hands lay the responsibility to manage that change, to help determine whether the future was one of bright and infinite possibilities or one where the planet was covered pole to pole with graves.

Each mutant was a scarlet candle against the darkness of forever—yet beside them glowed the golden candle of those who weren't mutants, equally bright, equally to be cherished. They were inextricably bound, these children of Mother Earth, and Xavier found here the proof of what he'd always known in his heart, what he'd always been unable to present to Eric Lehnsherr, that you could not safeguard the one without protecting the other.

At his direction, Cerebro came fully on-line and up to speed, making its presence known with a deep and resonant hum that gradually increased in intensity.

Hearing that hum, Stryker allowed himself a smile. He laid his hand on Lyman's shoulder.

"Guard this post, Mr. Lyman. That's the order."

"Yes, sir."

"From this point on, kill anyone who approaches. Even if it's me."

"Yes, sir."

"God bless you, men. God give us this day!"

Stryker returned Lyman's salute as though they were on a parade ground at West Point, trooping the colors before the massed corps of cadets, did an about-face, and strode away, Yuriko marching alongside in cadence.

Lyman watched them until they were both swallowed in darkness, then turned back to his men, to review their positions and their ammo loads. This would be a bear fight, he knew, but this was also what he and his men had trained for. They'd be ready, come what may, and they would prevail.

The explosion caught Mystique by surprise: the demo team was quicker than she'd anticipated. The door buckled inward as if it had been punched by some monstrous fist, and her ears rang with the shock wave of the blast. She dove for the MP5 she'd set on the console. She had few illusions about her chances for survival, but she also had three full magazines and a couple of grenades. At the very least, she'd give Stryker's bully boys a fight. She couldn't help wishing to be a little more like Rogue, though, so that when she manifested another's form and features, she also assumed their skills as well. Namely Wolverine's. Now would be a nice time to possess the runt's healing factor.

The first detonation didn't do the trick, it just warped the door in its frame and slightly popped one of the hinges. Mystique wondered what would come next and assumed it wouldn't be pretty. Any explosive strong enough to breach this door would create a blast effect capable of squishing every living thing inside the room to jelly. Cheerful.

Unexpectedly, the door started groaning as it was subjected to stresses well beyond its design tolerances. Like a
cork from a bottle of heavily shaken champagne, it
popped from its frame, outward into the corridor, to
land against the opposite wall with a crash so resounding
it shook this whole section of the complex.

She didn't need to be told who was responsible, and
when Magneto stepped over the threshold, she greeted
him with a round of heartfelt and appreciative applause.

The demo team and the guards, Mystique saw when
she peered outside, were safely in Jean Grey's custody,
squirming upside down in midair where her telekinesis
was holding them. Their weapons, the young woman
had separated into component parts and scattered. As
Mystique watched, Jean tossed her prisoners against the
wall. She didn't do it so very hard, they couldn't have
been much hurt, but from the way they collapsed to the
floor Mystique assumed she'd used her mental powers to
render them unconscious.

She reentered the room to find Magneto staring at the
console.

"Eric," she said to greet him as she joined him by his
side.

The look he gave her in return told her how glad he
was to see her alive and unharmed.

"Have you found it?"

She called up the power grid on the main display.

"The hydroelectric net is still functional and has been
reestablished by Stryker, with a large portion of it being
diverted"—she pointed to one of the sectors of the complex, an area where she had no video capability—"to
this chamber. It's new construction."

"My fault, I'm afraid," Magneto conceded as the

X-Men joined them. "Can you shut it down from here?" he asked Mystique.

"No."

Logan held back, his attention caught by familiar figures on one of the active security screens: Stryker and Yuriko, both in a hurry. He opened his mouth to report the sighting, then reconsidered and tapped a location query into the system. He looked toward Jean, then back to the monitor, and his dilemma was obvious: Should he go for Stryker or stay with the X-Men? He owed Jean the world, but Xavier?

"Come," Magneto said to Mystique. "We have little time."

Jean blocked him. "Not without us."

Mystique tapped the keyboard, and the kidnapped students appeared once more on their respective monitors.

"My God," Storm exclaimed, "the children! Kurt?" She didn't need to ask any more than that; he knew what she wanted, and he answered with a nod.

"Will you be all right?" Storm asked Jean, who was staring straight at Mystique. Jean knew exactly what was happening here, that Magneto had a private agenda, that Mystique had acted to divide the X-Men's forces and limit their ability to forestall his plan, whatever it was.

"Yeah," she told her best friend. "I'll be fine." Because she had Wolverine as backup. "Logan?"

No answer.

"Where's Logan?" Storm demanded when a look around the room and the hallway outside revealed no sign of him.

Jean had to confess to herself she wasn't surprised, but

there was disappointment in her voice as she replied, "He's gone. We'll have to manage without him."

For Xavier, thanks to Cerebro, the psychic links he'd established with the world's mutants were solid, had been from the first moment of contact. He'd never run Cerebro at such a level, nor stretched his power to such a degree, as much because of the risk to those he contacted as to himself. He knew already that the cost to himself when this session was over would be considerable, he already could feel the initial stages of what would be a killer of a migraine.

He'd done what had been asked of him, what he knew was necessary, yet he couldn't bring himself to tell the little girl.

"That's odd," he temporized. "I can't seem to focus on anyone." That was true. With all the contacts he'd made, none had been with any of his missing X-Men or with his students. He knew they were out there, he just couldn't *see* them—which bothered him, considering how clearly he could interface with all the others.

"Maybe you have to concentrate harder," the girl suggested.

Xavier increased the gain, and the hum from Cerebro grew deeper and more intense.

"Wait," Jean told her companions, holding out her hand to bring them to a stop. She, Magneto, and Mystique were deep inside the complex, a section that had been hollowed out of the rock right beneath the dam, which accounted for the dank air and never-ending seepage down the seams in the walls. She shut her eyes and concentrated a moment.

"I feel something," she said. And then brightened with a smile. "I think it's—*Scott!*"

Her call was answered with fire, a beam of glittering scarlet that erupted out of the darkness ahead to shatter a chunk of wall between Jean and the others with force enough to scatter shards of stone like shrapnel. As she dived clear of the beam's path, Jean threw a telekinetic cloak over her companions, to deflect the brunt of the debris clear of them, trusting the body armor components of her own uniform to protect her.

"My dear," she heard Magneto call from behind, "this is the kind of lovers' quarrel we cannot afford right now."

"Go!" she snapped over her shoulder. "I'll take care of him."

She had sight of him now. His face showed no expression, no reaction whatsoever to the sound of her voice calling his name. She tried reaching him with her thoughts but encountered a void whose only awareness was of an icy oblivion that radiated outward from a point at the base of his skull. She didn't need to see the circular scar on his neck to know that what had been done to Nightcrawler and to Magneto had now been done to Scott. Until the drug wore off, or she somehow broke its hold on him, he would keep fighting, without remorse or mercy.

Magneto and Mystique started to back away, and their movement caused Cyclops to fire again. This time Jean was ready, deflecting the optic blast to one side so that it gouged a shallow trench along the far wall. At the same time, she gestured with her own hand, radiating her telekinesis outward to slap him invisibly in the chest, hard enough to throw him off his feet.

She started running toward him, pushing him up and back through the air, increasing his speed as she did her own, gritting her teeth with the effort as he struggled— harder and with a lot more purpose than the soldiers earlier—to break her hold on him. Whatever control Stryker established allowed him to access all his victims' skills and training. Scott and she had often practiced how best to use her powers in combat, in part by figuring out how to compensate for them. Now he was turning that knowledge against her.

The corridor ended in a wall. She slammed him into it as hard as she could. Trouble was, he was wearing his uniform, and it protected him from the impact same as it had her from the shrapnel.

He fired again, forcing her to duck, and he hit a Humvee parked in an alcove, flipping the four-ton vehicle over onto the one parked next to it. As she scrambled up, she lost her hold on him, and Scott flipped himself over the balcony railing.

She rushed after him and found herself overlooking darkness, a room whose dimensions were totally hidden in shadow. Muttering a string of passionate curses that would have impressed Logan, she started to contact the others, to warn Magneto that she'd lost Cyclops. Only then did she realize that in the chaos of the moment, she'd lost her com set.

She stepped back from the railing and hunkered down to reduce her target profile while she considered her next move. She still had a sense of Scott's thoughts, enough to know he was unhurt and mobile, but she couldn't pinpoint his position. Worse, she still couldn't reach him, and the sound of gears and motors grinding from below would make the hunt downstairs even more difficult.

"Oh, Scott," she sighed. He was the strategist, the natural combat leader. It was more than training; it was something he excelled at, that he was born to do. She was the doctor, her role had never been more than backup. Every time they'd ever sparred, loser buys the beer, she was the one who ended up buying.

Slowly she got to her feet. It wasn't as if she had any real choice.

The kids were scared. The kids were bored. The kids were angry—at being left behind, at hearing no word, at not knowing when (not if, but *when*) some mook of Stryker's was going to find them. The grown-ups had promised to keep them in the loop, but all they heard from the radio was static.

John decided he'd had enough.

"That's it," he announced, and pressed the switch that extended the main ramp.

"Where d'you think you're going, John?" Bobby challenged.

"Where d'you think, moron? I'm tired of this kid's table shit."

Bobby started to his feet: "You'll freeze," he said, "before you make it to the spillway."

"I don't think so," John retorted.

"John, they told us to stay here," Rogue protested.

For a moment the two boys glared, ready to take out their tensions and frustrations on each other. Rogue wondered if Bobby really would use his ice power to stop John, and how hard John would use his flames to fight back.

"John!" she called, pleading, deliberately stepping between them.

That broke the moment. The look John gave Bobby was ugly and filled with warning, but what he offered Rogue was a grin, just like the Johnny of old, complete with a wink.

Then he was gone, at a trot across the hard-packed snow, defying the arctic temperatures. Rogue stepped past Bobby to the controls, but she made no move to raise the ramp. She knew how John felt, and a large part of her wanted to follow.

Jean descended the staircase at a run, hitting the floor in a roll that took her to cover amid the ranks of hulking, spinning generators, each the size of a modest one-story house.

She knew he'd be waiting and had an idea where he'd be. Most of all, she was fairly certain what he'd do.

He didn't disappoint.

There were two ways down to his level: either pitch herself over the balcony, as he'd done, or use the stairs. He'd want a position that gave him a ready line of sight of both options. Taking her on the fly was risky. Better to wait until she landed and was trying to get her bearings.

As she came up into a crouch, he fired, from off to her right. For anyone else, the time you saw his beam—moving at the speed of light—was the time it hit you. In Jean's case, her parry occurred at the speed of thought. Concept and execution happened instantaneously, so that Cyclops' optic blast crashed against the invisible barrier of her telekinesis.

The problem was, since his beam was trying its best to make like an irresistible force, she needed a way to brace the wall that protected her, to make herself the next best thing to an immovable object.

Didn't work. The telekinesis held, her feet didn't, and she felt herself slide backward along the floor.

Cyclops advanced on her, implacable as an automaton, adjusting his visor to hone his beam to maximum intensity.

The point of intersection where his energies met hers began to glow, like steel in a furnace, generating a radiance so bright Jean had to cover her eyes.

She was screaming, not in fear but in defiance, calling his name over and over again, trying every way she could imagine, with voice and thought, to reach him.

"Scott," she bellowed, as into the teeth of a hurricane, "please! Remember who you are! Who *I* am! Don't do this!"

She could feel his optic blast gnawing away at her shield, shattering the bonds of energy that kept her safe. There was a way to beat him, by splitting her teke and hurling it into him like worms, to burrow into the vulnerable places of his body. She was a doctor, she knew precisely where and how to do the most damage—to incapacitate or worse. She could block his airway or one of the valves of his heart or possibly interdict the smooth flow of neural transmissions along his central nervous system. But the initial attack had been too quick and too wild for her to make the attempt. She had had a chance when he came at her here on the floor, but she held back a fatal moment, afraid of her control—or lack of it. One thing to try this maneuver in the controlled conditions of the danger room, with sensors monitoring every conceivable aspect of the subjects' physiological condition and a full-spectrum medical facility only steps down the hall. Another to do it in the field, in a fight, where a single mistake could prove fatal.

She knew now how right that last was, only she was the proof, not Scott.

He'd upped the power ante faster and farther than she'd expected. She couldn't spare even one iota of teke to strike back at him, he'd break through her shields for sure. Yet doing nothing would have the same result.

She couldn't kill him.

She refused to be beaten.

And something awakened within her. A chord of celestial music that she'd always been aware of on the outermost edges of her being, from the moment she first used her powers, only now it wasn't a faint trill of notes but a full-throated symphony, a crescendo that rolled through her like a tsunami. She thought at first it would overwhelm her, but instead, with a joy so pure it could never be described or even remembered in full measure, she found herself riding the crest of this impossible wave, surfing creation the way she always yearned to do on water.

The air rippled around her as though it were a pool she'd just fallen into, and it began to glow, a roseate corona that flowed swiftly to her outstretched hand and beyond, to crash against the pinpoint needle of energy that was Cyclops' optic blast.

Jean bared her teeth and pushed herself to her knees, bracing one foot under her as she struggled upright, the raw emotion on her face in stark contrast to the total absence of any on Scott's.

The nimbus around her changed aspect as she fought, creating a suggestion more of fire than light and the sense of wings flaring outward from her back—not so much like an angel, although that would be an easy and under-

standable mistake. This was more akin to some predatory bird, a raptor, rising to the attack.

Between them though, the very fabric of reality twisted
under their combined onslaught. Cyclops' power was
considerable, but ultimately it was tangible. He actually
had limits. So did Jean, but where his were physical, hers
were solely of her imagination and of her will.

She took a halting step forward, pushing with her
thoughts as well as her body, and cheered to herself as
she moved Scott's optic blasts back toward him.

Her triumph was short-lived. These two combatants
weren't the only elements in this battle with limits. The
same applied to the physical world that lay between
them. They were battling each other on levels from the
paranuclear to the subatomic, and as Jean's resistance
surged to new and unexpected levels, as the energies employed increased exponentially, the heat and pressures
they unleashed triggered an equal and opposite reaction.

In effect, they created a molecular protostar, a local-
ized version of the Big Bang.

For a fraction of a nanosecond, a time so small it was
virtually immeasurable, they had a taste of creation.
Luckily for them and for their world, the fabric of reality—
already weakened by their struggle—tore wide open under
this incredible onslaught, allowing the bulk of the energies to vent into some other, wholly unfortunate plane of
existence. All the two combatants were aware of was an
impossible radiance that reduced the brightness of the
noonday sun to the level of a very dim bulb, and an explosion more impressive in every respect than one of
Storm's pet thunderclaps.

The concussion sent both of them flying. Scott, dazed
and shaken, went skidding and tumbling along the floor

for pretty much the length of the room. Jean wasn't so fortunate. Her flight was shorter, her landing harder, and she cried out as her leg caught on a corner of pipe and snapped like a dry branch.

The effects of the explosion radiated outward from the source, making themselves felt in every corner of the complex. The generator room itself shook like it was in the middle of an earthquake, the big machines rattling and groaning as they tried to cope with stresses that pushed the limits of their design specs. Dust and more fell from the ceiling, and off in the distance there was a resounding *clang* as a stretch of iron railing gave way.

High up in the shadows, unnoticed, a seam opened in the wall . . .

. . . and water began to leak through.

The shock knocked Stryker off his feet and would have left him bloody had Yuriko not been there to catch him. He muttered darkly as he brushed the dust from his clothes, then stopped cold as a drop of water splashed onto one lens of his glasses. He looked up to behold a spidery network of cracks in the ceiling, from which water was now falling in a steady drip. He actually shuddered at the sight.

A quick walk brought him and Yuriko to the one of the dam's monitor stations. A glance at the rusted, decaying, but still functional dials on the wall told him all he needed to know.

Early in his career, before Jason, before marriage, he'd been a field agent. Black ops. He'd attended a course in sabotage, a seminar on how to blow a dam. There were basically two ways to do it. You either dropped a really big bomb, or succession of bombs, in just the right place—

as the British did to the Germans in World War II—or you set off a much smaller bomb, also in just the right place, and let the dam itself do the rest. The key to a dam is its structural integrity, because the pressure of the water it's restraining is relentless. That's why public safety mandates that all such structures be scrupulously maintained. The slightest flaw, if unchecked, could lead to disastrous consequences.

This dam had essentially been left to rot. No one was interested in dismantling it, so the secondary spillway had been left open to drain the lake. Over the subsequent years, in part to hide what had happened here, the dam had been filed and forgotten. No one came to check on its condition, no one realized—until Stryker arrived to reopen the facility—that the open spillway had become hopelessly clogged and Alkali Lake itself had gradually filled almost to overflowing.

Now this explosion, whatever its cause, had provided the final, fatal catalyst. Because of the weight of water pressing on the dam, these cracks that now appeared miniscule would quickly grow and spread until the entire structure collapsed.

The complex was doomed. The only question was how long they had. He did some fast calculations, couldn't quite make them fit. Too many unknowns. So he decided then, as an act of will, that it would last until his work was done. He'd come too far, worked too hard, to accept even the possibility of failure. Or of defeat. His cause was just, therefore he would prevail.

"Time to go," Stryker told Yuriko, and they did, quickly.

\* \* \*

Jean heard him coming, boot heels striking the floor in a steady, robotic cadence that was totally unlike him, and she wailed silently to herself. He wasn't unconscious and he wasn't free and he was on his way to finish her off.

She tried to shift position, but her broken leg was agony. She couldn't muster concentration enough to neutralize the pain or to stop her lover.

*Screw that,* she thought, and tried again, marshaling her strength of body and will, first dampening the pain in her leg to a dull but manageable ache and then calling out to Scott, not with her voice, but with her mind.

She said his name, but what reached out to him was so much more. It was the sense of her, the emotions he stirred in her heart and those she sensed in turn from him. She took the world as it was when they were apart and then what it felt like when they were together, and it was the difference between a wasteland and a paradise. There was passion and comfort and need and joy, there was a strength that knew no boundaries, a sense of kindred souls made one, and that whole being far, far greater than the sum of its parts.

She opened her soul to him, holding back only that part of her that even now thought only of Logan, and realized as she did so that this was the part she would call upon if worst came to worst and she found herself with no other option but to kill.

Through the impenetrable fog of his mind she sensed him reaching for his visor and remembered absurdly the night they'd spent watching one of Scott's favorite movies, Robert Wise's classic *The Day the Earth Stood Still*. She remembered the climactic moment when Patricia Neal had been cornered by the robot Gort and how his visor glowed like Scott's as it opened to reveal the deadly beams within.

*Scott,* she called with her thoughts, *please—*
*Scott!*

His hand trembled, his mouth working as he struggled to speak. His breathing quickened, his hands clenched to fists, and there were flashes of light within his mind as he fought his way through the fog, calling out himself in answer to her cries.

Then, suddenly, he was crying aloud, desperate incoherent sounds like a man might utter clawing his way up from some abyss of the spirit, culminating in a great and awful scream that made her own pain insignificant by comparison.

He collapsed to his knees and sobbed, taking in breaths of air in huge, noisy gulps, a drowning man who'd finally reached the surface long after he thought all was lost.

He flinched when she touched him, curling in on himself, startled and terrified, too much like a dog who expected nothing but beatings. That made her angry, because this was her man and he was none of those things.

She touched him lightly once more on the face, but with her thoughts she enfolded him in warmth, in strength, in passion. She let him see reflected in her vision of him the man she knew he was, who made her complete.

*It's okay, Scott,* she told him telepathically and said the same aloud: "It's okay, it's me. It's *me*!"

And as he looked up in relief, she took him in her arms, burying her face in the hollow between neck and shoulder so he couldn't see her. That made her smile in-side, although there was no humor in it. It was easy to be strong for others but when it came to herself—well, that was a different chapter entirely. But she didn't want him to know what had happened, not yet. Let him heal just a little more, let him come a bit more wholly back to him-self, then he could handle it.

"You're hurt," he said.

"You're right," she grimaced. "Help me up, please."

"I'll carry you."

"Like hell. I'm a telekinetic, remember? I can make myself a splint and crutches all in one."

"Really?"

"If I'm wrong, sweetie, you'll be the first to know."

"Jean," he said, and then, haltingly, "I—I'm sorry."

She kissed him on the edge of his mouth, glad that the difference in height between them allowed her to keep her face shadowed.

"It's okay. It's okay. I . . . I was so afraid I'd lost you."

"Thanks" was all he said, but she could see the emo-tions that went into that single word, and she hugged him for it.

A moment later, her expression changed and she looked around the room in alarm.

"Scott," she said urgently, frustrated that she couldn't tell him why, "something's wrong!"

Mystique had printed out a map, showing the route to where the children were imprisoned. Storm and Night-crawler covered the distance in record time. Nightcrawler was right at home, racing as easily along the walls and ceiling as the floor, as limber crouched on all fours as standing erect on both legs. Storm wasn't anywhere near as confident, physically or emotionally. She didn't like being underground or in confined spaces. She thought she'd put those childhood fears behind her long ago and didn't appreciate discovering she might have been wrong.

At last they came to a room that was essentially the lip of a broad and deep pit. Surveillance cameras were mounted at intervals around the circular ceiling, allowing an unrestricted view of the hole. She'd seen on the control room monitors that deep parallel slashes had been gouged in the walls, at a height that suggested a man Logan's size. Such a person couldn't climb out, he couldn't jump out, there were no doors to be seen; the only possible mean of ingress or egress to the pit was a hoist on a sliding boom set in the ceiling. The room itself had a single doorway, and it was ringed by the ruins of a rubber gasket, which meant that in better days the entrance could have been sealed airtight. Alternating with the camera mounts around the ceiling were ventilation grilles. It didn't take much imagination to realize that gas could be introduced to the room instead of air, to deal with any prisoners who decided to get rowdy.

If this was a holding pen, it was designed by people who took no chances.

*Damn them,* she thought with unusual vehemence. *What did they want from him? What did they* do *to him?*

And then, more ominously, *What does Stryker intend with us?*

"Who's down there?" she called.

"Jubilation Lee," came the immediate reply. "Is that you, Ororo? Can you help us?"

"Hey, would I have come all this way if I couldn't?" She

looked sideways at Nightcrawler. "Kurt, could you—"
She didn't have to finish, he was already gone.

The kids, of course, had no idea who he was. Two girls
took one look at him and shrieked in terror, backing all
the way across the pit while Jubilee and Artie, one of the
boys, took station between them. The boy was ready to
fight—he even stuck out his forked tongue to try to scare
Nightcrawler, which he actually found quite amusing—
but Jubilee looked more curious than defiant. She assumed that if Storm was up top, then this had to be one
of the good guys. If it wasn't, since Stryker had given
them some kind of drug to inhibit their powers tem-
porarily, they were all pretty much screwed anyway.

Nightcrawler gently motioned her aside and spoke to
the frightened pair of girls.

"My name's Kurt Wagner," he told them. "Although
in the circus ring I'm better known as Nightcrawler. Perhaps you've heard of me?"

Blank looks all around.

"Ah, well. Some other time, perhaps. Come to me,
please," and he waved his fingers to urge them closer.
"It's all right. You've nothing to fear from me, I'm just
going to take you for a little jaunt."

"Can't Storm do this?" one of the boys asked.

"Don't be an ass," Jubilee told him. "There isn't
enough volume of air in here for her to generate sufficient wind. What're you going to do," she asked Nightcrawler, "climb the walls?"

"Not exactly," he replied. He wrapped arms and tails
around one of the frightened girls, who'd responded to
his call and stepped up close to him. "Now," he told her,
"close your eyes."

*Bamf.*

He was gone.

And a moment later, with the girl's excited cries echoing down from the floor above, he was back.

Logan didn't need a map, he just followed his nose. He had Stryker's scent, and since she was the only woman in the place, aside from Mystique and his fellow X-Men, he had no problem isolating Yuriko's scent as well. He could follow and find them anywhere now, no matter how cold the trail.

Suddenly he stopped. Another scent, one he never thought anything about, because it was a part of him.

He turned and thought about his first visit and the wolf he'd followed downstairs. This was a whole different section of the base, and a lot deeper. Nothing about the surroundings was familiar, and yet . . .

*Snikt!*

There were three slash marks in the wall, at the top of a flight of stairs. They reminded him of a book he'd read wintering up North of Sixty, waiting out a storm in a trapper's cabin. Jules Verne's *Journey to the Center of the Earth*. The explorers there had followed a trail left by their predecessor, a man named Arne Saknussemm, who'd blazed the way by leaving three parallel slashes in the rock.

He held up his claws. They fit as perfectly here as they had in the marks he'd found up top. He heard screams, but only in memory, and smelled blood that strangely seemed as fresh as if it had just been spilled. He'd fought his way out of here, of that he was certain.

Why hadn't they ever tried to find him? Why had he been brought here in the first place?

He clenched his fist, keyed the trigger in his nervous system, and put the claws away.

*Snakt!*

Only one man with the answers.

Moving fast, Logan descended the stairs.

Artie was the last. He looked a little wobbly as Night-crawler let him go, but then so did the indigo-skinned mutant himself, and Storm caught him by the arm as he swayed on his feet.

"It's harder with a passenger," he confessed. "And when I transport six—"

"I'm proud of you," she said. "Consider this a good deed to counterbalance all those sins."

He smiled in gratitude, but only for a moment as Artie protested, "I think I have to throw up."

"It's hard *for* my passengers, too, I'm afraid," he confessed further. "But the nausea will quickly pass."

Not soon enough for Artie, who bent double and promptly expelled all the food he'd ever gworfed in his life. Storm held his head until he was done, then manifested a tiny cloud of rain to wash his face clean. That's when the room shook around them, and when she decided the quicker they were quits of this awful place, the better for all concerned.

The stairs led Logan to a lab that, like the rest of the base, had seen better days. It was circular, with massive cylindrical columns supporting a large ring in the center. Unlike most of the other sections of the base, however, this one hadn't been stripped to the walls. It looked almost . . . operational.

In his mind's eye, the room wasn't empty. He counted at least a dozen ghouls on hand for every session, wearing a freakish kind of armored surgical moon suit that was designed to protect the wearer not only from biological contamination but from physical attack as well. By sight, he couldn't tell men from women, young from old. They all had the same face, and that was the visor of their helmets. Scents were how he told them apart, except for Stryker. He remembered now that Stryker was the only one unafraid to show his face. It was important to him to be seen, and Logan wondered now if that was why Stryker had seemed so disappointed when Logan didn't recognize him at the mansion.

This was a surgical suite, and as he circled the room, unconsciously keeping well clear at first of the tank in its center, he noted the carts on which the nurses had piled the necessary medical instruments. The usual collection of scalpels and hemostats, scissors and retractors and clamps, but that wasn't all, it wasn't even close. There were tools he couldn't name, whose purpose he didn't know, but the mere thought of them sent an unaccustomed thrill of horror up his spine.

Along the wall there was a bank of light boxes, where they would clip the X rays before going to work on him. They always let him see what was there, they always told him what they planned to do, they wanted him to know . . . they wanted him to know . . . they wanted him to know . . .

All that care and effort and . . . *consideration*—for nothing.

One of the X rays had been him. Some of them looked like monsters, all of them were of mutants. Maybe all of them were him? Maybe *he* was the monster? He didn't know.

He remembered what Xavier had told him—maybe he

didn't *want* to know? Right now, that didn't seem like so bad an idea.

Finally he forced himself to the tank. He'd thought it was empty, hoped it would be empty, but he was wrong. It was filled with an oily amber liquid and above it, suspended from the ring, a battery of instruments more appropriate to a slaughterhouse than a hospital. On pedestals beside the tank were what appeared to be molds: one with a set of three channels, needing no explanation, another with five, longer and slimmer and altogether quite elegant.

Next to the tank, at its head, was a large cylinder whose shape reminded him of a home hot-water heater, only this was made of a thick, transparent polymer that had the same transparent qualities as glass, but clearly much stronger. It had to be, since it was designed to hold molten adamantium, which came into the vat as hot as the core of the Earth. Attached to the cylinder were a number of long, snakelike tubes that ended in wicked-looking syringes built to punch through bone. The tank was half full of a silvery liquid.

He looked at that tank, at the cylinder, at the tubes, at the instruments—and knew at last where his nightmares came from.

"You know," Stryker said from across the room, though his presence came as no surprise to Logan. He'd scented the man's approach minutes ago. "The tricky thing about adamantium is that if you ever manage to process its raw, liquid form, you have to keep it that way. Keep it hot, keep it molten. Because, you see, once it cools, it's *indestructible*."

He paused a moment to let the implications of his words sink in, but Logan wasn't bothered. He'd already figured out that part. That had to be why they needed someone with a healing factor.

"But," Stryker continued, "I can see you already know that."

He was being very careful, keeping the full width of the lab, and as much equipment as possible, between himself and Logan.

"I used to think you were one of a kind, Wolverine. I truly did." He shook his head. "I was wrong."

Logan charged him and ran straight into Yuriko, who caught him by the arm and—using his own momentum as impetus—slammed him as hard as she could into one of the support columns. Stone cracked and powdered with the impact, but Logan wasn't even staggered.

Stryker caught Yuriko's eye, looked deliberately from her to Logan, and when she nodded, he took his leave, out a different doorway from the one he'd entered, taking time to lock it behind him.

Logan rose to his feet and extended both sets of claws. He had no interest in her, only her boss, but if she wanted trouble, he'd make it short and final.

In return, her own face looking bored, as though this sort of confrontation happened every day, she spread her fingers wide.

Logan was used to the reaction he got from other people when they saw his claws for the first time. Now, surprisingly, he learned how that felt as Yuriko's fingers elongated into eight-inch spikes. He didn't need to be told what they were made of, and he wondered how they'd managed the implantation. If she had a healing factor as well, this could be trouble.

"Holy shit," he said in amazement. She smiled, but it wasn't a human expression. In fact, nothing about her seemed human or connected; it was like she was some different species entirely, forever gazing at the world from the outside. She was predator, all others were prey. That was the natural order of things.

Her hand flicked out, faster than he could follow, and he felt a hiss of pain along his jaw, felt blood where she'd cut a shallow gash across his cheek.

He retaliated with a roundhouse swing that missed her by a mile as she ducked beneath it and came up like a jack-in-the-box, unleashing a powerful side kick to the belly that pitched him backward through trays of equipment, upending them on top of him as he tumbled to the floor.

With a banshee screech, she leaped after him, slashing at him with both hands, only to find her attack blocked by his own claws. Adamantium struck adamantium, creating its own unique brand of sparks as each of them fought to break through the other's guard and instead only managed to wreck the lab.

Stryker heard the sounds of battle and permitted himself a smile as he quickened his pace. Time, now more than ever, was of the essence.

Yuriko swung hard, but Logan slapped her aside. Before he could take advantage, she hurled herself clear of him, running straight at the wall and using it as a springboard to flip herself up and over. However, she made a slight miscalculation in her maneuver: As she twisted in midair, her finger claws ripped through a cluster of power cables fastened to the ceiling. They exploded with sparks, they were live and carrying a significant amount of juice, and they dangled and twisted in the air like manic snakes. That contact threw her fractionally off balance; she didn't quite land where she wanted to, or as smoothly.

It was the opening Logan had been waiting for.

Logan tackled her, and together they crashed through a glass wall into some kind of lounge. X-ray light boxes, equipment, computers galore crashed and shattered around them as they struggled. Logan had strength and a fair share of agility, but Yuriko possessed speed he couldn't hope to match. For every blow he landed, he took a dozen, and his uniform proved as effective at stopping her claws as a suit of air. Worse, her own healing factor seemed every bit as effective as his, only he was giving it a lot less work to do.

As they'd tangled on the floor, he'd caught a glimpse of the back of her neck, saw there the scar that marked both Nightcrawler and Magneto, and realized in that instant there could be no reasoning with her. In her own way, she was as berserk as he, and he knew she wouldn't stop until she killed him.

She hit him again, and again, using feet this time more than claws, choosing her blows with care so that she connected with soft tissue instead of bone. She wanted to wear him down, to strip him of the ability to defend himself, to remove all hope before she came in for the kill. That was what Stryker had asked of her, and she could deny him nothing.

She sent Logan crashing backward into the tank, and he tumbled into it, rearing up immediately only to collapse against the opposite end, eyes wide as his nightmares rioted up around him. He was clumsy and dazed, he had to be at the end of his rope.

With a ballerina's grace, Yuriko sprang onto the lip of the tank, striking a Kali-like pose, the fingers of both hands spread out before her like a pair of bloody fans.

Logan showed fear in his eyes, which was exactly what she wanted to see.

She struck, and as she made her move . . .

. . . so did he.

She slashed empty air, registering surprise and disbelief as Logan leaped straight up from the tank. Using all his formidable strength to defy gravity, he grabbed for the rack suspended above the tank and slashed through the wire tether that anchored it to the ceiling.

It dropped like a guillotine. He rode it down to crash on top of Yuriko and pin her to the bottom of the tank. She struggled and screeched, using her claws on the steel and concrete members that imprisoned her. It would only be moments before she was free.

They were moments Logan wouldn't let her have. On impact, he pitched himself clear of the rack and grabbed the syringes attached to the cylinder of adamantium, using the same movement to open the access valves. He spared her a quick and final thought—*I'm sorry*—and plunged the barbed needles between her unbreakable ribs and into her heart.

She screamed as the molten metal flowed into her body. She raged and struggled in a last desperate bid to escape, but she was doomed the moment Logan stabbed her. Adamantium oozed out her eyes and out her mouth, it burned through the very pores of her skin until she was coated from head to toe. Unable to maintain even a semblance of balance, she fell backward into the tank, creating a splash that emptied the vessel of half its volume of

amber liquid. Her fingers twitched spasmodically as she
sank to the bottom.

And then she was still.

Logan watched her, half expecting her to crack the
shell and emerge more powerful and deadly than before.
By rights she should be dead, from internal burns if nothing else, as the raw, fiery metal cascaded straight into her
heart. God knows what kind of damage had been done
to allow the adamantium to emerge from her eyes and
mouth. Covered as she was, she couldn't breathe. Perhaps that would do the trick?

He hoped so, prayed so. She was as much a victim as
he, and more. At least—and here he touched his fingers
to the back of his neck to make sure—he wore no scar to
brand him as Stryker's slave.

If he hadn't escaped, would that be him lying there?
Or taking Yuriko's place by Stryker's side, as his pet
assassin?

One thing more that Stryker owed him.

Time to collect.

He turned his back on this unholy place, and all it represented for his life, and started after Stryker's trail.

Nothing would stop him now.

# Chapter
# Fifteen

"You think they'll come?" one of the troopers, Grierson, asked Lyman.

Lyman nodded, automatically checking the other man's disposition. Grierson was hunkered down behind a concrete abutment, spare magazines at hand, spare weapons as well. He was on the young side for one of Stryker's men, but he had a superb personnel jacket, topped by a year spent as a platoon sergeant in the 82nd Airborne, humping the boonies in Afghanistan.

"They'll come," Lyman said.

"Can we stop 'em?"

"Those are the orders."

"No offense, but from what I saw on the video—"

"Those are the orders."

Grierson shrugged. "First time for everything, I guess." He hefted his long gun, a Barrett .50-cal sniper rifle, whose depleted uranium shells could punch through tank armor a mile away. "I get a decent shot with this!"

Lyman nodded again, aching for a cigarette. He never smoked at home, only in the field and only before a fight. Had to be nerves. Thirty years in the service, combat tours all over the world, and he still got nervous. He figured that was the difference between him and Stryker;

the commander had no nerves, or at least none that he ever showed his men.

One more time, for reassurance, and to give himself something to do, he made the rounds of his fire team, checked their sight lines and kill zones, made sure everyone had an abundance of weapons and ammo. In a fair fight, against an adversary like themselves, no matter how well trained and disciplined, he would have called the outcome no contest. His guys had ideal ground, anyone advancing up this corridor wouldn't even come close.

As it was . . .

He'd broken the cardinal rule of clandestine ops: He'd brought along some personal items. Only pictures—the wife, the kids, the grandchild-to-be. His dogs. He'd raised them from pups, a pair of mixed-breed shepherds that kept his wife good company when he was away. With the kids building households of their own, his own home was too empty too often. He knew she was lonely; he hoped the dogs made it easier to bear.

He wondered what they'd say, his kids, seeing him here? He thought of the children they'd taken from the mansion and how cavalierly Stryker had condemned them. Funny, even though he understood the broad outlines of Stryker's ambition, he always assumed—no, he always *chose* to assume—that the targets would be adults. Full-grown mutants.

He did a dangerous thing for a soldier. He put himself for a moment in the other man's boots and considered how he might react if they were *his* children who'd been stolen.

He took a breath and then another, even deeper, because the first was way too shuddery and he needed his

men to see him completely in control. He had to take
a third, because this time the fear wouldn't be banished
so readily; it had its hooks deep in him, and he had
to pry them loose one at a time. Lyman wasn't a brilliant
man; he wasn't into concepts. His skill was execution. Give him a mission, and you were guaranteed to see
it accomplished.

"I gotta go, sweetheart," he whispered to the pictures
in his hand, and he kissed each one in turn. One daughter, and her baby he knew he'd never see, three sons, his
two dogs, and the woman who was the center of his life.
He clasped his hands in prayer, bracing his wife's picture
between thumbs and fingers, staring at it with such intensity that by force of will alone he could almost make it
real.

That's when they heard the *hum* from inside the Cerebro chamber, a deep pulsing groan as if the world itself
were stretching sore joints. It wasn't so much heard as
felt, a frequency so low it made your insides quiver. At
the same time, the floor beneath them, the rock around
them, trembled, and every man in the fire team looked
around nervously, half expecting some monster to come
burning through the walls or the walls themselves to
come tumbling down.

"Remember the briefing," Lyman told them. "This is
part of the process. You guys may think this feels bad,
but I guarantee you it'll be worse for the muties. Stay
chill, people, stay alert."

"Five bucks says the gizmo nails 'em before we fire a
shot!"

"Save your money, Manfredi," Lyman shot back. "I'd
rather take it from you over poker."

He didn't get much of a laugh from his men, but it was

enough. Lyman tucked away his photos and checked his own weapons. If the muties had half a brain between them, that first pulse should bring them on the run. They'd know the stakes now.

It wouldn't be long.

"I have a valid target," Grierson announced, leveling his sniper rifle.

Lyman whipped his binoculars to his eyes and brought the approaching figures into focus. Magneto and Mystique, at a range of one hundred meters. The old man was a half step in the lead, marching up the hallway like he was leading a whole army into battle. He didn't seem to mind Grierson's laser sight resting right over his heart.

"You're cleared to fire," Lyman said, and immediately a resounding boom filled the hallway around him, so loud he couldn't help flinching.

The shell didn't hit its target; it never came close. Without lifting a finger, without a gesture of any kind, Magneto simply stopped it in midair.

The rest of the team opened up, and the air around Lyman filled with the stink of cordite and the sound of spent casings rattling off the walls and floor. Every man here was a crack marksman, and this was point-blank range. The only pause in the murderous volleys was when someone had to replace an empty magazine. In the space of a few frantic minutes, they expended better than half their munitions . . .

. . . and found themselves with absolutely nothing to show for it.

Not one of the bullets came closer to their targets than an arm's length. It didn't matter that they were forged of nonferrous materials, that some were super-dense plastic. If Magneto couldn't manipulate the shells directly, he warped the magnetic fields around them, and him, using force and pressure to accomplish his goal.

Too astonished to be scared, the troopers gradually stopped firing. A couple looked to Lyman, hoping for a Plan B.

He couldn't think of one; he was transfixed by the scene down the hall. They'd thrown literally thousands of rounds at the two mutants, and now Magneto was re-shaping them to his own requirements, pressing them so tightly together they formed a wall that completely obscured him and Mystique from view.

*Why would they need a shield,* Lyman thought. *He knows there's nothing we can do to him—*

He heard a faint *click,* followed the noise, and had his answer.

The bastard had just pulled the pin on his grenade.

Lyman grabbed for the bomb and pitched it clear, thankful for the seven-second delay on the fuse, but even as he did he knew it was a useless gesture—because those same fateful *clicks* could be heard all around him. They had a whole case of grenades, each man carried his standard allotment, and every one of them had just been triggered.

He saw his wife in his mind's eye and reached for her . . .

. . . and he was done.

Of course the explosion of the grenades ignited what remained of the rifle ammunition, which created quite a fireworks display outside the chamber. Mystique tucked her body close around itself at Magneto's feet, placing her back right against his metal shield as strays ricocheted all around them.

When the *ping*s and whistles and pops and crackles and booms had all faded, leaving Mystique coughing from the smoke and the stench of ruined flesh, her ears ringing from the shock waves, Magneto set aside his shield, and they proceeded on their way.

There wasn't anything left of the defenders worth looking at. Magneto paused a moment at the entrance, standing by a bloody mess that was unrecognizable as a man. Oddly, a photo had survived the slaughter, a little singed at the edges, a handsome woman of middle age and two bright-eyed dogs. Mystique kneeled for a closer look, but Magneto shook his head. He opened his hand, which was filled with the pins he'd pulled from the grenades, and let them fall, burying the photograph in steel.

Then his head jerked up and he staggered as if he'd just been physically struck, Mystique hissing in agony as a phantom ice pick went straight through her brain, as the *hum* radiating from inside the room got louder, grew deeper and more intense.

In front of Charles Xavier, a light appeared. In terms of the holographic globe being displayed by Cerebro, it was located at the core of the world. From that point, radiant spears stabbed outward to connect with each and every one of the scarlet dots that represented an active or potential mutant.

"Oh," Jean cried suddenly, and then she cried out in real pain as her concentration slipped and the teke splints vanished from around her broken leg. Psychically damping the pain didn't make it go away, it just made things feel worse every time she had to notice. But her injury was the least of her concern as her hand tightened on Scott's shoulder so tightly he winced, half wondering if she was going to crush his bones.

"Jean," he demanded, placing an arm around her waist, pulling one of her arms across his shoulder so he could better handle her weight, "what's wrong?"

"Voices," she gasped, "so many voices, can't you hear them, of course you can't what am I saying oh Charles oh *Charles* what have you *done?*"

"Jean!"

"Scott, it's Cerebro," she cried, and for the first time since he'd known her, Scott heard genuine terror in her voice. "We're too late!"

She screamed. He'd only heard its like once before, when he was young and hunting. It was one of the few memories that he knew dated from before the orphanage where he'd grown up. He was in mountains, so many they filled the horizon on every side, and though his dad carried a gun for protection, they were there to shoot pictures. Some poor fool in another hunting party had stumbled into a bear trap, and the metal jaws had nearly taken off his leg.

Jean collapsed to the floor, clutching at her head and howling. Scott knelt beside her, struck through the heart to see her in such pain, yet utterly helpless to alleviate it.

He heard a deep, basso profundo *thrum* that sounded to him like tectonic plates grinding, and then, just like that, he lost all ability for rational thought as his own head was overwhelmed by a sleet storm of pain. His eyes were burning and his brain with it, the fire coursing down his spine and along every path and linkage of his nervous system.

His last, desperate, marginally conscious act was to

throw himself clear of Jean, to wrap his arms around his head and tuck his body in as tight upon itself as he could manage. His beams couldn't punch through his own flesh; this way, he hoped, he prayed, he wouldn't unleash them on anyone else. He wouldn't hurt Jean—any more than he already had.

Storm and the children were making good time through the bowels of the complex. For once, even Artie was behaving. No smart remarks, no haring off on his own, he held her hand tight and kept pace, even though her legs were twice the length of his and she was walking fast. Nightcrawler was on point and so far, thankfully, the way ahead was clear.

She sensed the psi wave before actually hearing it, in the same way she sensed changes in the weather. The shape of the air, the energies coursing through it, bulged and rippled as though they were being shunted aside by the approach of a power far more massive than themselves.

Nightcrawler felt it, too. He dropped from the ceiling, bracing a hand against the wall to steady himself. He looked dizzy and felt far worse. In his whole life he'd never suffered from vertigo and now, suddenly, he was glad for what he'd been spared all these years. He tried to focus his eyesight, and when that failed, he realized it was getting harder to form coherent thoughts as well. It was as though every cell in his body had acquired the ability to teleport independently of one another, and they'd all decided to go their separate ways.

He started to turn, to warn Storm, to cry out to her for help, but that simple action proved beyond his capability as he stumbled over his own feet and flailed desperately for a handhold to stop himself from falling.

"Storm!" he cried with the frantic desperation of a drowning man, but she was in no position to help.

She was already on her knees, hands clutched to her head, caught in her own whirlwind and shot through with lightning that exploded from her eyes and circled right around to strike her back. Always before she'd been immune to the elements she wielded, but that was no longer the case as wicked arcs of electricity exploded over and *through* her. She writhed with every impact, and while the winds attacking her swept away the smoke raised by these repeated attacks, they couldn't dispel the quickly rising stench of burned uniform. Or the certain knowledge that in very little time, her flesh would be burning, too.

The children were screaming now, howling like souls being tormented by demons, Nightcrawler's eyes going wide with horror, his mouth forming the words—part demand, part prayer—"Stop it! Please, *stop it!* For the love of God—*stop!*" But no sound emerged. He was beyond the ability to speak.

He knew, as Storm did, that this was just the leading edge of the nightmare coming for them, the merest prelude to what lay ahead. He prayed for mercy, not only for himself and his companions, but for the souls of those responsible.

He forced one hand in front of the other, climbing along the floor as he would up a vertical rock face, determined to reach Storm, to give her what shelter and comfort he could so that together they could try to protect the children. There'd been no one to protect him growing up. He'd learned early how to fight and, far more importantly, how to defuse a fight, and he'd sworn afterward he would never allow anyone to be without a protector.

He stretched his right arm forward, a distance that seemed to his disoriented eyes to be miles. It was so hard to move, to think, there was a tremendous numbing pressure right behind his eyes that threatened to pop them from their sockets and he was sure his brain was swelling from the onslaught of the energy pulse.

Then the *hum* enveloped them, and all that came before faded to insignificance.

Nightcrawler's last conscious thought was of wonderment. He'd always believed you had to be dead before you went to Hell.

Logan tried to snarl, but it came out more like a scream. Claws emerged from both his hands, but they extended no more than an inch before retracting. This time, though, Logan's healing factor didn't close the wounds behind them, and blood sprayed from the open cuts. Indeed, it appeared that all the wounds he'd ever endured were coming back to haunt him as a score of gashes opened across his flesh, splashing the floor around him scarlet. Some were random and messy, the legacy of knives or bullets or the cruel vagaries of nature, but many were neat and purposeful, the incisions of careful men who'd abandoned all allegiance to the Hippocratic oath they'd taken as medical students to do no harm. They'd laid Logan open to the bone and now, in the place Stryker implied he had been born, it was happening all over again.

\* \* \*

Magneto staggered under the onslaught of the psychic pressure wave, standing against it as he would against the full force of a hurricane's winds. Step by determined step, he advanced on the doorway to Stryker's version of the Cerebro chamber.

"Eric," he heard from behind and to the side, Mystique's voice, shattering between one syllable of his name and the next, between that word and the one which followed. *"Hurry!"* Feminine for one, masculine for another, plunging from soprano to bass and back again.

He didn't look back, he couldn't spare the effort—and besides, he could imagine what was happening. Somehow Cerebro was attacking them through their very powers, turning what made them unique against them and consuming them with it. Mystique was a metamorph, a shape-shifter, able to mimic any conceivable human form perfectly. Size, age, gender, none of these were obstacles.

Now, as with Logan, her past came back to torment her. Cerebro made her flesh pliable, like soft wax, and then like mercury, as she underwent change after involuntary change, revisiting every face and form she'd ever copied. Even though she made it seem easy, it really wasn't. Her apparent speed came with years of training, of practice, of preparation. Each transformation was an effort, and the more she executed, the faster she did them, the greater the toll. If she needed to grow taller, she had to bulk up to provide the raw material. Shorter required burning off mass. Flesh was comparatively easy to sculpt, bones less so, and internal organs the most demanding of all. That's why most gender shifts were cosmetic.

None of that applied now. The shifts came so fast that

she presented herself as multiples. Her own coloring, Jean Grey's face, Robert Kelly's torso, Rogue's legs, Xavier's face, Rogue's hair, Jean's torso, Wolverine's hands, claws sprouting from fingers, from between her toes, Magneto's face rising from her belly, someone else's from each breast, arms becoming legs and feet growing fingers, all these mad alterations accompanied by a rising chorus of howls from mouths that popped into view all over her body, each capable of independent speech and all of them shrieking in agony under the relentless and crushing pressure of the wave.

Soon, terribly soon, the transformations would come so quickly, the pain would grow so great, that Mystique's consciousness—her sense of fundamental self—would shatter. In effect, on both a cerebral and a cellular level, she would forget who and what she was. Most likely, she would genetically discorporate into a muddle of mindless cells, and that would be the end of her.

Magneto knew all that, knew she was but one victim of far too many, knew something similar lay in store for him—unless he stopped it.

He lifted a hand and a new sound rose to challenge the *hum* of the Cerebro wave: the basso groan of metal finding itself subjected to stresses well beyond design tolerances. He couldn't do this at Mount Haven; the part of the complex where he'd been incarcerated had been constructed of nonferrous materials and revolutionary plastics. But Alkali was much older, built in a day when the likes of him hadn't been a factor. There was a lot of metal for him to play with, and even though the Cerebro wave presented a significant—for some, insurmountable—obstacle, he was determined to prevail.

He had survived Auschwitz. He had lived to see his

captors in their graves, had helped deliver more than a few of them to that end by himself. This would be the same.

He flashed teeth with the effort, almost a snarl, and metal started to warp and tear around him. The timbre of the *hum* emanating from inside faded ever so slightly, and the pulse of the Cerebro wave . . . slowed.

Charles Xavier was aware of none of this. He stared up at the globe circling around him, transfixed by the firefly display of scarlet dots, paying not the slightest attention to the trickles of blood from nostrils and ears and the corners of his eyes as stress ruptured the pinpoint capillaries that fed his brain. These were the most minor manifestations of being at the wave's source, of being the focal point of the power being unleashed, and at this moment they represented no lasting physical trauma.

That wouldn't last, of course. Mutant 143 knew that, somewhere in the deepest recesses of his own twisted psyche. In short order, as the pulse built to its peak, the greater vessels would burst, and he would be consumed by a massive and all-encompassing cerebral hemorrhage. He would die from the ultimate stroke—but not before bearing witness to the brutal and merciless slaughter of every person on earth who Cerebro considered a mutant. This was Stryker's revenge—not only would Xavier himself die, and all his precious students, but the future they represented. The murder of his dream would be the death of him, and before his own end Mutant 143 would make sure that Xavier realized the full import of what he had done.

And then, of course, 143 would die. Stryker appreciated the neatness and elegance of this resolution; it was ideal for a covert operation, one of his hallmarks. He didn't like loose ends. In one stroke, this eliminated not only the threat to the world but the weapon used to deal with it. As for 143 himself, the realization of his fate didn't bother him. Partly, he didn't really believe it would happen to him. He still retained a child's absolute faith in his own immortality. He couldn't conceive of coming to an end. What mattered for him now, as always since the manifestation of his mutant powers, was playing with his toys. They were mortal, they were fragile. He was God. And He had work to do.

So 143's eyes pulsed, casting their demented light into the core of Xavier's being. Around them, what was normally heard as whispers, the background susurrus of all the myriad thoughts Cerebro allowed Xavier to perceive, rose to a chorus of screams.

Cyclops wrapped his hands as tight as he could across his eyes, but he was sick at heart at the realization that he couldn't hold back his optic blasts much longer. Already they were reaching the containment capacity of his ruby quartz visor and little flashes of energy were beginning to pop through the spaces between his fingers, too small to do much damage but serving as eloquent harbingers for the devastation soon to follow.

Jean wasn't doing any better as she clutched her hands to her ears in a vain attempt to block the same threnody of desolation that enveloped her teacher. She swung her broken leg against a stanchion, not caring about any lasting damage she might be doing, praying instead that the pain she caused herself might serve as a bulwark against the assault from outside.

And she succeeded, although not quite in the way she had planned. Her teke slugged into high gear, stealing a page from Logan's book as her body remembered on a cellular level what it was like to be whole and set her power to work bringing that about. All the shards of bones, large or small, visible or microscopic, were plucked from where they'd landed in her leg and pressed back into their proper position.

She thought she'd experienced pain in her life, either directly or vicariously as an aspect of her power, when she synced into the minds of patients to ease their suffering, but she realized now that she'd never even come close as all those pieces of bone tore their way through her flesh to set themselves. She howled, thankful for the respite from Cerebro, struggling to find a way to reach Charles through this nigh-unbearable sleet storm of acid, to join her own strength to his and together find a way to neutralize the wave.

There was a fire within her, and she assumed that it had to do with her leg, that her power was somehow finding a way to fuse the bone back together, but as it grew, as her thoughts splintered and the fear blossomed that she wouldn't be equal to the task before her, it became a radiance too astounding to be described, too powerful to be measured, as though she were witnessing within herself the primal moment of creation, the lighting of the first spark within the infinite firmament.

With a cry of joy and longing, Jean Grey spread wide the arms of imagination and reached out to embrace the stars.

She knew then she was mad, but she refused to yield, to the pain or the madness. If this fire represented power, then she would find a way to harness it, to use it to save those she loved. If she was truly dying, she would find a way back from the ashes. She would never go quietly into the dark night of eternity.

Aboard the *Blackbird*, Rogue was struggling to reach the controls, to do as Storm had told her, but she couldn't make it. She couldn't even rise from the deck where she'd collapsed. Tears on her face, she couldn't stop Bobby from grasping her by the hand—in a grip that froze her to the shoulder, as he'd coated every visible surface on the plane with a sheet of glittering hoarfrost. His skin was transparent, she could see right through him, with him looking like a three-dimensional X ray—only this one was made entirely of ice. She could see his skeleton, and faint hints of what must be his heart and lungs and other organs. No sense of blood, no visible nerves, and he crackled faintly with every move, with every breath. His voice was arctic, biting and cold and nothing like he usually sounded.

Ice shattered as he wrenched her glove off her arm, she begged him to stop—at least in her mind—but nothing emerged from her mouth, there was this huge crowd crushing in around her, all the people she'd ever imprinted rising up inside her skull in rage at what she'd done, ignoring her apologies, her attempted explanations, demanding instead that she yield control to them. She knew he was trying to save her, offering his strength to give her a better chance of surviving, no matter the cost to himself. She didn't want that, she couldn't bear her own survival at the cost of his, and she knew as well that he didn't care.

He held her bare hand in his, deliberately initiating contact—and imprinting—and her eyes bugged wide as it turned to ice the same as his, while his started to look more and more normally human.

*"Bobby, stop it!"* she shrieked, and from lips that tasted chill as the pole came a voice that was a match for his, cold and remote and unhuman as space itself.

And from her eyes, as she saw from his, fell tears that froze to both their cheeks.

Thunder rocked the tunnel around Storm, wind howled, rain fell, and lightning continued to strike. She wasn't moving, sprawled on her face as bolt after bolt crashed against her body. Nightcrawler, by contrast, couldn't stop as he teleported in place again and again and again, faster and faster and faster, until he flickered like a strobe image.

John Allardyce hadn't made it to the entrance of the complex, hadn't even come close, before the wave dropped him. He hadn't moved from where he fell as breath kept coming in an ever-greater rush. He was hyperventilating, gulping huge amounts of air to fuel the raging conflagration within him, so much so that his skin was glowing— and the snow around him quickly melting away.

Henry McCoy was in his lab, measuring coffee grounds into a beaker while a nearby Bunsen burner had the water merrily boiling. Using gloves, he added the water to the grounds and savored the heady smell. This was what made every morning worthwhile, because a superb cup of coffee was for him the precursor to a successful day of research.

Without warning, his hand twitched so violently that

the beaker went flying, shattering glass and steaming hot water across the worktable. McCoy convulsively threw himself back from the table with such force that his stool upended and he crashed head over heels against the wall. His body spasmed as though he'd plugged himself directly into an electrical outlet, and he cried out in horror and disbelief, and no little pain, as nails bulged from the tips of his fingers into cruelly hooked claws. His arms doubled in width, splitting the seams of shirt and lab coat, the pigmentation of his skin turning a deep blue as he sprouted hairs of the same color all over his body.

He tried to call for help, but what emerged from his mouth was a roar, like a lion's.

What he saw reflected in the polished steel of his refrigerator was no longer anything that resembled a man. Hank McCoy was now a beast.

Kitty and Siryn were shopping for food, as much as two kids could buy with the handful of bucks they had between them. In the blink of an eye, Kitty found herself at the far end of the aisle from her friend. Another blink, she was through a wall and across the street. Another blink, she was inside a tree and partially sunk into the ground. She tried to move, but hands and feet could find no purchase, and with a wail of horror she realized that she wasn't the one who was moving. She'd suddenly become so intangible that gravity itself had no more effect on her. The Earth was spinning on its axis and leaving her behind. Worse, it was also revolving in its orbit around the Sun. How long before she found herself floating in space, while the world that was her home went on its merry celestial way?

Siryn didn't know quite what had happened to her

friend. She heard a yelp of surprise, caught a glimpse of Kitty disappearing ghostlike through the back wall of the store, and then she was shrieking across the full range of her accessible frequencies, calling forth a lunatic choir of howls from every dog within earshot as, at the same time, she managed to shatter every piece of glass in the store.

In a back room at Delamain's on the Rue Rogue in New Orleans' Vieux Carre—the French Quarter—the usual high-stakes game of poker was well under way, in defiance of the paddle-wheel casinos moored along the Riverwalk at the foot of Canal Street. The casinos had the flash, this game had substance, not so much because of the size of the bets but because of the quality of the players.

Remy LeBeau was a regular and one of the best. The cards, it was said, loved him the way he loved the women who invariably went out of their way to mix with his life, which could be a wild and risky thing. He was a thief by trade, and better at it than at cards, which was saying quite a lot. Stealing hearts was for him far more interesting and a whole lot more fun than stealing jewels or whatever, especially since the trick was always to make sure the stolen heart was never broken. In that regard, he had no equal. When the affair was over, his ladies loved him more than when they met.

This had been a fair night thus far in terms of winnings, but only because he'd been taking his measure of his fellow players. Now was the time to get down to business and make a killing.

Alas, this time, no joy. It was not to be.

He was dealer and from the deck came the joker, the

jack of hearts, to complete his full house. But as he flicked it from his hands a spark popped between his fingertips, igniting the card not with fire but with some kind of energy that made it blaze brighter than a maritime searchlight and strike the table with force enough to split the thick wood right across the middle. At the same time, as the other players reeled back in shock and alarm, the other cards he held likewise ignited.

He had a split second to look at the others, his face marked with confusion, his free hand reaching out for help—but all they saw were his eyes blazing red as fresh blood, and so none of them reached back. Then his cards exploded, shattering the remains of the table to kindling and scattering everyone to the walls.

Mystique wasn't moving anymore. That wasn't a good thing. Like the Wicked Witch of the West in *The Wizard of Oz* after Dorothy splashed her with water, she was melting. Flesh was liquefying, puddling beneath her, the shape of her skeleton starting to stand out in sharp relief. Soon, very soon, the bones would be exposed. Would she be aware of that? Would she be conscious to the end? She didn't believe that Stryker had an ounce of mercy in him, only that he was thorough. Whatever it felt like, the process would be final.

Magneto was still on his feet, glaring hawklike at the sealed door before him. He wasn't interested in the door any longer; he could breach it at his pleasure, with hardly any effort. His focus was on the configuration of the energy patterns that made up the Cerebro wave. Manipulating energy was what he did best. All he had to do was nail down the frequencies and signal characteristics of the wave. . . .

He set up a countervailing pulse and watched the two collide. Close, but not quite there.

He made the necessary modifications and repeated the process, creating in effect a wall of white noise around the entire chamber, a resonance field that utterly neutralized the Cerebro wave at its source.

Just like that, all around him, there was silence.

Blessed silence.

# Chapter
# Sixteen

Inside Stryker's Cerebro chamber, Charles Xavier sat straighter in his wheelchair as the globe around him stopped spinning and the entire system progressed through its shutdown cycle.

"That's strange," he muttered, and paused a moment to consider why that simple phrase seemed to have two meanings for him. The obvious related to what was happening around him and to why Cerebro suddenly seemed to acquire a mind of its own. The other, disturbingly, also seemed to relate to that nagging, persistent sense of *wrongness* that had plagued him ever since his escape from Alkali Lake.

He looked suddenly and sharply at the little girl, as though to catch her by surprise. She looked apprehensive, indicating that the shutdown wasn't what she'd expected, either. Xavier made a comforting gesture, spoke some comforting words, to reassure her that he was still in control, that everything would be all right. That appeared to help, although her mismatched eyes of green and blue still glowed disconcertingly bright.

*To work,* he decided. Identify the problem and resolve it, that was the ticket.

Still, as he reached for Cerebro's controls, he found

himself hesitating, he found his eyes returning to the girl, his thoughts reaching out to her through the veil that surrounded him. Something about her . . . felt . . .

He shook his head, dazzled by the afterimage of her eyes like blinkers in his mind. He knew what had to be done, and his hands moved with practiced skill over the controls. Someone was jamming the scanning wave. He had his suspicions who was responsible and, from there, what was necessary to break free.

Seeing him hard at work, the girl looked away, toward the massive door at the end of the gallery. This wasn't part of the program, and she didn't like it.

Magneto needed a little time to gather his strength. The battle against the Cerebro wave had been as hard for him as for the others and, in its way, had taken as great a toll.

At last he turned, and because she couldn't see him, wasn't aware of anything beyond herself, he allowed his face to show the sorrow Mystique's pitiful condition brought forth in him. Over their time together, he'd grown used to having her by his side, strong and utterly fearless, indomitable in will and surprisingly indestructible in form. He hated to think of her being vulnerable, and hurt.

He knelt beside her, unsure of what he'd find. Her eyes were opaque, as blank and lifeless as a doll's. She looked like a wax figure who'd been exposed to raw flame, so much of her lay in congealed folds beneath her body.

Then an aspect of her eyes changed. Still opaque, but no longer blank or lifeless, they took on the otherworldly depths of a shark's eyes.

She blinked, and color returned to those eyes, as it did to the whole of her body.

She flexed her muscles and stretched, to remind herself of how the parts of her all properly fit together, and flowed upward to a sitting position to look her companion in the eye.

He didn't say a word, nor did she. There was no need.

He stepped over the threshold and along the gallery to the scanning platform, roving his gaze until he'd taken stock of every part of the huge, circular space, impressed at the degree of accuracy that Stryker had achieved.

Xavier sat on his dais, facing a creature that made Magneto's lip curl in reflexive disgust. It had nothing to do with outward appearance. In his time, Magneto had seen more than his share of mutants who did not conform to baseline norms of human physiognomy. In his time, Magneto had also come face-to-face with living embodiments of what he chose to call evil, and that was what he was responding to here. The creature in the other chair, whatever his origins or upbringing, would have been right at home working by the side of Josef Mengele.

Under the circumstances, given what he had in mind, Magneto thought that quite appropriate.

"Hello, Charles," he said companionably.

The celestial song had ended. Jean was herself once more. She was whole, she was alive, more fulfilled than she could ever remember, and yet hollow and aching with a need more keen and primal than she had ever known, without the slightest clue how to answer it.

Instead, she woke up.

She looked toward Cyclops, who was lying nearby,

telepathy revealing instantly that he was fine—battered but fundamentally unbroken—and she welcomed him awake with a radiant smile. As he gathered himself, she continued taking stock. The substance of the walls within the complex had been designed to inhibit telepathic communication, so she found herself pretty much isolated, with only a vague sense that the others were all right and a growing disquiet whenever her thoughts turned to Xavier. Whatever had happened, they weren't out of the woods yet, not by a long shot.

She shifted her broken leg and winced, the lance of pain up the length of that limb making her breath hiss through her teeth. Her subconscious had done a superb job, every piece had been placed precisely where it was supposed to be—but the task wasn't quite finished. The bone bits still had to knit themselves together, and with a doctor's inherent caution, she didn't want to rush the process, even though she suspected she could.

That automatic realization gave her pause. She hadn't magically acquired Logan's healing factor, but somehow she'd tapped into a part of his psyche that allowed her to mimic it on her own terms. She had done consciously what he did as an autonomic function of his own body, and that—disturbingly—implied a measure of rapport between them she didn't care to think about.

She shook her head in dismay. If she'd wanted complications, she'd have gone into psychiatry. Oddly, but understandably for some whose powers were wholly invisible to the naked eye, she preferred tangible solutions to tangible problems. Like fixing a broken leg.

Push the process now and she risked messing up all her good work, leaving herself functionally lame.

*Thank Heaven,* she thought of Scott, *for having you to lean on, baby.*

And immediately felt a rush of shame, as though she'd been caught cheating on a commitment that wasn't even formal!

Worry about that later . . . if there *was* a later.

Nightcrawler was praying, curled into a ball of indigo, borderline invisible where the dim light from the corridor bulbs ran out of energy, hands curled protectively around his head, which, in turn, lay against his knees in a pose of abject supplication.

"What's he saying?" Artie asked.

"Our Father," Storm replied, "Who art in Heaven . . ."

"That's not what it sounds like."

"He's praying in German, and French, and in Latin."

Storm winced as she rose to her feet, trying to ignore the rude smells rising from the back of her uniform where the lightning had struck. Her nerves were a mess, as though a legion of fire ants were roaming beneath her skin, leaving a trail of itches the size of a superhighway that she couldn't scratch. She moved gingerly, like an old woman, taking care with every step and gesture—especially any that required turning her head—lest she lose a precariously maintained balance. She envied the children their resilience and used that as a goad to maintain a confident and solid facade.

She knelt beside Nightcrawler and stroked her hand down his back from neck to the middle of his shoulders, enjoying the richly delicious sensation of his luxurious skin. She'd never felt anything so smooth or plush, even the fur of newborn lion cubs.

He caught her with his tail, taking a couple of wraps

around her palm and giving her a gentle squeeze of thanks and reassurance that he was all right.

She turned to look at Artie and past him to the others.

"Everyone else okay?" she asked. Whether they were or not, they'd be moving in a minute, faster than before. The sooner they were quit of this place, and far away, the happier she'd be. Unless, in departing, she could scourge the landscape with her lightning right down to the bare rock, wiping away all trace that the Alkali Lake installation had ever existed. That would be a real pleasure.

And if William Stryker happened to be inside at the time, so much the better.

Stryker's escape tunnel ended at a small clearing on the periphery of the main complex, about a mile downriver from the dam. A helicopter was waiting, gassed and ready to go.

Quickly, because he was never a man to waste time, Stryker released the chains that anchored the vehicle to the landing stage. He pulled the safety flags free of all the flight control surfaces, cleared the air intake of the twin jet engines, and at the last, removed the wooden chocks from the landing gear.

In a matter of minutes, he would be safely away, and not long after, if his mental estimates were correct, the dam itself would eliminate all evidence of what had happened here.

Perfect.

Magneto spared Mutant 143 a momentary glance and smiled humorlessly at the creature's evident frustration.

He tapped his helmet and said, "You can't come in here."

Then, drawing a magnetic field close about him, he rose into the air to the core of the holographic globe, doing a slow pirouette and letting his excitement show as he beheld all the mutants revealed on the display. He'd never dared dream there were so many, and he remembered how people felt in the internment camps after the war—on the one hand, cut to the soul by the realization that so many had perished in the camps, and yet at the same time restored by the discovery that, despite the Nazis' best efforts, there were survivors. Enough to form the bedrock of a nation. He thought then of Moses, standing on the shores of the River Jordan, gazing across a promised land that he would never reach.

How would posterity judge him, he wondered.

If that posterity was mutant, he didn't mind. That he had succeeded, that they survived and prospered, was satisfaction enough. If it wasn't, he didn't care, because that meant he had failed. Either way, he would do today what needed doing.

Xavier paid no notice of him, so entranced was he by the glamour cast by Stryker's pet mutant.

Magneto shook his head in sorrow. "How does it look from there, Charles?" he wondered aloud, and while there was pity in his voice for his old friend, there was also an edge to his words, a contempt for the weakness that had brought Xavier to such a state. Here was a rich irony. If not for Xavier, Magneto would not have been captured and used by Stryker to crack open the secrets of Xavier's School—and most especially, of Cerebro. Yet, that selfsame act had in turn presented Magneto with the means to deliver his people forever from the threat of annihilation. Each act required the sacrifice of the same man. To Magneto, that was a more than fair exchange.

"Still fighting the good fight?" he mocked, turning away from Xavier to examine the device around him. His assessment completed, he used his power to begin a global reconfiguration. At his direction, Cerebro began to deconstruct and rebuild itself, the air filling with ceiling panels, metal braces, conduits, cabling, every key component that went into the construction of the machine, all moving swiftly and purposefully to their new destinations.

"From here, old friend, it doesn't look like they're playing by your rules."

The work finished to his satisfaction, he descended to the platform.

"Perhaps it's time to play by theirs."

On the far side of the doorway, Mystique smiled and strode briskly into the chamber. By the third step, when she emerged from the shadows, she was a perfect match for William Stryker.

She paused for a cruel and dismissive glance at Xavier, still oblivious to everything other than what 143 was feeding him. Then, she crouched beside 143, taking care not to touch him as she whispered into his ear: "There's been a change of plans. . . ."

As she spoke with Stryker's face, in Stryker's voice, 143's eyes bulged and a measure of saliva drooled from the corner of his mouth. He actually looked excited by the prospect.

Still presenting her masquerade, Mystique returned the way she came, reverting to her true form only after she was clear of the chamber.

Magneto stood before his friend one final time and tried to think of something to say. At Ellis Island, he'd been willing to sacrifice a child—Rogue—to achieve his goals. Now it was a friend. Nothing he could say, precious little he could imagine doing, would ever make that right. Some scales simply could not be balanced.

"Good-bye, Charles," he said.

Mutant 143, eager to begin, cocked his head to one side and glared once more into Xavier's skull.

Around them both the great globe flared once more brightly to life—only now, where its surface had been decorated by a random scattering of scarlet icons, representing the mutant population, now there was a multitude of pristine white ones, which stood for everyone else. Magneto had given them both access to every non-mutant sentient mind on the planet.

The better to destroy them all.

True to his nature, recovery for Logan was quick and complete. He was a little unsteady on his feet, but that was due to blood loss, as he could plainly see from the Jackson Pollock mess he'd made all around him on the concrete. He popped his claws and retracted them to make sure they were in good working order, and flexed his limbs and back to smooth out any kinks.

He had one clue to Stryker's trail: the man's scent, heavy in the air. That was all he needed. Without any specific memory to back it up, he instinctively understood that a man like Stryker would cover every contingency, including failure. He wouldn't want to be stuck here amid a whole passel of superpowered mutants who hated his guts. He'd have a convenient backdoor and waiting transportation. All he needed was time to make his getaway. All Logan had to do to stop him was catch up.

Silent and purposeful as a hunting cat, only far more ferocious, Logan picked up the pace.

\* \* \*

"*Was ist?*" Nightcrawler wondered as they rounded another corner in what was turning into an endless series of identical corridors—to find themselves confronting a slaughterhouse of a battlefield. Quickly the two adults blocked the children's path and shunted them back the way they had come.

After stern injunctions to the kids—especially Artie—to stay clear and, above all, not peek, Storm took another look, taking stock of the circular vault door that had obviously been ripped from its hinges, then just as obviously put back in place, much like a cork into a wine bottle.

"What is this place, Storm?" Nightcrawler asked again.

"Cerebro," she replied, and she didn't bother to hide her fear. Whoever had been here—and she needed no hints to come up with that identity—clearly didn't want anyone else going inside. And if the ultra-low-frequency hum she could feel as much as hear emanating from within was any indication, the system was still very much operational.

Of Xavier there was no sign, and she knew then that Magneto had remained true to his nature where the X-Men were concerned; he had found a way to betray their trust. No doubt for the most "noble" of reasons.

She sensed movement in the air that warned her of others approaching well before they actually came into view, so that when Scott helped Jean around the corner, Storm was there to greet them and shoulder part of the burden herself.

"Jean, what's going on?" she demanded.

Jean narrowed her eyes, holding her head for Storm as

she had for Scott, so that her eyes were mainly masked in shadow.

"The professor is still inside," she told them, using both their shoulders for support as she hopped toward the doorway on her good leg and tried not to relate to the gore that surrounded them. "With . . . another mutant. Another psi, very powerful, very twisted. Very dangerous. I've got to steer clear of him, too much chance of being snared like Charles. There's some kind of illusion, Charles is trapped, he thinks he's home, at the school!" She focused some more, and when she spoke, the words came in a rush. "Magneto's reversed Cerebro, it isn't targeting mutants anymore."

"Thank goodness for small favors," Cyclops muttered.

"So who's it targeting now?" Storm demanded at the same time.

*Who do you think,* Jean thought, and said aloud, "Everyone else."

Of course Artie had ignored everything Storm told him, and as a consequence had just heard what the others said. He had his own instant solution.

"You've got your optic blasts, Cyclops," he piped up. "So blast the door open!"

"I can't," was the reply.

To the other adults, as much as Artie, Jean explained, "Once the professor's mind is connected to Cerebro, opening the door could kill him." There was a moment's pause as all of them considered that as suddenly a very real possibility.

"We'll have to take that chance," Scott told them, even though he loved Xavier as a son does his father.

Abruptly, once more, Jean took charge: "Kurt, you have to take me in there. Now."

Cyclops, true to form, protested: "Jean!"

Nightcrawler shook his head. "I told you, it's too dangerous. I cannot teleport blind. If I can't see where I'm going, I—"

"Who is this guy?" Scott demanded.

In part because he felt flustered and pressed and wanted to defuse the growing tension of the moment, Kurt launched into his spiel: "I'm Kurt Wagner, but in the Munich Circus—"

"He's a teleporter," Storm said simply, holding up her hand to forestall Nightcrawler's introduction.

"We don't have time for this," Jean cried urgently.

"Wait," Storm said in a tone that wouldn't permit argument, backed by a will that was a match and more for anyone present.

Something in what Kurt had said, in the way Jean carried herself, caught Storm's attention. She reached forward to take her friend's chin in hand and turn her head up and around to meet her own eyes.

What she saw there broke her heart. "Oh, Goddess," she breathed, and didn't know who needed comfort more right then, Jean or herself.

"What's wrong?" asked Nightcrawler.

"Jean's blind," Scott said.

"I'm a telepath, damn it! I don't need eyes to see—" she began.

"Great," Scott snapped back at her. "So long as there are conscious minds around, you can tap into their visual receptors as surrogate eyes. But you've got a bum leg as well, remember?"

"I'll go," Storm said simply, and when the others looked at her, she repeated it, an unassailable statement of purpose. "I'll go." And then, with a look straight at Nightcrawler, "*We'll* go."

"Storm," he pleaded, "I can't!"

"Kurt, I have faith in you."

"Kurt," Jean said, "if Stryker's replicated the Cerebro chamber, then where you're going is essentially a huge, empty room. I'm projecting a mental image of the space into your head. Use that for your benchmarks. Stay clear of the walls, stay clear of the platform, you've got room to spare. Do you see it?"

Nightcrawler nodded and gathered Storm into his embrace, arms around her shoulders, tail wrapped snugly around her waist.

"One last thing," Jean said, "don't believe what you see in there. Remember, Charles' adversary traffics in illusions."

"This just keeps getting better and better," Nightcrawler grumbled in Storm's ear.

"If you're not clear in five minutes," Cyclops said warningly, "I'm coming in after you."

Storm nodded, and so—reluctantly—did Jean.

"Are you ready, Kurt?" Storm asked him. He wouldn't meet her eyes, but not because he was avoiding her. For the moment, his mind—and prayers—were elsewhere.

"Our Father," she heard him whisper, "Who art in Heaven, hallowed be Thy Name, Thy kingdom come, Thy will be done, on Earth—"

And just like that, they were gone.


"—as it is in Heaven!"

Just like that, they were somewhere else.

Storm had never jaunted, and after this ride never wanted to again. She didn't know how Nightcrawler

could stand it. She felt like she'd been turned inside out
and left a trail of body parts all the way back to where
they started. It was like she'd thrown up, horribly, but
only inside herself, and was left feeling all twisted and
out of sync.

They'd materialized right where Jean had suggested,
in the air about half a body length above the gallery.
Storm was in no condition right then to notice, or do
anything, so Nightcrawler continued to hold her as they
dropped to a landing.

They expected to find two figures: Xavier himself and
the mutant who was controlling him. But—surprise—no
Xavier, no command console, no command helmet.

The only other presence in the vast and empty room
was a young girl, standing right at the edge of the platform. She was all peaches and cream, her hair a glorious
gold blond, pretty as a picture, sweet as can be, a dream
made flesh. Her eyes, though, were an eerily mismatched
blue and green that seemed to glow with some intense inner light, and her face was that of someone whose will
was absolute.

Having no idea what to expect, but taking his cue
from Storm that something was wrong, Nightcrawler
looked around, eyes narrowing at the way the curvature
and coloring of the sphere made the room seem like a
limitless space.

"Hello," said the little girl brightly, as though she was
welcoming guests to her house.

"Storm," Nightcrawler wondered aloud, "have we
come to the right place? Is this Cerebro?"

She nodded, her attention focused, not on the girl, but
on the space a little beyond her where normally Xavier
would be sitting.

"Is it broken?"

"No."

"What are you looking for?" asked the girl.

"Professor!" Storm called. *"Charles!"*

The girl smiled sweetly, but there was a hollowness to her eyes, an edge to her stance, and the whole shape of her face around that smile, that made that sweetness a lie.

"I'm sorry," she said, "he's busy."


For Charles Xavier, every time he synced Cerebro was as marvelous and exciting as the first. It was the ultimate rollar-coaster ride against a backdrop as varied and spectacular as the clearest of night skies, if only the naked eye came with the range and sensitivity of the Hubble telescope.

His eyes and mouth opened in amazement and delight as he beheld the globe of the world from the inside; it circled serenely around them, its surface covered with a multitude of white lights, creating a display more crowded and, in its way, more beautiful than the stars. There were more than he could count, so he didn't even try.

He heard a great pulse from the heart of the machine, and the lights on the globe grew brighter, in tandem with the deepening pitch and increasing frequency of the pulses.

"Professor," he heard from the greatest distance imaginable, *"Charles!"*

He heard her as a whisper among the multitude, just as he had years ago during a trial run of the Cerebro prototype when his questing consciousness discovered a long, lean whip of a girl sitting on the summit of Mount Kilimanjaro, taking a break from herding cattle by tossing snowballs and seeing how far her winds could take them. (She'd already reached the Indian Ocean, now she was throwing the other way and trying for the Atlantic.)

"Did you hear that?" he asked excitedly.

"No," said the girl, shaking her head for emphasis.

It made Xavier's heart sing to know Storm was alive, but that awareness only increased his frustration when he couldn't lock in on her position. There was too much interference from these other voices. He had to find a way to screen them out.

Storm stepped toward the little girl.

"Professor, do you hear me?" she called, more loudly than before. "*Listen* to me, Charles! Whatever you're seeing, whatever you're experiencing, it's an illusion! You're in an *illusion*!" She heard no reply, and when she spoke again, there was a faint roll of thunder to her voice. "You have to stop this—you have to shut down Cerebro—*now!*"

The girl actually laughed.

"Who are you talking to?" she asked, in all innocence and rich amusement.

Xavier shook his head, as the word "now" echoed and reechoed through the spherical vault of the Cerebro chamber. For a moment he was sure Storm was right in front of him, close enough to touch—but all he could see was empty air. Save for the little girl, he was alone. His X-Men were lost, they were in deadly peril, he had to find them, save them.

And yet . . .

Always, his thoughts circled like vultures back to this same persistent, nagging question.

And yet . . .

Suppose *he* was the one who was lost?

"I hear them," he repeated, before voicing his own frustration. "But—I can't find them."

"Then concentrate harder," the little girl replied in a firm and commanding voice, in that special way that girls have that makes them sound as if they're merely stating an irrevocable natural law.

How could he be lost? He was in the heart of his mansion, of his school. He knew what had to be done.

Storm thought for a moment that she'd gotten through to him, but then the breath gusted out of her in a huff as she met the girl's gaze.

She wondered for a moment why the girl wasn't doing something more serious to stop them and answered her own question just as quickly. She probably needed most of her energies to maintain her hold on Xavier. As far as the girl was concerned, they posed no significant threat. All she needed to do to win was delay them long enough for Xavier to finish his work. After that, it wouldn't matter.

Nightcrawler started forward, intending to confront the girl physically—perhaps considering teleporting her out of the chamber—but Storm stopped him.

"Kurt, don't move," she told him. There were better ways to tempt the Gorgon.

"She's just a little girl," he said.

"No," she said flatly, "she's not." Because any entity capable of suborning Charles Xavier had to be considered as supremely dangerous as Magneto.

"Oh."

"Good advice," said the girl.

She breathed a small prayer of thanks that her own elemental powers—mainly her ability to wield lightning—created a level of background "static" in her own head that made it virtually impossible for a telepath to pick her thoughts. The first times that Xavier tried he came away with a devil of a headache.

With any luck, her adversary would have no idea of what was happening until it was too late. But this would be an all-or-nothing play. Once she acted, and revealed herself as a legitimate threat, the girl would have to strike back just as ruthlessly.

The girl smiled. "I've got my eyes on you!"

Stryker had his hand on the door handle when Logan's fist caught him upside his face. It was worse than being hit by an iron bat. Stryker dropped, stunned, his thoughts reeling before a fresh avalanche of incredible shock and pain, blood thick in his mouth from a broken lip, and he thanked whatever fates there were that Logan's punch hadn't shattered teeth and jaw as well.

He didn't wonder why the mutant hadn't used his claws. That reason was made plain when Logan rolled him over on his back and dropped beside him in a duck squat, almost daring Stryker to make a move to defend himself.

"Now," Logan said, with an edge of threat to his voice, "you were about to tell me something about my past?"

Looking up at him, William Stryker began to laugh.

"Why did you come back?" he asked, spitting blood.

"You cut me open! You took my life!"

"Please," Stryker said, and for the first time he looked actually disappointed. "You make it sound as though I stole something from you." He smiled suddenly, acknowledging a sudden surprise memory, or perhaps inspiration. "As I recall, it was you who volunteered for the procedure."

*"Who am I?"*

"Just an experiment," Stryker told him, playing every card in his hand, "that failed. If you really knew about your past, what kind of person you were, the work we did together—" He took a breath, wondering if he'd pushed Logan too far, if this would be his last. "People don't change, Wolverine. You were an animal then, and you're an animal now. I just gave you claws."

Throughout the control room, there wasn't a green light to be seen. The telltales on every console were flashing red, with alarm chirps and honks and sirens to add to the din. A set of displays showed the inside of the vast generator room, and a secondary phalanx of monitors presented data to show how dire the situation was.

The initial cracks had grown exponentially, in perfect concert with the original computer stress model. The jammed spillway had caused Alkali Lake to fill to the danger level, placing the dam under tremendous stress to begin with. Given the circumstances, it was already only a matter of time before it failed. The blast in the generator room had served to accelerate the process. Now, thanks to the relentless and incredible pressure of all that water, the worst-case scenario was about to reach fulfillment.

The complex shuddered—not very much, hardly enough to notice, just enough to stir some dust into the air—as blocks of stone the size of sofas crumbled from the ceiling. Then, as water jetted across the room with the force of a high-pressure fire hose, masonry fell in chunks the size of cars. Pipes, wrenched from their mountings, ruptured. Gas lines failed, filling the air with a heady mix of steam and other elements. Severed electrical conduits showered the room with sparks. Hydrogen ignited, setting off thunderclap blasts that only added to the chaos and destruction.

A torrent of water and stone and reinforced rebar cascaded onto one of the generators, jamming the turbine blades, which not only shattered but tore the whole assembly loose from its axis. Those blades flew every which way like scythes, and in their wake came a chain reaction of explosions that nobody in the complex failed to notice.


There it was again.

"Professor!"

Storm.

He still couldn't find her. Hardly surprising, considering the din. Voices in his head, the hum of Cerebro deafening in his ears, this was proving far more challenging and arduous than he'd ever imagined.

"Professor!"

Strange that the voices he was hearing seemed to be in pain. That couldn't be right. Cerebro was never intended to cause anyone harm. That was where he and Eric Lehnsherr had had their final falling out: What Charles Xavier saw as a tool, a means of bringing the human family together, Magneto wanted to use as a weapon, to cleanse the planetary genome once and for all. Having lived through one Shoah, he had vowed never to allow another, by whatever means were necessary. He understood the irony full well, this child of the Holocaust using the same methods as his own oppressors, the murderers of his family.

But somewhere along the way, he'd decided not to care.

He wasn't right, then.

This . . . wasn't right now.

Could anything be done about it?

*"Professor!"*

The chamber that housed Dark Cerebro shuddered from the tremendous shock wave. Overhead, the smooth curve of the dome came to an abrupt end as the vicious torque sheared through a line of retaining bolts and rivets. With a shriek of tortured metal, whole sections of ceiling plating collapsed, some falling straight past the gallery platform to and on the floor below with a resounding crash, while others tumbled lazily through the air as potentially deadly chunks of flying debris, especially dangerous for those like Nightcrawler and Storm who were essentially oblivious to them.

For that fateful moment, though, all of 143's illusions slipped—the setting reverted to its normal dimensions while the integrity of the holographic globe spasmed with static. Xavier coughed and started to raise his hands to remove his helmet.

But the moment was all the time he had, and it wasn't enough. The creature in the other wheelchair once more became the girl. The globe once more grew to the size of the planet itself. The room remained whole and intact, with none of those present allowed to have the slightest inkling of their danger while Charles Xavier unwittingly continued to bring about the annihilation of the human race.

The lights on the globe burned far brighter than before; Cerebro's *hum* was louder and more pervasive. Mutant 143 had accelerated the process.

Logan felt the explosion before he heard it, as a seismic transmission through the earth and a pressure wave a fraction of an instant ahead of the sound.

"What the hell was that?"

Stryker didn't answer at once, mainly out of defiance.

"Damn you, Stryker," Logan roared, grabbing the man up by the shirtfront, "what's happening? What is it?"

"The foundation of the dam has been compromised," he told Logan. "Some kind of rupture. Started in the turbines, and now it's spreading to the intake towers. The dam is releasing water into the spillway, trying to relieve the pressure . . . tying to stop the process . . . but it's *too late*! In a matter of minutes, we'll *all* be under water."

Logan looked back at the escape tunnel.

Stryker grabbed him, a drowning man to a life preserver: "Still want answers, Wolverine? Like how old you really are? If Logan is even your real name? If you have a family?" He knew the words were having an effect, and he glared at the mutant, willing him to listen, and to obey.

"Or," he said forcefully, putting all his strength into this final ploy, "is *she* still alive?" That one, that implication, hit the mark, dead center. "Then why don't we just get in the helicopter and fly away. I give you my word, Wolverine, come with me and I'll tell you *everything*. You owe these people nothing. You're a survivor, you always have been!"

Stryker gasped in pain as Logan delivered a wicked punch to the kidneys, one that was meant to hurt. He yanked Stryker close and tucked a fist under his chin, making his threat plain.

"I thought I was just an animal, Billy," he said.

Stryker flinched at the *snikt* of the claws extending from their housings and thought right then that he was dead. When he realized a second later that he wasn't, he had to face the shame of tears staining his cheeks, and far worse staining his trousers back and front. The outside claws bracketed his cheeks, close enough to dent the skin but not yet break it. The middle claw remained retracted.

Logan was smiling.

"With claws."

In the hallway outside Stryker's Cerebro chamber, with the kids stirring nervously as the floors and walls trembled enough to send a scattering of dust and some random splashes of water falling from the ceiling, Jean found her right hand closing into a fist. She felt a tension up her forearm, like a spring-loaded mechanism about to release, and her teeth bared fractionally in delight.

"Logan," she said, almost exclusively to herself, but mentally it was a full-throated shout.

He heard her, as if she were standing right beside him.

"Jean," he said, speaking as quietly as she and just as sure of being heard.

"Just tell me what you need, Wolverine. Tell me what you *need*. Tell me what you *want*!"

It was a simple choice: his past, or—and here Logan looked up toward the dam, which still showed no outward effects of the series of explosions deep underground; to the naked, untutored eye, it looked like it would stand forever—his future. To Stryker, the two had to be mutually exclusive. Maybe that was true?

Logan raised his fist, forcing the other man to rise to his feet, to tiptoes, both of them knowing that what he wanted more than anything was to pop that third claw and use Stryker's severed head as a soccer ball.

Stryker winced again at the distinctive sound of metal on metal, but this time the claws weren't extending. They had been retracted.

"I have what I need," Logan told him.

Before he could fall, Logan pitched him up against a nearby anchor post, where chains were used to hold the helicopters secure against the worst of the local winter storms. In a matter of seconds he had Stryker wrapped tight.

"If we die, you die."

As Logan raced back to the tunnel, Stryker pulled angrily on the chains and shouted after him: "There are no answers that way, Wolverine!"

A sudden rattle of metal caught his attention, and his eyes dropped to the chains. He thought at first it was some ground tembler related to the explosions that were shaking the dam, but he was wrong. His hands were trembling.

No big deal, he told himself, residual effect of his confrontation with Wolverine. He was scared, now he could afford to show it.

He sneezed, and the surprise outburst sent starbursts of pain through his skull that were worse than when Wolverine had punched him. He saw blood on the chains and snow in front of him. He wiped his face on a sleeve and left a scarlet trail that looked as though he'd used a decent and well-saturated paintbrush. But when he stuck out his tongue, he tasted a steady flow of it from his nose.

His face went pale as the snow, and a chill colder than the absolute of space closed around his heart.

*"Impossible,"* he breathed, and found himself wishing the mutant had used his claws.

That end at least would have been quick.


Alicia Vargas sat trembling on the floor of the Oval Office, her back against one of the two sofas that bracketed the presidential seal that was worked into the carpet. Ten minutes ago she'd been fine, and then it was as if she'd been knifed and gutted like a fish. She'd never felt such pain and thought, in that first rush of agony and terror, that all the nuns' stories of Hell had reared up to claim her. She was dimly aware of the President calling for help, of other agents and staffers laying her on the couch, making way for the medics and doctors . . .

. . . and then, as suddenly as it had struck, the pain went away. She felt fine. She was making apologies all around, her boss insisting on a full debriefing, someone mentioning what they all feared, that this was some new kind of mutant attack . . .

. . . and then, everyone around her dropped, pretty much the same way she had. She felt fine, but they were dying, and that staffer's offhand remark about mutants took on a whole new coloration that made her want to flee the building, that made her wish she *had* died moments ago. She was dying, they were fine. Now they were dying and she felt great. Did that mean, God forbid, she was a mutant?

She decided then and there it didn't matter. She was an agent of the United States Secret Service, assigned to the protective detail of the President. That made him her sole concern.

She drew her weapon from its holster and levered herself across the floor, collecting a couple more guns along the way. She couldn't quite muster enough strength yet to stand. The President had collapsed behind his desk and lay partially covered by his chair. With a convulsive heave, Alicia shoved it clear and, bracing her back against the wall, moved it to where she had a clean line of sight of both entrances. As gently as she could, she gathered the President's head into her lap, keeping her own Glock in hand while laying the other ones aside—but keeping them in quick and easy reach—to use a handkerchief to wipe his face of the blood that was now leaking from nose and eyes.

"Alicia," he choked. "My God, what's happening?"

"Sir, I don't know," she told him. "But I'm here, I'm okay, I'll keep you safe."

George McKenna didn't care about himself in that instant, because he knew Alicia's words were a lie. He didn't matter anymore, not as President, not even as a man; the only roles that had any substance were husband and father, and the bitterness he felt at this terrible moment was at being so far from those he loved. And even though he had no real hope of a miracle, he prayed for his wife, he prayed with all his heart and those coherent thoughts that remained to him for his children, that they be spared this awful end. He asked for mercy. . . .

Below the pontiff's balcony, three Vatican and CitiRoma ambulances stood on the periphery of St. Peter's Square. Some among the crowd gathered below had apparently been taken ill just before the pope's appearance. He'd signaled a secretary to make the proper inquiries, then proceeded with the day's events.

Now that handful of people were the only ones left standing, on the plaza and inside the Vatican itself. Elisabeth Braddock, who was taking a free day before driving to Milan to showcase Giorgio Armani's couture line for the fall show, picked herself up off the gurney and carefully stepped off the back of the ambulance. There was blood on her face and on her new dress—linen, expensive, designed exclusively for her by Kay Cera and now utterly ruined—and her shapely lips curled as she saw more pouring from the noses and eyes and ears of everyone in sight.

Bracing herself for what she knew was out there, Betsy opened the gates to her own mind and cast a telepathic net out across the plaza, hoping to find some clue to the cause of this mass affliction. She staggered as if she'd been physically struck and grabbed desperately for the handrail on the back of the ambulance to keep from falling. It was worse, so much worse, than she had imagined.

This wasn't just happening here in Vatican City. People were dropping throughout Rome itself.

She thanked her stars her mutant power had limits, sensing that no matter how far she cast her perceptions she'd just find more of the same.

Only the people in the ambulances appeared unaffected. Yet initially, they'd been the ones who were struck down by what was essentially the same effect. She knew one of the others was a mutant. It didn't take a rocket scientist to put the rest of the pieces together. Someone had tried to take out mutants, possibly the world over. And now those tables had been turned.

"No," she breathed. "*No, please no! Don't let this be happening. For God's sake, for mercy's sake—stop!*"

Her pleas fell on deaf ears, or perhaps they had just been drowned out by the screams of the multitude as extinction reached out to claim them.

This was Bobby's fault, Ronny Drake knew that for a fact. His brother must have figured out that Ronny had called the cops and this was some kind of mutie revenge, only he never dreamed his brother could be so cruel as to actually kill him. Brothers were supposed to look out for each other, that's what Mom and Dad always said, that's the way Bobby used to act before he went away to that damn school. Ronny was sobbing through the pain, clutching at his bedspread, calling weakly for his parents, why couldn't they hear, why didn't they answer? He'd never been so scared, he'd never understood before this moment how awful and all-encompassing a thing real fear could be. He grabbed for every breath, counted every heartbeat, cherished every thought, weighing them all against scenes from the movies and TV shows he'd seen, the video games he'd played. He knew this wasn't make believe, he knew there was no reboot, he didn't want to die, he said that over and over and over again, hoping repetition would guarantee his supplication being heard by the Almighty.

He was sobbing, and wailing, making hard, racking noises that tore at his throat and gut as hard as the energy waves that caused them. His face was streaked with blood, and it had splashed all across his pillow and sheets and the wall beyond. His vision was smeared and he expected to go blind before the end, he wished the end would come quickly, anything to take away the pain.

He told his brother he was sorry.

He wished he was a mutant, too, so at least they'd be together. And, with his life reducing fast to flickering embers, he found the capacity to hate Charles Xavier with all his young and passionate heart, blaming Xavier for stealing Bobby away from the home that had raised him, the parents who loved him, the brother who so desperately needed him.

On the floor of the New York Stock Exchange, hundreds of traders lay screaming. . . .

A thousand feet below the Pacific, the crew of the fleet ballistic missile submarine *Montana* lay screaming. . . .

A hundred fifty miles above the continental United States, the seven astronauts comprising the crew of the space shuttle *Endeavor* stood in silence as their commander tried to reestablish contact with the ground. They'd been in the middle of routine housekeeping traffic with Mission Control at Houston's Johnson Space Center when they'd heard a succession of increasingly garbled outcries and what sounded like screams.

After that, nothing.

"I say again, Houston, do you read? *Endeavor* to Houston, do you read?" The mission commander switched channels on the selector. "CapCom, do you read?" Switched again. "Edwards flight control, do you read?" One more time. "Cheyenne Base, do you read? NORAD ops, this is *Endeavor*, please respond." And finally, switching to 121.5, the international distress frequency: "Any station, any station, please respond. For God's sake," Peter Corbeau said, "is anybody there?"

The only answer was the static of an open carrier wave.

As far as they knew, they were all alone. And possibly the only human beings left alive.

Stryker wanted to scream, to shriek, to howl, but he couldn't. His mind, his body, his soul felt like they had all been snagged by monstrous barbed fishhooks that were now pulling away in every direction, determined to tear him apart. Something had gone terribly wrong. The only answer that made sense to him was that somehow the Cerebro wave had been reprogrammed to affect not mutants, but baseline humans.

All his work, all his planning, all his sacrifice—all for nothing.

With the whole world in his grasp, no power on earth could persuade Jason to stop. Strange that, after all this time referring to the boy as Mutant 143, Stryker could only think of him now by the name he'd given him. His father's name. It didn't seem . . . proper to call him anything else. As if this moment, with Stryker himself facing death, compelled him to accord his son the dignity, the identity, the . . . *humanity* that had been denied through the whole of his adult life. And Stryker felt a pang of grief, of misery, at the memory of the first time he'd held the boy, less than five minutes old, and marveled at how small and precious a gift he was. That had been Stryker's moment of sublime hope, when he had sworn to keep his boy safe, to stand by him no matter what. There'd been no hint then of what was to come, just this small and achingly vulnerable miracle who was the recipient of all the love that William and Karen Stryker had to give.

Ironically, humanity's only hope was now the dam. The shocks that set the ground to trembling were coming faster and stronger as water punched through the lowest levels of the complex like a pile driver, each collapsing section further undermining the foundation of the dam itself. Its collapse would destroy the complex and bury Jason. Stryker was no structural engineer—he couldn't build things worth a damn—but he'd spent a professional lifetime perfecting the art of destruction. Regardless, he was doomed, but survival for the world could now be measured in minutes.

Then a new but terribly familiar voice turned even that small hope to ashes.

"William," Magneto said, greeting him as an old friend, his rich and cultured English accent rolling the syllables of his name like a tiger savoring its prey.

Stryker glared up at him.

"How . . . good to see you again," Magneto continued as if he genuinely meant it.

Wolverine hadn't searched him, hadn't noticed the backup gun Stryker wore in an ankle holster. Molded plastic with plastic bullets that could kill a man as effectively as metal, designed to be totally impervious to Magneto's power.

Stryker grabbed for it, faster than he'd ever moved in his life.

Magneto let him clear the gun from its holster and almost—but not quite—bring it to bear before he used his power to wrap a length of chain around Stryker's gun hand like a whip, yanking it aside just as Stryker pulled the trigger. There was a flat report, and the bullet went way wide, into the trees. Mystique quickly stepped forward and wrenched it from Stryker's grasp, twirling it around her finger like a cowboy as she sauntered over to the helicopter and climbed aboard, leaving Magneto and Stryker to make their final farewells in private.

Magneto smiled.

"It seems that we keep running into each other," he said. "Mark my words, it will never happen again."

Another length of chain wrapped itself around Stryker's throat as Magneto pronounced his final sentence: "Survival of the fittest, Mr. Stryker."

Storm and Nightcrawler stood within Cerebro, and as far as they were concerned nothing whatsoever was happening. The great machine was silent.

But then Storm knew different. As the shock wave thundered past, the girl had lost control of her illusion, allowing them to see things as they truly were. Around them was a vast holographic construct of the globe, festooned with an uncountable number of blinding lights that Storm intuited at once represented the nonmutant population of the Earth. Remembering what she had endured when the Cerebro had been calibrated for mutants, she closed her eyes in empathy. Even if they found a way to save everyone, what could they do about the traumatic scars left on their memories? In some ways, that would be far worse than death because with it would be the constant terror that it could happen again.

That couldn't be her concern right now. First and foremost, she had to save them.

The momentary disruption of the illusion had revealed one thing more: the true identity of their adversary, not a little girl at all but a misshapen creature in a wheelchair, whose mind had latched onto Xavier like a lamprey.

Her initial, her main, reaction was sorrow that something so damaged could come into the world and never find the help needed to make it whole, in spirit if not in flesh. Much like Magneto, she dealt with the primal energies of the world. It gave her perceptions far beyond those of normal vision, and those in turn gave her an insight into people that was almost as effective as Logan's physical senses. She had seen cruelty in her life and once, when she was very young, had encountered a being that became for her the living embodiment of *evil*. She had known that at first glance, the same way that her first awareness of Xavier told her that he was a man to be trusted.

The man in the other wheelchair was *not* to be trusted. There was a *wrongness* to his spirit that made the patterns of energy cast off by his body as twisted as his body itself.

And for the second time in her life, staring at the false face of the little girl, Ororo Munroe knew that she was face-to-face with evil.

"He'll be finished soon," she said in a voice rich with satisfaction, a glutton enjoying the feast of a lifetime. The agonies—the ones she remembered, the ones she imagined—that tore at Storm's heart only filled his with delight. "It's almost over."

"This is not good," Nightcrawler muttered, looking up and around them nervously in the vain hope he might find a way to pierce the veil that the girl had cast around them. It bothered him to know that the place was collapsing about their ears and yet be unable to see any part of it.

Storm nodded agreement. They were out of time. "Kurt," she told him, "it's going to get very cold."

He nodded back to her, understanding that she was talking about more than the usual winter chill.

"I'm not going anywhere."

"When the times comes, we'll likely have to hurry— and there won't be any margin for error."

"In my whole life on the trapeze, I've never missed a catch. Do what you have to . . . Ororo. Trust me for the rest."

She spared him a glance and a smile that had nothing to do with business. "I like the way you say my name."

She couldn't see him blush, not with his indigo skin, and for that he was supremely grateful. "I like saying it."

As he spoke, he saw mist on his breath and realized she'd started what she had planned. Her warning was no joke; the room's ambient temperature had already dropped enough to make him shiver.

Her eyes were silver, highlighted in a crystalline blue, the rich color of the Earth's sky as seen from space, standing out dramatically against her chocolate skin. Her hair stirred in a breeze of her own creation, and Nightcrawler knew that this represented the calm center of an increasingly powerful whirlwind.

"There are winds you find in the wastelands of both poles," he heard her say, as though she were conducting a seminar. "Gravity grabs hold of cold, dense air and pulls it down the slopes of mountains and plateaus. In a volcanic eruption, the same thing happens with a pyroclastic flow. The air picks up an incredible amount of speed and that speed makes it colder. It's a dry wind, there's no precipitation. You can consider it a sandstorm of ice and snow. This wind cuts. It can freeze you in a heartbeat, not by coating you in ice but by turning the marrow of your bones to crystal. You don't fight this wind, you go to ground, you endure. You find a way to survive."

"What are you doing?" the girl wailed.

Nightcrawler, already shivering violently because Ororo couldn't spare the concentration or the effort to shield him, clutched at her arm.

"Storm," he cried, "she's a child."

"She's an illusion."

"Does that give you the right to condemn the being who created her?"

"Do we have a choice, Kurt? That mutant's life for the professor's, and likely the world!"

"That's a decision Magneto would not hesitate to make, I know. Nor have the slightest regret over it," he replied.

Storm said nothing, but her eyes blazed like silver beacons against the darkness.

"I'm *freezing*," the girl shrieked, her voice breaking, turning masculine and adult, then back to a girl once more. "You're hurting me. Make it stop!

"Stop it," the girl cried. And then, in 143's own voice, *"Stop it!"*

Just like that, the illusion flickered, faster and faster, like a manic strobe. The girl vanished, as did the illusion of the silent room and the deactivated Cerebro. They found themselves in chaos, with chunks of scaffolding and shielding plate tumbling all around.

Feeling frozen solid, Nightcrawler ducked as a piece the size of a limo took out a portion of the gallery back by the doorway. Storm ignored it all and stood her ground, her eyes fixed on her adversary.

Mutant 143 sat hunkered deep in his chair, eyes radiant with fury as he tried to grab hold of Storm's thoughts, only to discover what Xavier had learned years before—and just as painfully. That when she was fully in tune with her powers, when they were active on this level, it became virtually impossible to access her mind. The energies she manifested created too much psychic interference. To the unwary telepath, it was much the same as trying to grab hold of a bolt of lightning.

Mutant 143 cried out, so staggered by the backlash that his leash on Xavier also slipped.

Xavier felt the chill and knew it at once for what it was. He sensed the ripples of static on the fringes of his awareness and understood at once what Storm was doing. He beheld the hologram of the globe at life-size and the lights that blazed across its surface, bright, so bright, like candles on the brink of going out forever.

And he knew, with a realization that would haunt him to the end of his days, what he was doing here.

His first instinct was to shut down the Cerebro wave at once, but he held back. The process of disengagement had to be gradual, to allow the afflicted bodies and psyches to decompress, lest the shock of instant recovery do as much damage as the attacking wave itself.

To do that, though, he had to deal once and for all with—

"Jason," he said quietly as he turned. He didn't ask Storm to temper her winds. The young man who sat across from him knew too many pathways into his mind, he dared not allow him another opportunity to reassert control.

"No," the girl pouted defiantly, narrowing her eyes, shaking her head, fiercely trying to compel obedience.

"No," she repeated.

There was no inhibitor on Xavier's thoughts now; with it in place he couldn't operate Cerebro. That was why he had to be completely under 143's influence before he was allowed into the chamber. The pathways that 143 had used to worm his way into the core of Xavier's being now provided equal access to their source. The young man was gifted, and powerful, but Xavier acknowledged no equals, especially with the survival of humanity at stake.

"No," she cried again, with tears. "Stop! You're hurting me!"

The air rippled outward from her, looking much like the heat flow from a jet-engine exhaust, and in its wake the substance of the room's reality once again changed. It reminded Xavier of some of the classic cartoons, where the animator would swipe his brush across the screen, unleashing a cascade of color like a waterfall, which in turn would transform the scene into something altogether different from what had come before.

They found themselves on a battlefield, an image Xavier recognized from his own past, before the X-Men, before he lost the use of his legs, when he'd found himself cut off from his unit and caught in the middle of a firefight that was rapidly turning into a major pitched battle. Death came from all sides: It claimed men with stakes buried in the grass, with bullets, with cannon shells, with splinters blasted every which way by exploding trees, by a carpet of bombs tumbling from planes that flew so high no one knew they were in danger until the world erupted around them. They died from fire, they died broken, they died in agony, they died weeping and screaming and cursing and lost and lonely.

There were more images, none, thankfully, from Xavier's life, all of them skewed toward the cruel and the painful. As Xavier had sensed during that first interview, there was no empathy in Jason, no acknowledgment of the people around him as living, sentient beings worthy of even the slightest respect. To him, they were a different order of interactive toy. He took his pleasure from "mounting" them as the practitioners of voodoo believed their gods did when possessing their worshipers. He created scenarios that literally put his victims through Hell and gloried in the agonies that resulted.

There was nothing in him that responded to joy or that even recognized its existence. He considered his life a misery, and by sublimating those feelings through the torment of others, he made himself feel not so much better as less awful.

Had Xavier worked with him from the start, perhaps things might have been different. But Stryker had closed that door. Perhaps he had been right. Perhaps Xavier had been afraid of Jason. Had he only wanted those students at his school who could be saved?

*"Get out of my head!"*

"No," Xavier said. All those years ago, when he wasn't so sure of his vocation, or his own abilities, he'd made a terrible mistake. Could that be explained, could it be excused? That didn't matter to him now. Those options didn't exist today. He could no more abandon Jason now than one of his own. Succeed or fail, he had to try now, as he'd refused to then.

The ripples bounced off the wall, shunting all the images they carried with them into an incredible collision that made it impossible for a moment to tell which pieces of wreckage and shattering realities were illusion, and which were actual pieces of the room that was collapsing about their heads.

Through all the chaos, the only constant that remained was the facsimile globe, but at long last even that seemed to lose form and substance. Its outlines smeared, as transmitted images do when overtaken by static. Unnoticed in the ancillary din, the hum put forth by Cerebro gradually faded, as did the lights on the globe.

Xavier took a deep breath, mustering his strength for a last effort, and sent a thought pulse of his own along all the linkages that had been established between his mind and the rest of the world. Deep down inside there was a part of him that was tempted to try a global rewrite, something on the order of "love thy mutant neighbor as thyself," but it was an enticement easily resisted. Storm was fond of telling him that nature moved at its own pace, that some things had to be taught—and learned—in their own time. Short-circuit the process, shortchange the result, little good would come of it.

Having just endured firsthand what that meant, he had no desire to compound the resulting mess, just to try as best he could to set things right.

What he sent was a little bit of energy, or personal grace. A psychic aspirin. He couldn't banish the physical effects of the Cerebro wave, but at least he could ameliorate the residual pain. The victims might remember that pain, but they would no longer feel it. Quite the contrary. They'd actively feel better, like waking at the dawn of a fresh and beautiful day, whose sunrise contained the promise that anything was possible. And that those possibilities were good ones.

He reached up and removed his helmet, and with that severed his direct contact with Cerebro, which obligingly completed the full shutdown process. The globe vanished as if it had never been.

With it went Storm's winds, her eyes reverting to normal as Nightcrawler took her by the hand. Because the air was so dry, there was no evidence of the terrible cold she'd created beyond the residual chill itself.

Jean must have been monitoring the situation with her own telepathy, because the moment the helmet cleared Xavier's head, the vault door blocking the entrance was blown wide open, taking with it a fair chunk of surrounding wall.

Hot on its heels, Cyclops plunged into the chamber, only to backpedal frantically as a new series of explosions deep within the complex dropped another length of ceiling on the entrance, hopelessly blocking it.

The room shook as if it were a ball being worried by a playful puppy, and this latest assault proved far more than its structure could bear. As the platform and gallery began to twist alarmingly, Xavier chose to ignore the risk as he pivoted his chair and pushed toward Jason. The young man, grotesque as he was, had taken on the aspect of a waxworks mannequin. There was no expression on his face, no emotion in his eyes. Xavier sent thought after thought to him, but the harder he reached, the more defiantly Jason pushed him away.

He wanted no part of what Xavier had to offer.

A massive plate clipped the edge of the platform, and Xavier looked up to see most of the upper hemisphere crashing down on them. He knew what had to be done and lunged forward in his chair, attempting to grab Jason by the body or the chair—by some part of him—in hopes of creating a daisy chain of physical contact that would allow Nightcrawler—whose capabilities he could see clearly in Jean's mind—to teleport them all out of harm's way.

Jason would have none of it. Using the motor controls of his own chair, he backed out of reach just as the huge pieces of wreckage smashed into the gallery.

Then they were all falling as the platform gave way. Xavier felt Storm's arms, and something else that he belatedly realized was Nightcrawler's tail, but he didn't really register their touch. He had eyes only for the tortured, and now broken, semblance of a man whom he prayed had finally found his measure of peace.

The next thing he knew, after a moment of altogether sublime misery—which Jean's thoughts had *not* warned him about—he was in her arms, with Storm, Cyclops, Nightcrawler, and the stolen children crowded close around.

# Chapter
# Seventeen

While Magneto climbed aboard and settled into the copilot's seat, Mystique finished the start-up sequence. A rapid press of three buttons in sequence was rewarded by the rising whine of the twin jet engines coming on-line and spooling up to speed. She checked the gauges, satisfying herself that performance was nominal across the panel, and then engaged the rotors. Above their heads, through the clear canopy, the big blades began to spin.

One hand on the control yoke, the other on the secondary, Mystique was about to lift off when she nudged Magneto with an elbow and thrust her chin off to the left. He followed her direction and quickly found the figure of a boy standing on the tree line, face expressionless as he watched the helicopter prepare to leave. The only part of him that moved was his right hand, flicking open the lid of his Zippo lighter and snapping it closed, over and over, steady as a metronome.

Mystique looked at Magneto, wondering which way he'd jump.

He watched the boy for perhaps a minute, until Mystique found herself about to remind him that it was past time to go. The longer they stayed, the greater the risk of being caught by the dam when it collapsed. Not a good thing.

As if intuiting her thoughts, Magneto nodded once and beckoned once.

The boy just stood there.

John was thinking back to Boston, to how Bobby Drake had looked on the *Blackbird*'s ramp, staring up at his parents and his home as if he were saying good-bye to them forever. He'd ditched his own family ages back, and forgotten them, so for him the guy's hesitation had no meaning. Totally bogus moment. Now he found his cynicism and contempt thrown back in his face as he came face-to-face with the exact same choice. Walk away from Xavier's now, he knew, there'd be no turning back. Things would never be the same. The friendships he'd made would probably come to an end. Rogue . . .

What did he care about Rogue, really? The girl had the hairy wow-wows for *Bobbeeee*, for God's sake, talk about your total lack of taste! That pair of lames were made for each other, and both of them made perfectly for Xavier's. No way would John Allardyce turn out like them.

Pyro was made for better things.

He dropped the lighter into his pocket and headed for the open door of the helicopter.

The smile he saw from Magneto when he came aboard made it all worthwhile. He'd made the right choice.

As the helicopter lifted over the trees and Mystique accelerated toward the nearest line of mountains, Pyro had no regrets. And no worries, either, about the X-Men. He didn't believe they were in any danger. After all, they had their *Blackbird*—and here he uncorked a wicked nasty grin—that is, assuming Rogue or Bobby found enough gumption to fly that puppy to their rescue. Of course, that would mean breaking the rules, disobeying Storm's order. Fact is, Pyro didn't think they had it in them.

That thought didn't bother Pyro at all.

Storm led the way, wishing there was sufficient volume of air within the tunnels to generate a wind capable of carrying them all. The complex hadn't seemed so huge going in, but now the tunnels seemed endless. Fast as they hurried, she knew this was taking too long.

Nightcrawler was closest behind her, carrying Xavier in his arms as if the X-Men's mentor weighed next to nothing. Poor Kurt didn't look happy, either, probably because he wasn't altogether comfortable moving on two legs. He could make much better time galloping upside down along the ceiling on all fours.

Next came the children, with Scott and Jean bringing up the rear. She had one arm across his shoulders to take the burden off her broken leg.

After what Storm decided was just shy of forever, they reached the loading bay. They'd felt no more big explosive shocks the past few minutes, but it was clear that something just as bad was taking their place. Dust and small bits of debris were falling from every surface.

Their plan was to leave the way they had come, out the massive double doors at the far end of the loading bay and then along the spillway to the forest and, ultimately, the *Blackbird*. It wouldn't take long, because the moment they were outside Storm planned to take to the air and rocket her way back to the X-Men's hidden aircraft. She'd be there and back in a matter of minutes, and they'd be free of this terrible place.

Ten minutes, she prayed to any diety who cared to listen, that's all they needed. Fifteen, max. Not so hard a thing to ask for, was it? Hey, they'd just saved the world, that ought to be worth a tiny break from the fates.

The doors were wide open, and as they crossed the broad expanse of the loading bay, the kids commenting excitedly on the smashed and burned-out wrecks they passed along the way, Artie and Jubilation Lee raced ahead, ignoring Storm's cross *"Stop!"*

There was a taste to the air she didn't like, plus a low-frequency rumble that reminded her of one of the great herds of wildebeest on the African savanna suddenly going stampede. She could see a violence to the eddies and currents around the entrance and beyond that raised the hackles on her neck and made her break into a dead run of her own, filling the room with a bellow that grabbed everyone's notice. This seemed like a voice that could very well call down thunder.

*"I—said—stop!"*

And they did, right at the bottom of the approach ramp to the doors. As Storm caught up with them, snatching them off their feet and into her arms, her conscious mind caught up with the clues her subconscious had been processing, and she felt almost overwhelmed by an avalanche of despair. The air outside these doors was being assaulted by the leading edge of an air ram, a pressure wave compressed to the point of being an almost solid mass, by the force that was pushing it down this channel. It wasn't a stampede she was witnessing. The gates to the dam had been opened. The spillway was flooding.

She saw Jean separate herself from Scott and take a stance at the foot of the ramp, gritting her teeth as the air before her started to shimmer. Her red hair stirred without the slightest breeze and Storm knew that her friend was going to pit the whole of her telekinetic ability against the unimaginable force of the water coming down that huge funnel. Even if she could buy them time to escape the loading bay, almost certainly with the sacrifice of her own life, they'd still have to find some escape route from the complex itself. And if the spillway was flooding, then the dam itself had to have been compromised. Once it collapsed, dumping the whole of Alkali Lake into this valley, no power on Earth—certainly none available right now to the X-Men—would save them.

A great grinding noise filled the room, and everyone first assumed it had something to do with the onrushing flood, building its own runaway train crescendo outside.

Then the kids, and Storm, and even Jean, jumped as the double doors slammed shut.

"Trust me, darlin'," she heard Logan say, "you don't want to go out there." And she turned to find him a short way along the wall, with one fist jammed up tight against a sparking junction box that looked as big as his own chest.

Then an even more resounding *BOOM* shook the space, knocking most of the mutants present off their feet as it made the room shudder so hard it felt like a real earthquake. The doors bowed slightly from the impact shock, and water spurted from the central seam with the force of a high-pressure fire hose.

*Snakt!*

Logan retracted his claws, and the kids, who'd never seen him use them, who'd only heard—and mostly mocked—the stories they'd heard from Rogue, stared in silent awe.

"Everybody here?" he asked. "Everybody okay?"

His eyes told him the answer to the first, his senses cataloged the rest, and he zeroed in on Jean.

She didn't give him a chance to say a word but turned her face to him, to show him her ruined eyes, and said, "We're fine, Logan." The fingers of one hand were interlaced with Scott's. It wasn't just that she was leaning against Cyclops for support, it was the body language of the way their bodies melted seamlessly together. Even in these dire circumstances, it suggested a relaxed intimacy that spoke volumes about their relationship and the true depth of their feelings.

"Please," she told Logan, with a gentle empathy and a plea for understanding that had nothing to do with the words she was actually speaking, "help the professor."

He nodded, and let Cyclops half carry her away. She'd made her choice.

Storm watched him, with full understanding of what had just happened and how he might be feeling. He didn't try to put a brave face on the moment, or anything like that. His emotions were as plain and primal as Jean's; he'd never be ashamed of them. Just because she'd chosen Scott as her go-to guy didn't mean Logan would care for her any less. Or that the decision was final.

"Come on," he told everyone, maybe a little more gruffly than he'd intended. The adults chose not to notice. "There's another way out."

The spillway wasn't enough to save the day or even slow the process of collapse. Quite the contrary. The sudden and tremendous rush of water had the same effect on the underground complex as the earlier explosions. Wherever there was a weak bulkhead, wherever access portals had been left open, wherever doorways failed, water crashed into Stryker's base, further under-mining the foundation of the dam itself.

The first spiderweb series of cracks began to splinter the face of the dam itself, minute fissures that extended up from the initial breach underground in the generator room. They didn't look like much, nothing very impres-sive at all, until it became evident that the only way wa-ter could be leaking through them was if they extended clear through to the lake. That meant a crack right through better than ten meters of reinforced concrete.

Once more, the inexorable laws of physics and hydro-dynamics came into play. Water burst through the holes at tremendous pressure, backed by the full weight of a lake miles long, a mile wide just behind the dam, and hundreds of feet deep. This water ground away at the concrete as it poured through the cracks. With every passing second, as the very structure of the dam eroded, those cracks widened. More water escaped. More of the dam was washed away. The force of the water increased, thereby accelerating the process.

For all intents and purposes, though the X-Men didn't know it yet, they were out of time.

Well clear of the complex, but still below the dam, the team emerged from Stryker's escape tunnel. Logan pointed them over the crest of the hill to the helipad, and Storm hurried ahead to prep the vehicle for takeoff.

They found her on the edge of the trees, staring at the empty platform.

"Logan?"

"Son of a bitch," he growled, and charged across the clearing.

They caught up with him where he'd left Stryker. Logan was kneeling by the body, tapping one extended claw against the chains that had wrapped themselves so tightly around the man's throat he'd been virtually decapitated.

They didn't need an explanation, but he provided one anyway. "Magneto."

And again, with dark and deadly feeling, "That son of a *bitch*!"

"After what he'd done, Logan," Xavier said quietly, "small wonder he wouldn't face me, or any X-Man."

"Charley," Logan growled, "you don't understand—"

"If you say so."

Logan looked up and around, back in the direction of the dam, reacting to cues only his enhanced senses could perceive. Well, not quite his alone, because Storm was looking, too.

They started up the slope together, intent on reaching the top of the hill and having their eyes confirm the disaster that had befallen them. What they would do next was anybody's guess.

At last a chunk of facing larger than a freight car bulged outward from the body of the dam. Girders and rebar held it somewhat in place for a span of seconds as the stream of escaping water erupted into a raging torrent, but the stresses it endured went far beyond the limits imagined by any of the design team. Steel snapped like breaking strings, and these countless tons of concrete went spinning along the crest of a brand-new waterfall as lightly as a flat stone skimming the surface of a tranquil lake. It flew through the air at a slight angle and shattered against one of the pump houses with the force of a good-sized bomb.

In its wake, cracks as wide as roadways exploded across the face of the dam, rapidly reaching all the way up to the summit so that the next section to go involved a significant area of the wall. All pretense of integrity was gone. One collapse triggered the next as inexorably as a falling line of dominos, so that by the time Storm and Logan, with the irrepressible Artie close behind, reached the crest of the hill with its unobstructed view, there was virtually no dam left to see.

Just countless billions of gallons of water, thundering down the valley straight toward them.

"What is it?" Artie asked in breathless disbelief.

"Alkali Lake," Logan told him. "All of it."

He turned to Storm. "How many can you carry?" he demanded. She wasn't sure, and said so. "How about the damn elf, what's-his-name? How many can he carry, how far can he jump? And Jean, her mind thing, the teke, can she use it to make some kind of boat?" He was speaking in a rush, hand on her arm, Artie—who for once kept his mouth shut—tucked under his other arm as he propelled her down the slope. They had maybe a minute to act, and he wasn't about to waste any of it.

"What about you?" Storm demanded of him.

He snorted with derisive laughter. He could take care of himself, even in a flash flood of such immensity.

The rescue was doable—it had to be; they all knew that any other outcome was utterly unacceptable. They didn't have to go far, just clear of the wave front.

Just then, a tremendous wind blasted the clearing from above. It was too soon for the pressure ram leading the flood to reach them, and this downdraft was accompanied by the shriek of high-performance jet engines that sounded definitely *not* in a good mood.

\* \* \*

Skimming the surface of the treetops, when it wasn't actually plowing through them, the *Blackbird* sideslipped through the air toward them with a pale and terrified Rogue doing her best at the controls. All around her in the cockpit, displays flashed red and presented ominous messages in both text and voice, telling her in unmistakable terms that she was not flying the big jet at all properly or well. She couldn't help herself, she yelled right back at the telltales, agitation bringing her lower Mississippi accent to the fore with a vengeance. "I'm doing the best I can, damn it! Leave me the hell alone!"

They didn't listen. They kept right on yammering—about airspeed, flight profile, engine temperatures, hydraulic pressure, ground proximity, the landing gear. At least the last warning was something that made sense. She slapped the big lever on the front panel, the same way she'd seen Storm and Jean do it, and was rewarded by the hollow *thunk* of the struts lowering from their wheel wells. Unfortunately, that also screwed up the plane's balance and performance, creating additional drag that she wasn't expecting and didn't know how to cope with.

One of the main bogies snagged the crown of a fir, creating drag enough to pivot the plane right around and tip it to one side. Rogue tried to compensate, twisting the control wheel and applying power to the throttles, but she overdid both elements so that when the plane wrenched itself loose it slipped immediately into a flat spin that overwhelmed the ability of the vertical thrusters to compensate.

Fortunately, the plane only had about twenty meters to fall, not a lot of distance for a vehicle whose length was close to double that.

As everyone below scrambled for cover, the *Blackbird* made about half a revolution—Rogue sensibly chopped the throttles to zero—before the impact. It was a hard landing, and the only saving grace was that it landed in deep snow instead of on frozen earth. Even better, while the leading edge of the port wing buried itself in a patch of ground that was fully exposed, that ground was nowhere near solid. For this was where Pyro had collapsed when the initial Cerebro wave had struck. His wildly out-of-control power had melted all the snow for three meters and more around him. All that water had soaked straight into the ground, resulting in a boggy quagmire of mud.

The good news: The wing hit without substantial damage.

The bad news: Like any vehicle lodged in deep mud, it was likely stuck fast.

As heads all around the clearing cautiously poked up to make sure all was well, the *Blackbird*'s main hatch cycled open, and Bobby Drake emerged.

"What're you waiting for?" he yelled. "The dam's collapsed, we've got to *go*! *Hurry!*"

Storm was first in with Jubilee and the children. While the others came aboard behind her, she scrambled to the flight deck.

Rogue hadn't let go of the yoke, she was sitting stock-still, teeth chattering, pale as Storm's own hair, convinced that she'd doomed them all.

Storm took a moment she couldn't really afford to ruffle the young girl's hair. "You did great, Rogue. I am so proud of you."

\*    \*    \*

Aft, Cyclops helped Jean into one of the passenger seats, but as he reached over to fasten her harness, she waved him away.

"I've got it," she told him, and proceeded to buckle herself in without any hesitation or difficulty. Cyclops spared a quick glance to make sure the others were doing the same, then followed Storm to the flight deck. Rogue hadn't moved.

He crouched down and took her by both shoulders.

"It's okay, kiddo," he told her. "Storm and I, we'll handle things. Grab yourself a seat and strap in."

Convulsively, she released her harness and popped out of the chair, making sure not to touch either Cyclops or Storm as she sidled past them and rushed to where Bobby Drake was waiting.

Cyclops took her place, fidgeting a moment as he discovered that the sheepskin-covered seat back was so ice cold he could feel it even through his insulated uniform. There was the thinnest sheen of hoarfrost on the yoke as well, something he was used to finding wherever Bobby Drake hung out.

"What the hell—" he muttered, then relegated the concern to the back burner of his mind as something to worry about and deal with later.

He didn't waste time with preliminaries but initiated an emergency hot start. The engines obligingly spooled up to speed . . .

. . . and then went silent.

He started again, Storm gently manipulating the throttles, both of them watching the displays like hungry hawks to make sure that this time there'd be no loss of power.

"Thrusters four and six are out," she reported. It wasn't

anything Rogue had done; this was left over from the Air Force missile that had knocked them from the sky.

"We should still be able to fly," Cyclops told her.

"If we were level, absolutely. But we're stuck fast, and the thrusters we need to punch us loose are the ones we're missing. There's not enough power available to pull us out of the ground!"

"You got a better idea?"

She advanced the throttles, and the great aircraft began to tremble violently. Seeing a clutch of tree trunks flipping toward them through the air, Storm reflexively ducked her head into her shoulders, whistling as they bounced harmlessly past. They'd been torn loose by the flood and pitched on ahead. The mutants had only a few moments before the water was on them. It was now or never.

Xavier sensed the children's agitation and used his telepathy to ease their fear. If this was indeed the end, he would make sure that, for them, it would be peaceful and without pain.

Nightcrawler clutched his rosary and offered up the most heartfelt prayers he knew.

Jean closed her broken eyes and went to that place within her where the celestial song could be heard. Now, more than ever before, that strength was needed. In her mind's eye she rose once more from the ashes of creation and spread wide her arms, turning them to wings of fire and glory, that the *Blackbird* might fly, that these friends—who she loved more than her own life—would live.

In the base's loading bay, the closed doors finally gave way under the onslaught of this latest and most terrible fall of water, together with a major stretch of ceiling as well. Like starving hounds after a deer, floods poured down every corridor.

Far below, Yuriko Oyama lay unmoving in her cocoon of adamantium at the bottom of the augmentation tank. The room was mostly in ruins, but there were redundancy systems galore, and that meant some of the monitors were still active. The bionics that replaced much of Yuriko's purely organic components came with their own dedicated suite of sensors, and even though the images on the screens were wobbly and shot through with static, it was evident that she was still alive.

Not that it mattered. Encased in an adamantium shell, she was wholly incapable of movement. She wasn't going anywhere of her own volition or under her own steam.

A few moments later, as the flood waves reached this section of the complex, the whole question became moot. Walls shattered from the torrential impact, and that, in turn, collapsed the entire ceiling. In a heartbeat, the lab was filled with water, and the augmentation chamber itself, together with the Weapon X tank, was buried under hundreds of tons of steel and rock and earth.

Elsewhere, the same happened in the Cerebro chamber.

Outside, an avalanche of water hundreds of feet high cut a remorseless swath through the valley below Alkali Lake, annihilating every trace of the complex that had been constructed beneath the dam. The pressure wave of air that preceded it made trees that were meters thick bend almost double for the few seconds it took the water to reach them and snap them like kindling. Mist and foam rose from that leading edge of the wave, partially obscuring the awful fury of the event and the devastation it was causing.

Directly in its path, mere seconds from destruction, lay the *Blackbird*.

*No,* Jean thought to herself. More than an article of faith, this denial became for her its own irresistible, indomitable force of nature.

On the flight deck, both Storm and Cyclops reacted with surprise as switches and controls began to operate by themselves. Before their eyes the plane once more set itself for vertical takeoff.

Realizing who had to be responsible for this, Cyclops turned in his chair to call out, concern evident in his voice, "Jean?"

He reached for the release on his harness, but Storm laid her hand on his arm to stop him. It was the only card left to play.

Jean raised both hands, her face eerily serene, revealing none of the murderous concentration of will and effort this had to be demanding of her. Xavier's eyes narrowed. He couldn't gain access to Jean's mind, to determine precisely what was happening or assist in any way. The power she was manifesting created a scrambling field around her thoughts unlike anything he'd ever encountered, which he found himself unable to penetrate.

At Jean's bidding, the vertical thrusters fired. Mentally reviewing the plane's schematics, she cast forth a piece of her awareness to take a look directly at the problem, smiling to herself at how much simpler it was to do the work this way than it would have been with her hands.

No more squeezing through impossibly small spaces and getting cut and scraped by wayward outcrops of metal. She identified the problem and, using telekinesis, fixed it.

Obligingly, the engines roared to full power.

"The thrusters are back on-line," Storm told Cyclops, grabbing her controls and pulling back on the yoke. He took care of the throttles, advancing them to full emergency power, while keeping a wary eye on their appropriate telltales.

Of course, it wasn't quite that easy. Jean walked the psychic image of herself underneath the hull, where the wing was still stuck fast. Reminding herself to apologize later, she slipped the throttles out of Cyclops' grasp and eased back on the power to minimize the risk of structural damage. Another asset of working this way, she discovered to her delight, was that she could multitask at the speed of thought, accomplishing a number of objectives in no time at all, so that for her the onrushing wave appeared to be frozen in place, like one of Bobby's ice sculptures.

She set her phantom shoulders against the wing root, planted her phantom feet firmly enough on the ground to leave an actual imprint, and applied power in much the same way as Cyclops did by advancing the throttle. She called it from this magical place within herself, and reveled in the celestial song that enveloped her as she mated imagination to will and found the place where there are no limits.

The smile she gave, on her real face as on her phantom one, as the wing slipped free of the ground, was as radiant as if she were witnessing the birth of the very first star in the heavens.

The engines roared, gravity pressing everyone aboard

into their seats as Storm grabbed for altitude, racing ahead of the flood wave at a steep upward angle that bought them the time they needed to rise above the crest of the water. At the same time, she brought a wind right into their face, to create an even greater amount of lift for the wings.

At the back of the plane, Logan stood by the open ramp as the valley fell farther and farther behind. A light was *pinging* insistently beside his head, Storm on the flight deck pointedly telling him to close the damn door. He ignored it, for the moment.

He looked around suddenly, sharply, as if someone were standing right beside him, and more slowly his gaze swept the passenger section of the jet until his eyes came to rest on Jean. She didn't respond, but he knew she was aware he was looking at her. He suspected she was aware of a lot of things, and capable of far more than any of them even imagined. She'd need someone strong to walk beside her, and he flicked a quick glare to the right-hand seat on the flight deck. Cyclops better be equal to the task. Jean deserved the best, and if she figured Logan didn't fit that bill, he'd make damn sure whoever she chose was worthy of her.

That made him chuckle, and he looked back toward what had been Alkali Lake. The water was down by more than half, though with any luck the flood would slacken over time and distance, and the towns downriver would survive. Probably worth suggesting to Charley that the X-Men help out, though.

Then his mood darkened. No more Stryker, thanks to Magneto. Whatever secrets he possessed were lost to Logan now. Same went for the base. If the past was indeed prologue, like Shakespeare said, then all Logan was left with right now was a book full of blank pages.

Stryker had called him an animal.

He looked at his dog tags and knew that wasn't entirely a lie, or even an exaggeration. But man was an animal. Did that make what Stryker said true, the way that Stryker meant it?

Logan turned once more into the body of the plane until his eyes came to rest again on Jean.

Animals didn't feel the way she made him feel, or inspire the feelings he knew he did in her. Animals didn't give a damn about feeling . . . worthy.

A new movement caught his eye; Rogue had turned in her seat to look from Jean to him. He gave her a smile, acknowledging that his epiphany cut both ways, that much of what drove Rogue was the desire to feel worthy of him. That had never happened before, either.

There was more to this new world he'd found than Jean, no matter how signal a part of it she was. And some other parts were just as precious.

He didn't look back as he pressed the control that raised the ramp and sealed the hatch. He didn't look down as he dropped the dog tags into his pocket.

He made his way forward, shaking his head in amusement as he saw Jones curled up around Nightcrawler's tail, playing with it the way a kitten might a ball of string. Rogue and Bobby were looking after the kids, most of whom had crashed the moment the *Blackbird* was airborne. No one said a word about John.

Logan had marked the boy's scent on the tree line, followed its trail to the helicopter pad where it mingled with Magneto's and Mystique's. As best his senses could report, they'd taken off together. The boy had joined up of his own free will.

Then there was Charley.

They met each other's eyes, but only for a moment. They had a lot to talk about, and it had to be talk. Logan wasn't sure when he'd allow the other man inside his head, only that it would be a while. And Xavier knew better than to visit uninvited. They were both wary, they were both wounded; it made sense under the circumstances to put things off until they'd had time to heal.

Not as if Logan was planning on going anywhere. Not solo, anyway. Not anymore.

He climbed up to the cockpit and slipped into the seat that Scott had vacated, watching him tenderly begin to apply bandages to Jean's eyes, while Xavier leaned close, probably using his own mental powers in concert with hers to determine the full extent of the damage.

Storm was looking at him, and he was surprised to see there was no sign of concern on her face. Made him grin to realize that it wasn't because she didn't care, but rather because he didn't need it.

The book of his past was closed. Didn't matter to the X-Men who or what he was; he'd proven by character and actions that he belonged. They accepted him wholeheartedly and without question. Now that ball was in his court.

The book of his future was waiting to be written, and wherever it might lead in days to come, Logan knew that for the present his life was bound to theirs.

He reached out his left hand, and with a smile full of promise and delight, Storm took it, indicating that he place his right hand on the yoke.

Together they pulled back on the sticks and sent the *Blackbird* soaring toward the stars.

# Epilogue

Ten minutes before, the news anchors of all the major networks had solemnly introduced the President, live from the White House in Washington, D.C. The graphic of the presidential seal was displayed, and the image dissolved to George McKenna sitting at his desk. The housekeeping staff had been busy in the week since the attempt on his life, and the office looked good as new. The desk itself, carved from the timbers of a British frigate captured during the war of 1812, had been swept of its usual clutter. The only items in view were a stack of files, in leather loose-leaf binders adorned with the seal, and the knife with its scarlet banner: MUTANT FREEDOM NOW. And of course, the speech.

The copy he held was just for show. He was actually reading from the TelePrompTer right in front of him, speaking to the nation as he would to his own children. It was a good quality he had, this ability to convey the most complex of issues in terms that everyone not only understood but which also made them relevant to their own lives.

He just wished—with all his heart—he had a different topic.

The office was crowded—broadcast technicians, staffers,

military, Secret Service. There was a palpable air of anxiety
to the room, and McKenna prayed that didn't show on his
own face. He was asking a lot of his country, to in effect de-
clare war on some of its own children.

He had a bust of Lincoln on his desk, out of camera
shot, and a photo of John Kennedy. The one, because he
led the Union in and out of a Civil War; the other, because he had stood with the world on the brink of nuclear Armageddon and brought it safely home. He
thought he knew now some of what they had felt during
those fateful days and weeks and, for Lincoln, years. He
looked at the knife and wondered as well if the road of
his life would come to the same end.

Dying wasn't such a horror; he accepted it as a natural
part of life. Being killed, though, especially having survived a combat tour in a serious shooting war, that was
something he'd hoped he'd never have to worry about
again.

There'd been no word from Stryker since their meeting
in this very office. No contact, in fact, with any of the
man's senior staff. That was worrisome to McKenna, especially in light of the reports that filtered out of Westchester, about military helicopters and kidnapped and
terrorized children. They represented everything McKenna
feared most about Stryker's operation and his methods,
and he'd been on the brink of ordering him to stand
down when the whole of the human race had apparently
come within a heartbeat of extinction.

He couldn't really recall much of what had happened,
beyond collapsing, and then finding himself cradled in
the lap of one of his female Secret Service detail, while
she leveled her pistol at the doorway. Today she was
standing off in the corner, to his left, back to the wall,

where she had a clear view of everyone present and an equally clear run at McKenna himself. If anything happened, he knew that Alicia Vargas would give her life to save him, without hesitation.

She hadn't seen the speech, almost no one had, although its substance had been the focus of scores of rumors ever since he had asked for airtime. He'd worked on it with his wife—who'd been with him most of his political career and who actually served as his de facto chief speechwriter—and ended up writing most of the text himself. There were no copies, other than the one scrolling through the camera mount in front of him, and no advance material had been released to the press. Whatever he would say tonight would come to the nation as a surprise.

He thought of his children as he spoke, and of how he'd feel if he were to discover one of them was a mutant. Could he stand by and see them condemned? How fiercely would he resist? And yet, it was only by the smallest yet most profound of miracles that the world had survived at all. Did not the needs, the very survival, of the many justify the sacrifice of a few?

Stryker's indictment of mutantkind was damning, but that's what indictments were supposed to do, make the case for conviction. McKenna would have felt better, though, if someone had been able to mount a defense.

Maybe he needed one more bust on his desk, of Pontius Pilate. Or would old Ramses be better, condemning the Hebrew firstborn?

Movement caught his eye, but it was only his chief of staff pouring a glass of water.

". . . in this time of adversity," McKenna read, "we are being offered a unique opportunity—a moment to recognize a growing threat within our own population, and take a unique role in the shaping of human events."

He took a deliberate look at the pile of folders Stryker had given him.

"I have in my possession . . . evidence . . . of a threat born in our own schools, and possibly even in our own homes. . . ."

He jumped, just a little, as a surprise burst of thunder rattled the room. Staffers moved quickly to the door and windows out of camera view, to close the curtains. Unfortunately, the broadcast was live; there was nothing to be done about the windows right behind him as a sky that the Weather Channel had guaranteed would be clear suddenly darkened with angry clouds from horizon to horizon. Lightning flashed spectacularly and often, and the glass was pelted by a torrential downpour of cold and driving rain. Nothing would be flying today, not in the vicinity of Washington. If people had half a brain, they wouldn't even try driving.

". . . a threat we must learn to recognize, in order to combat it . . ."

A display monitor was mounted to one side of the camera, allowing him to see how he looked. But with another, even more daunting burst of lightning and thunder like the wrath of God, that screen abruptly dissolved into static.

"What the *hell*?" McKenna demanded, as much a reaction to the atmospheric display outside as to what was happening here. The lights had flickered as well. Just perfect, just dandy, the most important speech of his administration gets skunked by wild weather that just whistled up out of nowhere.

"What the *hell*?" he repeated, rising slightly from his

chair, because he'd just then noticed that the red light atop the camera was no longer glowing. The camera was off, he wasn't broadcasting. He was about to call to the cameraman, only to realize that the man was standing stock-still, as if he'd been flash frozen.

He looked around the room and saw that the same applied to every person present. They weren't moving, not a one. And yet it wasn't time that had stopped, only the people—water was still pouring from the pitcher Larry Abrahms was holding, overflowing the cup and pouring over his leg to the floor.

McKenna grabbed for his phone but couldn't find a dial tone on any of the lines, not even the direct, secure, untappable link to the National Military Command and Control Center in the Pentagon. He pressed the crash button, to indicate an imminent threat inside the Oval Office. By rights that should have set off alarms throughout the building and brought armed agents at a dead run.

Nothing happened. In a room crowded with people, he was suddenly quite alone.

Something stirred over by the fireplace, but because of the bright TV lights right in his face he couldn't quite make out what he was seeing until they stepped forward.

Six in all. Three men, three woman. One man in a wheelchair, everyone but him clad in form-fitting leather that bore the look of a uniform. He wore a suit, as conservatively respectable as McKenna's own.

"You," he said to the man in the wheelchair, immediately recognizing the familiar face from various news programs, the networks' go-to talking head when it came to the subject of mutants. Stryker's file had made the reason plain.

"Good afternoon, Mr. President," said Charles Xavier.

"What are you doing here?" McKenna demanded, rising to his feet.

"We're mutants," Xavier said, "but we aren't here to harm you. Quite the contrary. My name is Charles Xavier. These are the X-Men. Please sit down."

"I'd rather stand."

He had names for all of them, mainly from Stryker's files: the redhead, whom he'd met when she testified before Congress, was Xavier's associate, Dr. Jean Grey. The silver-haired woman was one of the teachers at Xavier's School, Ororo Munroe. The younger girl had been referred to in Stryker's files only by a code name: Rogue. One of the men was also a mainstay of the School, Scott Summers; the other, surprisingly, as McKenna remembered from some particularly nasty CIA files, shared ops with, of all organizations, the Canadian Special Intelligence Operations Executive. He was Logan. He hung a little back and apart from the others, his eyes never resting as they ceaselessly swept the room for any signs of trouble. He was the team's cover, just as Alicia Vargas was for her President. If there was a problem, McKenna understood that he'd be the one to deal with it.

Dr. Grey's eyes were strangely milky, lacking iris and pupil, and McKenna realized with a start that she must be blind. She made a small gesture with a hand, and an imposing stack of files floated through the air to McKenna's desk, landing right beside the folders already there.

"These are files from the private offices of William Stryker."

"How did you get them?"

"Let's just say I know a little girl who can walk through walls."

"Where is Stryker?"

"Regrettably," and Xavier sounded like he actually meant it, "no longer with us."

"You killed him!"

"He was killed, yes. While trying to annihilate every person on this globe who possessed the mutator gene."

McKenna's eyes flashed to his left, to Alicia Vargas, as he remembered how shockingly she'd collapsed, writhing on the floor as if in the throes of a grand mal epileptic seizure, blood gushing horribly from her mouth and nose and eyes and ears and the pads of finger- and toe-nails, as though her whole body had suddenly become obscenely porous. She hadn't moved from her post, but he could see that, unlike everyone else in the room, she was aware of what was happening. She could hear Xavier and see him. She had her hand on her gun, but she hadn't yet drawn it. To his credit, McKenna didn't once doubt her loyalties. Mutant or no, she would be true to her oath.

"I didn't know," he said. "My God." He shook his head, vainly trying to grasp the enormity of Stryker's ambition. "Do you think I would—do you think I *could*—sanction such a thing?"

"If I did, sir," Xavier told him, "we wouldn't be here talking."

McKenna flipped through the dossiers, speed-reading enough to make him sag atop the desk, resting his full weight, plus that of the office, plus that of the world, on hands and shoulders. Atlas had nothing on him when it came to bearing burdens.

"I've never . . . I've never seen this information."

"I know," Xavier said quietly.

McKenna glared up at him from lowered brows.

"But I don't respond well to threats."

"This is not a threat, Mr. President, of any kind. This is an offer." He rolled forward in his chair and indicated the bust of John Kennedy. "I remember those days, as you do, and the fear that came with them, that through no fault or action of our own, the world would end. It wouldn't even be a matter of someone's choice. It could just as easily happen as a mistake."

McKenna nodded, thinking of how he'd helped his father dig a bomb shelter in the backyard and how utterly futile that shelter would have been if the worst came about.

"You and I, Mr. President," Xavier continued, "and the people we represent have had a taste of our own version of doomsday. How close did we all come to the abyss? And what have we learned from that terrible experience? John Kennedy and Nikita Khrushchev found a way to lay the foundation for a lasting peace between their two nations—or at least a way to lessen the possibility of outright war. Can we not try to do the same?

"I realize"—he indicated the files Stryker had provided—"you may have information about me. About my school. About our people. Grown mutants like me, like the X-Men, like . . . Magneto, are but a comparative handful. Most mutants are children, and what are children but the promise of the future made flesh? What shall we promise our posterity, sir? A world based on hate and fear, whose ultimate outcome is a genetic Civil War that will likely be the death of us all? Or can we find a better way?

"I'm willing to trust you, Mr. President, if you're willing to return the favor.

"As we both have seen firsthand, there are forces in

this world, mutant and nonmutant alike, who believe that a war is coming. That it is inevitable. You'll see from these files how diligently some have worked over the years to start one.

"If we wish to preserve the peace, to guarantee our posterity, we must work together. Do you understand?"

McKenna looked at his chief of staff. The pitcher was empty, the flow of water reduced to a trickle of drops. Larry was such a fashion plate, he was sure to go totally berserk when he discovered his sodden trousers and ruined shoes.

Then he looked back at Alicia Vargas. There was such a look of longing, and apprehension, in her eyes that—as father and grandfather both—he wanted to take her in his arms and reassure her that there really was no bogeyman in the world, nothing she need ever fear, save as Franklin Roosevelt warned, fear itself.

"Yes," the President said, after a long pause for thought. "I think I do."

He held out his hand across the desk, and from his chair, Xavier took it. He had a strong grip with calluses that told McKenna that, like himself, here was a man who liked to work with his hands. Clearly the man was a good teacher, and George McKenna hoped he wasn't too old and too set in his ways to learn.

"I'm glad," Xavier told him. "We are here to stay, Mr. President. The next move is yours."

McKenna nodded—and wasn't surprised to see, when he looked up a moment later, that Xavier and his X-Men were gone.

He turned to the window and saw that the storm was passing. Just as in the "Pastoral" sequence of Disney's original *Fantasia*, the gods of thunder and lightning, having had their fun, were moving on, leaving a bright and beautiful day in their wake. He wondered which of Xavier's—what had he called them?—X-Men was responsible, and for no reason he could articulate, fixed on the image of the black woman, Ororo Munroe, tall as he was, with the most incredible blue eyes and hair of burnished silver.

Alicia coughed, ever so gently.

Larry Abrahms yowled with fury, just as McKenna expected, which made the President smile.

Immediately in the room, there was a ripple of surprise and agitation. As far as anyone else was concerned, the President had been making his speech and then—presto!—suddenly he was standing where he'd been sitting, and everything was in a small kind of chaos.

McKenna took his seat and waited for a semblance of order to be restored, a matter of some hurried and small-voiced exchanges between the camera crew and whoever was handling the network feeds. The commentators and anchors had evidently been vamping like crazy since the signal was lost.

Nobody noticed the new pile of folders on the desk, and as McKenna took his chair, awaiting his cue to continue, he looked from one to the other.

The stage manager held up five fingers, then quickly folded them one by one into a fist. At the last, the red light above the camera blinked on again, and the Oval Office was once more live and broadcasting.

At first George McKenna didn't say a word, a silence that began to make those watching start to feel distinctly nervous, unaware that he was marshaling thoughts and arguments and rewriting frantically in his head. Nobody understood the quirky, self-deprecating smile he made, or the look that accompanied it toward the bust of Lincoln. Nobody, save perhaps Charles Xavier, caught the wayward thought that came to him then: *At least you had a train ride and the back of an envelope handy when you wrote the Gettysburg Address; me, I've got to wing this! Extempore and live to the whole damn country!*

But he had no doubts. He knew now what he wanted to say, and as with all such moments, this was something best said from the heart and from the soul.

Taking the files Xavier had given him, McKenna placed them on top of Stryker's and, looking straight into the camera, and into the homes and offices of the American people and, he prayed, especially into their hearts, the President of the United States began to speak.

Along Pennsylvania Avenue, tourists and locals began hesitantly to venture once more out of doors, commenting to one another about the downpour and collectively grumping about the miserable state of weather forecasting.

A family from Utah gathered on the grass of Lafayette Square for what they figured was a spectacular Kodak moment, with the White House as a backdrop and not another pedestrian in sight to mar the photo. Dad gave everyone their cue, they all said, "Cheeeeese," with grins galore, he clicked the shutter . . .

. . . and nobody moved. Not here, not anywhere within a radius of blocks. Flags flapped in the crisp autumn breeze, fountains burbled, birds fluttered through the air. All the mechanical elements of life in the nation's capital functioned as they were supposed to. But none of the people noticed.

Then, apparently out of nowhere, a sleek ebony aircraft rose into the sky from the helicopter landing stage on the South Lawn of the White House. The *Blackbird* held position for a moment above the executive mansion, then rocketed silently away.

In its wake, Washington woke up and continued with the normal course of what had started as a normal day. Only a few would ever know the truth, of how a handful of heroes had stood between the world and those who would leave it a wasteland, of how their struggle would inspire a leader to achieve greatness and an immortality all his own, to rival those of the predecessors he so admired.

Decent people, striving to do the right thing. That's all it takes to save the world.

Some call themselves human, others mutant.

And some of those mutants are the X-Men.

Thanks to them, their world has a future.

With their help, that future may be glorious indeed.

# Acknowledgments

Thanks to Stan Lee & Jack Kirby, for coming up with the concept in the first place; to Len Wein & Dave Cockrum, for revamping it and then handing over the writing reins to a young punk who probably didn't know any better; to Louise Simonson & Brent Eric Anderson, for "God Loves, Man Kills"; to Eleanor Wood, for reasons that need no explanation; to Betsy Mitchell, for having faith; and Steve Saffel, for keeping both book and writer superbly on-track. Sometimes, it takes a "village" to write a book, and for that I am extremely grateful.